TOM SHARPE

Tom Sharpe was born in 1928 and educated at Lancing College and at Pembroke College, Cambridge. He did his National Service in the Marines before going to South Africa in 1951, where he did social work before teaching in Natal. He had a photographic studio in Pietermaritzburg from 1957 until 1961, when he was deported. From 1963 to 1972 he was a lecturer in History at the Cambridge College of Arts and Technology. In 1986 he was awarded the XXXIIIème Grand Prix de l'Humour Noir Xavier Forneret. He is married and lives in Cambridge.

Tom Sharpe

Grantchester Grind

A PORTERHOUSE CHRONICLE

PAN BOOKS

in association with

André Deutsch and Secker & Warburg

First published 1995 by André Deutsch Limited
and Martin Secker & Warburg Limited

This edition published 1996 by Pan Books
an imprint of Macmillan General Books
25 Eccleston Place, London SW1W 9NF
and Basingstoke

Associated companies throughout the world

in association with André Deutsch Limited
and Martin Secker & Warburg Limited

ISBN 0 330 32307 5

579864

A CIP catalogue record for this book is available from
the British Library.

Typeset by CentraCet Limited, Cambridge
Printed and bound in Great Britain by
Mackays of Chatham plc, Chatham, Kent

To my daughters
Melanie, Grace and Jemima
without whom this book would
never have been written

1

'Godber was murdered,' said Lady Mary. 'I am fully aware that you refuse to believe me, but I know.'

Mr Lapline sighed. As Lady Mary's solicitor he was forced twice a year to listen to her assertion that her husband, the late Sir Godber Evans, Master of Porterhouse College, Cambridge, one of the University's oldest foundations, had been deliberately done to death by or on the orders of the Dean, the Senior Tutor or one of the other Senior Fellows. Mr Lapline, a Cambridge man himself and a keen respecter of old institutions, particularly of old persons who had become institutions in their own lifetimes, found the accusation most distasteful. With a less wealthy and well-connected client he would have said so. Instead, and as usual, he prevaricated.

'It is not that I refuse to believe it,' he said. 'It is just that, in spite of every effort we have made, and as you know we have employed private detectives at great expense to your good self, we have been unable to find a shred of evidence. And frankly – '

Lady Mary cut him short. 'I am not in the least interested in what you have not been able to find out, Lapline. I am telling you my husband was murdered. A wife knows these things. All I require from you is proof.

I am not a young woman and since you seem incapable of providing that proof . . .' She left the solicitor dangling. It was all too obvious that she was not a young woman and, in Mr Lapline's opinion, it was doubtful if she ever had been. It was the unspoken threat that was alarming. Ever since her recent illness she had, as Mr Lapline liked to put it – he was fond of borrowing the sayings of famous men – become an old woman in a hurry. In her present mood she was capable of anything. Mr Lapline was nervous.

'In view of what the coroner said . . .' he began but she cut him short again.

'I know perfectly well what the buffoon said. After all I was there at the inquest too. And quite frankly it wouldn't surprise me to learn that he had Porterhouse connections. Either that or he had been nobbled.'

'Nobbled?'

'Bought off. Bribed. Got at. Call it what you will.'

Mr Lapline shifted uncomfortably in his chair. His stomach was playing him up again. 'I'd hardly call it any of those things,' he said, 'and I'd strongly advise you not to either. Certainly not in public. The damages for criminal slander can be enormous. Of course as your legal adviser I am prepared to listen but – '

'But not, apparently, to act,' said Lady Mary. 'I have become fully aware of that.' She got to her feet. 'Perhaps I would be better advised by a more enterprising firm.'

But Mr Lapline was already out of his chair. 'My dear Lady Mary, I assure you I have only your best interests at heart,' he said, conscious that those best interests included the Lacey fortune she had inherited from her father, the Liberal peer. 'All I am trying to impress on you is the need for discretion. Nothing more. Now, if we had any evidence, no matter how slight, any evidence at all that Sir Godber was . . . well, murdered, I would be the first to put the case before the Director of Public Prosecutions, if need be, in person.'

Lady Mary sat down again. 'I should have thought the evidence was there already,' she said. 'For instance, Godber could not have been drunk. He was most abstemious. The Dean and the Senior Tutor were lying when they said they found him totally intoxicated.'

'Quite so,' said Mr Lapline. 'The fact remains . . .' He stopped himself. Lady Mary's gaze was most unnerving. 'I mean there doesn't seem any doubt that on the evening of his . . . murder he had consumed a quantity of whisky. I really don't think we can dispute the autopsy report. The medical evidence was very clear on that point.'

'It was also clear that he had drunk it between the time he was attacked and his death, not before the so-called accident. The argument that he had fallen and fractured his skull because he was drunk doesn't hold water.'

'True, very true,' said Mr Lapline, glad to find something he could agree with.

'Which brings us to the bottle,' Lady Mary went on.

'Bottle? What bottle?'

'The bottle of whisky, of course. It was missing.'

'Missing?'

'Yes, missing, missing, missing. How many times do I have to repeat myself?'

'No need to at all, dear lady,' said Mr Lapline hurriedly.' But can you be quite sure? I mean you were naturally extremely distraught at the time and – '

'I am never extremely distraught, Lapline,' Lady Mary snapped.

'Upset then, and it may not have occurred to you to look for the bottle at such a very distressing moment. Besides, one of the servants might have thrown it away.'

'It did and they hadn't.'

'It did. And they hadn't,' said Mr Lapline involuntarily and before realizing he was repeating her words again. 'I mean – '

'It did occur to me to look for some whisky that night, and the bottle had gone. I spoke to the French au pair and it was perfectly obvious she had no idea what had happened to it. It wasn't in the dustbin either.'

'Really?' said Mr Lapline incautiously.

'Yes, really,' said Lady Mary. 'If I say I looked in the dustbin and it wasn't there, it wasn't.'

'Quite so.'

'What is more, whoever murdered Godber deliberately forced him to consume the contents of that bottle, when he was helpless and dying, to make it look as though he was drunk and had had an accident. Do I make myself plain?'

'Absolutely,' said Mr Lapline with no misgivings. 'As a pikestaff.'

'The murderer then made the mistake of removing the bottle to prevent the police finding his fingerprints on it. I hope that too is as plain as a pikestaff.'

'Oh yes. Most convincing,' said Mr Lapline. 'It's such a pity this evidence wasn't presented at the inquest. If it had been, the coroner would surely have postponed the verdict to allow the police to make further enquiries.'

Lady Mary bridled. 'Considering how quickly the inquest was called and considering my own state of mind at the time, I find that remark most unhelpful. As it was, I stated unequivocally that my husband had been murdered and that I meant to obtain justice.'

'You did indeed. No question about it,' said Mr Lapline, recalling the scene with considerable distaste. Outbursts in a coroner's court in which an hysterical client accused the Dean and Fellows of a famous Cambridge college of murder were definitely not his forte. 'On the other hand – '

'Then there is the question of the telephone,' Lady Mary went on implacably. 'Why had it been dragged off the table? Obviously to stop Godber calling for help. Finally, the fact that none of the whisky glasses had been touched is proof that he was forced to drink the stuff. What more evidence do you need?'

'Well, I suppose he might have . . .' Mr Lapline stopped. It did not seem advisable to suggest that Sir Godber could have drunk straight from the bottle. Lady

Mary might espouse every cause that purported to help the lower orders and the deprived, but she was hardly likely to take at all kindly to aspersions on her late husband's sense of social propriety. Gentlemen did not drink neat whisky out of bottles. Not that Mr Lapline considered Sir Godber Evans to have been a gentleman, merely a failed politician and Minister of Technological Development who had been relegated to the Mastership of Porterhouse. And to get even that far he had married this most unattractive woman for her money and influence. Looking at her thin lips and pointed nose, Mr Lapline wondered, not for the first time, what their sex life had been like.

He dragged his thoughts away from this unsavoury topic and tried to concentrate less morbidly on the damned man's death. 'I'm still afraid that the evidence, while undoubtedly enough to convince me, is nevertheless circumstantial, altogether too circumstantial to persuade officialdom to take further action at this late stage. Unfortunately, as you well know, bureaucrats are most tiresome . . .'

'Nobody knows better than I do how obstructive bureaucrats can be, Mr Lapline. I need no telling.' She paused and leant forward. 'Which is precisely why I have decided on an entirely new course of action.'

She paused again to let Mr Lapline wonder what this course of action might entail for him. She hitched her chair forward. 'I intend to create the Sir Godber Evans Memorial Fellowship at Porterhouse. For this purpose I shall donate six million pounds to the College. Don't interrupt. Six million pounds. Very well, they will undoubtedly accept it, and you will make the necessary arrangements. You will ensure that no one knows that I am the benefactress and the sponsor of the Fellow I will choose. You will find the applicants for the post . . .'

For the next twenty minutes Mr Lapline listened and the state of his stomach grew worse. It was clear she had every intention of choosing just those qualities in the successful applicant that would make the Sir Godber Evans Memorial Fellow exceedingly unpopular in Porterhouse. Even if the man failed to prove conclusively that Sir Godber had been murdered, and Mr Lapline couldn't see how he could do anything else, his enquiries were bound to have the most alarming effect on the Senior Fellows.

'I shall do my best, Lady Mary,' he said gloomily when she had finished. 'I shall do my best.'

Lady Mary bared her teeth in a smile. 'My best, Lapline, my best,' she said. 'And you will act expeditiously. I will interview each applicant you think suitable and I don't want any mistakes. I am sure you take my meaning.'

*

Mr Lapline did. He left the house in Kensington gripped by a sense of despair. Once back in the offices of Lapline & Goodenough, Solicitors, The Strand, London, he took another pill and went to the extraordinary and almost unheard-of lengths of consulting his partner. It was not something he liked doing. Goodenough's expertise lay in helping the firm's less respectable clients, particularly those with problems that involved the Inland Revenue or, worse still, the police. A number of titled bankrupts continued, thanks to Goodenough's efforts, to live in remarkably unreduced circumstances and a number of gentlemen Mr Lapline would have preferred behind bars remained at liberty. Mr Lapline did not approve of Goodenough. For such a very respectable firm he was too facile.

'My dear chap, you mustn't take such threats at face value,' Goodenough said when Mr Lapline told him what Lady Mary had demanded. 'The fact that she is so evidently demented as to continue a vendetta against the Dean and Senior Tutor should be a source of great satisfaction to you.'

'Goodenough,' said Mr Lapline severely, 'the gravity of the situation calls for something more constructive than flippancy. She undoubtedly means to go to another firm unless I follow her instructions to the letter. What are we to do?'

Goodenough considered that note of appeal and was gratified. It was about time Lapline learnt to respect his contribution to the firm. 'Well, in the first place we must humour her,' he said.

'Humour her?' said Mr Lapline. 'Humour her? She's not someone you can humour. She is demanding action and speedily.'

'Then we'll give it to her. We'll find some dreadful fellow she'll be bound to choose and let the brute loose on Porterhouse.'

Mr Lapline shuddered. 'And what possible good do you think that is going to do? Except to stir up a hornets' nest of scandal and lead to the most appalling series of actions for defamation.'

'Precisely,' said Goodenough. 'Nothing could be better. If the Dean and Senior Tutor and so on can be provoked into taking legal steps against the beastly woman, we will have her eating out of our hands. You have no idea how the issuing of writs and the likelihood of enormous damages endears a client to his, or in this case, her legal advisers. She will come to depend on us to get her out of the mess.'

Mr Lapline fastened pedantically on the verb. 'Endear? Endear? Your use of words is as indefensible as your ethics. I find your attitude frankly alarming.'

'Of course you do,' said Goodenough. 'That is why we are such excellent partners. I, in my own exemplary way, deal with the horrid realities of our profession while you maintain our reputation for professional rectitude. I am merely pointing out that if we wish to retain Lady Bloody Mary as a client we must give her what she wants.'

'But she can't possibly want to be sued by a whole host of furious dons who have been accused of murder.'

'I can't see why not,' said Goodenough. 'From what you've told me there isn't a hope in hell of re-opening the inquest on her husband after all these years, whereas a case for criminal slander would give her the opportunity to prove her point. It is known in common parlance as putting the cat among the pigeons. And think of our fees, Lapline, think of our fees.'

'I am thinking of our reputation,' said Lapline, 'for probity. What you are suggesting is entirely contrary to –'

'Come off it, old chap, come off the high horse. And don't talk to me about probity. After a long day dealing with tax-evading morons who wouldn't know probity from the back end of a bus, I am not in the mood for a dose of professional self-righteousness. Either you want to keep the Lacey account or you don't. Make up your mind.'

But Mr Lapline already had. Lady Mary and the Lacey account were by far the most important concerns of his professional life. The Lacey fortune was not a vast one. It didn't compare with the really big ones, but it was substantial. Mr Lapline appreciated that. And besides, it was old money and fitted in very nicely with his own views on what was right and proper. To that extent he felt it was real money as opposed to the other sort, the unreal money that Goodenough seemed to understand. Unreal money drifted about the world from one country to another and in and out of currencies and tax havens in the most unseemly fashion. Mr Lapline disapproved of it in much the same way that he disapproved of Goodenough. In his opinion they both lacked substance. The Lacey money didn't. It was safely invested in solid British institutions, in land and in well-run industries. It was not to be trifled with. But above all Mr Lapline needed to represent it. The Lacey account was the touchstone of his professional reputation.

'Oh well, so be it,' he said. 'I'll have to leave it to you. My stomach . . . And in any case I wouldn't know where to look for the sort of so-called scholar she would accept as the Sir Godber Evans Memorial Fellow.'

'I'm sure I'll find someone,' said Goodenough. 'You leave it to me. And if I were in your position, I'd have that wretched gall bladder out.'

Mr Lapline sighed and shook his head sorrowfully. 'It is all very well to talk,' he said. 'My wife won't allow it. Her mother died during a gall-bladder operation. It's a damned nuisance.' He got up to go. 'And do please bear in mind that there must be nothing shady about this business. Our responsibility lies in protecting Lady Mary from herself.'

It was a remark calculated to annoy Goodenough. 'Of course it does,' he said. 'The fact that the old bird is dotty is beside the point. Half my clients are off their trolleys, but I still manage to keep them solvent and out of jail. Ask Vera.'

But Mr Lapline preferred not to. Goodenough's secretary possessed physical attractions that were rather too obvious for Mr Lapline's taste and were, he suspected, used in part to distract the Special Income Tax investigators from concentrating at all closely on the dubious accounts of Goodenough's clients. He chose not to speculate on the other uses his partner might put them to. He went back to his office and thought wistfully about having his gall bladder out after all.

*

That evening Goodenough explained the problem to Vera. 'She's an old woman who has seen everything she believed in proved wrong and it has made her even more bitter than she was before. In any case, she's got more money than she knows what to do with and now she's out to raise hell in Porterhouse. She's already put Lappie in a spin and his gall bladder is playing up again. It always does when he's under stress. I've said I'll find the applicants for him.'

'Meaning that *I* will,' said Vera, helping herself to another gin and tonic.

'Well, I was rather hoping . . .' said Goodenough with a look of mock guilt.

Vera arranged herself on the sofa. 'I shall need time off,' she said. 'And expenses.'

'No problem. Bloody Mary's account will see you right. And you're an angel.'

2

That wasn't the way Vera saw herself but she was away for only a fortnight during which time Mr Lapline felt far worse. 'Are you sure you know what you're doing?' he asked Goodenough several times, only to be told that everything was under control. Goodenough chose not to mention whose control that was and Mr Lapline chose not to question him too closely.

In the event Vera returned with a list of twenty academics who would be happy to become Fellows at Porterhouse. Goodenough studied the list doubtfully.

'I had no idea there were so many universities,' he said. 'And who's this man in Grimsby whose research is into Psycho-erotic Anal Fantasies? I can't see Porterhouse accepting him even for six million.'

'I can't see Lady Mary Evans taking to him either,' said Vera. 'Unless of course she approves of early-morning drinking. On the other hand, his thinking is undoubtedly radical.'

'And Dr Lamprey Yeaster at Bristol? His curriculum vitae seems very sound. "Historical Research into Industrial Relations in Bradford".'

'I don't think he's quite right for her, somehow,' said

Vera. 'He's a member of the National Front and his views on blacks leave rather a lot to be desired.'

'In that case she won't touch him with a bargepole. There's no one here she's going to choose.'

'Oh yes, there is, my dear,' said Vera. 'I think she'll like Dr Purefoy Osbert.'

Goodenough looked at her suspiciously. 'You mean you've ring-fenced him? Why? What's so special about him apart from his name?'

'Nothing very much except that he'll do what I tell him. Have a look at his list of publications.'

Goodenough read them. 'He seems to have a thing about executions,' he said. 'Particularly hangings. There's a book here called *The Long Drop*.'

'That's Purefoy's magnum opus. I haven't read it myself but I'm told it's strong stuff. He has made a study of every hanging in England since 1891.'

'And you think Bloody Mary is going to approve of him? She is violently anti-capital punishment.'

'So is Purefoy. You've no idea how many innocent people he believes have gone to the gallows. That's his whole thesis.'

'What's this about Crippen? *The Innocence of Dr Crippen*? The bugger wasn't innocent. He was guilty as hell.'

'Not according to Purefoy,' said Vera. 'Mrs Crippen committed suicide and the doctor panicked and buried her in the cellar.'

'What, after cutting her up into small pieces or

14

whatever he did? The fellow is off his head. Still, I can certainly see him getting on with Lady Mary like a house on fire. But tell me, why do you always refer to him by his Christian name?'

Vera smiled. 'Because he's my cousin,' she said.

*

It was not something Goodenough mentioned to Mr Lapline. In fact he amended the list of Dr Osbert's publications. Mr Lapline was in a bad way without having to cope with the innocence of Dr Crippen and what happened when they hanged Mrs Thompson. He was having trouble with his own bowels. 'I can't honestly say I begin to like the sound of any of them,' he said, 'and as for this one in Grimsby . . .'

'You don't think he's right for Porterhouse?'

Mr Lapline expressed the opinion that he wasn't right for anywhere except hell. Goodenough went away to make his next move. Having studied the notes Lady Mary had made on the Senior Fellows – there wasn't a faintly benevolent comment among them – he decided it would be best not to discuss the possibility of the new Fellowship with the Bursar. The Dean (what she had to say about the Dean was vitriolic) and the Senior Tutor, 'a wholly unintelligent person whose interest in rowing suggests obsessive adolescent interests' in her words, clearly distrusted the Bursar who 'sided with Godber on financial grounds'. There was independent evidence of this dislike in the reports of the two private detectives she had employed to investigate her husband's death. One report, written by an unfortunate operative who had spent two hellish months working as a human dishwasher in the College kitchens and who had developed a most unpleasant skin condition thanks to the scouring powder and detergents he had been forced to use, described the Dean as the real power in Porterhouse with the Senior Tutor as his deputy.

'I have decided to make the offer through the Senior Tutor,' Goodenough told Vera. 'If I took the idea to the Bursar, the Dean would turn it down flat. He'd smell trouble. Got a nose for it. In any case, from what I hear the Bursar is so desperate for money we're bound to have his support. It will look better coming from the Tutor.'

*

In fact the stratagem was unnecessary. The Dean was already making plans to spend some time away from Porterhouse. He was going to find a rich successor to Skullion, preferably from among the Old Porterthusians. He had always been fond of Skullion, but in view of the financial situation in Porterhouse the need to find a new Master, one with financial pull and a very large private income, seemed imperative. At least to the Dean. That was how they had dealt with the financial mess Lord Fitzherbert had got the College into. Fitzherbert had been a rich enough man himself, and they had made him Master. That had always been the preferred Porterhouse method, and the Dean meant to use it again. The real difficulty lay in finding a way to remove Skullion. It had never been supposed he would live so long after his stroke and now the Dean could only hope he would pass quietly away after an excellent dinner. The Dean had in mind the special Duck Dinner. Skullion had always loved *Canards pressés à la Porterhouse*. All the same the Dean had been to see the College doctor in the hope of an unfavourable prognosis for the Master, but Dr MacKendly was more concerned with the Dean himself. 'Now what is it this time?' he asked. 'The old prostate giving you trouble again?'

'Hardly,' said the Dean, 'since it has never given me the slightest trouble before.'

'Well, it was bound to happen at your age,' said the doctor, putting on a surgical glove and indicating the examination couch. 'Now this may be a touch uncomfortable but hardly painful.'

'It certainly won't,' said the Dean, remaining rooted to his chair. 'I have not come about my own condition. I am concerned about Skull . . . the Master, that is.'

Dr MacKendly sat down regretfully at his desk but did not remove the surgical glove. 'Skullion? Can't say I'm entirely surprised. All that sitting about in a wheelchair and so on and widdling into a bag is bound to have an effect in the end. Of course we could operate, but that can cause problems you know. Sometimes one ejaculates backwards into the bladder.'

'I hardly think Skullion ... the Master is likely to ejaculate anywhere,' said the Dean bitterly, 'particularly as he doesn't need a prostate operation. What I want you to tell me is your opinion on the Master's general fitness.'

The doctor nodded. He still hadn't removed the surgical glove. 'General fitness, eh? Well, that's a different matter altogether. I mean at our age we can hardly expect to be entirely fit and – '

'I am talking about the Master, Skullion, for goodness sake,' the Dean snapped. 'His general fitness.'

'Point taken,' said the doctor. 'And I have to say that he is not at all well. The Porterhouse Blue he had, you know, was a very bad one. It's amazing he survived at all. He must have the constitution of an ox.'

The Dean eyed him very unpleasantly. 'And would you assess his ability to perform his duties as Master of the College at the same bovine level?' he asked.

'Ah, there you have me, Dean. I have never really known what a Master's duties are, apart from dining in Hall and being around for official occasions and so on. Otherwise there is practically damn all to do as far as I can see. Skullion has proved that, hasn't he?'

The Dean made a final attempt to get an answer that made sense. 'And how long do you think he's got? Got to live, I mean.'

'There you have me again,' said the doctor. 'It is almost impossible to say. Only a matter of time, of course.'

But the Dean had had enough. 'Have you ever known when it wasn't?' he asked and stood up.

'Wasn't? Wasn't what?'

'A matter of time. From the day we are born, for instance.' And leaving Dr MacKendly to work that out – the doctor's speciality was rugby knees, not metaphysics – the Dean went down the steps into King's Parade and walked back to Porterhouse in a very nasty temper. Around him tourists stared into shop windows or sat on the wall under King's College Chapel or photographed the Senate House. The Dean disregarded them. They belonged to a world he had always despised.

Two days later, explaining that he had a sick relative in Wales to visit, the Dean set off in search of a new Master for Porterhouse. Something told him he had to hurry. It was a gut feeling, but such a feeling seldom let him down.

*

The feelings that Mr Lapline had in his stomach were by now so acute that it was some two weeks before Goodenough had sufficient time to spare from his partner's work to travel to Cambridge to meet the Senior Tutor for lunch at the Garden House Hotel overlooking the Cam. 'I'd have invited you to my club in London, but it gets very crowded these days and we can talk more privately here. Besides, it is always a pleasure to visit Cambridge and I'm sure you're a very busy man. I hope you don't mind lunching here?'

The Senior Tutor didn't in the least mind. He had heard good things about the Garden House, and Wednesday lunch in Hall tended to be rather meagre. He accepted a very large pink gin and studied the menu while Goodenough spoke about his nephew in the Leander Club, his own college, Magdalen at Oxford, and anything but the matter he had come to discuss. It was only after he had persuaded the Senior Tutor to have another very large pink gin and then had primed him with a sizeable helping of pâté, an excellent fillet steak and a bottle and a half of Chambertin and they were sitting with their coffee and Chartreuse, that Goodenough finally got round to the topic of the donation. He did so with an air of slight embarrassment.

'The fact of the matter is that we have been instructed by someone in the City who wishes to remain anonymous to sound out the Senior Fellows about the creation of a new Fellowship, and frankly, knowing your reputation for discretion, I thought a quiet chat with you might be the best way to start.' He paused to allow the Senior Tutor to choose a cigar to go with another Chartreuse. 'The funding for the salary of the new Fellow would of course be paid for by our client and the donation to the College would run into seven figures.'

Again he paused, this time to allow the tutor to calculate that seven figures made one million. 'In fact the client has mentioned six million pounds with possibly more to follow on her . . . his death.'

'Six million? Did you say six million?' asked the

Senior Tutor rather huskily. If it hadn't been for the meal, and the cost of the Chambertin and the Partagas cigar, he would have wondered if he was being subjected to some fiendish practical joke. Nobody had ever offered Porterhouse such an enormous sum before.

'Oh yes, at least six,' Goodenough said, sensing the Senior Tutor's bewilderment. Taking advantage of it, he went on. 'But on condition that the donation is not made public. I'm afraid my client is an eccentrically private person and insists on anonymity. I have to make that point.'

For a moment the thought crossed his mind of hinting the client might be Getty. He did better. 'You've heard of Getty?'

'Yes,' said the Senior Tutor almost in a whisper.

'Unfortunately my client does not possess that degree of wealth but she . . . he' (damn that second Chartreuse) 'has a very considerable fortune all the same.'

'Must have,' muttered the Senior Tutor, and made the mistake of inhaling the Havana too deeply. When his gasping coughs stopped, Goodenough went on. 'I'm telling you all this privately because of your reputation for discretion. It is essential that nothing leaks out. Your influence in Porterhouse is well known and I feel sure that with your backing . . .'

The practised words wafted happily into the Senior Tutor's mulled consciousness. The client was particularly anxious that the Bursar, whose reputation was not so . . . well, to be a little indiscreet, not so reliable, must not be consulted, but if the Senior Tutor could give his assurance that the donation would be accepted – the Senior Tutor could and did – and the Fellow appointed – the Senior Tutor had no doubt about that – then the matter was settled, and Mr Goodenough's client would proceed. A letter putting forward the terms of the appointment would be drawn up and sent to the Senior Tutor, who would make the necessary arrangements, presumably through the College Council, and confirm the decision in writing. By the time Goodenough had finished, the Senior Tutor was in a state of euphoria. Goodenough gave him a lift back to Porterhouse in his taxi then caught the train to London.

*

'He did what?' said Mr Lapline next day.

'Lapped it up,' Goodenough said.

'Lapped it up? Are you sure?' Mr Lapline couldn't imagine any of the Senior Fellows at Porterhouse lapping anything, apart from soup, up. From what he had seen of the Dean and the Senior Tutor at the inquest into Sir Godber Evans' death, they might well chew but they were definitely not of the lapping sort.

'Absolutely,' Goodenough assured him. 'Swallowed the proposal hook, line and sinker, along with an excellent bottle of Burgundy and an underdone steak – '

'For heaven's sake, Goodenough, don't talk about food. If you knew what my stomach is doing to me – '

'Sorry, sorry. All I'm trying to tell you is that you've

got no reason to worry about losing Her Ladyship's account. She will find someone on that list who will prove just the sort of person she wants, and Porterhouse will accept him with open arms. Whether they like what they get is another matter altogether. That is not your problem, nor mine.'

But Mr Lapline continued to be pessimistic. 'I wish I had your confidence. I just hope to God she doesn't choose that anal-erotic swine from Grimsby. With a list of publications like that the sod ought to be in jail.'

*

For the next few weeks the firm of Lapline & Goodenough resumed its normal and most respectable routine. Mr Lapline's gall bladder quietened down, and Lady Mary was sent the list of candidates along with their curricula vitae. It was left to her to invite them down to her house to be interviewed. Goodenough refused to have anything to do with that side of the business. 'I wouldn't dream of involving the firm in such matters,' he said. 'We are not a scholastic employment agency. In any case, I have yet to receive written confirmation of the contract from Porterhouse, though the Senior Tutor did write to thank me for lunch and said he was sure the Fellowship would be approved.'

All the same, Goodenough's curiosity had been provoked by his reading of *The Long Drop*. Even to his hardened sensibilities Purefoy Osbert's book was deeply disturbing. He had sat up late for two nights running, transfixed by the anatomical consequences and the details of hangings with which Dr Osbert seemed most at home.

'Are you sure this cousin of yours is entirely sane?' he asked Vera. 'That beastly book of his has to have been written by someone with a pronounced taste for S and M.'

'You're just an old fuddy-duddy. Purefoy isn't in the least like that. It's just that the poor darling is deeply committed to social justice.'

'Could have fooled me,' Goodenough muttered. He hadn't much liked that 'poor darling' when applied to a man who could describe so graphically the consequences of too long or too short a drop on victims who were either too short and fat themselves or too tall and thin. There was also the evidence – and Dr Osbert's facts could not be faulted – that since the abolition of capital punishment a great many people found guilty of murder and condemned to life imprisonment had later been shown to be wholly innocent and had been pardoned. It followed from these incontestable statistics that a considerable proportion of those who had been hanged before abolition had also been entirely innocent. The lawyer in Goodenough found this conclusion most upsetting. He wondered how the argument would go down with the Dean and the Senior Tutor.

'I suppose it doesn't matter what happens once he's been appointed,' he told Vera. 'All the same I can foresee some extremely heated arguments.'

'Which Purefoy will win,' said Vera, 'because he is obsessed with facts and certainties.'

'Not the only thing he's obsessed with. And anyway, it is not a fact that Crippen didn't murder his wife. It's an assumption, and a false one.'

But Vera wasn't prepared to argue. 'He is an excellent researcher and a genuine scholar. You'll see that when you meet him.'

'I don't intend to,' said Goodenough.

*

Nor, it seemed, did Lady Mary. The strain of interviewing the previous applicants for the Sir Godber Evans Memorial Fellowship had told on her failing health. Never a very sexual person herself, she had found the interview with the psycho-anal-erotic fantasist from Grimsby deeply disturbing. Owing to an extremely painful attack of sciatica she had had to conduct it while lying on a chaise longue, and Dr MacKerbie had arrived smelling very strongly of beer and whisky. In fact he was plainly drunk at ten o'clock in the morning and had evidently got the impression that she was lying there waiting to enjoy his particular fantasies and even to experience anal eroticism herself. She had been saved by the housekeeper who heard her screams and by Dr MacKerbie, whose drunkenness made the business of undoing his trousers altogether too hazardous.

After that nightmare interview, Lady Mary invariably sat behind a substantial desk with a tape recorder running and the housekeeper's husband standing in a corner of the room for protection. The interview with Dr Lamprey Yeaster went fairly well to begin with. The historian was at least sober and his knowledge of Historical Research into Industrial Relations in Bradford before the War was impressive. So in a way, though in an entirely different way, were his opinions on post-war immigration policies and the consequences of allowing hundreds of thousands of West Indians and Pakistanis into Britain. Lady Mary Evans had him hustled out of the house after twenty minutes and had to lie down on the chaise longue again, this time with nervous prostration.

The next six applicants all failed to satisfy her and the only one who appealed to her at all said he'd changed his mind and wouldn't go near Porterhouse because it was a bloody snob college and anyway he was quite happy doing research into potato pathology at Strathclyde and Cambridge didn't have anything to offer him. By the time she reached the vivisectionist from Southampton and had had to listen to a perfectly foul account of his work with cats, Lady Mary was on the point of abandoning the entire project. But her sense of duty prevailed. She phoned Mr Lapline, and was put through instead to Goodenough.

'I do see the problem,' he said when she complained bitterly about the quality of the applicants and wanted to know why she had been sent a man who made it his life's work to torture cats to death when she was particularly fond of cats and . . . 'I really do, Lady Mary, but the fact of the matter is that Porterhouse has a perfectly dreadful reputation, as you are probably aware, and – '

Lady Mary pointed out that as her late husband had been Master of Porterhouse and had been murdered there of course she knew it had a dreadful reputation and what had that got to do with sending her a lot of psychopaths.

'The thing is,' said Goodenough, 'that it has proved extremely difficult to find genuine scholars who want to go near the place.'

'So far you haven't found a single scholar. That awful man from Bristol who wants to send every black person back to countries they've never come from . . .'

'You mean Dr Lamprey Yeaster? I had no idea he held such disgraceful political views. My remit was to – '

'From now on your remit, as you choose to call it, is to vet the applicants yourself. I am not a well person, and I refuse to have to meet people who are either mad or thoroughly repulsive in some other way. Is that clear? And anyway, why are you dealing with the matter? I have always dealt with Mr Lapline.'

Goodenough sighed audibly into the phone. 'I'm afraid Mr Lapline is undergoing medical treatment for his gall bladder. A temporary condition but a very painful one, I'm told. In the meantime please be assured that I shall do everything necessary . . .'

He put the phone down and went through to Vera. 'Well, that has simplified things,' he said. 'You can tell Cousin Purefoy he has the Fellowship. She doesn't want to see any of the others. I suppose I'll have to meet him after all.'

3

In Purefoy Osbert at Kloone University the news that he was about to become the Sir Godber Evans Memorial Fellow at Porterhouse aroused mixed emotions, though only slightly. He was perfectly happy at Kloone where he had first studied and, having graduated, had gone on to his doctoral thesis, 'The Crime of Punishment', on the inequities of the penal system in Britain. On the other hand he had no doubt he would be perfectly happy in Cambridge. And the move would have its advantages. The University Library there had many more books than that at Kloone and to Purefoy it was in libraries that he could acquire certainties. Certainty was essential to him and the written word had a certainty about it that everything else in life lacked. Like an intellectual sniffer-dog, Purefoy Osbert kept his nose close to documents, collected information and felt confident in the certainty of his conclusions. Theories and certainties protected him from the chaos that was the universe. They also helped him to cope with the chaotic inconsistencies of his late father's opinions.

The Reverend Osbert had been of the eclectic persuasion. Brought up as a Presbyterian, he had in his teens switched to Methodism, then to Unitarianism and from that to Christian Science before being persuaded by a reading of Newman's *Apologia* that Rome was his spiritual home. The homecoming did not last long, although it contributed to Purefoy's naming. Tolstoyan pacifism was more manifestly the answer and for a while the Rev. Osbert toyed with Buddhism. In other words Purefoy's childhood was spent on a roller-coaster of changing philosophies and uncertain opinions. He would go to school one morning knowing that his father believed in one God, only to come home in the afternoon to learn that God didn't exist.

Mrs Osbert, on the other hand, was entirely consistent. So long as her husband paid the bills – he had inherited a row of small houses and rented them to reliable tenants – and provided the family with a comfortable living, she did not mind what opinions he held or for how long. 'Just stick to the facts,' she would say when one of his digressions went on too long, and she was frequently telling young Purefoy, 'The trouble with your father is that he is never certain about anything. He never knows what to believe. If only he could be certain about something, we'd all be a lot happier. You just bear that in mind and you won't go the same way.' Not wanting to go the same way as his father, who had died quite terribly on his return from a pilgrimage to a Buddhist shrine in Sri Lanka where he had made the mistake of attempting to befriend a rabid dog, Purefoy had never forgotten her words. 'I told him one of those days he would go too far,' she explained to

Purefoy after the funeral. 'And he did. To Sri Lanka. And all in search of holiness. Instead of which . . . Well, never mind. You just stick to certainties and you won't go far wrong.'

Purefoy had done his best to follow her advice. All the same, he had inherited his father's tendency to seek for meaning in abstractions. At Kloone University he had been particularly affected by Professor Walden Yapp, who had once been wrongly convicted of murder. The Professor's account of his time in prison and the psychological trauma resulting from a sense of his own innocence had affected Purefoy deeply and had influenced his choice of a doctoral thesis. Professor Yapp's innocence could not be doubted. Had capital punishment still been in existence when the Professor was sentenced, he would certainly have been hanged. 'From my own experience I can say with absolute assurance that other men, as innocent as I am, have undoubtedly gone to the gallows.'

Professor Yapp's statement had inspired Purefoy Osbert to spend five years working on his next book, *The Long Drop*. He acknowledged his debt to Professor Yapp in his dedication and then went on to do further research into innocent victims of the criminal system and the brutalizing effect of prison life on prisoners and prison officers alike, for a book he intended to call *This Punished Breed*. It was a work he hoped would put an end once and for all to the pernicious and positively mediaeval public belief in crime as a punishable offence.

He went further. He did not subscribe to Professor Yapp's belief that theft, murder, muggings or any other criminal activity were the products of poverty and social deprivation. He blamed the law itself. As he never tired of telling his students, 'Crime is the consequence of the system of law and order established to root out the social disease it creates. By defining that which is unlawful we ensure that the law will be broken.' It was a concept that naturally found favour with his students and had the merit of forcing the more intelligent ones to argue vehemently with one another, and even occasionally to think. This was a notable achievement at Kloone, and added to Dr Osbert's already considerable reputation. But for the most part he spent his time in libraries or at the Public Record Office going through box after box of documents in pursuit of the information he needed.

But if his father and mother had influenced him, so too had his cousin Vera. From his earliest childhood he had always done what she wanted. She was five years older than he was and, being a kindly if slightly promiscuous girl, had been only too ready to show him the certainty of her sex. From that moment of adolescent revelation Purefoy had been ambiguously devoted to Vera. He had spent many hours thinking about her and had been sure he was in love with her. But she had gone her own way and Purefoy had pursued other less uncertain quantities. It was only much later, when he met Mrs Ndhlovo, that he knew himself to be truly in love.

One evening, in the mistaken belief that he was going to hear a lecture by a leading authority on Prison Reform in Sierra Leone, he found himself sitting in the front row of an evening class Mrs Ndhlovo was giving on Male Infertility and Masturbatory Techniques. The class was well attended and while Purefoy had learnt some of the facts of life from Vera, he learnt a great many more from Mrs Ndhlovo. She was particularly interesting on *coitus interruptus* and means of avoiding *ejaculatio praecox*. Above all she was beautiful. It was not solely her physical beauty that appealed to him so much: she had a beautiful mind. In a curiously unnecessary pidgin English she spoke in detail about clitoral stimulation and fellatio with a calm assurance that left him almost breathless with admiration. And desire. Within the course of that first hour he had found his true love and when the following week he was there in the same seat looking adoringly up at her splendid lips and eyes while she showed some particularly horrible slides of the effects of female circumcision on mature women in East Africa, he was certain he was in love. After the lecture he introduced himself and their relationship began.

Unfortunately for Purefoy Mrs Ndhlovo, while fond of him, did not reciprocate his feelings. Her first marriage in Kampala had not been an entirely happy one. The discovery that Mr Ndhlovo already had three wives and that the first wife had been the one to suggest that he marry again had rather spoilt the honeymoon. All the same she had loved him in her own way and felt genuine sorrow when he disappeared and was rumoured to be among the other contents of General Idi Amin's freezer. The fact that they were no longer there when the General was ousted and fled to Saudi Arabia had done nothing to set her suspicions to rest. By then she had left Uganda and had come to Britain to start a new career in education. Within a few months she had gained a considerable reputation at Kloone by stating openly at parties that her Johnny had almost certainly been part of 'that black bastard Idi Amin's late-night snack'. Such outspokenness on interracial matters had until then been unheard at the University, but no one could find fault with Mrs Ndhlovo. She obviously had every right in the world to talk like that about the man who had murdered and consumed her husband. She had been there in Uganda and she had suffered terribly. The fact that she was very attractive and knew so much about sexual practices in Africa and, it seemed, just about everywhere else in the world also helped to make her a popular figure. Besides which, she was a very practical woman.

'All very well you say you love me,' she said, maintaining the curious English Purefoy found so delightful, 'you don't earn enough to keep two and have kids too. You got no ambition either, Purefoy. No money, no ambition, no Mrs Ndhlovo.'

'But Ingrid, you know – ' Purefoy began.

'And don't call me that name. I no like it. I Mrs Ndhlovo. Different.'

'You can say that again,' Purefoy said. 'But one of these days I'm bound to get a professorship and – '

'One of these days too late,' said Mrs Ndhlovo adamantly. 'I don't have kids by that time. Get the pause.'

'The paws?' said the mystified Purefoy.

'Manopause. Don't know why they call it manopause. Have to pause now once a month. After manopause, no pause at all. No kids either. I go find proper man. Ambition. Money. Not just sit ass on chair reading books. Make some big thing. Got to have ambition.'

From these grim discussions Purefoy came away disheartened but he still attended her evening classes and had watched in an agonizing ecstasy her demonstration of the use of the double-strength condom as a means of delaying the male orgasm. The sight of her long tapering fingers sliding the thing over the plaster-of-Paris penis and then stroking the scrotum left him limp and wishing to hell he'd taken the precaution of wearing one himself. The following week he had come better prepared, only to find that her lecture was purely theoretical and dealt entirely with an historical review of medical and religious objections to so-called self-abuse or onanism. There had been none of those practical demonstrations that had made the condom necessary and, far from saving Purefoy Osbert embarrassment, the thing had been the cause of it. His efforts to prevent the device making its way down his trouser leg had caught the attention of the women on either side of him, who were evidently as bored as he was by historical objections to masturbation. Purefoy's spasmodic movements were far more intriguing. Purefoy smiled bleakly at the woman on his right and was misunderstood. 'Can't you wait until afterwards?' she asked in a whisper that was audible several rows behind. For the rest of the hour he sat staring rigidly at Mrs Ndhlovo and hardly moved at all, but at the end of the class he was forced to stand up.

'After you,' said the woman on his left. The one on his right had already hurried off.

'No, please, after you,' said Purefoy and squeezed back against the chair.

The woman shook her head. She had no intention of passing at all closely to a man whose sudden attention to his upper leg had been so peculiarly spasmodic and intense. She hadn't liked his bleak smile either. 'Look,' she said, rather unpleasantly. 'You go out first. All right?'

It wasn't all right, but Purefoy went. So did the condom. For a moment it clung to his knee but only for a moment. As he stepped forward it dropped out of the bottom of his trouser-leg and lay supine on the toe of his shoe. Purefoy tried to kick it off but again his movements were too peculiar to ignore. Conscious that he was the object of amused interest he hurried down the hall and out into the comparative anonymity of the parking lot where he could deal with the thing in private. After that Purefoy abandoned the condom method and took matters into his hands before attending Mrs Ndhlovo's classes.

*

It was shortly after this and several more vain attempts to get Mrs Ndhlovo, if not to marry him, at least to become his partner, that Vera phoned to tell him about the Fellowship at Porterhouse. Purefoy Osbert was not interested. 'I am perfectly happy here and I have no interest in going to Cambridge. And anyway why should anyone offer me a Fellowship at Porterhouse just like that? You have to apply and explain your special area of research and – '

'Purefoy, darling, of course you've had to apply. That is all taken care of, and your application has almost certainly been accepted.'

'It can't have been. I haven't made it.'

'But I have,' said Vera sweetly. 'On your behalf.'

'You can't go round making applications on other people's behalf. You've got to get their consent and anyway you don't even know what I've published or my curriculum vitae. Or what my present studies are.'

'Of course I do. I got it from your Faculty secretary. She was extremely helpful.'

'What?' squawked Purefoy, now thoroughly alarmed and angry. 'She had absolutely no right to give confidential information away like that. I've a good mind – '

'A very good mind,' Vera interrupted. 'In fact an excellent one, which is why you are going to Porterhouse.'

'I'm most definitely not,' said Purefoy. 'I want to know why Mrs Pitch gave you details of my curriculum vitae. You can't go round revealing – '

'Oh, do hush up. She didn't do anything of the sort. I'm your cousin, remember, and I know just about everything about you. Besides, it's all on the Kloone University computer and I know your password so I went straight in and had it all printed out.'

'My password? You don't know it. You can't have got it from Mrs Pitch either because she doesn't know it.'

'I'm certain she doesn't, but I most certainly do.'

'What on earth do you mean?' Purefoy demanded.

Vera giggled. 'Purefoy, dear, you're so transparent. "Certainty" is your password. I knew it had to be something like that. You're obsessed with it.'

Purefoy Osbert groaned. Vera had always been smarter than he was. 'In that case I'm going to change it,' he said. 'And I am definitely not going anywhere near Porterhouse College. It's got a dreadful reputation for snobbery and all sorts of other things.'

'Which is why you have been given a Fellowship there. To change things for the better,' said Vera. 'They need some serious scholarship, and you are going to provide it. Your salary will be more than three times what you're getting at the moment and you will be free to do your own research work with no obligation to do any teaching.'

Purefoy Osbert's silence was significant. Only that day he had had to attend an extremely boring Finance

Committee meeting at which the possibility of financial cuts had been discussed with the mention of a freeze on salaries, and that had been followed by a seminar on Bentham with several students who were convinced that prisons built like Dartmoor on the panopticon principle were far more suitable for murderers and sex-offenders than the more modern open prisons Purefoy advocated. Some of them had even argued that child molesters ought to be castrated and murderers executed. Purefoy had found the seminar most distressing, particularly the way the more prejudiced students had refused to accept the facts he had given them. And now suddenly he was being offered a Fellowship that involved no teaching and with a salary that would surely satisfy Mrs Ndhlovo.

'Do you really mean that?' he asked cautiously. 'This isn't some sort of joke?'

'Have you ever known me to lie to you, Purefoy? Have you?'

Purefoy Osbert hesitated again. 'No, I don't suppose I have. All the same . . . you're talking about a salary – '

'Of nearly sixty thousand pounds a year, which is far more than any professor gets. Now give me the number of your fax machine and I'll send you a copy of the letter you will be receiving either tomorrow or the next day from your sponsor's solicitors, Lapline & Goodenough.'

'But that is the firm you work for,' said Purefoy.

'Which is how I happen to know you're being offered the Fellowship,' said Vera and, having taken his fax number, rang off.

Ten minutes later a bewildered Purefoy Osbert sat reading the most amazing letter he had ever received. It was on Lapline & Goodenough, Solicitors, official note-paper and was signed by Goodenough, and while it was only a fax copy there could be no doubt about its authenticity. Purefoy considered the stated conditions very carefully. 'As the Sir Godber Evans Memorial Fellow you will be required only to establish the facts of his life with a view to the possible publication of a biography. His tenure as Master of Porterhouse was a very short one and ended with his death . . .'

Purefoy Osbert read on, trying to see where the snag was. There didn't seem to be one. He could pursue his own studies, he could, if he wished, take a post in the University proper as opposed to Porterhouse College, and his stipend of £55,000 was guaranteed from funds provided by the sponsor, who wished to remain anony-mous. In short he was being offered a sinecure and, as far as he could see, there were no awkward strings attached to it. He was particularly interested in the repeated emphasis on the sponsor's respect for his methods. Purefoy Osbert spent the evening in a state of euphoria and even considered going round to visit Mrs Ndhlovo with his amazing news. But he didn't. He still couldn't be certain this wasn't some sort of hoax. If it turned out to be true there would be no more talk about his lack of money or ambition. And she certainly wouldn't be able to say he wasn't a proper man.

4

At Porterhouse too there was some delay. Goodenough's insistence on the need for no publicity and his praise of the Senior Tutor's reputation for discretion had placed the latter in something of a quandary. For one thing he couldn't discuss the proposed Fellowship with the Bursar because he wasn't, in Goodenough's opinion – which the Senior Tutor shared – to be trusted, and for another the Dean was away from Cambridge, supposedly visiting a sick relative in Wales. And without the Dean's presence at the College Council no decisions could be made. The Master would never ratify the new Fellowship without the Dean's consent. And while Skullion had recovered his power of speech and some movement he had never lost the sense of deference, particularly to the Dean, that forty-five years as a College Porter had instilled in him. Besides, the Senior Tutor himself tended to defer to the Dean. They had never liked one another and there were times when they had quarrelled so badly they were not on speaking terms, but together they had prevented Porterhouse from following the example of every other college in Cambridge. Or to put it more accurately, they had slowed change down to a pace that would allow the past to catch up and reimpose old values on new ways. After much argument in the College Council it had been agreed that Porterhouse would finally admit women undergraduates, though with a qualifying motion proposed by the Senior Tutor that this should in no way diminish the accommodation provided for male entrants. This motion had passed unnoticed. The Dean's conversion to the notion of women in Porterhouse had so amazed the younger and more progressive Fellows – he had been adamantly opposed to the idea for years – that they hadn't foreseen the consequences of the Senior Tutor's addendum or the Praelector's support for it, which he was by custom entitled to make in Latin. It was only much later, when the question of the numbers of women to be admitted to the College came up, that the progressive Fellows led by Dr Buscott realized the crisis facing them. Porterhouse was a poor college. It had once been a rich one but all that wealth had been lost by the then Bursar, Lord Fitzherbert, who had gambled the money away at Monte Carlo. Since that catastrophic moment Porterhouse had sunk into poverty.

Even the Bursar, who had voted for the changes and for the inclusion of women, had been appalled at the suggestion that a new block be built for them behind the Chapel. 'Of course I support the proposal in principle,' he said, 'but I must point out that it is totally impractical. Such a building programme would cost millions. Where do you suppose we could find the funds?'

'Presumably in the same way as other colleges go about these things,' said Professor Pawley, Porterhouse's most eminent scholar, an astronomer whose life's work had been concentrated on an exceedingly remote nebula known as Pawley One. 'Other Bursars have recourse to banks and commercial loans. It is surely not beyond our intellectual resources to make use of similar means?'

The Bursar had swallowed the insult and had taken his revenge. 'It is not our intellectual resources which are in question, but our practical ones. We don't have any means of obtaining loans. The cost of rebuilding the Bull Tower proved far higher than had been foreseen by those on the Restoration Committee' – Professor Pawley had been its chairman – 'who failed to distinguish the difference between the cost of modern building materials such as bricks and the vastly more expensive price required to replace extremely old materials. In the circumstances, if anyone can explain how I can obtain any additional funding, I shall of course be most grateful.'

*

In the face of this unanswerable question the new building never materialized and while women had come to Porterhouse their numbers were negligible. And since the Senior Tutor was in charge of admissions as well as the Boat Club, those women who were admitted had certain characteristics that distinguished them from the girls in other colleges. Even the Chaplain, always a broad-minded man, had complained.

'I know the world is a very different place these days and I try to keep up with the times,' he had said over the kidney ragout at dinner one night, 'but I draw the line at young men wearing lipstick in public places. There is some man on my staircase who is distinctly odd. I found a tube of lipstick in the lavatory this morning and whatever aftershave lotion he uses is most disturbing.'

'I don't suppose there is any point in explaining,' said the Praelector, keeping his voice down. The Chaplain was deaf, but it was as well to take precautions.

'Definitely not,' said the Dean. 'If he ever found out their real sex, Heaven alone knows what he might get up to.'

'I suppose we must be grateful he's not interested in boys. A lot of the dons in other colleges are, I'm told.'

'It's amazing he can get up to anything at all at his age,' said the Senior Tutor a trifle mournfully. 'Still, it was obviously a great mistake to put any women on his staircase.' They looked accusingly at the Bursar who was in charge of room allocations.

'I only put two there,' he protested, 'and I made sure they passed the Test.'

'The Test? What is the Test? Apart from matches and rivers and things,' enquired the Praelector.

The Bursar hesitated. Dr Buscott and some of the younger Fellows were down the table and he had no desire to be linked in their minds with the 'Old Guard'. 'It is an exceedingly outmoded way of ensuring – ' he began, but the Dean seized his opportunity.

'The Bursar means that he has to examine the creatures before employing them as bedmakers to make absolutely certain that they are sufficiently repulsive to stifle the sexual urges in even the most desperately frustrated undergraduate,' he explained in a loud voice. 'That is why it is called the Bedder Test. The aim is to keep them out of the beds they are paid to make.'

In the silence that followed, Dr Buscott at the far end of the table was heard to wonder aloud what century some people thought they were living in. The Senior Fellows chose to ignore him. Dr Buscott held a post in the University and that, as the Dean had said, made him no sort of Porterhouse man.

'Not that the system always works, if memory serves me,' said the Praelector finally. 'That young man who blew up the Bull Tower with gas-filled condoms was found to have been fornicating with his bedder at the very moment of the explosion. Name of Zipser, I seem to remember. Now what was the bedmaker's name?'

'Biggs. Mrs Biggs,' the Chaplain shouted suddenly. 'Big Bertha Biggs I remember they called her. Wore tight boots and a shiny red mackintosh. A splendid woman. Most ample. I shall never forget the way she smiled.'

'I doubt if anyone else will either, come to that,' said the Dean grimly, 'though whether she was smiling when the Tower exploded we will, I am glad to say, never know. Not that I am in the least interested. Any sexual deviant, and a young man who could find Mrs Biggs in any way desirable must have been a pervert, deserves to die. It was the other consequences I found deplorable. Quite apart from the enormous cost of the restoration, it gave that damned Master, the late Sir Godber Evans, the chance to exert his authority over the College Council. The only good thing to come out of the whole ghastly affair was that he died of drink not long afterwards.'

'I always understood that he had an accident and fell over,' Dr Buscott intervened from the far end of the table.

'He would not have fallen had he not been drunk.'

But Dr Buscott hadn't finished. 'And saddled the College with a Head Porter as Master. I have never been able to understand why he named Skullion. If, of course, he did.'

The Senior Tutor almost rose from his chair and the Dean's face was suffused. 'If you are accusing us of lying . . .' the Senior Tutor began but the Chaplain provided a diversion.

'Dear Skullion,' he shouted. 'I saw him sitting in the garden the other day wearing his bowler hat. He seemed to be much better and certainly much happier.'

'Did he have his bottle with him?' asked the Praelector.

'His bottle? I didn't notice. He used to have a bag,

you know. It was on the end of a pipe and sometimes would slip out. I once stepped on it, quite by accident of course, and the poor fellow – '

'For God's sake, shut up,' snarled the Senior Tutor and pushed his plate away.' I really don't see why we should discuss Skullion's bladder problems over the kidney ragout.'

'I entirely agree,' said the Dean. 'It is a most unsavoury topic, and not at all suitable at table.'

'Savoury now?' the Chaplain shouted. 'But I haven't even finished my main course.'

'I think if someone would switch off his hearing aid . . .' said the Praelector.

*

The Dean's first port of call in his search for a new Master was Coft Castle, the training stables belonging to the President of the Old Porterhouse Society, General Sir Cathcart D'Eath, to consult him.

'Seen this coming,' said the General. 'Bad show having to have a Porter as Master. Worse still a chap in a wheelchair. Makes a bad impression in a sporting college, don't you know.'

'Quite,' said the Dean, who didn't share the General's view of Porterhouse. For him the College was the repository of traditional values. 'The fact of the matter is that our finances are in a dreadful state. We need a very rich Master to put us in the black again. Can you think of anyone who might be suitable?'

'Daresay you could try Gutterby down in Hampshire. Good family and plenty of money,' the General said. 'Things haven't been good for anyone lately, though. Difficult. Difficult.'

They sat in Sir Cathcart's library late into the night. From inside the cover of Sir Walter Scott's *Rob Roy* the General had produced a bottle of Glenmorangie. The Dean on the other hand was drinking Armagnac which came from *The Three Musketeers*. It put an idea into Sir Cathcart's head.

'I don't suppose you've considered Philippe Fitzherbert,' he said. 'Old Fitzherbert's boy. Said to be extremely rich. Got a place down in Gascony and lives there. Odd chap. French mother.'

The Dean looked puzzled. 'Rich? Considering the way his father practically bankrupted the College and finished the Anglian Lowland Bank on which we relied, I'm amazed to hear his son is rich. He can't have inherited it. The College had to soak old Fitzherbert as Master.'

Sir Cathcart sipped his drink and his ginger moustache twitched. Behind the bloodshot eyes something was happening. 'Heard something,' he said, resorting to the staccato that best expressed his important thoughts. 'Rum. Very rum. After the war.'

The Dean sat rigid in his deep armchair. He recognized that the General too was following his instincts. This was no time to interrupt.

'Tell you who might know more. Anthony. Anthony

Lapschott. Financial wheeler-dealer. Never quite sure what. Went into publishing too, made a small fortune. Writes books in his spare time. Tried to read one once. Couldn't make head nor tail of it. Something about the loss of power. I've never quite known what to make of him but he seems to have known everyone. Spends his time these days down in Dorset. Portland Bill. If anyone knows, he will.'

The Dean considered Anthony Lapschott. He remembered him as a strange young man whose friends were for the most part in other colleges. An Arty, not a Hearty. On the other hand he had the reputation of being one of the few serious thinkers to have emerged from Porterhouse. Yes, he would go and see Lapschott. The Dean had that gut feeling again.

5

The Bursar's feelings were strong too, but of a different kind. Unlike the Senior Tutor, whose relationship with the Dean had its up and downs, the Bursar couldn't be said to have any relationship with either of them that was not down. The Dean and the Senior Tutor despised and hated him, and he in turn detested them. Ever since he had sided with the late Master and Lady Mary over the changes they had wanted to introduce in Porterhouse, they had regarded him as a traitor and the man who had given Skullion the sack. What Skullion himself thought of the Bursar couldn't be put into words even by someone who wasn't in the Master's awful condition. In the circumstances Goodenough had made a wise decision to approach the Senior Tutor and to leave the Bursar well alone. On the other hand the Bursar, who was responsible for the College's so-called finances, knew only too well the situation had reached crisis point. The actual fabric of the College, the roofs and gutters, the stonework and the old wooden floors, all needed urgent attention and, while every other Cambridge college had been able to afford general repair and cleaning-up, Porterhouse remained as grimy and smoke-blackened as ever. A piece of guttering had fallen into the street near the Main Gate, fortunately not hitting anyone, and there were leaks in the roof of the Chapel and parts of Old Court.

In short, unless funds were found quickly Porterhouse would fall apart and once again the Bursar would be blamed. In a last-ditch attempt to avoid this and learn how to raise funds he had recently attended a seminar on 'Private Fund-raising for Establishments of Higher Education etc.' in Birmingham. For three days he had sat through a series of lectures on the subject and had been impressed by what he heard. For obvious reasons he hadn't spoken himself but late one afternoon, when he was leaving a lecture entitled 'Private Influence on Education in Donational Usage' which had been given by a don from Peterhouse, the Bursar was approached by a man curiously dressed in a black blazer, a light brown polo-neck sweater, white socks and moccasins. His eyes were almost invisible behind dark blue sunglasses.

'May I introduce myself, Professor,' he said, producing a card from his breast pocket. 'My name is Karl Kudzuvine, Personal Assistant to Edgar Hartang of Transworld Television Productions and Associated Enterprises.'

He spoke in a strong American accent and the card certainly did say he was Karl Kudzuvine, Personal Assistant and Vice-President of TTP etc. There were a number of telephone and fax numbers and an address in London with another in New York.

'As Vice-President and Personal Assistant to Mr Hartang it is my privilege to say how inspirational I found your comments on the need for Private Influence in Donational Usage. I want you to know that Edgar Hartang shares your opinions without reservations and I am instructed to say that he will appreciate meeting with you to discuss this issue at your convenience on Wednesday twelfth at twelve forty-five over lunch.' And before the dumbfounded Bursar could explain that he hadn't said a single thing about Donational Usage or Private Influence, and in any case he wasn't a Professor, the extraordinary American had seized his hand and shaken it, had said he'd been deeply honoured to meet him, and had hurried from the hall. The Bursar watched him get into an enormous car, with black windows and what appeared to be a satellite dish on the roof. As it disappeared into the night he read the words 'Transworld Television' on the side.

The sight galvanized the Bursar. He wasn't sure that he knew who Mr Edgar Hartang was but he was evidently a person with money to burn on huge cars. The Bursar went back down the hall to the financial expert from Peterhouse, who was arguing with several Principals of Poly-Techs who found the idea of any private interference in educational policy deeply offensive.

'I wonder,' said the Bursar in his most ingratiating manner, 'I wonder if I might borrow your lecture notes for a moment. I found what you had to say remarkably to the point.'

'More than some did,' said the lecturer, looking grimly at the backs of the retreating Principals. 'You can have the whole lecture. I've got it on hard disk and can print it out any time.'

The Bursar went back to his hotel room and read the lecture very carefully. He didn't fully understand the financial jargon, but as far as he could make out, the man was arguing that benefactors had the right to control the educational policy of establishments they'd funded. It might well have been entitled 'He Who Pays the Piper Calls the Tune'. It was not a doctrine the Bursar found at all unreasonable. All he wanted was funds.

On the way back to Cambridge by train he read the lecture several more times and memorized its more salient points. Next day in his office he altered two letters in one word on the title page and removed the author's name and made several copies.

The following Wednesday at 12.30 precisely he entered the headquarters of Transworld Television Productions near St Katherine's Dock and was surprised to find himself confronted by Mr Kudzuvine. He was standing behind the reception desk and appeared to have grown a ponytail. He also seemed to have developed a sizeable pair of breasts. On the other hand he was wearing the same blue dark glasses, light brown polo-neck and black blazer with chrome buttons. Even more disconcerting was the sight of two more Kudzu-vines, this time without ponytails or breasts, coming towards him through a metal frame that looked just like an airport metal-detector.

'I've come to see Mr Hartang,' the Bursar told the person – he could see now that it was definitely female – behind the counter.

She checked the computer screen and handed him a plastic card. 'If you will just follow the brothers,' she said. The Bursar turned to find the two large men just behind him. The next moment he was emptying his pockets of any metal objects and his briefcase had disappeared through an X-ray machine. Neither of the men spoke and it was only when he was through the metal-detector and was filling his pockets again that Karl Kudzuvine appeared. He too was wearing dark glasses, brown polo-neck, white socks and moccasins. 'I got to apologize, Mr Professor sir,' he said as the Bursar was hustled into a tiny photographic booth and a Polaroid was taken of him, 'but we get a lot of terrorist threats on account of some of the series we've made like on the rainforest and wildlife and whales and baby octopuses. You know.'

The Bursar didn't but it was clear that Karl Kudzu-vine was determined to tell him. 'You know they eat baby octopuses some places like Spain mainly. Places like that. They don't even give them their youth and growing up and all. We done a series on baby octopuses one time . . .' He paused for a moment and checked the plastic card with the microchip and the Bursar's photograph on it. The Bursar was about to say that baby octopuses were delicious when Kudzuvine went on, 'Had a lot of trouble. Threats and all. So now we got to check out identities anyone enters the building. You got your ID now. Like you can come in no trouble. OK?'

They went across to an elevator and Kudzuvine pressed the button for Floor I. As the lift shot up ten floors, according to the indicator above the door, the Bursar had the terrible idea that something had gone badly wrong with the thing and that he was about to die. But the elevator stopped and Kudzuvine spoke to a microphone and a camera in a corner of the roof. 'K.K. and Professor Bursar Guest to Executive Suite Zero,' he said. The very next moment the lift dropped – plummeted was the way the Bursar would have described it if he'd had time to think and hadn't been so alarmed – to some other floor which didn't register at all on the indicator. Again Kudzuvine spoke to the camera. The doors opened and the Bursar stepped out into a large office with an enormous glass-topped desk and some very small and heavily glassed windows. The room was almost entirely bare of furniture except for a number of green leather chairs and a huge sofa. The floor appeared to be made of marble, and there were no rugs. Behind the desk a small man who looked almost exactly like everyone else he had seen in the building and who wore a brown polo-neck sweater, dark blue glasses, white socks and moccasins and what appeared to be a rather ill-fitting wig, got up and came round to greet him.

'I am so pleased you could come,' he said in an almost reedy voice. 'I hear from Karl here your ideas most interesting and I have so much wanted to discuss the question of funding institutions of the highest learning with you. Do come and sit down.' He led the way to the green leather sofa and patted one end to indicate that that was where the Bursar was to sit.

'It is very kind of you to invite me,' the Bursar said and hoped he was about to quote the parts of the lectures he had memorized correctly. 'It is just that I feel there has been too much stress laid upon the avoidance of influential input on the part of fund-providers. As fund raisers we are not in any position to . . . either morally or realistically to decide the intended educational provisos of benefactors. Research should be orientated towards the social needs of industry and . . .'

At the far end of the sofa Edgar Hartang nodded agreement, his eyes invisible behind the blue glasses. 'I think what you say is so very right,' he said. 'My own life has, I am sorry to have to admit, been without formal education and it is perhaps for that reason I feel the need to make my little contribution to the great institutions of learning such as your famous . . . er . . . college.'

The Bursar decided he was hesitating for the name. 'Porterhouse College,' he said.

'Naturally. Porterhouse College is well known for its

high standards of . . .' Again Hartang paused and for a moment the Bursar almost said 'Cuisine'. He couldn't for the life of him think of any other high standards Porterhouse might possess, except perhaps on the river and in sport. But Hartang was already ploughing on with platitudes and clichés about his hopes and intentions and the need to establish relationships, meaningful relations to the mutual benefit of all concerned and caring institutions like . . . like Porterhouse.

The Bursar sat mesmerized by it all. He had no idea what the man was talking about except that he appeared to be inclined to make a financial contribution. At least the Bursar hoped so. He couldn't be sure, but a man who could be so concerned about the fate of forests and baby octopuses to the point where he had to take extreme measures to protect himself from the murderous attentions, presumably, of Amazonian lumberjacks and Spanish fishermen, had to be amazingly philanthropic. Or mad. Some of his utterances suggested the latter, and one in particular he was never able to forget or begin to understand. It had to do with 'the need to create an ephemera of permanence'. (In fact the expression or concept or whatever it was did not simply stick in the Bursar's bemused memory, it positively lodged there and made itself so thoroughly at home that in later life the Bursar would suddenly start from his sleep and alarm his wife at three o'clock in the morning by demanding to know how in God's name ephemera could be made permanent when by definition they were precisely the opposite. Not that the Bursar's wife, who had been to Girton and was a dreadful cook, could help him. And it certainly did nothing for his peace of mind to be told the statement was a paradox. 'A paradox? A paradox? Of course it's a bloody paradox. I know it's a fucking paradox,' he screamed at her. 'I'm not stupid. What I want to know is what that appalling man was ... what meaning he attached to the statement.' 'Perhaps he didn't mean anything in particular,' his wife said sensibly, but the Bursar would have none of it. 'You didn't meet him,' he said. 'And I'm telling you he meant something.')

But at the time the Bursar merely sat looking attentively into the dark blue glasses and nodding occasionally while part of his mind wondered why a man as obviously rich as Edgar Hartang should wear such an obviously cheap wig. He was even more puzzled when the lunch trolley was wheeled in and he found himself obliged to eat five enormous courses of what was evidently the tycoon's idea of *ancienne cuisine* while Hartang himself toyed with the most delicate plates of *nouvelle*. Even the wine, a very heavy Burgundy, was rather too rich for the Bursar and he glanced several times almost enviously at his host's bottle of Vichy water. But at least the clarity of Hartang's conversation improved over the meal.

'I guess you must be wondering why it is that I choose to dress in the same informal way as everyone else who works here at Transworld Television Productions.' He paused and sipped his mineral water.

'The thought had crossed my mind,' the Bursar agreed, though he was still more preoccupied with that damned wig. It was such a very obvious one.

Edgar Hartang blinked weak eyes and smiled softly. 'Okay, I'll tell you,' he said and cocked his head to one side in the process, partly dislodging the wig which tilted to the left. 'I don't choose to dress like them. I permit them to dress like me. I have always liked the polo. Most comfortable, and, of course, silk. And the colour has taste with the black blazer. I designed the buttons myself. They are embossed with the Transworld logo. You see a little tree?'

The Bursar peered at one of the tycoon's buttons and saw what looked like a small bush.

'So tasteful,' Hartang went on. 'And of course the polo is of silk.'

The Bursar had already heard that. 'And the blazer is naturally of cashmere. White socks so clean and fresh. And for the feet the ethnically correct American moccasin shoes which are again so comfortable. I like it for myself and what is good for me is good for my staff.' Again he paused and waited for the Bursar to approve.

'What a nice touch,' said the Bursar and immediately regretted it. Edgar Hartang's vocabulary might be curiously eclectic and his accent uncertain, but it was clear that he was having difficulty distinguishing between 'nice touches' and 'soft' ones. He took off his glasses for a moment and this time the Bursar didn't think his eyes were weak.

'You think a nice touch?' Hartang asked. 'You think so?'

'I meant of course it is a delightful idea. I am sure very few men in your position would have been so considerate.'

'None of them would,' Hartang insisted. 'None.'

'None,' said the Bursar, sensing agreement was obligatory.

For a time he was left to eat in silence while the great man made some calls to Hong Kong, Buenos Aires and New York and sucked what looked like an antacid tablet. It was only when the Bursar had finished an unpleasantly sticky jam tart, which played havoc with his dentures, and was drinking his coffee that Hartang announced his intentions. 'I got to see you again next week to discuss the funding requirements. Karl will coordinate with you and the accountants. I do not involve myself in details. Only in end outcomes. Like it has been a great pleasure meeting with you. We talk about funding requirements next week.'

And before the Bursar could say anything by way of thanks, he had disappeared through a small door in the wall disguised as a mirror. Karl Kudzuvine was waiting with the elevator. 'Same time same place and don't forget your ID,' he said. 'And the College account print-outs.'

'Print-outs?'

'Sure. We got to see what we're getting. Okay?'

'Well, actually we . . .' the Bursar began, but he was

already being helped into a taxi which he directed to Liverpool Street Station. The whole experience had been most peculiar and a little disturbing. All the same the Bursar could congratulate himself. He might not – he certainly didn't – know what on earth was going on, but at least he seemed to have got some extremely rich and eccentric man, whose national, racial or linguistic origins he hadn't begun to fathom, interested in Porterhouse, and the repeated use of 'funding requirements' augured well.

*

During the following week he made a number of enquiries about Transworld Television Productions and Mr Edgar Hartang and, while some of the answers were reassuring, others were less so. TTP had been a small television and publishing company which had started off making educational and religious cartoon movies mainly for the US market, but had suddenly broadened its activities with the advent of satellite TV and what must have been an enormous injection of capital though the source of the funding was unknown. The company was a private one and owned by some sort of trust which operated through Lichtenstein and possibly the Cayman Islands and Liberia. In short no one – certainly no one the Bursar could ask – no one knew who Edgar Hartang was, where he came from, or even where his home was. In London it was thought he had an apartment in the Transworld Centre, but since he invariably travelled incognito and by private jet what he did outside Britain was a mystery. What Transworld Television Productions did was also a bit of a mystery. They still made religious movies, though for so many different religions and denominations that no one had any idea what they themselves really stood for. To make things even more obscure they marketed whatever they did produce through so many subsidiaries in so many countries that it was impossible to know.

'But what about the whales and the baby octopuses?' the Bursar asked one man he knew who had connections with Nature Programmes at the BBC.

'Whales and what?'

'Baby octopuses,' said the Bursar, who had never got over Karl Kudzuvine's explanation of the extraordinary security measures at Transworld Centre. 'They made a series that had some pretty dramatic effect on the Spanish fishing industry. They received death threats and things.'

'Christ. I never heard about it, but if you say so. Try World Wildlife. They'd know. I don't.'

But the Bursar hadn't bothered. From his point of view the only thing to matter was that Transworld Television Productions obviously had funds to spare. A company that could make religious movies for the Vatican, for several extreme Protestant Churches in the Bible Belt in America, for Hindus, for Buddhists and various sects all over the world as well as documentaries on rainforests, whales and baby octopuses, had to be

incredibly rich. The Bursar began to think he had found
a private gold-mine. All the same he remained puzzled
and his bewilderment increased when he went down to
London the following Wednesday.

This time he did not meet Mr Hartang. 'He's busy
with Rio right now and then Bangkok want him so he's
non-available,' Kudzuvine told him when he'd been
through the metal-detector and the Porterhouse
accounts ledgers had been screened in the X-ray
machine. 'You got me and Skundler. Skundler does the
assessmentation.'

'Assessmentation?' said the Bursar.

'Like money. Okay?'

They went up in the elevator to Floor 9 and then
down to 6. 'Got to be careful. Drill,' said Kudzuvine by
way of explanation.

'Are you still having trouble about the baby octopuses?' asked the Bursar. For a moment Kudzuvine
looked a little uncertain.

'Baby octopuses? Oh, sure, those baby octopuses. Are
we ever. Those fucking wop fishermen in Italy. They've
given us more trouble than you can imagine. Man, death
threats.'

'Italians? Italian fishermen too?' asked the Bursar.

'Who else?' said Kudzuvine, but the Bursar hadn't
time to answer. They had reached Floor 6. Kudzuvine
carried the ledgers into Skundler's office and introduced
the Bursar as Professor Bursar.

'Ross Skundler,' said the man, who looked exactly

like Edgar Hartang the week before, but without the hairpiece. The desk was glass-topped too but far smaller than Hartang's, and while the chairs were the same green colour the leather was clearly artificial. There was no sofa. But if the Bursar was taking in the details of Ross Skundler's office with its computers and telephones, the Assessmentation Officer was finding it difficult to take in the Porterhouse ledgers. They were extremely large and quarterbound in dark red leather. 'Jesus,' he muttered and looked from them to Kudzuvine. 'What's with those? Where'd you find them? Ararat?'

'Arafat?' said Kudzuvine. 'What's the PLO got to do with it? Says on them Porterhouse. You only read figures or something?'

'Ark,' said Skundler, who evidently didn't like Kudzuvine's manner any more than he liked the look of the ledgers. 'The Ark on Mount fucking Ararat. Animals two by two, okay? You can't count or something? Makes like four.'

The Bursar was about to intervene with some light remark about baby octopuses and Noah, but remembered in time that octopuses – or was it octopi? – could swim. He was feeling decidedly uneasy in the company of these two men who clearly hated one another.

'I can count,' said Kudzuvine, 'but Professor Bursar don't have no print-out. Isn't that right, Prof?'

The Bursar nodded. 'I'm afraid we aren't into computers,' he said, trying to match their way of talking.

'You can say that again,' said Skundler, still looking very warily at the huge ledgers. 'These have got to be fiscal archaeology. Like dealing with the Fuggers.'

But even the Bursar was beginning to get annoyed. 'I beg your pardon,' he said coldly.

Mr Skundler looked up at him very suspiciously. 'What for?' he asked.

This time it was Kudzuvine's turn to intervene and pacify things. 'Just because the Prof isn't computer-literate don't mean you got to call him that. Old guy can't help it.'

'Call him what, for fucksake?'

'You know. You've just used it again.'

'Used it again? You mean . . .' The light dawned. 'I didn't call him a fucker. What's he done I got to call him that? *Fugger*, dummy, F-U-G-G-E-R-S. Kraut bankers way back in the Dark Ages. Like . . . like the Crusades or something. Used quills. Jesus, what a way to run a business. Got to catch a fucking goose every time you make an entry. You use a – ' But something about the look on the Bursar's face stopped the question. 'Okay, let's go,' he said instead and opened the first ledger. 'Just hope you're into double entry.'

The Bursar hit back. 'As a matter of fact we are,' he said. 'And what's more we don't use quills.'

Mr Skundler pushed his blue glasses up onto his forehead and ran his eyes down the pages for several minutes, while the Bursar sat and glared at him, and Kudzuvine peered over his shoulder at the figures. It was clear they were having difficulty believing what they were seeing. Finally Skundler looked up.

'I got to tell you something, Professor Bursar,' he said in a tone that was almost kindly, 'I got to tell you. With figures like these you're wasting your time. You don't need double entry. This is all one way. Like financially temperaturewise it's absolute zero.' He shook his head. 'I never seen like it since Maxwell took a swim in the sea some place.'

'Don't you mean BCCI?' asked Kudzuvine. 'They buried Maxwell Mount Olive.'

'Popeye,' said Skundler. 'Of Olives. O fucking F, for Chrissake.'

In his chair the Bursar looked on miserably. All his hopes had been dashed. 'I'm very sorry,' he said, 'but there you are. We are a very poor college and I'm obviously wasting your time . . .'

Skundler raised a hand. 'Wasting our time? Professor Baby, you are not wasting our time one microsecond. You need us. That's what we are here for. You're not wasting our time. I haven't seen anything better than this since the Berlin Wall came down. Suddenly it's freedom all the way for guys like Soros.'

'Really?' said the Bursar. 'How very interesting. You do mean Soros the financier who sold sterling . . .? Oh well, never mind. You actually think Mr Hartang will provide some funding for Porterhouse?' He said it uncertainly and Kudzuvine laid a kindly though heavy hand on his shoulder.

'Think, Professor Bursar? We don't think – and I heard that, Skundler – we know. The thing is wrapped up right now.'

'Shrinkwise,' said Skundler, 'solid plastic. You've got it made, no question.'

'Well, there is just one question,' said the Bursar, feeling suddenly extremely happy and confident. 'I mean . . . I mean why should Mr Hartang be so very generous?'

'Generous?' said Skundler. 'Of course he's generous. He's got rich being generous. He's a philanthropist.'

'He's that too,' Kudzuvine agreed, 'though since he had that heart coronary thing he's had to go easy on the girls. Takes it out of him. I said to him one time, "Mr Hartang you want to go easy. Take it the Clinton way like they're on their fucking knees praying to the thing."'

'Well, I must say . . .' the Bursar began but Skundler stopped him.

'Don't. It's better not to with K.K. around. Like he gets everything wrong. It's because he's a moron.'

'Mormon,' said Kudzuvine. 'It's got an M in it.'

'See what I mean?' Skundler said to the Bursar. 'Like ignorance is a religion with him.'

'That ain't ignorant. We did a series one time on Mormons outside Salt Lake City. Real nice.'

By the time the Bursar went back to Cambridge the ledgers had been copied with some difficulty and he was feeling both elated and peculiar. In so far as he had been able to understand what Kudzuvine and Ross Skundler had been saying, Transworld Television Productions and Edgar Hartang were going to pour money into Porterhouse not only because Hartang was into philanthropy but, as Kudzuvine had put it, 'Cambridge is where it's at. You got it all.'

'It's nice of you say so but – '

'Listen. You live there. Cambridge. Place has got it over Disneyworld every which way. History, DNA, professors, a whole bunch of churches and stuff. Geniuses all over town like Hawking. You read *The History of Time*. Great book. Teaches you. I been up to take a look-see and it was something else with all those cunts on the river and lawns like they give them facials every day. Cambridge. Man, Cambridge makes virtual reality look like it's not happening.'

The Bursar felt rather the same way about Transworld Television. He still couldn't see how a man like Hartang could get rich by giving money away. It didn't make sense.

6

Purefoy Osbert's trip to London was pretty peculiar too. Purefoy wasn't sure why or rather how he had been chosen to become the Sir Godber Evans Memorial Fellow at Porterhouse and Goodenough wasn't sure he wanted to meet him face to face and had to be forced to do so by Vera who said he'd be pleasantly surprised; and Lady Mary made it a condition of her interviewing Dr Osbert that either Lapline or Goodenough – preferably both – should inspect him first to make sure that he was hygienic, wasn't an alcoholic, wasn't a raving racist who advocated mass transportation of black people like Dr Lamprey Yeaster from Bristol, and, most importantly, wasn't from Grimsby.

'Grimsby? What's she got against Grimsby?' asked Mr Lapline when he read the letter. 'Perfectly respectable town. Cold in winter of course.'

'If you remember the candidate from Grimsby was into – ' Goodenough began.

Mr Lapline had remembered. 'Oh God,' he said violently. 'You don't mean to tell me Lady Mary actually interviewed him?'

'I think he tried to get into her too,' Goodenough

went on. 'As she told it, she was lying on this chaise longue with a bad leg – '

'I warn you, Goodenough, if you lose Lady Mary Evans' account, I'll ... I'll ...' Another gall-bladder spasm silenced him.

'That's why we've got to inspect Dr Purefoy Osbert,' said Goodenough. 'I thought if we took him out to lunch at the Savoy Grill ... Now what's the matter?'

Mr Lapline explained what the matter was and why he bloody well wasn't going anywhere near the Savoy Grill or any other restaurant in London and if Goodenough seriously thought ...

'All I meant was we'd be able to tell whether he's house-trained and knows how to use a knife and fork properly and that sort of thing. We can't possibly have some ghastly uncouth fellow going up to Porterhouse. Or molesting Lady Mary.'

Mr Lapline looked up at him curiously. 'Goodenough,' he said finally, 'there are times when I wonder if you are entirely sane. If you can think back that far, you may remember that when I first read that list, I said they were all impossible candidates and that swine from Grimsby ought to be behind bars. And now you have the gall to tell me we can't have some uncouth fellow going to Porterhouse. The whole damned lot aren't even faintly couth.'

'But no one else wanted to take the post and we had to find her some candidates,' said Goodenough. 'Anyway I'll wine and dine this Purefoy Osbert chap and tell you what it was like. I think I'll have Omelette Arnold Bennett.' And on this unfortunate note he left the office.

*

In the event he was pleasantly surprised by Purefoy who was relatively well dressed for an academic and was actually wearing a tie for the occasion and wasn't unduly impressed by being taken to the Savoy Grill. Having passed that test with flying colours – Purefoy had accepted a glass of dry sherry rather than the extra dry martini Goodenough had offered him and had then quietly had two glasses of wine with the meal – Goodenough insisted on taking him to an extremely low strip joint. Purefoy expressed the opinion that he had never been into anywhere like it before and didn't think he wanted to ever again. And anyway the girls were absolutely nothing to write home about though, come to think of it, some of them were so dreadful trying to describe them in a letter might help to exorcize the memory of them. As a result of that remark – Goodenough had found one or two of the strippers rather attractive – their next stop, after Purefoy had practically been forced to have two double Scotches, was at a gay bar filled with transvestites and men in leather where Purefoy was touched up by someone who might have been a lesbian but probably wasn't. By that time Goodenough was almost convinced, and there was no 'almost' about Purefoy's opinion of Goodenough.

Goodenough's next question, put as he leant negligently against the bar, clinched it. 'Are you by any chance interested in anal-erotic fantasies?' he asked.

Purefoy backed hurriedly away from him and bumped into a man wearing a leather thong who seemed to enjoy the encounter. 'Sorry,' Purefoy muttered, still keeping a very wary eye on Goodenough.

'Don't be,' said the man in the thong. 'The pleasure's all mine.'

Which was, for once, true. Purefoy Osbert wasn't enjoying himself at all. In fact the whole evening had been excruciating. He had been taken to an extremely expensive restaurant by a lawyer in rather too light a suit and grey suede shoes who had tried to get him drunk on a huge export-strength gin martini which he had had the good sense to refuse, had then eyed him most oddly throughout the meal, and had seemed particularly interested in his hands and his mouth. After that, presumably to soften him up, the bloody man had made him sit in a filthy strip joint and look at repulsive women taking off their clothes and squirming. Then there had been the insistence on two double whiskies and a bar filled with homosexuals where he wanted to know if Purefoy was interested in anal-erotic fantasies. No wonder the bastard had been looking at him so peculiarly all evening. Purefoy wasn't waiting around to find out what was going to happen next. Not that he needed to be told. And he had a pretty good idea why he had been offered the Fellowship at Porterhouse when he hadn't even applied for it.

Purefoy Osbert headed for the door and had several more distasteful encounters on the way. Behind him Goodenough followed but Purefoy had had enough. 'Now you just hold it,' he said menacingly, backing into the road. 'You just stay away from me.'

'But my dear chap,' Goodenough said by way of apology, 'I only wanted – '

'Well, you're not getting it and that's for sure. I don't know how you got the notion . . . oh yes I do. It's that bloody cousin of mine – Vera's idea of a practical joke. My God, I'll make her pay for it. Dragging me all the way to London.'

'No one is dragging you, I can assure you of that,' said Goodenough. 'It's obvious you've got hold of the wrong end of the stick.'

'I haven't,' said Purefoy with a slight slur. Those two double Scotches were having an effect. 'The stick I've got hold of . . .' He looked around for a weapon and was nearly run over by a taxi. As he lurched forward Goodenough took his arm.

Purefoy shook him off. 'Let's get this absolutely straight,' he said and clenched his fist. 'You may be a fucking poof . . . gay but I'm not and if you touch me again I'll – '

He got no further. A very large person in a loud check suit appeared in front of him. 'Who are you calling a poof?' it asked, and promptly delivered a knock-out blow to Purefoy Osbert's chin. Goodenough caught him and hailed a taxi.

'Earls Court,' he told the driver and gave the address of Vera's flat. By the time they arrived there Purefoy's nose had stopped bleeding and he wasn't at all sure what had happened. They went up in the lift.

'I don't think I'd better be around when he wakes in the morning,' Goodenough told Vera when they'd got Purefoy to bed. 'It's been a perfectly ghastly evening.'

'I can see that,' said Vera. 'What on earth happened?'

'He thought I was out to seduce him. It's all the Grimsby bastard's fault.'

'And you went and hit him because . . .?'

'I didn't hit him. That wasn't me,' said Goodenough. 'Some weight-lifting lesbian slugged him for calling me a poofter. And I'll tell you another thing. He thinks you put him my way so that I could make a pass at the brute. He swore he was going to kill you. You don't know what it was like. As though I wanted to bed him.'

'And I'll tell you something,' said Vera. 'You're staying the night and you're going to bed me. It's the only way out.'

They went through to the bedroom and began to undress.

'I have to hand it to you,' Goodenough said. 'You certainly pick the perfect candidates. Lady Mary is going to love your Purefoy, and he's going to cause havoc in Porterhouse.'

*

Two days later, and only after a great deal of persuasion and cajoling, Purefoy Osbert went to be interviewed by Lady Mary. He still wasn't entirely happy about Goodenough's sexual inclinations. 'If you'd seen that gay bar,' he told Vera. 'I mean I don't care what people do but it was like a vision of Hell by Hieronymus Bosch. And why did he have to look at me like that?'

'He just had to be sure,' Vera said.

'Well, I hope to hell he's sure now. And don't ever leave me alone with him. He may be as straight as you say he is but if you'd seen the way he looked at my mouth . . .'

'I can assure you he's all right. Now let me tell you about Lady Mary Evans . . .'

Purefoy Osbert spent an hour with Lady Mary, who still felt safer behind her desk and with the housekeeper's husband close by. 'Dr Osbert,' she said, 'I see from your application that you have been at Kloone University for eleven years. Isn't that a long time to remain in the same university? Haven't you ever wanted to advance your career?'

'My career consists of researching what actually happened,' said Purefoy, looking without any warmth into her strangely blue eyes. 'I am not interested in any other approach and I can research the facts I need as well at

Kloone as anywhere else. Certainties are to be found in primary source materials and to some extent from secondary opinion, though only where such opinion is confirmed from a separate and wholly unconnected source.'

Lady Mary nodded, perhaps approvingly. 'And I see that your area of research is in the methods of penal restraint or, in simpler terms, prisons.'

'With particular reference to capital punishment,' said Purefoy.

'Of which you approve?'

Purefoy Osbert almost stood up. 'Of which I entirely disapprove,' he said. 'In fact the word "disapprove" is not adequate to express my convictions. Capital punishment in any form is an act of the utmost barbarity and – '

He would have gone on but Lady Mary stopped him. 'I am delighted to hear that,' she said. 'Dr Osbert, what you have just said confirms the opinion expressed to me by Mr Lapline, my solicitor, who has been handling the choice of applicants for the Fellowship I am sponsoring at Porterhouse College.'

Purefoy Osbert stirred in his chair. He wanted the salary the Fellowship would bring with it but he felt it only honest to tell this strange person what he truly thought. 'I think you ought to know,' he said, 'that I have grave reservations about Porterhouse College. It has, I am sorry to say, an exceedingly unpleasant reputation and I am by no means certain I want to go there.'

In front of him Lady Mary was smiling, if you could call what she was doing smiling. Her yellow teeth gleamed. There could be no mistaking her feelings. 'My dear Dr Osbert, I trust you won't mind my calling you that, but your opinion of Porterhouse so entirely concurs with my own feelings about the College that I am prepared to say now that the Sir Godber Evans Memorial Fellowship is yours if you will do me, and of course my late husband, the honour of accepting it.'

She sat back in her chair and allowed Purefoy to savour the approval she had given him. Purefoy Osbert thought about it.

'I am afraid I need to know rather more before giving my answer,' he said firmly. 'I am grateful to you for the offer but my area of concern is not in vague hypotheses and, to be frank, I need to know why I am being offered this post and what the actual nature of your intention is. I have been told it is to prepare material for a biography of your late husband, but in view of the salary or stipend . . .' There was no doubt now about Lady Mary's beam. It was radiant. In fact had she been anyone else, and Purefoy Osbert more perceptive and sensible to the feelings of any woman other than Mrs Ndhlovo, he would have said she had fallen in love with him. Instead he listened while she explained the purpose of the Fellowship.

'I have created it and am offering it to you because my husband's work at Porterhouse did not receive the recognition it deserved. We . . . he had intended to make the place one of academic excellence and met a quite astonishing degree of opposition from the Fellows. I want him to have the posthumous recognition and esteem he deserves. And I want to see his policies put into effect.'

'But I don't really see that I can make any positive contribution,' said Purefoy.

'I am sure that your presence will be a first step,' said Lady Mary, leaning forward across the desk very earnestly. She paused and stared with those pale blue eyes into his. 'And, of course, for the purpose of a biography you need to find out everything about his life and, I may say, his death. You may find it fanciful of me but I am not happy with the official explanation and I want to know exactly what happened. The truth, Dr Osbert, that is all. I acknowledge that I am supposed to be a weak and fallible woman but this is a world dominated by men and that is their opinion. For once I am prepared to accept that judgement. I am asking you to establish the facts of the matter. If you uncover certain evidence that proves my darling Godber's premature death was due to natural causes I shall accept your verdict. All my life I have had to accept unpalatable truths and I have done so on the basis of facts, some of them quite terrible.' Purefoy Osbert already knew that. The evidence for her past idealism was there on the walls in the signed portraits of some of the twentieth century's most murderous leaders. Even Purefoy Osbert, who had never taken a very great interest in politics or politicians, was conscious of their presence. Lady Mary's ideals were evidently those he was used to at Kloone.

'I am sure you are quite the right person for the position,' she went on. 'Mr Goodenough will provide you with any additional information you need. There are a number of documents you will find most informative.' And on this practical note she ended the interview. There was no point in setting out her real aims now. It was much better to let him get to work quickly. Which was what she told Mr Goodenough on the phone when Purefoy had left Kensington Square. He had agreed to go to Porterhouse on the terms stated in the letter and with the guarantee that his researches or investigations into the facts of Sir Godber's life and death were to be free of any restrictions. Lady Mary had said that she would do nothing to prevent him finding the facts but implied that other people might.

'I was most impressed with Dr Osbert,' she told Goodenough. Mr Lapline had refused to accept the call ('Tell her I'm out or dead or in hospital or something,' he had told his secretary) on the grounds that her impressions of a man who thought Crippen was the innocent victim of a Scotland Yard conspiracy might be as violent as his own.

'I'm so glad,' Goodenough said. 'I must say I thought him quite the best of the bunch.'

Lady Mary tried to tell him what she thought of the rest of the bunch, but had some sort of seizure.

*

'Anyway, she seems happy enough with your lovely cousin,' Goodenough said to Vera. 'Yes, I quite agree. I won't use that adjective in his presence. He still treats me like some sort of animal that ought to be in quarantine. And pursuing that particular simile she has instructed me – those were her words – to get him into Porterhouse immediately. No, she didn't bother with "expeditiously". She said "immediately" and with six million in the kitty, I don't think we're going to have all that much trouble with the College Council.'

He was right. After a phone call to the Senior Tutor followed by a letter and another phone call and a fax, Goodenough felt satisfied. 'I think he has prepared the ground very well already,' he said to Mr Lapline. 'The Dean is away and cannot be contacted and according to the Senior Tutor he would be the main stumbling-block to any Fellow named after the late Master. So they're going ahead without him.'

'I should have thought the main stumbling-block would be the present Master himself,' said Mr Lapline gloomily. 'It cannot be easy to get Council decisions ratified by a Master who has difficulty speaking and can't write. Do you think they get him to make his mark? It's going to look very odd to future historians of Cambridge during the twentieth century if they do.'

'Oh I don't know. I must be more optimistic about the future than you are,' said Goodenough. 'Probably by that time nobody will be able to read at all. In any case I understand he can talk again.'

*

The College Council did approve the appointment of Dr Purefoy Osbert and Skullion was brought in to sign the document, though it was thought best not to let him know the bit about the Sir Godber Evans Memorial.

'Just say it is a new research Fellowship,' the Praelector advised the Senior Tutor, who was standing in for the Dean. 'His feelings for Sir Godber were not, as I recall, of the fondest.'

'He loathed the man,' said the Senior Tutor, 'and I can't say I blame him. I detested the late Master myself. What I never could understand is what the Bursar saw in him. I suppose it was money.'

'Of course it was money, though it was Lady Mary's money. Hadn't got a bean of his own. Married the stuff, and I don't think it was much of a bargain. Which brings me to my next point. I cannot begin to imagine what City financiers sponsored Dr Osbert and the Fellowship. I should have thought they would have preferred to forget Sir Godber ever existed. The damage he did to the country's commercial interests as Minister of Technological Development was enormous. Cut funding on what is now called superconductivity. It was in its infancy in those days.'

The Chaplain took up the challenge erroneously. 'Before I came to Porterhouse I conducted a great many baptisms of infants,' he said, 'but I wouldn't have called any of them "super". It has been one of the blessings of my life as College Chaplain that I am no longer required to bless any babies. Looking into what I suppose must be called their faces almost convinced me that Darwin was absolutely right. I remember one particularly horrid little boy who made me think of Occam's Razor rather wistfully.'

'Occam's Razor? But that's for circumcision, surely,' said the Senior Tutor.

Dr Buscott shuddered but kept silent. He knew what Occam's Razor was but it was too late to try to educate the Senior Fellows now. In any case the Chaplain, who was dozing off, was murmuring something. 'I've always felt very sorry for Abelard, you know. They used something like Occam's Razor on him. Most unpleasant.'

7

In a grey stone house on Portland Bill the Dean and Anthony Lapschott finished dinner and took their coffee in a long room overlooking Lyme Bay. It was late. Lapschott kept curious hours and did himself well – in the Dean's opinion, very well. Not that he would have chosen to retire to Portland Bill. It was too grey and grim and dingy for him, the streets too empty and steep and the wind coming off the sea had been gusting to Force 9 when he drove up the hill past the prison earlier in the day. It had risen further during the evening and howled round the house thrashing the few shrubs in the garden, but in the long panelled room the storm seemed strangely distant. Everything there – it was as much a study and library as a drawing-room – was luxurious, almost too luxurious, with thick Persian rugs and deep armchairs and a massive leather-topped desk and a couch on which Lapschott could spend hours reading while beyond the window storms at sea and the ceaseless wind battered the coast without affecting his comfort.

It was this contrast between the grey and grim world outside and the one Lapschott had created for himself in the house that disturbed the Dean. Besides, he had never liked modern paintings and he particularly disliked

Bacon and Lucian Freud. Lapschott's tastes were too sophisticated for him and something of his distaste had evidently communicated itself to the other man. During dinner, served by two Filipino maids and a manservant, Lapschott had explained his own reasons for living where and how he did and the Dean had found them as disturbing as the house itself.

'I find it amusing to observe the end of the world,' said Lapschott. 'Perhaps I should say the ends of the worlds.' The Dean would have preferred him to say neither. Still, the underdone lamb was surprisingly good and the claret was excellent.

'And in many ways Portland Bill allows me that melancholy perspective. Geographically it is the end of England. Land's End is in Cornwall and the Cornish are Celts, and besides Land's End is very commercial these days. But here there is only rock and the lighthouse and beyond it the Race and the open sea. And to the west is Dead Man's Bay. That's what Hardy called it. A sailing ship too close inshore would be trapped by the wind coming up the Channel. Unable to round the Bill, it would be driven onto the Chesil Bank. Hundreds of dead men out there, Dean. Behind us more dead men. Two gaunt prisons and the stone quarries that went to make the Gibbs Building in King's College and St Paul's Cathedral. The convicts built the breakwater round Portland Harbour, hauling the stone from those quarries in the nineteenth century to protect the world's greatest fleet. For them Portland was the end of the world too. I can go and look down at the Harbour and find some curious satisfaction in its emptiness. What fleet there is could fit into a tiny corner of it. That world has ended now, though I have just been reading the most interesting life of Fisher by Jan Morris. A madman of sorts, Fisher built the Dreadnought and began the naval arms race with the Kaiser's Germany, a foolish and romantic duel that ended in stalemate at Jutland. The British lost far more ships and men and the German Navy never put out to sea again until it sailed to Scapa Flow and was scuttled there. Such a pointless war fought by men who were thought to be civilized.'

'The Germans started it,' said the Dean. 'They invaded Belgium, with whom we had treaty obligations.'

'Yes, but, as the Dutch say, "Belgium doesn't exist." It was created only in 1831,' Lapschott agreed rather dismissively. 'But in any case the enemy always starts wars. One cannot sacrifice millions of men without offering them some good reason. I have a recording somewhere of the Kaiser's message to the German nation along similar lines in 1914. He quotes Shakespeare and Hamlet's soliloquy. I'll get it out for you later if you'd like to hear it. *"Um sein oder nicht sein,"* to be or not to be. He repeats the lines twice. Germany was faced with no other alternative and millions of men went off to fight, convinced that was indeed the case, only to find that they were *nicht sein*. Pathetic romanticism. No one was thinking at all rationally. Reason slept and out of that sleep was bred the monster, Adolf Hitler.

And of course Lenin, another monster. And what have we achieved for Britain? What?'

The Dean had no answer. He could not share his host's melancholy interest in history. It was too abstract for him. Britain was still the finest country in the world. 'I suppose we saved the world from barbarism,' he said.

Lapschott looked at him with a sardonic smile. 'One form of barbarism undoubtedly. Or two. But there still seems an inordinate amount of it about these days. I was thinking rather of what Britain has lost. Or given away. I don't mean the Empire. No. We opened the way for the Japanese to become what we once were.'

'For the Japanese to become what we once were?' said the Dean, thoroughly mystified.

'The Anglo-Japanese Alliance of 1902. They were to safeguard our interests in the Far East and free our Pacific fleet to protect the British Isles. We treated them as equals and they fulfilled their side of the bargain by declaring war on Germany in 1914 and seizing all the German possessions in the Pacific. Very sensible. Another island race, a sea-faring people who followed our example by sinking the Russian fleet at Port Arthur without declaring war.'

'Treacherous devils,' said the Dean indignantly. 'They did the same at Pearl Harbor.'

'And Nelson sank the neutral Danish fleet at Copenhagen. And Churchill used the same method against the French at Dakar in 1940. The comparisons are almost exact. Why do you suppose as long ago as the seventeenth century the French called us perfidious Albion? Because we were treacherous.'

'That was Napoleon,' objected the Dean but Lapschott shook his massive head.

'It was Bossuet, in a curious sermon on circumcision.'

The Dean finished his lamb. He found the conversation most distasteful. He had come to seek advice about a new Master and was being treated like an undergraduate in a tutorial. Worse still, the wretched man was confronting him with a view of history so cynical that it made his own self-congratulatory realism seem nothing more than nostalgic sentimentality. For the rest of the meal he kept silent while Lapschott spoke of poets and politicians, of men and affairs so far beyond the Dean's little ken that he was pleased to find the drawing-room so vulgar.

With regained confidence he raised the question of a new Master. 'Cathcart suggested you might be able to tell me something of Fitzherbert, the son of our disastrous Bursar,' he said.

'Philippe? Nothing much to tell. The stupid son of an avaricious father. Lives in France on the money Fitzherbert *père* stole from the College.'

'Stole?' said the Dean. 'He was supposed to have lost it at Monte Carlo.'

'That was his story. I happen to know otherwise. But that's of no use to you now. The son has wasted his inheritance. There is no point in your trying Philippe if you want a rich Master,' Lapschott told him.

'Gutterby, Launcelot Gutterby perhaps?' the Dean asked less confidently.

'Have you met his wife?'

'No, I have never had that pleasure. I've kept in touch with Launcelot but I've never been invited down.'

Lapschott raised a massive eyebrow. 'If you ever are, I advise you not to go. Lady Gutterby is not a pleasant woman and she holds the purse strings very tight indeed. Very wise, considering how very vague he is, but there are limits. Mine is Fitou with cold mutton. And I happen to know there is some excellent wine in the cellar.'

The Dean shuddered. He would definitely avoid Lady Gutterby's hospitality. 'I've made arrangements to stay with Broadbeam. After your time, but a fine rugby player. Lives down near Bath.'

Lapschott nodded. He had heard well of Broadbeam. For another hour the Dean described his itinerary and the problems facing Porterhouse. When he finally went to bed, leaving Lapschott lying with his feet up on the great sofa reading Spengler, he was thoroughly depressed. Lapschott had held out little hope of finding any OP who had the money to rescue the College and no suggestions to make. He seemed to view the plight of Porterhouse as nothing more than another interesting example of decline resulting from smug stupidity and idleness. The Dean's view of Lapschott was simpler: the man was conceited and decadent and possibly effete. His name seemed suspiciously foreign. To add to his discomfort his bedroom faced west and was not isolated from the elements outside by heavy curtains. Worst of all there was an open fireplace and a chimney. The Dean lay in bed and listened to the wind howling.

In the morning he was up early, wrote a note thanking Lapschott for his hospitality and left after breakfast. With a sense of escape from something he did not understand or like, he drove down the steep hill away from the old prisons and the great stone quarries into the soft, rolling countryside of Dorset. He took his time and kept to narrow country roads. His next stop would be with another Old Porterthusian, one of the more likeable ones, Broadbeam. Then he had several more wealthy OPs to visit up the Severn Valley. Finally he would go up to Yorkshire and call on Jeremy Pimpole, who had been his favourite almost as much as he had been Skullion's. Launcelot Gutterby and Jeremy Pimpole had been the brightest stars in the Head Porter's social firmament. Occasionally the Master could still be heard muttering 'Gutterby and Pimpole' over and over again in memory of their air of ineffable superiority as undergraduates. And in his own way Jeremy Pimpole had been the Dean's idea of a perfect gentleman too. Such a delightfully vague and charming young man. Now he would be a gentleman farmer and manager of the great Pimpole estate. The Dean smiled as he thought of the world of difference that separated the Pimpoles of this world from the Lapschotts, and stopped in a small wood to have a pee.

8

At Transworld Television Productions Kudzuvine had news for the Bursar. 'Mr Hartang wants to see the College, Professor,' he said. 'He's got to see for himself what he's funding. Right?'

'Most definitely,' said the Bursar. 'He is very welcome to come up and look around at any time.'

'Fine. Fine. Only trouble is he don't move except by Lear jet or his 125 and you don't have no landing field.'

'We've got Marshalls' airport. He could always land there and it's only a few miles away. We'll find a car for him.'

'Sure. Only happens he's in Bangkok and he's got business. Schedules as tight as a turtle's asshole and is that tight. Drown if it wasn't. You know that. We did a movie one time on turtles, some fucking island . . . Gal something.'

'Galapagos,' said the Bursar.

'Right first time. Got to hand it to you, Prof, you know your geology. Galap . . . What did you call it?'

'Galapagos. It's where Darwin first – '

Kudzuvine wasn't having it. 'Wrong. That's Australia some place. So he don't come to your Porterhouse. It goes to Hartang.'

'I don't see how that's possible,' said the Bursar, now thoroughly mystified. 'I mean you can't move buildings. It's out of the question. It really is, you know. We'd be delighted to have him come up – '

'You're not hearing me, Prof. What sort of business are we in? Transworld?'

'Transworld? Yes, I know that, but there are limits, you know, and frankly – '

'Transworld Television Productions,' said Kudzuvine. 'Satellite transmission. Okay?'

'Ah, yes,' said the Bursar, feeling slightly less insane. 'I see what you mean.'

'There in one, Prof Baby, there in one. We make the movie and E.H. sees it Bangkok or Lima, Peru or whatever, no sweat. Agreed?'

'Of course, of course. If that is what Mr Hartang wants, you are very welcome to come up with a video camera and take pictures of the College. I can't see any problems about that.'

'Great,' said Kudzuvine. 'So now we've got to pick a time.'

'Well, any time really, though at the moment the undergraduates are studying for Tripos and it would be better – '

'Studying for tripods? You got students studying for tripods? I didn't know . . .'

'Tripos exams. They are in three parts. Prelims, Part One and Part Two. Quite different from Oxford where they only take one exam at the end of the third year.'

'One?' said Kudzuvine, now as mystified as the Bursar had been a few moments before. 'Like monopods? Hell, that's really something. Three years to study for monopods. This system of yours is something else.'

'All I'm trying to tell you,' said the Bursar, 'is that it would be better if you could wait until after the exams and come up in June when we have May Balls. They are dances.'

'Why do you have May Balls in June?' demanded Kudzuvine.

'After the Bumps – '

But Kudzuvine had had enough. Bumps was too much. 'Like stick with these balls,' he said. 'It's safer.'

The Bursar agreed. He found trying to explain Cambridge customs almost impossible. 'We don't have a May Ball every year,' he said. 'They are very expensive to organize and the tickets cost £150. There are marquees . . . tents.' The thought that Kudzuvine might confuse marquees with someone noble in France was too awful. 'And we have two bands and – '

'This is terrific, baby. This is it. Man, we've got it made. Shit, E.H. is going to love it. I mean he's wild about parties and balls and stuff. We film this you'll have all the fucking funds you need to put you in orbit.'

The Bursar backed away from this enthusiasm. Funds were all he required. 'You mean you'd come up with a camera and film the May Ball? I'm sure that could be arranged.'

'Arranged? I'll say it will be arranged, you'd better believe it. What's today?'

'Wednesday,' said the Bursar.

'Right. We'll be up Sunday for a look-see. You know. Got to get the scenes right. Around 8 a.m. I'll be there.'

'I'm not sure . . .'

'You don't have to be sure, Prof Bursar. You leave it to old K.K. No sweat.'

And once more the Bursar found himself being helped into a taxi and driven to Liverpool Street Station. As usual after a meeting with Kudzuvine he was feeling distinctly uneasy and not very well.

*

But if Wednesday was bad, Sunday was absolutely awful. The Bursar seldom went to Early Communion, preferring to put in an appearance at Matins or Evensong, but in the knowledge that he was going to have to show Kudzuvine the College and in the process show the College Kudzuvine, and also knowing that Porterhouse preferred its Americans quiet and with some modicum of sophistication, the Bursar offered up a little prayer to the Almighty to see him safely and happily through the day. From the results, God had been in no mood to listen. The Bursar came out of Chapel just before 8 a.m. to find Walter and three other porters trying to prevent a number of men, and perhaps women, all dressed in brown polo-neck sweaters, black blazers, white socks, moccasins and those dark blue glasses, from opening the whole of the Main Gate so that they could back a video truck into Old Court.

'You can't bring that thing in here,' Walter was saying, 'you've got no permission.'

'We got Professor Bursar's permission,' said the familiar loud voice. 'You telling us Professor Bursar got no authority round here?'

Walter stared dementedly round at the identical faces, evidently trying to figure out which one to answer. 'I'm ... I'm ... I'm telling you you can't bring that thing in here is what I'm telling you. It isn't right,' he shouted.

Kudzuvine poked his waistcoat with a large forefinger. 'Listen, baby,' he said nastily (Walter was fifty-eight), 'listen, baby. I'm asking you a question. I'm asking you Professor Bursar got authority round here? Yes or no?'

'No, no,' said Walter, 'of course he hasn't. We haven't got a Professor Purser. You've come to the wrong college. Why don't you go along to ... well, wherever you're meant to be and – '

'Porterhouse,' said Kudzuvine. 'Porterhouse is where we're meant to be.'

'Are you sure you don't mean Peterhouse?' asked Walter. 'Peterhouse is down past Queens' and Pembroke. It's on the right.'

'You telling me I don't know where I'm meant to be?

Eight fucking a.m. I told Professor Bursar and now you're telling me you haven't got a Professor Bursar?'

'Yes. I mean no . . . and leave them bolts alone. They haven't been undone since Her Majesty. God Almighty.' Walter looked round frantically for help from higher authority and spotted the Bursar and several earnest undergraduates standing by the Chapel. 'We've got a Bursar but not a Professor – '

Kudzuvine turned and followed his gaze. 'What did I say?' he yelled. 'Professor Bursar, course you've got Professor Bursar. Hey Prof, you look great.' The Bursar was wearing a gown for Chapel, as was Porterhouse custom. Kudzuvine turned back to the group of Transworld operatives. 'Hey, you guys look at that for costume. Like for fucking real. Monks, man, monks. And look at this one!' The Chaplain had emerged from the Chapel and was peering happily at them. 'I mean who needs characters with these around? We got it made.'

The Bursar hurried forward. He had to stop the bloody man before the Senior Tutor appeared in his dressing-gown or something. 'For Heaven's sake, keep your voice down,' he said, grasping Kudzuvine by the sleeve. 'And you can't bring whatever that thing is in. It is out of the question.'

'It is?' said Kudzuvine, now almost whispering. 'Why?'

The Bursar looked round for some practical reason

and found it. 'The lawn,' he said. 'The lawn. You can't drive that in on the lawn.'

Kudzuvine and the group turned their startled attention to the Old Court lawn. 'The lawn?' he said, evidently awed. 'So what's so special with the lawn?'

'It's hundreds of years old,' said the Bursar suddenly inspired. 'It's . . . it's protected species. No one is allowed even to walk on it.'

Kudzuvine shook his head in disbelief. 'No one is allowed to walk on it for hundreds of years? So how come it's so short and green and stuff. Cuts itself too?'

'No, of course not. The College gardeners cut it but only dons are allowed to walk on it.'

'Jesus,' said Kudzuvine. 'Got a lawn hundreds of years old. That I understand. Whole place looks like it's been here hundreds of years, maybe thousands. Mr Hartang is going to love this.'

'I daresay he will,' said the Bursar, finally beginning to feel he had the situation slightly in hand. 'But not if you bring that truck thing in with those cables and ruin it.'

'Yeah, you could be right at that,' Kudzuvine admitted. 'Okay, you guys, leave it in the street.'

'And I don't think that's a very good idea either,' the Bursar continued. 'The police will – '

'So we move it some place else. Where's the campus parking lot?'

The Bursar tried to think. It had never crossed his mind that Porterhouse might have a campus or even be one. Walter came to his rescue. 'You can always try the Lion Yard,' he muttered. 'Though if you ask me I don't think you'll get it in.'

Kudzuvine turned his attention away from the lawn. 'Did you say . . . You did say the Lion's Yard?' he asked. Awe wasn't an adequate word now. Horror was more like it.

'He means the car park . . . the parking lot,' the Bursar explained. 'It has nothing to do with the College. And I assure you there are no lions in it.'

'There are,' said Walter. 'There's a great big red one.'

The Bursar looked at him and shook his head. He had never liked Skullion as Head Porter but there were times when he wished he was back. Skullion would never have allowed this situation to develop. 'Yes, Walter, but it's a stone one. A statue,' he explained with difficult patience. 'It's called the Lion Yard after the lovely old pub that used to stand there.'

'Oh, I remember the Lion so well,' said the Chaplain, who had joined the gathering outside the Porter's Lodge. 'Such a shame they knocked it down. It had a delightful walkway, almost an arcade with leather sofas on either side and little insurance offices and shipping agents behind them. I used to sit there and have coffee in the morning. And of course there was a bar. And I seem to remember some enterprising young man from Magdalene ran a sort of casino there with a roulette wheel. Such fun.'

Kudzuvine and the other polo-necks stood in silent

admiration and stared through their blue sunglasses. It was obvious they had never seen or heard anything like this before.

'Ah well, I must leave you good people,' the Chaplain said. 'Breakfast calls. Spiritual sustenance is one thing but, to change the emphasis of Our Lord's words slightly towards the practical, "Man cannot live by wine and biscuit alone." We are corporeal beings after all. So nice meeting you.' He tottered off in the direction of the Dining Hall following the scent of porridge and bacon and eggs and good coffee.

*

For the next twenty minutes, in the almost serene atmosphere that had been induced by the Chaplain's nostalgia, the Bursar got Kudzuvine to have the video van parked away from the College.

'We'll clear a space by the bicycle sheds, when you need to use it,' he explained, 'though I must say I never visualized such . . . well, it's like a pantechnicon.'

It was a most unfortunate word to use. Kudzuvine seized on it. 'Professor Bursar, have you said it?' he bawled.

'Well, I think so . . .' the Bursar began, but Kudzuvine had grabbed him by the arm.

'Pantechnicon it could be but that's small stuff. We go straight into thirty-five or maybe even seventy mill. We've got this Ball, see, and everyone dancing out in the open air . . .' He paused and looked puzzled. 'Where do they dance?'

The Bursar smiled. It was to be his last smile for some time. 'Well, mostly in the Hall of course,' he said. 'They clear the tables out, you know.'

'The Hall? Show me,' said Kudzuvine.

The Bursar led the way to the Screens and the Transworld Television team came bunched behind, gaping. 'These are the Screens,' he explained. 'On our left are the kitchens . . . well actually they are down below but the steps lead down to the Buttery. Now the Buttery – '

'Hold it there. Hold it,' Kudzuvine said, almost pleading. 'You mean you got a place you make your own butter? You mean in wooden churns with fucking handles and milkmaids and . . . This is beyond incredible. It's wayer out than way. Jesus, that I should have been so privileged. And you said you didn't use quills.'

'I don't, as a matter of fact,' said the Bursar coldly. He still felt very bitter about Mr Skundler's rudeness and the notion that he had to catch a goose every time he made a single entry. 'And the Buttery isn't for butter. It is where the bread and ale, and of course in years gone by some butter, was kept. Nowadays one buys one's sherry and wine there and the undergraduates can order beer or wine with their meals.'

Kudzuvine's mouth was hanging open. 'You mean you actually encourage kids to get alcoholic in there? I don't know what to say? This isn't happening. It can't be.'

'Not alcoholic. Just sensible drinking. It's all part of their education,' said the Bursar, who wished Kudzuvine's last two remarks had been true.

But Kudzuvine's short attention span had switched to the Hall itself, where a waiter had just come through for more coffee. 'Take a look at this, you guys,' he said and went in. Behind him the Bursar cringed. A small number of undergraduates were having breakfast and looked up in annoyance at the intrusion. Kudzuvine didn't notice. He was gazing in rapture at the portraits of past Masters hanging on the panelled walls and seemed particularly enraptured by Dr Anderson (1669–89) and Jonathan Riderscombe (1740–48), both of whom were decidedly fat.

'Shit,' said Kudzuvine, clearly now on some sort of higher than high. 'No wonder the place is called Porterhouse. It's a wonder it isn't Porkerhouse the way those guys look. And we think we've got obesity problems. That's human foie gras up there. I mean you can't get that way naturally. You've got to be force fed. And what's with their cholesterol level? Must been way off the scale like they sweated the stuff. And with porkbellies like those they can't ever have seen their John Henries. Except in the mirror of course. And look at the roof . . .'

By the time the Bursar had managed to get them out of the Hall he was in a state bordering on nervous collapse. 'We can't go round the College like this,' he said weakly. 'Couldn't your team go – '

'Right off first time, Professor Bursar. Man, we need your organizational skills,' he said and called the team into a huddle. The Bursar mopped his brow and prayed. It was no use. As the Hartang lookalikes scurried off in different directions, Kudzuvine turned back to the Bursar with even more terrible enthusiasm. 'So we've got them dancing in the Hall,' he said. 'Where else? You said two bands and . . .'

'Actually we lay a sort of wooden stage over the lawn in New Court and the Fellows' Garden and the marquees . . . tents are for the buffet and so on and the champagne . . .'

Kudzuvine listened avidly to the full explanation. 'Oh boy, oh boy,' he sighed. 'Oh brother. And all dolled up in gowns and tuxedos like it's Atlanta with Clark Gable and that Vivien Leigh and it's still Aunt Jemima Pancake Mix time.'

'I beg your pardon?' said the Bursar, as usual most unwisely.

Kudzuvine cringed. 'No, sir, I beg yours, Prof. You didn't hear me say that. I meant it was Afro-American Person time down south which is where I come from. Like Bibliopolis, Alabama, which I'm mighty proud of. That's where I was raised, sir, in Bibliopolis, Alabama, which as you will know is named after the Writer of the Good Book.'

The Bursar rather doubted it. He had never actually

thought of the Bible as having been written by one person but he supposed it was just conceivable. With Kudzuvine around anything was conceivable. The bloody man had moved on to helicopters and long shots.

'Okay, so we swing in over that church . . .'

'Chapel,' corrected the Bursar.

'Okay, chapel and we grab the lot with wide-angle like you've never seen and then head round by that tower and get the kids all dancing and the bands playing and . . . No, that isn't it. Chopper'd blow them all over the fucking place. We got to get something else. I'll give it some thought.'

'I'm not sure all this . . . What are those people doing on the roof of the Chapel?'

Kudzuvine turned and looked. Several people with polo-necks and blue glasses had climbed onto the lead roof of the Chapel and appeared to be measuring it. 'I guess they're looking for angles. Technicians. Difficult to tell who they are at this distance.'

The Bursar gazed at him in wonder. It was impossible for him to tell who any of these people in Hartang's clothes were at any distance. That was part of the horror. 'I really don't think they ought to be there just now,' he said. 'They are having Sung Eucharist in the Chapel this morning.' Again it was an unfortunate statement.

'Sung what? Sung You Christ? What, right now? This I've got to see.'

'No, don't, please don't. Please,' the Bursar begged.

But Kudzuvine was already striding off along the Cloisters hoping, the Bursar had little doubt, to see some more fucking monks in costume. He followed miserably, his mind functioning only vaguely and mostly in pictures of fearful genies and bottles. Or was it Pandora's Box? Something like that. Kudzuvine wasn't just one of the four horsemen of the Bursar's Apocalypse, he was the whole damned lot.

Inside the Chapel the full extent of the Transworld Television team's activities was only just beginning to be known. Only the Chaplain, deaf to the world, was unaware that something very odd was going on. The Praelector certainly knew. And the choir, who were singing 'Oh God our help in ages past, Our hope in years to come' in what had been an almost uplifting manner, were all staring at the ceiling. It had always been the weakest part of the Chapel and lack of finances had prevented its timbers being replaced or properly treated. Under the weight of Kudzuvine's angle technicians – several more had clambered up to have a good look round – the rafters seemed to sag and bounce slightly and, while the moccasins didn't thump or make much noise, in the silence that followed the end of the hymn they did sound as though a flock of extremely large birds – the Praelector thought of ostriches except that they didn't fly – had landed on the roof and were stalking about seeking what they might devour.

'Let us pray,' said the Chaplain, 'for all those sick and unhappy people who at this moment – ' He stopped. A large plaster moulding had broken away and had crashed into the aisle, but the Praelector wasn't waiting any longer.

'I think,' he shouted as another beam groaned above his head, 'I think we should all leave the building now.'

Another large piece of fine plaster moulding, this time of a vast cherubim, detached itself and slid down the wall, taking a marble memorial of Dr Cox (1702–40) with it, and almost killed an undergraduate in the pew underneath. Even the Chaplain was now conscious that something very like an earthquake was taking place. As the choir and the small congregation headed for the door – 'Now don't panic. Move slowly,' someone shouted – they were stopped in their tracks by the sudden appearance of Kudzuvine. He stood in the doorway, a menacing figure in his dark glasses and poloneck, and held up a hand.

'Hold it,' he shouted. 'Hold it.'

For a moment the Praelector looked round for something to hold. He had spent too many hours in the Rex and the Kinema in Mill Road not to know a gangster when he saw one, and Kudzuvine had all the hallmarks of a Mafioso about him. But the stoppage was only temporary. Another chunk, this time of solid masonry, dislodged by the end of a roof timber, hurtled down and landed on the lectern. No one was waiting any longer. The congregation surged forward, completely ignoring Kudzuvine's demand for a replay, and Kudzuvine himself, who was knocked to the ground and trampled on by some extremely large rugby players and a girl with a half-Blue for hockey. By the time they were clear of the danger zone only the Chaplain remained entirely calm.

'We must all pray for forgiveness,' he told the supine Kudzuvine, whose nose was bleeding profusely and who didn't know what the hell had hit him though it felt like a herd of steers in a movie he'd once helped make in Texas. In any case he had hit his head on the flagstones and had no clear idea where he was.

The Chaplain helped him to his feet. 'You come along with me, dear boy,' he said, and with the help of two undergraduates Kudzuvine was helped up the stone staircase to the Chaplain's rooms and laid on the bed. He was only partly conscious.

9

The Senior Tutor, on the other hand, was intensely
conscious. In fact, in a long life devoted in the main to
remaining unconscious of just about everything except
rowing and food and ignoring as much of reality as he
could, he had never been more unpleasantly conscious.
Like the Bursar, he wished to God he wasn't. He had
dined in Corpus the night before and while not exactly
wisely – the port had been particularly good but a whole
bottle of a '47 crusted port had put him in a state where
two large Benedictines had seemed a good idea – he had
dined extremely well. As a result he had woken late
feeling not so much like death warmed over as hell
heated up. It wasn't only his appalling headache, it was
his stomach. He didn't want to know what was going on
down there but whatever it was he wished it would
stop. Or come up. The desire to vomit was both
overwhelming and impossible to satisfy. And he could
only imagine that he had developed galloping hobnail
liver, one with spikes on. But it was his eyes that were
troubling most. When he finally got up – 'got up'
was wrong – when he managed to get to his feet, he had
to sit on the edge of the bed for ten minutes alternately
clutching his stomach and his head, and had slowly

crawled along the wall to the bathroom, the face that he could barely see in the mirror was not one that he had any desire to recognize. It seemed to be covered in floating spots which moved across its purple surface or hung like strands of some sort of detached and rather thick spider's web about the place. In fact everywhere he looked he seemed to be darkly mottled, and when he could focus sufficiently to look more closely at his eyes they resembled strawberries that had something the matter with them. For a moment he thought he must have caught a particularly virulent form of pink eye. Except of course that they weren't pink. The bloody things were scarlet and crimson and to talk about the whites of his eyes would have been absolutely meaningless. But it wasn't what he saw in the bathroom mirror that worried him most. As he went back along the wall towards his bed and, hopefully, death, he passed the window overlooking the Court and ... It was at that moment that the Senior Tutor knew he was suffering from the DTs and swore for the first time that, if he lived – not that he wanted to – he would never drink anything faintly alcoholic ever again.

There was a man in a polo-neck with a black blazer and white socks and dark blue sunglasses standing gazing up at the Bull Tower. That was fine in its way, though the Senior Tutor disliked tourists intensely. What really appalled him was that there was another man similarly dressed over by the Screens and yet another apparition – or was it two more? – gazing at the fountain. In fact, they were all over the place. The Senior Tutor clutched the sill in front of him and tried to count the swine. He'd got to about eight, though he wasn't sure there weren't sixteen, when he raised his eyes to heaven and caught sight of some more on the Chapel roof.

With a dreadful moan the Senior Tutor fell back against his desk and cursed himself, God, and that fucking '47 crusted port, not to mention the two Benedictines which until that moment he had forgotten. There was no doubt about it. He was in the last stages of delirium tremens. He had to be. Pink elephants were one thing. He'd heard about people with alcoholic poisoning seeing them. And spiders. And frankly he'd have given anything for some decent pink elephants or spiders. But that he should be afflicted by symptoms that produced seemingly dozens of men wearing dark sunglasses and white socks and polo-neck sweaters clearly indicated a degree of insanity he hadn't supposed existed. For a second or two he considered going back to the bathroom and putting an end to the horror once and for all and for ever and ever.

He was saved by a new and extraordinarily vivid illusion. Or delusion. There was another ghastly figure at the Chapel door and as he gazed in utter horror there was a sudden eruption of people from the Chapel who fought their way out and over the ghastly figure. The Senior Tutor shut his eyes and crawled back to his bed. At least in there he couldn't see anything very much.

He lay with his head under the covers and prayed for death.

He was in this condition when the Praelector arrived in a state of alarm himself. 'Senior Tutor, Senior Tutor, are you there?' he called out from the passage. The Senior Tutor whimpered and pretended not to be anywhere, but the Praelector was not to be misled. What was happening in the College was so dreadful he had to consult someone and none of the Junior Fellows was about and the Dean was absent and Professor Pawley, who had been doing something astronomical during the night, had sported his oak and refused to be woken. Only the Senior Tutor was available to help cope with the crisis. 'Senior Tutor, for Heaven's sake do get up. The most dreadful things are happening.'

The Senior Tutor knew that but he didn't want to talk about it. 'Go away, please go away,' he called weakly from the bedroom. 'I am very unwell.'

'Unwell? Oh dear, I am sorry. Do you want to have the doctor or Matron? I'll go and . . .'

But the thought that first the Matron and then Dr MacKendly should see him before he died roused the Senior Tutor. 'No, for God's sake, no,' he pleaded, emerging from under the bedclothes. 'And on no account turn on the light.'

Framed in the doorway, the Praelector hesitated. He had heard rumours about the Senior Tutor's sex life and he was afraid he might be intruding upon it in some way. 'When you say you are unwell . . .' he began.

'I am . . . I am . . .' the Senior Tutor struggled to find words for his state without mentioning the DTs and men in dark glasses and white socks. 'I am not quite myself.'

For a moment the Praelector, a man who was not easily affected by events and took things as they came, was distracted from his own recent experiences. 'So few of us are,' he said. 'I know that at times I am not entirely sure of my own real nature. It is a question of philosophical interest that – '

'It isn't,' the Senior Tutor protested. 'It has nothing to do with philosophy. I am beside myself.'

'Ah,' said the Praelector, reverting to his previous sexual theory that the Senior Tutor might actually be beside someone else. 'Now do you mean that literally or metaphorically?'

It was not a question the Senior Tutor felt in the least like answering. 'What the hell does it matter whether I mean . . . Oh God, the agony . . . Can't you tell I am out of my mind,' he almost shouted.

'Well, I can certainly tell you are not entirely in it,' said the Praelector. 'But then so few Cambridge dons are entirely in their minds all the time. In fact I'd go so far as to say some of them appear to have no minds to be in. That is surely where the expression "to be in two minds" comes from.'

'Does it fuck!' screamed the Senior Tutor, driven even further towards dementia by the abstract nature of the argument. 'I am out of the only mind I've got. Or had. I am mad. I am insane. Don't you understand simple language?'

'If you put it like that, I can't say I am entirely surprised,' said the Praelector, whose goodwill had reached its limit. 'To tell the truth I never believed you to be entirely normal. All that rowing and riding up and down the towpath shouting obscenities . . .'

The Senior Tutor shouted some more and provoked the Praelector to switch the light on. He had almost entirely forgotten why he had come to see the Senior Tutor. What he saw now served to convince him that his original premise had been the right one. Clearly the Senior Tutor had done something very nasty to himself sexually. The face that glowered at him from the bed was that of a man in extremis. The Praelector's concern came back. 'My dear fellow, what have you been doing to yourself? At your age masturbation can be very dangerous. Have you been using some – '

'Masturbation,' screamed the Senior Tutor. 'Bugger masturbation.' Again it was an unfortunate expression to use.

'Well, there is that,' said the Praelector, glancing round the bedroom to see if some young man was there, but he could only see the Senior Tutor's clothes all over the floor and what looked like a very full bottle of Californian Chardonnay beside the bed. Something about the aroma in the room suggested he was mistaken about its contents. 'All the same . . .'

But the Senior Tutor had been driven beyond the

bounds of endurance by the suggestion that he had been masturbating. He didn't exactly leap from the bed – he was incapable of leaping anywhere – but he certainly staggered from it.

The Praelector looked at his naked body with disgust. And fear. The Senior Tutor hadn't been exaggerating. He was extremely mad and extremely dangerous. 'All right, I'll go,' the Praelector said, backing through the doorway and now remembering why he had come in the first place. 'But before I do I think you ought to know that the College is filled with dreadful young men in dark glasses and polo-neck sweaters and white socks and...' To his amazement a change came over the Senior Tutor. From being very obviously a homicidal maniac he had suddenly switched to being something else.

It would have been going too far to say that he was looking happy. The '47 crusted port and the Benedictine were still having their effects on just about every part of his body and his eyes didn't look at all healthy but his relief had turned him back into something almost human. 'What did you say?' he whimpered. 'What was that you said?'

'I said the College is filled with dreadful young men in dark glasses and polo-neck sweaters – '

In front of him the Senior Tutor sank to his knees and raised his bloodshot eyes to the ceiling. 'Alleluia, praise be to God,' he moaned, and expressed his feelings by throwing up.

The Praelector left him there and went down into the Court to find that Walter, three other porters, Arthur, the Chef and the entire kitchen staff plus the gardeners supported by dozens of undergraduates, had rounded up the Transworld team and had hustled them out into the street. 'You come back in here like that and you'll get more than a bloody nose,' Walter told one of the team whose glasses had been broken and who was minus a moccasin. 'Next time you won't know what's fucking hit you.'

*

In the Chaplain's rooms Kudzuvine still didn't. The Matron, a heavy woman with large hands, had had a look at him and had advised calling Dr MacKendly. 'You never know, do you?' she told the Chaplain who was rather partial to her. 'Not with blows to the head, you don't. I daresay he'll be all right but it's best to be on the safe side.'

'I'm not sure that I want to be,' said the Praelector, who had joined the little group at the bedside. 'Anyone who can do what those men did to the Chapel doesn't come into any category I want to preserve alive.' He thought for a moment and then added, 'Oh, and by the way, Matron, I think it might be advisable for you to pay the Senior Tutor a visit. He's been acting very peculiarly and I think he could do with some assistance.'

Muttering to herself that he always did act peculiar, she left on the Praelector's mission of revenge. He still hadn't got over the Senior Tutor's disgusting behaviour or his language. The Matron would do him good. In any case he wanted to ask this awful gangster with the swollen nose what he and his mob had been doing in the College. 'It's not as though there is anything worth stealing, or we'd have sold it,' he told the Chaplain, who was trying to treat Kudzuvine's suspected concussion or fractured skull with brandy. Kudzuvine wasn't having any. He lay there staring up at the Chaplain in a glazed way.

'Now open your mouth, my dear chap,' said the Chaplain. 'A little of what you fancy does you good, as dear Marie Lloyd used to say.'

'I don't think he fancies Rémy Martin somehow,' said the Praelector, who felt like a drink himself.

'Ray Me who?' muttered Kudzuvine. 'What's happening? What's going on?'

'Nothing is going on. It's just that you've had a little accident and fallen . . .'

Kudzuvine concentrated hard and remembered. 'You call that a little accident? Being trampled to death by a herd of fucking monks and things? You call that little?'

'It's merely a term of . . . it's a slight euphemism, an understatement. Nothing to get excited about.'

Kudzuvine glowered. 'Nothing to get excited about? You got to be kidding. And understatement it wasn't. I was the fucking understatement. You ever been trampled to death by a herd of fucking – '

'Yes,' said the Chaplain with surprising authority. 'As

a matter of fact I was lock forward in the scrum, if you know what that means, and I have frequently been trampled on. There's no need to make such a fuss about it. You are obviously an American.'

'I am a citizen of the greatest super-power in the world,' said Kudzuvine. 'That's me. A born and bred natural citizen of the greatest super-power in the whole goddam world and proud of it you better believe me. We can take on the whole fucking rest of you and whip the hell out of you all no sweat.'

'I seem to remember you did particularly well in Vietnam,' said the Praelector, who had landed in Normandy and hadn't forgotten the platoon being bombed by Flying Fortresses near Falaise. 'A most impressive performance. Brilliant strategy and such excellently disciplined fighting men and generals, but then again you were only up against small men who didn't have any aircraft. I daresay if they'd bombed you as heavily as you bombed them . . .' He left the comparison for Kudzuvine to work out.

'What the fuck are you talking about? Vietnam? Hell, we didn't stand a chance. Those bastards are so small you can't find them to kill and they breed like flies.'

The Chaplain intervened with a different brandy, this time Hine. 'I'm sure you'll find this to your taste,' he said, only to be told to take the fucking stuff away because he was an American non-alcoholic and teetotaller from Bibliopolis, Alabama, and they'd better believe it.

'Oh, but we do,' said the Praelector. 'Now, if you'll just tell us your name?'

'What for?' Kudzuvine demanded belligerently.

For a moment the Praelector was tempted to say they needed it for his next of kin, but he decided on tact. 'It's just that we want to be friends and – '

'Shit!' said Kudzuvine. 'Trample me to death like I'm a fucking Iraqi or something and you want to be friends? Go fuck yourself.'

'I can see this is going to be difficult,' said the Praelector, who had had a trying day and was sick to death of being insulted.

'What I don't see,' said the Chaplain, who had drunk the Hine brandy himself, 'is what Iraqis have to do with being trampled to death.'

'One must suppose it refers to the world's greatest super-power using bulldozers to bury the poor devils alive in their trenches,' the Praelector said, and poured himself a glass of the Remy Martin.

'Goddam right we did. Those bastards didn't know what hit them,' said Kudzuvine.

The look in the eyes of both the Chaplain and the Praelector suggested that something of the same sort might be about to happen to Kudzuvine but, being the man he was, he had no idea it was coming. 'I don't know if you have a good lawyer,' the Praelector said very quietly and very distinctly, 'but I think I should tell you that when the police arrive and you have been charged with aggravated assault, criminal trespass with damage, and that damage deliberately done to a Listed Building of National Importance – '

'Listed Building of National Importance? What the fuck you talking about? Like what?' Kudzuvine shouted and tried to sit up.

'If you want a comparison with something in your own country, might I suggest deliberately causing the destruction of the Unitarian Church in Cambridge, Massachusetts, where Emerson preached. But then perhaps you don't know who Emerson was?'

'Sure I know who Emerson was. Invented the fucking electric light. Emerson!' Kudzuvine practically spat at them.

The Praelector smiled grimly. 'What I'm trying to get you to understand is that, following in the great tradition set by the lawyers and judiciary in your wonderful country, we are going to sue you for the damage you have caused to one of the oldest and most valued college chapels in Cambridge. Now I don't know what damages and costs we will be awarded but the courts in England are increasingly following the American custom of . . .'

There was no need to go on. The physical injuries Kudzuvine had suffered had paled into total insignificance. He knew about damages. 'Get me Hartang,' he whimpered. 'I've got to have Hartang.'

'I'm afraid I haven't got any,' said the Chaplain. 'Lapsang Souchong, yes, and Earl Grey, but Hartang no. I can't honestly say I've ever heard of it.'

The Praelector was less sympathetic. 'He's playing

the oldest legal trick in the world. Playing dumb and being of unsound mind. Not that it is going to help in the least. He brought whoever those dreadful men were into the College where they did the most monstrous damage and committed criminal trespass. Now what did you say your name was?'

'Kudzuvine,' said Kudzuvine.

'Really? How very interesting. And I suppose your mother's name was Ivy,' said the Praelector. 'Something botanical at any rate, and I daresay you have Swedish ancestry.'

'What the fuck you talking about my mother's name? Botanical? They called her Lily May. And what's with the Swedish shit? Nothing Swede about us. Free-born citizen of the greatest super – '

'Quite so. We've been through the virtues of America before *ad nauseam* and we don't need them again. What is your real name? And don't come up with ... a or Kentucky Bluegrass or anything Linnaean.'

Kudzuvine tried to get off the bed on the other side. He was clearly terrified. But the Praelector had already left the room.

'What's with the other guy, monk?' he asked the Chaplain. 'He always like this?'

The Chaplain seemed to consider the question seriously. 'I suppose he must be,' he said, 'though now you come to mention it ... oh well, never mind. It's probably that time of the month.'

'Time of the month? What's the time of the month

got to do with it? Guy thinks he menstruates or something?'

'I think it's mainly something,' the Chaplain answered. 'I'm most sorry about that tea. I do have some China. Are you sure?'

Kudzuvine didn't want tea and having some part of China wasn't doing him any good either. But his main worry was the 'something'. 'What's he do this time of month?' he asked as he tried to move towards the door. 'Turn into a werewolf like Frankenstein? We did a movie once on fucking wolves. They got a real tight social order, you know that?'

'How very interesting,' said the Chaplain, and tripped Kudzuvine up with a walking stick. He was still on the floor when the Praelector returned with the Head Porter and two assistants. He stared at their shoes and dark grey trousers and moaned.

'I think it is about time he had a strong drink,' the Praelector said, 'though I don't think we should waste good brandy on the swine. Something cheap and nasty. I'll get some from the kitchen.' He wandered off and presently returned with a large bottle. 'Turn him over,' he ordered and Kudzuvine was turned over and looked up frantically at five horrible faces and at the bottle.

'What are you going to do?' he whimpered. 'What's with the bottle?'

'What's with the bottle is a rather nasty cooking brandy which you are going to taste rather a lot of unless you tell us your name.'

'Kudzuvine, for fucksake. What you think it is? Clinton or Schwarzkopf or something?'

'No, those hadn't occurred to me,' the Praelector said, 'though now that you mention it . . .' He knelt beside Kudzuvine and the look in his eye was very cold. 'Now open your mouth.'

Kudzuvine clenched his teeth. 'I've told you before,' he said nasally and with the greatest difficulty, 'I'm a free-born citizen of the world's greatest su – '

The Praelector poured some brandy onto his teeth and Kudzuvine closed his mouth entirely.

'I can see this is going to be very difficult,' said the Praelector. 'We are going to have to prise his mouth open with something.' He rose immediately to his feet and looked round for a suitable instrument. He seemed to find one in the Chaplain's umbrella. 'Now then Walter, if you and Henry will just hold him steady . . .'

But Kudzuvine was on his feet again and backed against the wall with a wild look in his eye and a round ebony ruler in his hand. 'You lay one hand on me,' he squealed, 'I'm going to fucking kill you. Kill you, understand? You ain't going to make me drink fucking alcohol no way and you'd better know it. I want out of here and as a free-born natural – '

'He does go on about being free-born and natural rather a lot,' said the Praelector, but the Chaplain had disappeared into the next room.

He came back with a large pink rubber bag with a pipe attached to it. 'I wonder if this would be of any use,' he said. 'A very nice girl from Addenbrooke's comes occasionally to give me colonic irrigation . . .'

'Shit,' said Kudzuvine.

'Exactly. I find it helps a lot. You put the liquid in this bag here and this plastic bit on the end of the pipe goes up –'

'Oh no, it fucking doesn't,' yelled Kudzuvine. 'You think you're going to stick that thing up my ass and pour a quart of fucking brandy down a douche, you're out of your fucking minds. I'm telling you when I get on to the Embassy you bastards are going to learn what it means to be a citizen of . . . an American citizen . . .'

He stopped and stared. The Chaplain had handed the douche to Walter who was filling it with cooking brandy. As the bag swelled the Chaplain explained its mechanism. 'This sort of clothes-peg thing is what controls the flow,' he said, pointing to a plastic grip on the rubber pipe. 'Once we have inserted this rounded piece into his mouth –'

A yell from Kudzuvine stopped the explanation. 'Mouth? Mouth? That thing don't go anywhere near my fucking mouth. No way. It's unhygienic. You know where that thing has been?'

'As a matter of fact I do,' said the Chaplain, 'quite a number of times too. I suppose she's been coming here since 1986. A delightful girl called Daisy with such very delicate hands. I had constipation at the time I remember and –'

He was interrupted by Kudzuvine, who had hit

Henry with the ruler and was making a dash for the door. He was overcome and pinned to the wall.

'I think it would be easier to administer if he was lying down,' said the Praelector. 'Mind you, we don't want to spill any brandy on the bed. It will have to be the floor again.' There was a brief but violent struggle and Kudzuvine was held down on the carpet.

'You hold the bag, Henry,' Walter said, 'and I'll just insert this plastic bit . . . Funny shape it is too and a bit too long to get it right in. Does it matter if we spill a bit, sir? Because it's got these holes in the side and like I say it's a bit long to shove right in. I mean, we might pour the brandy down his lungs and that wouldn't do him a lot of good, like.'

They considered the problem for a moment and the Chaplain found the answer. 'Blu-Tack,' he said. 'I know I've got some somewhere. I use it for cleaning the keys of my typewriter and picking up pins off the floor, you know. Now if we block up the top holes we won't have to push it right down his throat.'

On the floor Kudzuvine's struggles redoubled and were coupled with the most terrible threats and what the American Embassy and Government would do to them and Porterhouse like . . .

'Grenada and Haiti? And of course we are an island and a small one too,' said the Praelector and wondered aloud why the United States always seemed to prefer wars with island nations. 'But never mind about that. Now then, Mr Mafia man, you are either going to tell us your real name and address and who you are and what you were doing with a team of . . .' He searched for a word.

Walter supplied it. 'Goons, sir?'

'Exactly. Thank you, Walter. A team of goons, or hoods. Who did very substantial structural damage to a building, namely the Chapel, which was built several hundred years before your charming country was so unfortunately discovered. Such a shame Columbus didn't go the other way. Now, if you tell us what we need to know, we will not have to put this rather peculiar enema contraption which, I agree, is not at all sanitary, to a purpose I cannot believe it was originally intended for. This is your last chance.'

'I've got the Blu-Tack,' said the Chaplain excitedly. 'Now if we just put it in these holes at the top of the plastic bit . . .'

'I don't think it's going to be necessary with some of the holes, sir,' Walter told him. 'Some of them are sort of blocked already with . . . well, I don't like to say, sir, but if you ask me . . .'

But Kudzuvine was a broken man. 'I swear to God my name is Kudzuvine, Karl Kudzuvine, from Bibliopolis, Alabama, sir,' he said, weeping copiously.

The Praelector was unimpressed. He had served as a recruiter for MI6 and knew some of its methods. 'A likely story,' he said. 'First Linnaeus and a very unpleasant convolvulus plant rather like Russian Vine or Mile-a-Minute used to prevent soil erosion on roadside cuttings in the South, and now a town called Bibliopolis which clearly doesn't exist. What will you think of next?'

'I swear to God it's true. I'm Vice-President of Transworld Television Productions and I – '

'Oh dear,' the Praelector interrupted, 'have you ever known an American who wasn't a vice-president of something or other? I'm sure I haven't. So terribly boring, all this self-importance.' He simulated a yawn. 'And can't you come up with something better than Transworld Television Productions? Such a very trite name for a company. Transworld indeed!'

'But I swear to God – '

The Chaplain intervened. 'This does happen to be Sunday,' he said, 'and I would be obliged if you would refrain from using that sort of language.'

Kudzuvine looked at him pitifully. The Chaplain was holding the end of the douche, which now had blue holes as well as brown ones, in a very threatening manner.

'Language? What language for Chrissake? You keep asking me questions how the fuck am I supposed to answer without language? I don't know no deaf and dumb. You know, with the hands and all.'

He lay and wept and the Praelector continued with his questioning. He had decided to soften his approach for the time being. 'Now I don't want to have to do this but – '

'You don't?' Kudzuvine broke in. 'You don't want it?

You think I do? You think I want that filthy thing in my mouth where it's been? You think that, you're wrong. Man, you couldn't be more wrong, sir.'

'Well, it's up to you,' said the Praelector. 'It's either that thing, as you call it, and frankly I don't know what to call it myself, or the brandy. I don't know if you are acquainted with cooking brandy but the taste isn't pleasant, not pleasant at all. I always stick to decent cognac myself.' He paused for a moment. 'Now then, which is it to be?'

Kudzuvine tried to consider the alternatives and found it very difficult. The Praelector seemed to have left something out. 'You mean between cooking brandy and cognac? Man, I don't know what to say. I keep telling you I'm a non-alcoholic teetotaller. I don't even touch beer. I don't smoke grass, nothing. Not any more. You know, keep my body clear and clean. Even gave up Listerine somebody tells me it's got alcohol. And you want to go easy on the under-arm stuff too. Some of that's got aluminum in it. Gives you Alzheimer's.' He paused as a new and more terrible thought hit him. 'You guys haven't got Alzheimer's, have you? Dear shit . . .'

The Praelector drew up a chair. He had reached the end of what little patience he had managed to retain. 'If you are ready, Walter,' he said to the Head Porter, but the Chaplain had remembered something.

'You know, I do believe he may be right,' he said.

The Praelector looked up at him. So did Kudzuvine. 'About what?' asked the Praelector, who couldn't for the life of him believe that this filthy American gangster could be right about anything at all.

'About the television thing. Weren't they trying to bring some sort of lorry with wires in through the Main Gate, Walter?'

'What, this morning, sir? Come to think of it, they were. Had Transworld Television written on the side. I wouldn't let them. I wasn't having that. I told them the last time them bolts was undone was when Her Majesty – '

'Is this true, Walter?' the Praelector interrupted. 'You actually saw this . . . these words?'

'Oh yes, sir, and Henry did too, didn't you, Henry?'

The Junior Porter nodded. 'He kept asking for Professor Purser and you said we didn't have no Professor Purser and the Bursar came along. Been to Early Communion the Bursar had and you said that wasn't like him to come so early . . .'

On the floor Kudzuvine managed to find words. Brandy had been dripping from the end of the douche onto his face. 'Professor Bursar,' he screamed, 'Professor Bursar gave me permission to take . . . to video the College for Mr Hartang. You ask him he'll tell you. I had his authorization. Okay, so not on the lawns.'

'Not on the lawns? What not on the lawns?'

'Like walk on them. They're hundreds of years old you know that? Hundreds and hundreds of years old.'

'Really?' said the Praelector, who happened to know they had been relaid ten years before. 'You know, I hadn't thought of it like that.' He was beginning to think that whatever had been going on the Bursar was going to have a quite staggering amount of explaining to do. In the meantime this man, whose name seemed as unlikely as his syntax, had to be handled with rather more care and sophistication than he had been shown to date. It would do the Porterhouse reputation no good at all if it leaked out – the word was unfortunately most appropriate – that he had been threatened with forced brandy-drinking by means of a douche that had for ten years been used for colonic irrigation purposes by the Chaplain. That sort of thing would not look good in the *Cambridge Evening News*.

The Praelector set out on a policy of appeasement. 'My dear chap,' he said, helping Kudzuvine to his feet. 'You were saying something about the lawn being hundreds of years old and . . .'

'Sure. Professor Bursar told me that. They're protected species like whales and stuff,' said Kudzuvine, still eyeing him very warily indeed. 'Didn't say nothing about roofs and chapels. They a protected species too?'

'More or less,' said the Praelector and changed his mind. This man Kudzuvine, if that was really his name, had very little grasp of English. 'In fact very much more. They are Listed Buildings under an Act of Parliament signed by Her Majesty the Queen and cannot be altered, touched, damaged or in any way interfered with without the duly obtained permission given in writing and after due consultation by Her Majesty's Commissioners for

Ancient Monuments which permission will only be given should the Monument or Listed Building be in serious danger of collapsing. I can assure you that the Porterhouse Chapel and the Monuments it contains come into the latter category as a result of the actions of the men you introduced into the College and for whom you are responsible. I cannot begin to imagine the full consequences of your action except that they will be extremely drastic. The issue may have to go to the Privy Council. I hope I have made myself clear.' By which the Praelector of course meant the opposite.

Kudzuvine was still gaping at him. 'The Privy Council?' he muttered. 'Did you say Privy Council?'

'Her Majesty Queen Elizabeth the Second's Privy Council deals with matters – '

Kudzuvine held up a shaking hand. 'Don't tell me,' he said, 'and I had romantic dreams about that Princess of Wales and the Royal Family. And now you tell me Her Majesty . . . Shit! You British. I'm never going to understand anything round here.'

'Few people do,' said the Praelector. 'We are, I suppose, an acquired taste. Am I not right, Chaplain?'

Kudzuvine turned to look at the Chaplain, who was helping Walter and Henry to drain the cooking brandy back into the bottle. 'Did you say "an acquired taste"?' he said. 'I shouldn't have thought so. It's only cooking brandy and I very much doubt that anyone will notice the Blu-Tack. In fact it might actually add a certain bouquet to the brandy which it presently lacks.'

'I got to get out of here but now,' said Kudzuvine and stumbled towards the door only to be tripped up again by the Praelector using the umbrella. As he slumped forward and hit his head Kudzuvine had the briefest moment of lucid thought. He had to get out of this terrible, terrible place before . . .

By the time Walter and Henry carried him across the Fellows' Garden to the Master's Lodge he was mercifully quite unconscious.

'I am afraid the creature will have to be our honoured guest for a few days until he has quite recovered,' the Praelector said. 'I can think of no better place for an honoured guest than the Master's Lodge. It is immensely secure and well protected, and besides he will be company for the Master. I am sure Skullion will see he is looked after properly. I shall send for Dr MacKendly and perhaps it would be advisable for Matron to move into the room next to his with another porter on hand and possibly even one or two of the larger kitchen staff to see to his needs and to ensure he does not leave the College. In the meantime, I think a word with the Bursar is called for.'

10

While Kudzuvine was stripped of his polo-neck sweater, his trousers and underwear, his white socks and his moccasins and put to bed stark naked (his clothes were sent to the College laundry for unnecessary attention), the exhausted Praelector gave orders that only undergraduates and Fellows were to be allowed to enter or leave Porterhouse. Then he went to see if the Senior Tutor was in a fit state to discuss matters with the Bursar. He found him sipping a cup of beef tea and in a very nasty mood indeed. But at least he was sober.

'I must have been insane,' he muttered, staring blankly into the empty fireplace.

The Praelector patted his shoulder sympathetically. 'You certainly acted most peculiarly, old chap, though I would not have gone so far as to say you were actually insane. Just not your usual self.'

The Senior Tutor started in his chair and looked at him with genuine hatred. 'Don't you start again,' he snarled. 'I had enough of that this morning. Whether I was beside myself or in two minds and whether I had a right mind or a left one. And then you accused me of masturbating. I wonder you didn't come out with it and say I was suffering from Wankers' Doom and ask if I had hair on the palms of my hands. And then to top it all you had to send that bloody Matron round when you knew I was lying naked on the floor and could hardly move. Have you ever been ... I won't say nursed by that foul woman because her methods of nursing pre-date Florence Nightingale. Do you know what she did to me?'

'No,' said the Praelector hurriedly, 'I don't. Anyway why did you say you must have been insane when I came into the room just now?'

'Because,' said the Senior Tutor with extraordinary venom, 'because I thought two large Benedictines taken after an entire bottle of 1947 crusted port at Corpus Christi, and that's not a name I'd use for that damned college, would settle my stomach nicely. Have you ever drunk an entire bottle of crusted port *and* two Benedictines?'

The look on the Praelector's face was a sufficient answer.

'Well, don't is all I can say. I wouldn't wish the consequences on my very worst enemy. And what damned fool told me '47 was a good year for port? It was a bloody awful year for everything. Whale meat and snoek and the coldest winter imaginable ... If anyone mentions 1947 to me ever again ...'

The Senior Tutor sipped more beef tea and gave the Praelector the opportunity he had been waiting for. 'On the topic of little problems,' he began and stopped.

The Senior Tutor had choked. 'Little? Little problems? You come in here and talk to me about little problems. This is the worst problem . . .'

He gave up and the Praelector went on. 'I'm talking about Kudzuvine and the damage done to the Chapel.' He stopped. The Senior Tutor was looking homicidal again.

'The leader of that group of hoodlums calls himself Mr Kudzuvine,' the Praelector explained.

Quite clearly the Senior Tutor didn't believe him. 'Why?' he demanded.

'I don't know why. I'm just saying he does. And I have to say I didn't believe him to begin with either.'

'I don't believe the bastard now. End of story,' said the Senior Tutor.

'Well, not quite, as it happens,' said the Praelector tentatively. The Senior Tutor's temper wasn't just uncertain – in fact uncertainty didn't come into it – it was extremely nasty all the time.

He had turned a furious face towards the Praelector. 'Go on. What do you mean "not quite"? You mean there's more?'

'I'm afraid so. You see, when the roof of the Chapel began to give way . . .' he began.

'You are a liar, a bloody liar,' shouted the Senior Tutor. 'You come in here and deliberately set out to torment me.' He rose from his chair and spilt some of the beef tea down his trousers. 'I've looked out of windows I don't know how many times today to make sure those ghastly figures weren't there and I'm not going blind on account of the masturbating you accuse me of and the Chapel roof is still there. It has not given way.'

'I didn't actually accuse you of masturbating, you know. I just thought that – '

'Thought? What's that if it isn't accusing?'

'Well, we all think things all the time but it doesn't mean to say we do them. God alone knows what would happen if we did,' said the Praelector.

'I don't need God to know what I'd do. I know damned well myself.' The Senior Tutor slumped back into his chair and spilt some more beef tea.

'Well, about the roof. You're quite right, it hasn't given way entirely, but thanks to those foul people stamping about on it this morning during the Sung Eucharist several large sections of plaster have come down – it's a miracle no one was killed – Dr Cox's Memorial Bust has gone and the Lectern has assumed a new and rather peculiar configuration.'

'But the Lectern is made of solid bronze. It's immensely strong,' said the Senior Tutor. 'Are you saying it's bent?' His disbelief was patent.

'Not so much bent as twisted. You know that bird on the front, I assume it's an eagle? Well, it's no longer flying forward so much as looping the loop.'

'Looping the loop? Are you out of your mind? The fucking thing never did fly. Couldn't even if it wanted to. Far too heavy and – '

'Oh, for goodness' sake,' the Praelector interrupted.

It was his turn to be furious. 'Stop taking figures of speech literally and listen. A huge block of solid masonry supporting one of the roof timbers came away and landed on the Lectern. In other words, we are now in a position to demand the most enormous damages from these people. It could run into millions.'

'Could do but it won't. Don't suppose we'll ever catch the swine and even if we did they'd weasel out of it somehow.'

'As a matter of fact Mr Kudzuvine is lying in bed in the Master's Lodge and is unconscious. I have sent for Dr MacKendly and the Matron is with him.' A shiver ran through the Senior Tutor. 'The point I am trying to make is that Mr Kudzuvine is Vice-President of a company called Transworld Television Productions who were here at the Bursar's behest to make some sort of film about the College. In other words – '

'The Bursar? You mean to say the bloody Bursar's responsible for . . . ? I'll kill the swine. I'll tear him limb from limb. I'll make him wish he'd never been born. I'll – '

'Sit down,' commanded the Praelector and, exercising his temporary physical superiority, pushed the Senior Tutor and the beef tea back into his chair. 'You will do nothing of the sort. Instead you will listen to me. We are strategically placed to force this Transworld Television company to make good the damage they have done and pay very large financial compensation into the bargain. I am now going to see if I can find the Bursar and I want you to come with me . . . No, on the whole I do not think that would be very advisable given your present condition. I shall find someone more rational.'

He went down the stairs and found Dr Buscott gloomily looking at a moccasin floating in the Fountain. 'I don't know what the world is coming to,' he said. 'I gather there was some sort of riot here this morning.'

The Praelector took him and a young physicist called Gilkes along to the Bursar's office. 'I want you to take careful note of what is said,' he told them. 'We are going to sue for damages and I need witnesses.'

They finally found the Bursar hiding in the little washroom behind the College Secretary's office and although it was Sunday she was there herself. 'Ah Mrs Morestead, have you seen the Bursar?' the Praelector enquired.

Mrs Morestead indicated the washroom with her head and the Bursar was brought out. He was ashen and in a state of acute anxiety.

'Now come along and sit down and tell us all about it over a nice cup of tea,' said the Praelector in his most kindly manner. 'Mrs Morestead is going to make a nice big pot of strong tea and we'll have some biscuits and you'll explain why you hired this Transworld Television Company to come and make a film about Porterhouse. Now it's all right. Nobody is going to hurt . . . to blame you and you are quite safe with us. Just tell us in your own words . . . No, there's no need to gibber and I didn't quite catch what you were gibbering about. No, the Senior Tutor isn't going to find you here. And yes, I daresay he is stalking about seeking whom he may devour, though I rather doubt he's in any condition to stalk anything and his desire to devour is notably absent today. Now here is Mrs Morestead with the tea. Yes, lots of sugar. Thank you, Dr Buscott, and the biscuits please, Mr Gilkes. That's nice, isn't it? Nice and cosy.'

The Bursar shook his head miserably. 'They'll kill me. I know they will,' he whimpered.

'I don't think so. Of course the Dean is going to be a trifle cross and the Senior Tutor – '

'I'm not talking about them. I'm talking about those terrible people down at Transworld Television. Skundler, for instance.'

'Skundler?' said the Praelector and asked for the name to be spelt so that Mrs Morestead could get it down.

'And then there is Edgar Hartang. He's the head of it all and a terrifying man and enormously rich and flies about the world in his own King Lear . . .' The Bursar stopped, conscious that there was a mistake somewhere.

'I see,' said the Praelector in tones that would have done credit to an undertaker at the bedside of a dying man. 'Do go on. In a King Lear? Does he have three daughters, by any chance?'

'I think he means a Lear jet,' said Gilkes. 'It's an executive jet and can fly anywhere in the world.'

'Very useful, I'm sure, and at least we now know that Mr Hartang is a person and not a brand of tea. But you still haven't told us why you hired them to film the College.'

'I didn't,' said the Bursar. 'They wanted to give the College huge sums of money and I was at this conference on fund-raising when Kudzuvine approached me and . . .'

While his story poured out the others sat listening raptly. As the Praelector told the College Council when it met some days later, it was at that moment that he felt Porterhouse had hit the jackpot.

11

It was hardly the most auspicious moment for Dr
Purefoy Osbert to arrive to take up his post as the Sir
Godber Evans Memorial Fellow. He had made special
arrangements with the authorities at Kloone and had
agreed to drive up once a month to do some Continuous
Assessment work on the students in his Department
without any cost to the University and the parting,
though sudden, had been an amicable one. Even Mrs
Ndhlovo had shown her admiration of him and approval
by allowing him to kiss her and fondle her beautiful
breasts. 'You are becoming a proper man, Purefoy,' she
said, giving up pidgin English for a moment. 'I can see
that you are going to make a great name for yourself.'

'You could have the same name if you married me.
You would be Mrs Osbert.'

Mrs Ndhlovo gave the matter some thought and
shook her head. 'No, not until you are famous and rich,'
she said.

'But I am comparatively speaking rich, and although
I may not be famous I am still the Sir Godber Evans
Memorial Fellow at Porterhouse College, Cambridge,
and that is not something to be sneezed at.'

Mrs Ndhlovo laughed and pushed her hair away from

her eyes. 'I not sneeze, Purefoy sweetheart. I not even sniff. I just say I wait see what happens you. I hear Porterhouse not such good place right now. Plenty bad things happen one time.'

'And I intend to find out for certain what happened to Sir Godber. That is why I got the post and the salary.'

'I know what the salary is. You told me and that don't make you rich. You just comfortable and can go find nice girl to jig-jig with now stead of beating your biltong way you do now.'

'Biltong?' said Purefoy, who wasn't familiar with Afrikaner eating habits.

'Meat, Purefoy, beating your meat. It means – '

'I know what it means. I've been to every lesson you've given on the subject of Male Infertility and so on and I – '

'I don't give lessons on so on. Ain't possible. So on. Got to end some time. Even Mr Ndhlovo got to stop coming. Come three, four, five times but not so on. And he proper man. Got balls. Wonder what happened to them.'

Purefoy wasn't even faintly interested in the destination of the late Mr Ndhlovo's testicles. 'All I'm trying to tell you is that I never think about any other woman except you when . . . when . . . well, when I seek relief from my frustration.'

Mrs Ndhlovo's eyes widened wondrously. 'My, oh my,' she said. 'I heard it called lots of things my time but I never did hear it called technical like that. Relief from frustration. You ain't frustrated, is you, honey?'

'Of course I am,' said Purefoy, whose own balls were beginning to ache. 'You know I am. For you.'

'Then you give me one more big kiss and I let you feel my mammaries one time more.'

'I really do wish you wouldn't use terms like that. You've got lovely breasts and it's wrong to call them mammaries.'

'That's technical like you saying relief from frustration 'stead of soaping the snake. I know others just as good.'

Purefoy Osbert misheard her and shuddered. 'Please,' he said, 'please don't use that awful word. You're not a cow. You're the most beautiful woman in the world. And you speak perfectly good English. Why do you have to pretend to be someone you're not. You are beautiful.'

'I ain't no such thing, Purefoy. I just a proper woman. Now you go be proper man and then maybe . . .'

'You'll marry me? Please say you will.'

'Possibly,' said Mrs Ndhlovo. 'But first of all you'll have to prove yourself a proper man at Porterhouse.'

*

In the event Purefoy had the greatest difficulty proving he had anything to do with Porterhouse. He arrived at the Main Gate to find it locked. He pulled the bell chain and waited. There were heavy steps inside and a man asked him what he wanted.

'As a matter of fact I want to come in. I'm expected.'

On the far side of the gate the Head Porter smiled to himself. 'That's right. So you are,' said Walter. 'I knew you'd be back and like I told you you'll get more than a bloody nose if you try to get in this time. Now get lost.'

Purefoy stood dumbfounded on the pavement. He understood now why Porterhouse had such a dreadful reputation. If anything, what he had heard had been an underestimation of its dreadfulness. And he could well believe Lady Mary's statement that her husband had been murdered there. For a moment he almost decided to return to Kloone but the thought of Mrs Ndhlovo gave him strength. To win her hand and all the rest of her he had to be a proper man. He would do anything for her.

'Listen,' he called out through the black door. 'My name is Dr Osbert and I am expected.'

There was a moment's hesitation inside. 'Dr Osbert? Did you say Dr Osbert?'

'Yes,' said Purefoy. 'That is precisely what I said.'

'We've already got Dr MacKendly in for that bloke in the Master's Lodge,' Walter called back. 'Are you a partner of Dr MacKendly or something? I didn't know he'd got a partner.'

'No, of course I'm not a partner of Dr MacHenry. I am Dr Purefoy Osbert.'

'And he sent for you from Addenbrooke's Hospital?' Walter asked. His tone of voice was less aggressive now.

'I am not that sort of doctor. I don't have any medical training. I'm the – '

But the Head Porter had heard enough. 'No, I had a funny idea you weren't a proper doctor,' he said. 'But I'll tell you what, you try getting into the College you're fucking well going to need one. Now buzz off.'

For the second time Purefoy Osbert's resolution faltered but he stood his ground. Inside the great gate he could hear a muttered conversation. He seemed to catch the words 'The buggers'll try anything in the book, Henry. Calls himself a doctor!'

Purefoy jerked the bell chain again. He was getting angry now. 'Listen,' he shouted. 'I don't know who you are – '

'That makes two of us, mate,' said Walter. 'I don't know who you are and what's more I'm not interested.'

'But,' continued Purefoy. 'I am the new Fellow.'

'He's a Fellow now,' said Walter. 'Or a fella.'

'I am the Sir Godber Evans Memorial Fellow and my name is Dr Purefoy Osbert. Do you understand?'

There was a long silence on the far side of the gate. It was beginning to dawn on Walter that he might have made a terrible mistake. All the same he wasn't taking any chances. 'What sort of glasses are you wearing?' he asked.

'I am not wearing any glasses. I can see perfectly well.'

The Head Porter wished he could. There was no peep-hole in the gate. He tried peering through a crack and could only see Purefoy's leather sleeve. 'And you're not wearing white socks?' he asked.

'Of course I'm not wearing white socks. Why on earth should I be wearing white socks? What does it matter what colour socks I'm wearing?'

'And you really are the Sir Godber Evans . . . whatever it was you said, Fellow?'

'Would I say I was if I wasn't?' Purefoy demanded. If this was the level of intelligence at Porterhouse, he was definitely going back to Kloone. Getting knowledge and understanding into people's heads there was infinitely easier than this.

Inside the gate Henry was telling Walter that the bloke outside didn't sound like a Yank. Walter had to agree, and presently the wicket gate opened slowly and a strange and rather alarmed face peered at Purefoy. In the Porter's Lodge Henry was trying to phone the Senior Tutor, who wasn't going to answer.

'I suppose you'd better come in, sir,' Walter said, switching from the threatening to the positively servile. 'And I'll carry your bags, sir.' Purefoy Osbert stepped through the wicket gate carrying them himself. If this cretin – and he wasn't going to waste time on euphemisms now – got hold of the suitcase containing his notes and manuscripts he'd probably never see them again.

'I'm ever so sorry, sir, but we've had a bit of trouble here today and my orders were not to let anyone who wasn't a member of College in or out. Praelector was very strict about it. I do apologize, sir. If you'll just step this way, sir . . .'

Purefoy followed him into the Porter's Lodge. It was unlike that of any other Cambridge college he had visited. Here there were no signs of the late twentieth century and a great many of the early nineteenth and even eighteenth. The pigeonholes looked as though generations of birds had actually nested there instead of letters and messages. But everything was clean and highly polished. Even the brass hooks on which keys hung were brightly polished and the sheen on Walter's bowler hat suggested that he treated it with reverence. Purefoy put his suitcases down and felt slightly better. The smell of beeswax was having a calming effect on his nerves.

All the same his reception had been so extraordinary and alarming that he kept a watchful eye on the Head Porter and on Henry, the junior one who wasn't getting through to the Senior Tutor on the ancient telephone in the far office. 'It's no use,' he said. 'He isn't in.'

'He is. Just not answering,' said Walter. 'And no wonder, state he was in last night when he come in from Corpus. Looked like a corpus himself, he did. What he must have been like this morning doesn't bear thinking about. Oh, he did look horrible.'

Purefoy listened to this exchange and found it disturbing. If the Head Porter, who was hardly a pleasant man to look at – he had a twisted and unnaturally gruesome way of eyeing people out of the corner of a strangely coloured left eye – could describe someone as looking horrible, the man must be utterly hideous. Henry's next remark was hardly reassuring either.

'Matron says he threw up all over the bedroom floor,' he said. 'Bollock naked he was too. Said she thought he was dead first of all. Had a Porterhouse Blue was what she thought.'

'If he goes on like that at his age, he will have one and no mistake,' Walter said, and emerged from the little office with an obsequious grimace that Purefoy hoped was a smile. 'I'm very sorry about this, sir. I wasn't told you were coming today and I had strict orders about them others. But I've found you in the book and you're all right. The Bursar's allotted you rooms overlooking the Fellows' Garden so here's the keys. Henry will carry your bags, sir, and show you the way.'

Purefoy bent to pick up his suitcases but Walter stopped him. 'Sorry, sir,' he said with another grovelling grimace that managed in some mysterious way to combine extreme servility with something distinctly threatening, 'but gentlemen Fellows don't carry their own bags in Porterhouse. Don't set a proper example. That's what Mr Skullion what's the Master now told me. Tradition, he said it was, going ever so far back.'

For a moment Purefoy felt like telling the man he didn't give a damn about Porterhouse tradition and always carried his own bags, but he had travelled a long way and he was exhausted. 'What do I do with my car?' he asked. 'It's on a parking meter down the road.'

'You give me the keys, sir, and I'll have it driven round to the Old Coach House which is where the Fellows' cars are kept. You wouldn't happen to know what make it is, would you, sir?'

To Purefoy Osbert it seemed obvious the Head Porter was taking the piss out of him but Walter's next remark changed his mind. 'I only ask, sir, because a lot of the Fellows don't know. The Dean's been driving an old Rover since I don't know when and he still calls it a Lanchester and they don't make them any more. Leastways I don't think they do. And the Chaplain's got an Armstrong Siddeley, though he don't drive any longer and I don't think he even knows it's there.'

Purefoy gave him the keys and told him it was a Renault and was green and had an A registration. 'I think it's A555 OGF,' he said.

'Very good, sir, and I'll put the keys in your pigeonhole. That way you'll know where to find them.'

'But I don't know which my pigeonhole is,' said Purefoy.

'Ah, but I do, sir. All you'll have to do is ask me, sir.' And with another terrible grimace he disappeared into the back where he could be heard telling someone that that new Fellow, Dr Oswald, had a foreign car and a Frenchie one at that which wouldn't go down well with the Senior Tutor because he didn't like ... Having a shrewd idea what was coming, Purefoy followed Henry and his two suitcases round Old Court and behind a very old block of blackened clunch and up a path to another building, this time of blackened brick. On the way they passed a number of students, all of whom looked rather too respectably dressed for Purefoy's liking. He was used to people in boots and with torn and patched jeans and with hair that was either very, very long and unwashed, or hardly existed at all. He was suspicious of clean young people with neat haircuts and a great many of the young men he saw seemed to be very large and muscular and to laugh too loudly. And the one young woman he met smiled agreeably, which he found most peculiar. At Kloone women didn't smile. On the whole they scowled and practised assertiveness on him.

At the bottom of a staircase marked O Henry stopped and pointed at a blank space at the top of a black nameboard. 'That's you, sir. Very nice rooms too. Next to the Senior Tutor's. Very fond of the young gentlemen is the Senior Tutor, sir.'

He climbed the staircase and Purefoy followed with a sinking feeling. The porter's statement had put him in mind of the ghastly evening he had spent with Goodenough and if he was going to have to endure the attentions of another bugger – for the second time in his life he dispensed with political correctness – he was going to insist on having rooms elsewhere. But as in the case of Goodenough he was proved entirely wrong. There was nothing in the least gay about the man who emerged from the doorway opposite Purefoy's rooms and demanded to know if they had to make that confounded din.

'Only dropped the keys, sir,' said Henry, 'and this gentleman's bag, sir.'

'Keys? Bags?' muttered the Senior Tutor. 'Sounded more like a troop of elephants with tambourines to me.'

He went back into his rooms and shut the door very gently. In the darkness Henry searched for the keyhole and chuckled. 'Loves his little joke, the Senior Tutor does. And of course his port. Regular port drinker he is, sir. You can always tell from the complexion. Now the Dean likes a tawny port and that is why he looks the way he does but the Senior Tutor is more a crusted man, likes his dregs I daresay, and of course that's what makes him look the way he is.'

But at least the rooms Purefoy had been allocated were very comfortable ones with a large study and sitting-room and a smaller bedroom with a window that looked out at a large Jacobean house across some lawns and past what appeared to be a large square block of yew.

'That's the Master's Lodge where the Master lives and that down there on the lawn is the Master's Maze. People have gone in there and never come out, they say. But that's just a little joke I'm sure, sir, though I wouldn't go in it myself. Best to be on the safe side, isn't it? And I don't suppose I'm allowed to. Can't walk on the grass, servants can't. Only Fellows can.'

Purefoy Osbert went back into the study and looked out of the window there. Again he was looking onto gardens but this time there were formal rosebeds as well as lawns and a rockery with a pond and something that looked like enormous rhubarb growing by it.

'That's the Dean's own garden, that is. Tends it himself when he hasn't got the arthritis or rheumatism or whatever it is he gets from the damp coming up from the river and the wind blowing from the east. Comes across the North Sea all the way from Russia that wind does and there's not an hill between the Gogs and some mountains they've got with a funny name like the public toilets they've got by the bus station. Ur . . .'

'The Urals,' said Purefoy, and wondered if all porters were so talkative in Porterhouse.

Finally, after showing him how to light the gas fire and work the little stove in the gyp room and where to find the bathroom, Henry left and Purefoy sat down and wondered if he had done the right thing in coming to Porterhouse. It was all quite unbelievably anachronistic and cut off from the world in which he had lived for thirty years. Porterhouse wasn't simply a Cambridge college: it was some sort of museum.

12

The same thought might have crossed Kudzuvine's mind when he came to the next morning, if Kudzuvine had had anything of a mind. In any case, because of his concussion and Dr MacKendly's medication, what little mind he had was working with the greatest difficulty.

'I think we'll give him something mildly soporific and hypnotic, Matron,' the doctor had said when he first examined the unconscious American. 'No need for an X-ray or anything like that. Waste of money. Chap's obviously got a skull like a steel ball and if he hasn't . . .' He left Kudzuvine's future well-being in the balance.

But the so-called soporific and hypnotic drug he injected twice into him exceeded the doctor's expectations. The effect was not in the least mild. When Kudzuvine came to he was virtually catatonic. He could see and hear and feel but that was about all. What he couldn't do was move. And what he saw made him extremely anxious to move. It did more. It filled him with the utmost dread. Close beside the bed, a bed Kudzuvine had never been in before and in a room he didn't begin to recognize, there sat the most malevolent creature he had ever seen since Quasimodo in a reshowing of *The Hunchback of Notre Dame*. In Kudzuvine's

condition this creature was infinitely worse to look at
and it was far, far worse to be looked at by it, whatever
it was. Kudzuvine had no idea. Worst of all, he was
incapable of shutting his eyes and cutting out the sight
of this thing that sat looking at him so malignantly. Not
only couldn't he shut his eyes but he seemed to be
paralysed. And naked. In a huge bed and bedroom he
had never been in before. In a desperate attempt to find
out if he was able to speak or had been struck dumb
into the bargain, Kudzuvine struggled to find words. So,
quite evidently, did the ghastly creature in the chair and
now that he came to look at it more closely, not that he
wanted to in the least, he could see that it was Quasimodo, updated to a clinically chromed chair that had
been provided by the Mayo Clinic or some other hospital for the Mobilely Challenged. Not that the expression
was at all adequate even if he had been able to bring it
into play. What was sitting a yard away from him didn't
just have a Mobility Challenge Problem. It had the
fucking works. It was, as Kudzuvine would have put it
had he been able to, man, but Totally Challenged,
Mentally, Physically, Vocally and Morally, extremely
Morally Challenged. Or, to put it in the sort of language
Kudzuvine personally preferred but hadn't got the courage to use, this thing was fucking evil, man, like the
fucking Devil in a bowler hat. And it was only two yards
away from him and making noises. In the ordinary way
Kudzuvine would have been relieved to know that he
could hear and hadn't gone deaf to add to all the other

system failures that had evidently occurred since he didn't know quite when. But not now. Now all he wanted to do was to cut out the sounds emanating with such evident effort and inarticulacy from the thing in the chair.

'You shouldn't have done that,' Skullion said. He had to repeat the sentence several times to make sure Kudzuvine got the message but Kudzuvine was way ahead of him. He knew that whatever he had done he shouldn't have done it. That was fucking obvious. Like he'd taken the wrong sort of dope, man, like crack cocktailed with LSD and Toad and fucking nerve gas. It had to be something catastrophic like that, it just had to be. But why the fucking bedroom with fat, very fat, white babies flying around the fucking ceiling and the Quasimodo update sitting there like he was waiting for fucking tenderloin to fry just right for eating?

'You damaged the Chapel,' said Skullion after another struggle. 'You damaged the Chapel.'

Some part of Kudzuvine's neural network stirred and died away. He knew the word 'Chapel', and he sure as hell knew the word 'Damage', though he usually used it with 'Limitation' and 'Exercise' and neither of the latter had the slightest relevance to his present situation. Kudzuvine stuck to 'Chapel' and was still hanging onto it when the Matron came into the room and said, 'Now, Master, you mustn't wear the gentleman out. Let him rest in peace.' Which would have been fine except that for a large woman in a nurse's uniform to call the Thing in the chair 'Master' gave rise to such appalling notions in Kudzuvine about the nature of the Thing's colossal power and influence that he knew with absolute certainty that it had to be the Devil. 'Rest in peace' didn't do much for him either. He put it together with Chapel and came up with Chapel of Rest, which explained his condition, the huge bed and the room and those fucking angel babies flying around the ceiling.

It also explained why he was stark naked. He was in a morticians' funeral home waiting to be buried or cremated and maybe embalmed first. That would explain why the Thing in the wheelchair had been looking at him like that. It had been measuring him up for the coffin or calculating how best to cosmeticize him for embalming. Above all it explained that black bowler hat and the fact that the Thing had been wearing a vest with a gold chain across it. If anything was needed to send Kudzuvine into a frenzy of terror, it was the notion that he was going to be buried alive. Or cremated. Or embalmed. Kudzuvine didn't know much about embalming people but he was certain it involved opening them up and taking all the organs out and then putting something else back inside. And all this was going to take place with him fully conscious – well, for part of the time, the first part, which was undoubtedly the nastiest. It wasn't. It mustn't happen. He had to show them he was still alive. Somehow.

Kudzuvine made gurgling noises and said 'Fuck' several times quite loudly and then made up for it by getting 'God' out quite a few more and 'Help' a great many. Then he lay back and went to sleep again, only to be woken some time later to find a tall thin and positively cadaverous old man and a shorter stumpier middle-aged man with ginger hair standing on one side of the bed. The big woman in the nurse's uniform stood on the other. But at least the Thing wasn't with them.

'And how has he been, Matron?' the man with the red hair asked. 'Any trouble?'

'None whatsoever, doctor,' said the woman. 'Slept like the dead.'

'Help, help,' Kudzuvine managed to gurgle.

'He seems to be trying to say something,' commented the tall thin man. But the doctor had sat down on the edge of the bed and was shining a torch into Kudzuvine's eye. He obviously didn't like what he was seeing. 'That new stuff I tried on him last night has done rather more than I'd expected,' he said. 'It's a synergistic combination of several major anti-psychotic tranquillizers with some muscle-relaxant drug in case there are any violent tendencies. Very new on the market and it certainly lives up to the maker's claim. You'd think to look at him . . .'

'Help. God. Help,' Kudzuvine tried to scream but failed pathetically.

'I'm sure he's trying to say something,' said the cadaverous old man.

'Yes, you'd think so, wouldn't you?' said the doctor. 'But it's merely some sort of reflex action. He's not with us at all. Ah well, I don't think I need give him another shot. He'll keep just as he is. Has he passed water or anything like that?'

The Matron lifted the bedclothes and shook her head.

'Well, just to be on the safe side,' he said and took out a tube. 'I always carry a spare one for the Master.'

The Praelector turned away and looked out of the window to avoid having to watch the distasteful process of feeding a catheter into Kudzuvine's penis. And Kudzuvine wasn't enjoying it at all.

The Praelector's next observation horrified him too. 'Ah, here comes the Chaplain,' he said. 'He'll be coming to have a chat with the Master. He usually comes over once a day. A curious relationship, I've always thought.'

But Dr MacKendly and the Matron were discussing the possibility of seepage from the back passage. 'It happens fairly frequently,' he said. 'I should put a piece of plastic under him. One of those black garbage bags will do nicely, and it will be very appropriate too.'

They looked at Kudzuvine one last time and left the room while he was still muttering, 'Help. God. Help.' It didn't do him any good at all.

*

His colleagues at Transworld Television weren't helping him either.

'Yeah, so Kudzuvine's in some kind of shit. Ever known when he wasn't?' was Skundler's comment when told about the incident at Porterhouse. 'So he's got to paddle his own. Not my business. You work in the media business you got to take risks. Some come back, some don't. That's the way it is.' And no one else argued with the Assessmentation Officer's judgement. As someone else said, as it happened with more prescience than she dreamed, 'So K.K.'s gone. So he's gone. What's new?'

*

In Bangkok Edgar Hartang sat with a six-year-old boy on his lap. That was new for the boy, but not for E.H. He tweaked the child's nipple and giggled and took off his blue glasses and his toupee. Good old E.H. He was having one hell of a time.

So was the boy. It was just a different sort of hell.

13

The Bursar's sort of hell was of an entirely different variety. He hadn't enjoyed having to explain his role in the Transworld invasion of Porterhouse, but at least he had been spared the presence of the Dean and the Senior Tutor. He hadn't seen the Senior Tutor and the Dean, thankfully, was away but he knew what paroxysms of rage Kudzuvine and his Transworld team would have induced in both men and what their attitude to him would have been. He'd have been out of his job and out of Porterhouse and he'd have been lucky not to have been horsewhipped into the bargain. The Senior Tutor was fond of saying he'd horsewhip some swine or other and, while these threats had been empty ones in the past, the Bursar was in absolutely no doubt that in the present case, and with the Dean egging him on, the Senior Tutor would have put the words into action. Instead the Praelector had treated him with tea and quite astonishing sympathy and had seemed to find his story of how he had met Kudzuvine and later had lunch with Edgar Hartang more and more interesting as it went along.

All the same, the Bursar had been conscious that the College Secretary was taking it all down in shorthand

and that the research graduate Gilkes was making copious notes. By the time the questioning was over the Bursar felt very much better. 'You've been very, very kind to me,' he told the Praelector emotionally. 'I don't know how to thank you.'

'There's no need to blub, my dear fellow. And it is our business to thank you. You have no idea what you have done for the College. And you need not worry about Mr Kudzuvine. He's in safe hands.'

'Did you hand him over to the police?' the Bursar asked.

'Of course not. He's in safer hands than that. Now you go home and have a good night's rest. We are going to need you at your intellectual best in the days to come.'

At the time the Bursar hadn't realized the full implications of that remark. He had gone home, hurrying out through the back gate for fear of running into the Senior Tutor on the way to the Main Gate, and had drunk several very stiff whiskies before taking twice the recommended dose of his wife's sleeping pills and going to bed. On Monday he had stayed at home and it was only on Tuesday, on his return to his office in Porterhouse, that he learnt what the Praelector had meant about Kudzuvine being in a pair of very safe hands. 'You mean he's laid up in the Master's Lodge?' he asked Walter in the Porter's Lodge. 'What? With Skullion?'

'I wouldn't put it quite like that, sir. He's more laid out than laid up, if you take my meaning.'

The Bursar didn't. The Master's Lodge at Porterhouse was beginning to sound like a charnel-house rather than any sort of Lodge. First the late Sir Godber and now Kudzuvine. 'What did he die of, for God's sake? Did the Senior Tutor hit him . . . ?'

'No, sir, nothing like that. Senior Tutor wasn't in any condition to hit anything. He'd already hit the bottle and wasn't very well himself. No, the American basta . . . gentleman had some sort of accident in the Chaplain's rooms and it was felt best if Dr MacKendly attended to him with the Matron. She's there now and Mr Skullion . . . the Master has been sitting by his bedside just to make sure he doesn't do himself any more mischief. After all, the College doesn't want no bad publicity, does it, sir?'

'No, I'm sure it doesn't,' said the Bursar doubtfully and wondered just how much publicity Transworld Television was going to give the assault – he didn't for a moment believe that Kudzuvine had had an accident – and battery of one of its Vice-Presidents. Presumably as far away as Easter Island they'd be seeing a bandaged Kudzuvine being carried from the College. They were bound to have satellite TV there, and it had just been installed on St Helena. The Bursar went off to his office and found the College Secretary waiting for him.

'Ah, there you are,' she said. 'Feeling better? No? Well, these things take time to get over, don't they? Anyway the Praelector asked me to tell him when you came in. He wants to come down and talk it over.'

'I don't really think I'm up . . .' the Bursar began but it was too late. Mrs Morestead had gone through to her office and had phoned the Praelector.

'They'll be down in a moment,' she said brightly when she came back and sat down with her pad and pencil.

'They? Who's coming with him?'

'I don't really know, though I did see Mr Retter and Mr Wyve crossing the Court just now.'

'Mr Retter *and* Mr Wyve?' said the Bursar, with a resurgence of panic. Things must be simply awful for both the College solicitors to have arrived. It had never happened before. Mrs Morestead's next remark increased his dread. 'And yesterday we had the men from the Ancient Monuments Commission up from London and Mr Furness the architect with them. Stayed all day, and the structural engineers have been shoring up the Chapel roof with great girders. They say the whole thing may have to come down.'

The Bursar covered his face with his hands and waited for the worst. It came in the shape of the Senior Tutor, the Praelector, Dr Buscott and the Chaplain. The Senior Tutor was looking particularly ferocious. He still hadn't got over his hangover and the 'hair of the dog' he'd taken in the shape of a glass of neat rum had given an even sharper edge to his temper. All the same, the Praelector remained in charge. He was far older and senior in Porterhouse rank to the Tutor, and with both Mr Retter and Mr Wyve in attendance it seemed unlikely the horsewhip would come into play. 'I don't think this office is large enough to hold us all,' said the Praelector. 'Perhaps we should adjourn to the Fellows' Private Dining Room.'

They trooped out across the Court, Mrs Morestead following with her pad and pencil, and it was only when they were seated round a mahogany table in the Private Dining Room that the Praelector explained the purpose of the meeting. He did so in a decidedly sepulchral manner.

'We are gathered here today,' he said, 'to take measures to deal with what can only be described as a major catastrophe both for the College itself and for the architectural heritage of the entire country. The Porterhouse Chapel is one of the finest examples of late mediaeval neo-Romanesque religious architecture in Britain. Its style is unique in owing very little to the influence of the Gothic. Constructed at a time when the Gothic style was predominant, it speaks volumes for the conservative nature of the College even in those days that our predecessors chose to celebrate the faith in the most traditional fashion. Porterhouse has always prided itself on being, in the truest sense of the expression, "behind the times" or, to be even more precise, to exist in a timeless world. It is therefore supremely important in an age in which change seems all-conquering, and the future seems to hold nothing but the stultification of the human spirit by the endless watching of television and the proliferation of appalling programmes to satisfy man's baser desires, that we should fight the company that has deliberately and criminally done such terrible damage to our Chapel. It is our bounden duty to extract the maximum in compensation from these people at Transworld Television not only for the physical damage done to the entire fabric of the College but for the mental suffering they have inflicted on members of the College. I for one will never recover from the shock . . .'

While the Praelector's peroration rambled on the Bursar tried to think what other bits of the College buildings had recently become unsafe and whose condition Transworld Television Productions could be forced to make good. There was a length of gutter behind the Cox Block that had recently dropped into the road, fortunately when no one was underneath. Not that any of those awful young men could have reached it, the pitch of the roof was far too steep for that and they'd have needed ropes, but all the same. Then there was the entire section of the Library that required repointing, and all the chimneys were in a dangerous state . . . The Bursar occupied himself by making an inventory of repairs needed.

Opposite him Mr Retter and Mr Wyve sat side by side and said nothing. They had inherited their position as legal advisers to Porterhouse with the firm Waxthorne, Libbott and Chaine, when they had joined it. They had been regretting the connection ever since. Waxthorne, Libbott and Chaine had all been dead a great many years before, but Mr Retter and Mr Wyve, being sound legal men, had insisted on keeping their

names. It provided them with an adequate cover for
their own legal inadequacies by allowing them to say
that Mr Waxthorne had given it as his opinion that . . .
Since Mr Waxthorne had been lying in the cemetery on
the Newmarket Road for sixty-five years he could be
said to act only in a consultancy role, and it was perfectly
reasonable and indeed proper for Mr Retter and/or Mr
Wyve to explain that he was unable to see any of their
clients personally. Exactly the same could be said on
behalf of Messrs Libbott and Chaine, the former having
chosen to be cremated rather than share the same earth
even approximately close to the partner he had loathed
for years, and the latter having bequeathed his body to
the University Medical Faculty for research purposes
and dissection, less out of a desire to advance medical
knowledge than to make absolutely sure he was well and
truly dead before he went to the crematorium on the
Huntingdon Road. Up to a point his wishes had been
fulfilled, though his skull was still used as a wine bumper
by a rather effete Drinking Club in King's called the
Chaine Males. And up to a point Mr Retter and Mr
Wyve had prospered. They had always specialized in
work for colleges and had never been known to under-
take any case that required them to appear in court,
although Mr Retter had had to appear once before the
magistrates for driving under the influence and had lost
his licence for a year. Faced with anything involving
litigation they invariably briefed other solicitors in
London who in turned briefed counsel.

In short, the fees of Waxthorne, Libbott and Chaine were extortionate. This was hardly surprising. They were the solicitors for Porterhouse and were forced to work for the College for nothing. There were days when they cursed the Praelector. He had known Mr Waxthorne as a young man and had attended his funeral and had for many years kept in touch with his widow and knew perfectly well that Libbott had been cremated and Chaine had gone to that part of the Medical School from which only bits and pieces return. Now, however, they felt they could be taking on a case which might just be so rewarding for Porterhouse that they would be paid. 'After all we've nothing to lose,' Mr Wyve had said. 'If they win against Transworld, an unlikely outcome I agree, they'll be in a position to make good some of our losses on their behalf.'

'But if they lose, as surely they must against such a vast company, the costs will be enormous.'

'Theirs, not ours,' said Mr Wyve, and the matter was settled.

All the same they said nothing at the meeting, and left it to the Praelector and the Senior Tutor to explain to the Bursar what they wanted him to do. They also felt it wiser to leave the meeting before the facts were placed before him. As Mr Retter put it to Mr Wyve, 'We cannot be party to any dubious actions they may take. It would invalidate our role in the case and do our reputation no good at all. I did not like the look in the Senior Tutor's eye. However, having read the Bursar's statement, I'm beginning to think they do stand a chance. Transworld Television Productions did make the approach to the Bursar, and he has lunched with this Hartang man. I cannot say I like the sound of any of them.'

Behind them in the Private Dining Room the Bursar was appalled. 'Go and sit with Kudzuvine?' he gasped. 'Go and sit with him? I don't want to go anywhere near him. I won't do it. I won't.'

The Senior Tutor stood up slowly. The neat rum was really eating into him now. 'Mrs Morestead, if you wouldn't mind leaving us,' he said with a terrible menace. 'We do not need a transcript of what is going to be a private discussion.'

For a moment the College Secretary hesitated. She was slightly fond of the Bursar, largely because he never shouted at her whereas the Senior Tutor almost always did. But she gave in and left the room. Dr Buscott didn't like either the Bursar or the Senior Tutor, but he was interested to see what was going to happen. He sat back in his chair and waited.

The Bursar didn't. He made a dash for the door but the Praelector, who had been sitting beside it, had already locked it and pocketed the key.

'Just let me get my hands on that bastard . . .' the Senior Tutor began but the Praelector stopped him.

'If you will be so good as to sit down,' he said. 'We need the Bursar in one piece if he is to sit with the man Kudzuvine and get him to answer the questions necessary for our case against his company. If you start knocking the Bursar about we'll merely have three sick men in the Master's Lodge. Besides, his own evidence is vital.'

'Oh, all right,' the Senior Tutor grumbled but he returned to his chair. The Bursar didn't. He stood ready to dash round the table if the Senior Tutor got up again.

The situation was calmed once more by the Chaplain. 'I must say that our guest, Mr Kudzuvine, did not strike me as being in much of a condition to answer questions when I visited him the other day. He made some most peculiar noises, especially when I asked him if he wanted to make his Confession before taking Communion.'

'The man is a fanatical teetotaller,' said the Praelector, and was surprised by the Senior Tutor's suddenly expressed wish that he was too. 'I don't suppose Holy Communion is up his street.'

'Something is up somewhere,' said the Chaplain. 'He's got the same filthy pipe and bag that Skullion wears. Do you suppose everybody who stays at the Master's Lodge is obliged to wear one?'

'Let us get back to the original point of discussion,' said Dr Buscott, 'in other words that the Bursar is going to use his influence with this Kudzuvine person –'

'I'm not,' said the Bursar. 'I'm damned if I am. In any case I haven't got any influence with him. You don't know what he's like.'

'I've got a bloody shrewd idea,' snarled the Senior Tutor. 'Wears blue sunglasses and a polo-neck sweater – '

'Quite,' interrupted the Praelector, 'but I don't think the Bursar is talking about his appearance. I think he means his psychological make-up, his mentality in so far as he has one, though increasingly they do say that the higher anthropoids are capable of rational thought ... Not that I'd put Kudzuvine among the higher anthropoids. Much lower than, let us say, a brain-damaged baboon. Now where was I? Yes, the Bursar's objections to sitting and chatting with the creature are, I presume, based upon the fear that Mr Kudzuvine may feel that his present condition has resulted from his association with the Bursar. I can give you every assurance that he will regard you as a true friend.'

'Why should he? And what is his present condition?' demanded the Bursar, who had been horrified that whatever that condition was it required Kudzuvine to wear a catheter and bag.

'Let us take your second question first. It has some bearing on the question of his fondness for you. Unfortunately what occurred on Sunday in the Chaplain's rooms rules out any feelings of affection Mr Kudzuvine might have felt for the Chaplain and me. In our efforts to get the man to tell us who he was we perhaps went about it the wrong way.'

'Ah, of course that explains everything,' said the Chaplain. 'When I enquired about the bagpipe he acted most peculiarly. Of course, of course! I'd forgotten about the cooking brandy and I can see that my remarks about the benefits of colonic irrigation – '

'What the hell is he talking about?' asked the Senior Tutor, reacting to the mention of cooking brandy.

'Nothing, nothing. The point I am trying to make is that while, thanks to Dr MacKendly, Kudzuvine does not know what hit him, by the time he comes to his senses he may recognize who hit him. That rather rules the Chaplain and me out.'

'Are you seriously saying that you and the Chaplain actually assaulted this man?' Dr Buscott asked. He was enjoying himself enormously.

'No, I am not saying that,' said the Praelector coldly. 'I am using the word "hit" in a metaphorical sense of his not understanding what was going on. Have I made my meaning absolutely clear, Dr Buscott?'

Dr Buscott nodded. He was astonished at the transformation that had come over the Praelector now that there was a crisis in Porterhouse and the Dean wasn't there to exert his authority. The Praelector was a very old man indeed who had previously always stayed in the background. Dr Buscott found it all exceedingly strange. He would never understand what made the Senior Fellows tick.

The Bursar, on the other hand, was still trying to understand why the hell Kudzuvine should feel any fondness for him. 'When you say "thanks to Dr Mac-Kendly" . . . ?' he said, and left the question unspoken.

'I mean that the College doctor has administered some mild medication, thus reducing Mr Kudzuvine's mania and criminally intrusive behaviour to a gentle docility and calmness that is, I am told, quite remarkable. Skullion . . . the Master sits beside his bed a lot of the time and they seem to have hit it off quite well together. As you know the Master is not an easy fellow to get on with.'

'Nor is Kudzuvine,' said the Bursar, who still didn't like the Praelector's repeated use of the word 'hit'. 'He's bloody nasty.'

'He was very nasty, I agree, but now he's not,' said the Praelector. 'So we will come with you as far as the bedroom door and you will . . .'

There was some brief resistance on the Bursar's part but it was overcome by the Praelector's promise that someone would be within striking distance all the time. And by the Senior Tutor's description of what would happen to him if he didn't go.

'When you say "within striking distance",' said Dr Buscott, 'are we to take it that you also mean that in a metaphorical way?'

'No,' snapped the Praelector, 'I mean it literally. You will be manning the tape recorder on the landing and the porters are there too. So if we are ready, gentlemen . . .'

But the Bursar still prevaricated. 'What sort of questions am I to ask?' he said and helped himself to a very large whisky from the decanter on the sideboard.

'You've read the list Mr Retter supplied, haven't you?' said the Praelector. The Bursar nodded. 'So there is no need to waste time.'

'Can't I just have another quick one?'

'No,' said the Senior Tutor, 'you can't.'

14

The little group went out into the morning sunlight and made its way across the Fellows' Garden and past the Master's Maze to the Lodge and presently the Bursar was ushered into the bedroom where Kudzuvine was lying propped up against the pillows. The Bursar approached him warily. Kudzuvine didn't look at all vicious. On the other hand he didn't look at all well. Something about his eyes.

'Hullo, Karl,' the Bursar said huskily, breathing whisky fumes. 'You don't mind me calling you Karl, do you K.K?'

'No, Prof, I don't mind. I'm just delighted you call me anything. Man, Professor Bursar, am I glad to see you. Have I had one hell of a trip. I mean I didn't know they came that bad. This was a trip like nothing I've ever known and I've had some way-out ones in my time.'

'Well, I suppose all this gadding about and going to the Galapagos Islands must have made you an experienced traveller.'

'Traveller? Galap . . . What you say? Gal . . .'

'Where the turtles are.'

'What turtles?' The panic-stricken look was coming back into Kudzuvine's eyes.

The Bursar decided to steer the conversation back to more immediate problems. 'And how do you feel now? Are you feeling any better? In yourself I mean.'

Outside the bedroom door the Senior Tutor recoiled from the expression. He had had enough discussions about the Self to last him a lifetime. The Praelector and Dr Buscott continued to listen intently. Kudzuvine's literal selfishness was becoming more and more obvious. 'In myself? How do I feel in myself? You mean "in" like in, man?' he muttered. 'Hell shoot, I don't know how I feel any fucking place. I don't even know where the fuck I am and I've got this fucking ogre comes and looks at me like I'm in an iron lung and can't move a damn bit of me and my eyes won't shut and you ask me how I feel in myself? Shit, there ain't no answer to that one. Ain't no words I can find any place.'

'But you're feeling better now surely?' said the Bursar. 'You are sitting up and talking and opening and shutting your eyes quite normally.'

'Now. Sure I am. I can move again and of course I keep opening and shutting my eyes just to make sure I can because, Prof, some of the things I've seen around here I don't ever want to see again. No siree. Not this side of hell I don't. And I got to tell you I don't smoke even joints after this trip. I don't know what it was I took but I OD'd on something fucking awful. I mean the Chemical Warfare guys ought to take some of my blood and look into it see what the fuck it was. They could scrap the Marine Corps with that stuff in the arsenal. And the battle tanks and win wars no problem. Jesus it was something else I can tell you. Still is half the time. I keep having this feeling I'm dead or something.'

'How extraordinary,' said the Bursar. 'It must be most unpleasant.'

Kudzuvine stared at him in horror. 'Unpleasant?' he squeaked. 'Unpleasant it isn't. It's ... it's ... hell, I don't even know what it is. Some old guy I think I've seen someplace comes in and starts fucking praying like I'm really dead and I can't move or say anything and I'm trying to but he won't listen and there's another guy and a nurse and Quasimodo in a wheelchair looking like he's measuring me up for something and when they're gone I have these terrible dreams about cooking brandy. You know what cooking brandy is, Prof?'

The Bursar said he had a shrewd idea but Kudzuvine disagreed. 'Not this cooking brandy you don't. Not the way I know it. You can't, it's not possible because it's in my fucking head. It's got to be the only place it is. Man, you know any good shrinks round here? Because when I have that dream I know I've got to be schizoid and I need help but bad.'

'I'm sorry to hear that,' said the Bursar to keep on the right side of him. 'I take it it's a very nasty dream then?'

'When?' said Kudzuvine, getting disoriented again.

'When you have it,' said the Bursar.

'Is it ever. Jesus it's the worst, man, the worst. There's this monk, man, and a terrible old guy and I mean old and mean and terrible and I'm being held down on the floor and they've got this fucking rubber douche bag and . . .'

'I think we can miss this dream out,' said the Praelector loudly from the landing. Kudzuvine's mouth dropped open and he started violently. So did the Bursar.

'Did you hear that?' Kudzuvine demanded when he could speak.

But the Bursar had had time to think. 'Hear what?' he enquired.

Kudzuvine shrank down the bed. He had to be insane.

The Bursar changed the subject. 'There's been something I've been wanting to ask you for some time,' he said. 'Mr Hartang told me he allows his staff to wear exactly the same clothes as he does because he wants the staff to be comfortable. I think that's very considerate of him, don't you?'

Kudzuvine came to life again. The mention of Hartang seemed to have galvanized him. It had certainly taken his mind off his own sanity or lack of it. 'He told you that? Hartang, old E.H. told you that?'

'Yes, that's what he told me,' the Bursar agreed. 'What I was wondering is why he wears such an obviously cheap wig.'

'Well let me tell you something, Prof,' said Kudzuvine, evidently warming to a subject close to his heart. 'Comfort, zumfort. That old bastard doesn't give a hound-dog's shit for the comfort of the staff. Most of the time like twenty-four hours in the day he don't know they're even there. Pays them – has to because they work the money for him – but they drop dead in front of him he don't even notice except there's a mess on the floor. Happens one time I was there and he's bawling this guy out because he's lost a consignment some place, an island some place . . .' He tried to think where and for once the Bursar had the good sense not to mention the Galapagos Islands and turtles. 'Cayman or Bahamas somewhere there like the Bermuda Triangle. Whole fucking twenty million gone play hookie. So E.H. is going to have this guy down the Bermuda Triangle too after he's been through the shredder first. And he's telling him his fucking fortune and the guy don't like what he's hearing and he's got a weak heart or something so he gets death first before the independents arrive to fly him out in a body-bag. Lying there cold meat and you know what old E.H. is worrying about?'

'No,' said the Bursar, utterly appalled by what he was hearing. 'What was he worrying about?'

Kudzuvine smiled fondly at thé memory of the occasion. 'Guy's pissed himself on the carpet and E.H. is saying get the whole thing up he isn't going to have the room stink of fucking piss is all he cares. Goes out for his lunch. Comes back and there's a new carpet but he don't like the fucking colour so that's got to be changed too. You think that's all? Changes his mind again. Got to be a marble floor. Guy pisses on it you can wipe it up. Same with blood. Don't show. That's good old E.H. for you. Lovely man. Right?'

It was hardly the word the Bursar would have chosen. He glanced nervously at the door but remembered that the Senior Tutor was out there and in any case Kudzuvine was in an obviously amiable mood and was still fond of him. Not that the Bursar wanted his fondness but he was stuck with it. 'So what happened to the man who had died?' he enquired.

'Nothing. Too late. Cancelled the independents from Chicago and had him cremated real nice. Natural death and all so there's nothing to worry about.'

'I suppose not,' the Bursar agreed. 'But if he doesn't care about the people he employs, why do you all wear the same clothes he does? You want to look like him? Is that it?'

Again a strange smile lit up Kudzuvine's face. 'Prof Bursar, you got it the wrong way round,' he said and there was no doubting his affection for the Bursar now. 'Who the fuck wants to look like old E.H? Man's as ugly as a fucking pig. Just not going oink all the time, is all. And pigs is what it's all about.' He paused to let the Bursar come to grips with this information.

The Bursar failed to. 'Pigs?' he said. 'How do pigs come into it?'

Kudzuvine laughed this time. He really was feeling much better. 'Wrong again, Prof baby. Pigs don't come into anything. It's what goes into pigs he don't like one little bit. Like he's phobic about pigs. Some guys in his situation get phobic about bridges or new expressways. Knew a guy once had this bad thing about crocodiles 'cause they eat just about anything and every little bit. Said to him one time, "Harry, so why fucking worry? You're living in Atlanta, Georgia, not up the fucking Nile, Africa." Didn't do no good. They took the poor bastard shark-fishing one day, like for bait. Got some big monsters too with him. Took them hours to wind those babies in.' He paused again at the memory of this extraordinary feat. 'So with old E.H. it's pigs. He don't want to end up in their swill tub like the wife of some guy he read about some time. He says to me one time we're going some place he won't eat Chinese not if he's starving and I say, "That's real nice of you, Mr Hartang. Is that because they eat hound-dogs and puppies and all?" and you know what he says? Says, "Karl K." – always calls me that when he is in a good mood – "Karl K. you're so fucking dumb and you don't even know it. Try thinking sweet and sour." So I try thinking and I'm out of the tunnel. "Oh, pork, you mean pork." Man, he went a funny colour and was I glad that fucking plane was pressurized or I'd have been deepsixed right then. But I got him calmed down by the time we landed Miami some place. Learned not to mention pigs or pork. And bacon is a no-no too. Even weaner is off the fucking menu. We had some dealings with a Heinie once called Weaner only they spell it different like with an I and an E and old E.H. pulls the rug on the deal because someone tells him a weaner is a small pig. And you got to be careful with fucking. I don't use that sort of language with E.H. in case he don't hear too good.

Tom Sharpe

Yes sir, Prof Bursar, he and anything piggy don't mix good.'

The Bursar felt extremely uneasy now but fear and curiosity kept him glued to his chair. 'Yes, I see that,' he said hesitantly, 'but I still don't understand about the white socks and polo-neck sweaters and the blue sunglasses which you wear.'

'Shoot, that's easy. Like with the metal detectors and the I.D. cards, it's for protection. Someone gets in the fucking building with an Uzi ... No, with an Uzi he could probably do a total but there's no way an independent is coming in the precautions we take, not with an Uzi. Got to be real small and plastic and with maybe one slug and he'd have to hide the thing up his ass and no independent I know would do a thing like that. Blow his ass off with an unreliable plastic .38 no proper trigger? No way. So he gets in the building, who's the target? Everyone looks the same. Goes round asking if you're Edgar Hartang and he's got no ID. Hey, Prof man, tell you something. I wouldn't want to be that guy. Like they'd Calvi him like they did that other guy under Black Monks Bridge only this time they'd meathook him if he was lucky. Right? So that's why old E.H. has the Transworld staff wear the same clothes he does. You don't get where Edgar Hartang does in the multi-media finance business without you cover your ass pretty damn good and E.H. has his covered every which way.'

'But why does he wear a cheap wig like that?' the

Bursar asked in spite of himself. He had never heard such horrible stories before in all his life.

'Why's he wear the wig? And he sure as hell does wear it all the time I've been with him. Same as the shades. No one knows what he really looks like. He takes it off, could be someone else no one knows. Yes, sir, Prof Bursar, got to get up real early like the day before yesterday to catch that old motherfucker because he don't sleep far as I can tell and he's always some place else or like in the bunker we got over here.'

'The bunker being . . .'

'Transworld Television Production Centre. Boy, is that place fireproof. Take a megaton to blow that baby away, know what I mean?'

The Bursar knew something. He should never have had anything to do with Kudzuvine. That fund-raising seminar had been the biggest mistake of his life. Until now he hadn't even known such people existed and, if they did, they shouldn't be allowed to. All the Americans he had met had been polite, educated people. But this was a mad, horrible, sadistic and monstrous world he had been introduced to. And into. He had to get out before his reason failed completely. Very slowly and with the utmost caution he got out of his chair and moved towards the door.

'Hey, Prof Bursar baby, you ain't going? Hey, no, stop, I need you. I got to need you.'

But the Bursar wasn't waiting to find out what Kudzuvine got to be needing him for. He wanted out, and Kudzuvine needed a hole in the head. Instead he got Skullion.

'I think we should allow the Master to sit with him,' said the Matron as the gibbering Bursar tumbled through the door. 'He usually has a definitely calming effect on the patient and I'll phone Dr MacKendly. I think it would be best if he were given something to quieten him down.'

*

'I've always been amazed at the Master's ability to exert his authority over the most unpleasant people,' said the Praelector a few minutes later as he and the Senior Tutor went downstairs in the wake of the Bursar who was being comforted by the Chaplain.

'That wasn't an unpleasant person,' said the Senior Tutor, 'the swine is a bloody gangster.'

'I knew that from the very moment I set eyes on him,' said the Praelector, 'but what a very useful gangster he is proving to be.'

Above them Dr Buscott was carefully removing the long reel of tape on which every word Kudzuvine had said had been recorded and was replacing it with a fresh reel. But before doing so Dr Buscott had taken the additional precaution of ending the recording with his own sworn statement and that of the Chaplain that what had been heard was a true and authentic record of what had been said at the time and date.

15

To Purefoy Osbert the comings and goings at the Master's Lodge were of only visual interest. He had no idea what was going on over there but from the window of his room he watched the Senior Tutor and the Praelector and the Chaplain come and go across the lawn and past the Master's Maze in their various ways. The Senior Tutor strode now that he felt better, the Praelector stalked slowly and meditatively with his head bent like some long-legged water bird, possibly a heron, watching for a fish. The Chaplain trotted, and the Bursar had to be helped. But the strangest figure to emerge from the Lodge was the Master himself who came, usually at dusk, though occasionally, when his presence by Kudzuvine's bedside was not required, in the morning or afternoon to sit by the Back Gate as he had done when he had been Head Porter, watching and waiting for the young gentlemen, as he still called the students, to climb in after hours. Not that 'after hours' could be said to exist any longer. The College gates, when not closed against intruders, were left unlocked all the time. But traditional ways persisted at Porterhouse to the point where the Night Porter kept a list of every undergraduate who came in after midnight and the list went to the Dean who would summon persistent late-nighters and threaten them with fines or even rustication if they continued staying out late. Not that the Dean really objected. As he put it many times to culprits, 'There is a right way of doing things and a wrong way. And the right way after midnight is over the back wall next to the Master's Lodge.' The fact that the back wall was topped with a double bank of revolving spikes to prevent undergraduates climbing in provided the sort of challenge the Dean approved of.

'Besides, it provides the Master with an interest and something to concentrate his mind on,' he had said at a meeting of the College Council when one of the younger dons had proposed that the spikes be removed as constituting a dangerous relic from the past. That proposal had been defeated and the spikes remained along the top of the wall and the great wooden gates. Below them Skullion did too, sitting in his wheelchair or sometimes managing to hobble across to lean where he had leant so many years before against the trunk of an old beech tree with the words 'Dean's report in the morning, sir' ready on his lips. With the full moon Purefoy Osbert could make out that dark shape even at one o'clock in the morning when he turned his lights out, and he found it sinister. He couldn't begin to fathom what went on in the former Head Porter's mind, or the sheer persistence of the man. But then Porterhouse baffled him completely. It wasn't simply that it was unlike any other college in Cambridge. It was that

Porterhouse seemed to refuse to accept that any changes had occurred since . . . well, since before the First World War, or to recognize the astonishing achievements in science and medicine that were being made year after year by people in Pembroke and Christ's, in Queens' and Sidney Sussex, in fact in every college in Cambridge. Except Porterhouse. In Porterhouse the emphasis was always on the Arts and, if the War Memorial was anything to go by, on the Martial Arts. Hundreds of Porterhouse men had gone to their deaths obediently on the Somme and at Loos and again in the Second World War. And everywhere he went in his exploration of the College he encountered large muscular undergraduates who greeted him politely or, in the case of those who hadn't heard he was the new Sir Godber Evans Memorial Fellow, as though he were one of the College servants.

'Hey, you with the face,' one young lout had called out to him, 'come and help me shift the desk in my room. It's too damned heavy for me.' And Purefoy had obliged him, only to point out most coldly and politely that he was in future to be addressed as Dr Osbert and not as The Face, if you don't mind. But his main interest lay in fulfilling his mandate and doing his research into the life and times of Sir Godber Evans. As usual his first visit was to the College Library, an oddly shaped octagonal structure of stone standing apart from the other buildings in its own walled garden behind the Chapel. Inside, a central iron circular staircase went up from floor to floor and the shelves radiated out from it. At the very top a lantern let in the light.

Purefoy Osbert recognized the system immediately. 'Bentham's Panopticon,' he said to the Librarian, who ought to have been sitting at the circular desk under the staircase but who had made himself more comfortable in a small side office.

'Quite right, but, since no one ever bothers to read in here or to take books out, it seems an unnecessary precaution,' the Librarian told him. 'I can't imagine that it crosses anyone's mind to steal a book. The only thing I have to do round here is dust the shelves occasionally and turn the lights on and off in winter.'

'But how do you occupy your time? I see you are writing something,' Purefoy said. An ancient black enamel typewriter with glass panels on the sides stood to one side of the desk, and there were typed pages in a wire basket.

'Oh, I'm mucking about trying to revise Romley's *History of Porterhouse*, which is completely out of date – it was published in 1911 – and full of the most dreadful inaccuracies. For instance, he actually goes so far as to claim that Porterhouse predates Peterhouse which was the first college in Cambridge as everyone knows. Not the late Mr Romley. No, he's convinced the original foundation was Porterhouse and that a school for Franciscan monks was established here in 1095.'

'But the Franciscan Order wasn't founded until the thirteenth century,' said Purefoy. 'That can't be right.

He must have meant some other Order, like the Benedictines who were founded much earlier.'

'In AD 529, to be precise,' said the Librarian, and
immediately won Purefoy's heart. The Librarian was
obviously a man who placed a special emphasis on
certainties.

'But surely this man Romley must have known that?'

'Heaven alone knows what he knew. From what I've
seen of the older Fellows he probably thought Benedictine was only a liqueur.'

'Well, if all his facts are as bad as that I should forget
the revision and write your own history of the College,
warts and all.'

'I have more or less decided to, though I think I won't
mention warts. That's what really brought me here.
Warts and eczema and skin diseases in general. Actually
I graduated from Glasgow as a medical doctor. It was a
great mistake. I wasn't cut out for the contemplation of
skin conditions and I wasn't any good in any case. I saw
this post advertised and I thought it would be a much
pleasanter life and I've always loved reading and I cannot
stand inaccuracies. That was another reason for not
staying in medicine. Diagnosis is largely guesswork and
while the effect is obvious the cause very seldom is. No
one really knows what causes eczema and I don't think
they understand very much about warts either. Some
people can charm the things away. Well, I just wasn't
prepared to be a medical water-diviner. Or I suppose I
should say a blood-diviner.'

They talked on and Purefoy told him about the work he was supposed to be going to do on the life of the late Master, Sir Godber Evans. 'Actually, I was meaning to ask you if you knew where any of his papers are,' he said.

'I suppose they might be in the archives,' the Librarian said with a derisory laugh. 'Though knowing what the Dean and the Senior Tutor thought of him, it wouldn't surprise me if they had burned them.'

Purefoy was shocked beyond belief. 'What?' he exclaimed. 'But you can't do things like that. It's sacrilege to destroy documents. That's the only stuff of history there is, and the facts ... You can't destroy knowledge like that.'

'You can in Porterhouse. You try reading Romley's *History* and you'll see what he thought about facts. I don't suppose he'd have known one if he'd had it handed him on a plate.' He paused and thought for a moment. 'Though come to think of it, the only fact he'd be likely to recognize would be on a plate with lots of sautéed potatoes round it and a glass of excellent claret to go with it. Anyway we can go down into the Crypt and have a look.'

'The Crypt? Under the Chapel?'

'No, under here. It's really just an enormous cellar but they call it the Library Crypt. Don't ask me why. They call everything in Porterhouse by some peculiar name. Have you seen the Dossery?'

Purefoy said he hadn't, and had never heard of such a place.

'It was part of the original lodgings where the scholars used to sleep. Now they've split it up into separate rooms but they still call it the Dossery.'

He unlocked a door in the wall and they went down a steep flight of stone steps. The Librarian tried to switch the light on but nothing happened. 'It's the damp,' he explained. 'The whole place practically drips and the wiring hasn't been replaced since God knows when. That's why I wear rubber-soled shoes and keep those heavy industrial gloves here. It's safer and, if you're going to come down here, I'd advise you to use them. You don't want to get electrocuted.'

He tried the old metal switch several times more and finally the lights came on. They were very dim. 'The Bursar insists on fifteen-watt bulbs to save money but if you need more light I've got some one-fifties in my office, though frankly I don't know what they'd do to the wiring. Probably set it alight and burn the place down.'

But Purefoy was looking in horrified amazement at the enormous pile of old tea-chests with which the cellar was filled. 'These are the archives? These are really the College archives? It's insane, it's criminally insane. Look at the mould.' He pointed to some fungal growth on the side of one of the boxes.

'I know. I've tried to do something about it but every

time it rains we get several inches of water down here because some drain is blocked and they won't spend money unblocking it. I've tried putting bricks under some of the boxes but it doesn't seem to help very much.'

They went along the great pile and Purefoy felt inside some of the boxes and touched damp paper. He shook his head in disbelief. Even if the Librarian was right and the Dean and the Senior Tutor had burnt Sir Godber Evans' papers they'd have been wasting their time. All they had to do was leave them down here. The damp would do the rest. Anyway he had found something to do. He would go through these tea-chests and take their contents up into the Library and dry them out one by one. He wasn't going to see facts turn into mould and he'd have something to say to the Bursar and the Dean when he got a chance. He was going to insist that some part of Lady Mary's benefaction was spent creating a proper and dry and temperature-controlled archive for the Porterhouse Papers.

16

In fact the Dean was already on his way back to Cambridge. His visits to Broadbeam and the other OPs had proved fruitless. No one had been able to think of any really wealthy man who might be honoured to be Master of Porterhouse.

'It's this damned recession, you know,' Broadbeam had told the Dean. 'Property prices have tumbled, there's been the Lloyds fiasco and Black Wednesday. I can't think of anyone with the sort of money you're talking about. I don't suppose you want another ex-Minister as Master? No, I can see you don't.' The Dean had gone a very odd colour. 'I daresay you could find some American academic who'd think it great to be called Master of Porterhouse, but you'd have to be pretty careful who you chose. Some of our transatlantic friends take education very seriously and you don't want to spoil the character of the College by having a Master who is too clever by half.'

It had been the same everywhere he had visited. He had been utterly appalled to find Jeremy Pimpole, who had inherited millions from his South African mother, living in a gamekeeper's cottage on the estate that had been the family home since the middle of the eighteenth century. The house and land had been sold and all Pimpole seemed to be interested in now was his dog, a wall-eyed cross between a bull terrier and a sheepdog, and the local pub, neither of which was to the Dean's taste. And Pimpole's addiction to things canine was not limited to the old dog. In the pub he insisted on ordering two large Dog's Noses which, the Dean was horrified to learn, were made up of two parts gin to three of bitter. When he protested that he couldn't possibly drink a pint of the filthy stuff and couldn't he have a half or better still none at all, Pimpole had got quite nasty and had pointed out that it had taken him years to train the pubkeeper to get the proportions right.

'Bloody difficult to get the fellow to understand that a pint has twenty ounces to it and that means you've got to take seven ounces of gin to thirteen of best bitter to get a proper Dog's Nose. Start asking him to make it a half would confuse the poor fellow. Thick as two short planks, don't you know.'

The Dean didn't know. He was totally confused by Pimpole's calculations. 'But if it's two parts gin, and I sincerely hope you're joking, how on earth can the three parts of beer be thirteen. And seven ounces of gin . . . Dear God.'

'You calling me a bloody liar?' Pimpole demanded angrily.

'No, of course not,' said the Dean hurriedly. He understood now why Pimpole's own nose was the way it was and almost certainly why he had been reduced to living in the gamekeeper's cottage.

'You see those three enamel jugs he's using, the big one and the two small ones?' Pimpole continued, pointing a grimy finger down the bar where the barman was apparently filling the larger of the two with the contents of a gin bottle. 'Well, half of that big one is seven and two small ones make thirteen. Got it?'

The Dean hoped not but he was no longer prepared to argue. The wall-eyed dog was lying by the door eyeing him maliciously. 'I suppose so,' he said, and watched while the barman levered the beer into the small jugs and then, having poured what was presumably half a bottle of gin into each glass, added the two small jugs of beer. The Dean made up his mind that he wasn't going to drink a whole pint of Dog's Nose on anybody's account. It wasn't a dog anyway. It was a Hound of Hell's Nose.

'Well, down the hatch, Dean old boy. Good of you to come and see me.'

'Yes,' said the Dean bitterly. It wasn't good of him to come and see this ghastly drunk. It was damned bad. He took a tentative sip of the filthy stuff and recoiled. Whatever the proportions of gin to beer were meant to be, they didn't even approximate to two to three. It was more like five to two. And anyway he'd never liked gin. It was a woman's drink, he used to say, and of course it had always been called Mother's Ruin. The Dean took another sip and revised his opinion. It ruined more than mothers. It completely ruined a perfectly decent pint of beer. Pint? Of course it wasn't a pint of beer. From what he could make out it was a third of a pint of beer topped up with gin. And it had obviously ruined this bloody man Pimpole. He'd been such a charming young man, a little vague, it was true, but with that delightful air of innocence about him that made up for his superior attitude to those around him. There was nothing in the least charming about Pimpole now and, the Dean thought, not even the publican found his company pleasant. Still, if he drank gin in these quantities every day, and from the look of his nose he must have done for several decades, he had paid for a good many of the pubkeeper's holidays in Benidorm or wherever such people went. Only the superior attitude remained and that had turned to irritable arrogance. He sipped again and found Pimpole watching him rather contemptuously.

'Come on, Dean old chap, drink up like a man,' he said. 'Where is the old Porterhouse spirit. Pass the port and all that sort of thing. Can't keep the other chaps waiting. Not done.'

'What other chaps?' demanded the Dean, having just swallowed another disgusting mouthful, and on an empty stomach.

'Me,' said Pimpole. 'Old Jeremy Pimpole.'

'Oh yes, of course,' said the Dean and was further disturbed to see that Pimpole's glass was empty. Nothing was going to induce him to pour a pint of this stuff down his throat like water.

He changed his tactics and tried subterfuge. 'Look, Jeremy dear boy . . .' he began.

'Don't you "dear boy" me,' snarled Pimpole. 'I'm fifty-two if I'm a day and I don't have soft fair hair and the rosy cheeks you used to like looking at so much.'

'True, very true,' said the Dean meaning to refer to the soft fair hair and not to the latter part of the sentence. 'I mean . . .' he tried to correct himself.

'First you sip a properly concocted Dog's Nose like a fucking poofter sipping tea and now you begin – '

'No, I most certainly don't,' said the Dean furiously. No one had called him a fucking poofter to his face before. 'I was referring to the very obvious fact that you are as bald as a coot, and I'd do something about that nasty scab you've got up there before it gets any worse, and also to the fact that what you called your rosy cheeks look more like the map of the world when we still had an Empire. Mostly red but with nasty bits of green and yellow where the French or Germans were. Now get that into your head.'

For a moment the Dean thought Pimpole was going to hit him. But instead he jerked his head back and roared with laughter. 'One up to you, Dean, you old bastard,' he roared. 'That's more like it.' He turned to what the Dean regarded as some yokels down the bar. 'Hear that, you chaps? The bloody old Dean says my face looks like a map of the fucking world when we still

193

had an Empire and . . .' He turned back to the Dean. 'What did you say the bits of green and yellow were?'

'Oh never mind, never mind,' said the Dean, who had no more intention of discussing Pimpole's complexion with a bar full of farm labourers and tarts than he had of drinking the rest of that beastly Dog's Nose.

'Oh but I do mind,' said Pimpole, whose mood changed from second to second. He stuck his face right up to the Dean's. 'I mind very much. And what about my snout? What's that look like?'

'A snout,' said the Dean. 'I think you've covered it very nicely with that word. Snout, sir, snout.'

Pimpole jerked his head away and roared with laughter again. 'That's the stuff, Dean. That's the stuff to give the troops. That's Porterhouse talking. Straight between the eyes and no bullshitting about. Now, get that Dog's Nose inside you and we'll have another. I'm thirsty.'

The Dean looked back at his glass and found to his horror that he had accidentally drunk almost half of it. He wasn't drinking any more even if the man Pimpole tried to force it down his throat. He'd die fighting rather than die of Dog's Nose.

He struck back. 'You may be thirsty, Pimpole,' he said, 'but I happen to have an ulcer.' He didn't, but it was the only excuse he could think of on the spur of the moment. 'I am not drinking any more of that muck on an empty stomach and there's an end to it.'

It wasn't. Pimpole had the matter well in hand. Or appallingly. 'Barman,' he yelled and, when the man went on talking and pulling beer for some other customers, changed it to 'Fred, you shit!'

'Fred you shit, Dean here's got an ulcer. Go and tell that wife of yours, you know, the one with the squint and the bloody great boobs, to make herself useful for a change and rustle up some of those awful cheese sandwiches of hers. And make it snappy.'

For a moment, a terrifying moment, the Dean thought he was about to be involved in an affray or whatever they called bar-room brawls. The look in the pubkeeper's eyes certainly suggested that he knew which wife Pimpole had been referring to and he didn't entirely agree with his assessment of her physical charms. But the look died away to mere hatred and he went off muttering something about Lord Muck and doing for him one of these days.

A minute or two later he was back. 'Says she hasn't got any of that awful cheese you're so fond of. Will a nice bit of cold mutton do?'

'Yes, yes, of course it will. Very nicely, thank you,' said the Dean politely but Pimpole hadn't finished.

'Where did she get the sheep from?' he demanded.

'I don't know,' said the publican, 'and frankly I don't see that it matters much, does it?'

'Oh don't you? Well I do,' said Pimpole. 'If she gets it from old Sam, I don't think the Dean would want to eat it. I know I wouldn't.'

'Not fresh enough for you, Mr Pimpole?' said the publican sarcastically.

Pimpole leant forward with his empty glass. 'Too fucked for me, Fred, too fucked. Ever since his wife died two years ago, Sam's been into sheep when he can't get someone else's wife, don't you know. Likes his meat cold, does Sam.'

'Christ,' said the Dean, and even the publican recoiled. But still Pimpole hadn't finished his discourse. 'Of course if you're not fussy, I don't suppose it matters very much. And it does come cheaper from Sam. Been well hung, too. You ask your Betty Crosseyes and see if she don't agree.' The publican lurched away while the Dean tried to find words to say that he didn't want mutton sandwiches after all. He'd lost his appetite, and in any case he had no doubt whatsoever that the woman would do something quite disgusting to the sandwiches to get her own back. In the kitchen he could hear some very unpleasant words being used, mostly by the husband.

'Struck the right chord there, Dean old boy,' said Pimpole with a hideous wink. 'And don't you worry about your mutton. Old Sam's been into Betty more times than he has sheep and anyway he likes them live with their fur coats still on. I only said it to rile Fred.'

'By the sound of things you have succeeded only too well,' said the Dean. 'All the same, with my ulcer . . .'

'Of course, your bloody old ulcer. Got to do something about that, haven't we? Now Mummy always used to say peppermint . . .' Pimpole leaned right across the bar and seized a bottle of crème de menthe and a large wineglass.

'For God's sake stop,' shouted the Dean as Pimpole began to pour. 'You can't be serious. After that half pint of gin?'

Pimpole ignored him. He had filled the wine glass and spilt some of the crème de menthe on the bar. 'Now look what you've made me do,' he said accusingly.

'I didn't make you do anything,' the Dean protested. 'And I'm damned if I'm going to drink that bloody stuff. And don't – '

'Come on now, there's a good Deanie boy, take Mummy's lovely medicine like a good little man and tum-tum will feel much better.'

'It bloody well won't. Take the stuff away from me. I detest it. And what is more, I detest this beastly pub of yours. You can stay here if you want to but I am going home.'

'Where the fucking heart is,' said Pimpole and drank the schooner of crème de menthe as the Dean, no longer caring what the wall-eyed dog did to him, marched out of the pub, stepping on the animal's tail as he went. Outside he looked around for his car and was about to get into it when he spotted a police car with two policemen in it watching him. The Dean veered away from his car and tried to walk unconcernedly down the road in the hope of finding a hotel or at least a Bed & Breakfast to spend the night in. There wasn't one.

'Only the pub,' a man he stopped to ask told him. 'The Leg of Lamb. But I wouldn't recommend it. Used to be The Pimpole Arms but they had to change it on account of His Lordship's habits. Sheep, you know. Some of these old families go a bit queer.'

'I've gathered that,' said the Dean and, adding sheep to the addictions of Jeremy Pimpole, walked on disconsolately in the direction of Pimpole Hall and the gamekeeper's cottage. It was not a pleasant journey. The cottage lay a mile and a half from the village and the muddy lane was not lit. Only the moon helped and then only fitfully, most of the time being hidden behind clouds. In the hedges on either side of the lane night creatures went about their business and somewhere an owl hooted. In the ordinary way the Dean wouldn't have minded quite so much, but the mixture of gin and beer and the awful atmosphere in the pub where so much latent violence had been almost palpable, not to mention Pimpole's sudden changes of mood, had frayed the Dean's nerves so that every sound startled him and every dark shadow filled him with alarm. Cursing himself for not having tried to find a taxi, though it was almost certain the village didn't have one, and cursing himself even more for having come to see Pimpole in the first instance, the Dean trudged on, stopping every now and again to listen. He could have sworn he had caught snatches of the Porterhouse Boating Song wafted on the night air from the direction of the village. The third time he stopped there was no doubt about it. The words were clear now. 'Bump, bump, bump, bump the boat before us. Bump, bump, bump, join the jolly chorus. There ain't no boat, there ain't no boat, there ain't no boat before us, So all drink up and off we'll go to Hobson's Conduit whorehouse.'

Again, in the ordinary way the Dean would have found pleasure in the sound of that old song which he had heard so many times, and sung himself in his youth, though he had never known where Hobson's Conduit whorehouse had been and had supposed that in years gone by it might have been at The Little Rose opposite the Fitzwilliam Museum. But now in the darkness – it had begun to rain – and in the knowledge that the man singing it had added a very large wineglass filled with crème de menthe to his first Dog's Nose and had probably had another 'for the road' and that this foul-tempered man was accompanied by a large wall-eyed dog on whose tail the Dean had stepped only half an hour before, the sound of the song held no magic for him. None whatsoever. It merely served to cause the Dean to fear for his immediate future. For a moment, a long moment, he considered sleeping out under the hedge or in a haystack but they didn't make convenient haystacks any more and anyway it was still raining and the Dean had no intention of dying of pneumonia under some hedge. Perhaps if he hid and let the drunken Pimpole go past the brute might fall asleep and allow him to sneak up to his room . . .

The Dean found a gateway and was about to scramble

over – the damned gate was locked – when he discovered it was also topped by barbed wire. With a muttered curse he turned and hurried on until he reached a dark copse to his right and, scrambling down into the ditch and then dragging himself painfully into the hedge itself, tried to blend in with a holly tree which seemed suitably black. The sound of Pimpole's ghastly voice was quite close now and he was singing a revoltingly rustic song, an adaptation of 'Old MacDonald Had a Farm' so filthy that the Dean began to wonder about Pimpole's relationship with that beastly dog, and concluded that no animal could possibly be safe in his presence. Unfortunately the wall-eyed dog had similar feelings about the Dean and, while Pimpole staggering up the lane might well have mistaken the Dean in his black suit for part of the holly tree, the dog's nose knew better. The dog stopped and peered into the darkness and growled. Pimpole halted and peered too.

'Some fucking thing in there,' he mumbled. 'Better go have a look at it.' He came forward and the Dean decided the only thing to do was to come out of the hedge as gracefully as he could.

'It's only me, Jeremy old chap,' he called, and stepped away from the holly and fell headlong into the ditch. It was, he was quick to discover, a ditch in which stinging nettles grew in profusion. In his agony the Dean got on all fours and looked up at the swaying figure of Pimpole silhouetted against the drifting clouds.

'What the fuck are you doing down there?' Pimpole asked. 'And anyway what gives you the right to call me "Jeremy old chap"! I'm Lord Pimpole to you, and don't you forget it. And who the hell are you?'

'I'm the Dean, you know the Dean of Porterhouse, Jeremy dear . . .'

'Lord Pimpole to you,' Pimpole yelled and called the dog, 'Scab, Scab go fetch!'

But the Dean had had enough, enough of the stinging nettles, of the ditch, of Pimpole, of the whole bloody situation, and he had not the slightest intention of being fetched by that filthy dog. He scrambled to his feet and shot out of the ditch and was only stopped from falling flat on his face in the lane by Pimpole who caught him in his arms.

'Hold hard there,' he yelled. 'Steady the Buffs. No need to take off like a scalded bloody cat. Why, my goodness gracious me, if it isn't the Dean. My dear fellow, what on earth were you doing in that ditch? I mean one's heard of hedge priests and all that sort of thing but I've never seen you in that role, old fellow-me-lad. Marrying someone down there, were you? What a rum show.' And breathing crème de menthe, gin and draught beer fumes in the Dean's face he put his arm through his and off they staggered together towards the cottage. Behind them, disappointed by the missed opportunity to get its own back for its stepped-on tail, slouched the dog. But at least Pimpole had regained some of his old warmth and friendliness, probably due to a second or even a third Dog's Nose. He was obviously very drunk indeed and waxing maudlin.

'Don't know what the fuck the country's come to, Dean my old dear,' he said, practically weeping. 'Gone to the dogs. Not that I mind dogs. Love the little buggers. And the big ones too, of course. Irish Wolfhounds. Lovely beasts. Knew a chap in Spain who bred them. Bloody good judge of a dog. Didn't much care for me though. Can't think why. I'm not a bad sort of dog, am I Dean?'

'No, of course not. A very good one,' said the Dean.

'Lost all my bloody money though. Can't think how. It just stopped coming in. It was Mummy's, of course. Copper and stuff like that in Northern Rhodesia and places like that. Just stopped. Couldn't pay the butler. Bugger took to drink. And I thought, that's not a bad idea, so we used to make Dog's Noses and have some laughs together I can tell you but I had to give it all up. Polo ponies. Used to like polo and then some blokes came along. Called themselves bailiffs or receivers or some such. Never seen them before in my life. Offered them a Dog's Nose. Don't really know what happened after that. Live by myself now with Scab of course. Bloody loyal friend, Scab. Old Barney Furbelow's wife comes in and does for me now three times a week and I do for her when I can. Used to be the Under-Gardener Barney did. And his father before him. The good old days, Dean, bloody good old days.'

Somehow they went into the cottage and Pimpole tried to show the Dean up the stairs to his room and failed. The Dean helped him to his feet.

'Sleep on the sofa in the front room,' Pimpole muttered. 'Lavatory is out the back when you want it.'

The Dean went up to his room and, having undressed, got into bed. It was an iron bedstead of a sort the Dean had forgotten existed and the mattress was thin and lumpy. His hands still stung from the nettles, his face did too, and the sheets smelt peculiar, but he was glad to be alone and under a roof. It had been an appalling day.

It wasn't a very pleasant night. A sleepless hour later he needed to pee and the lavatory was out in the back garden. The wall-eyed dog wasn't. It was sleeping with Pimpole in the front room and as the Dean came down the stairs it poked its horrid head out of the door and growled. The Dean stopped and the dog came further out and growled again. The Dean backed miserably up the stairs and shut his bedroom door hoping that a room equipped with such an ancient bed might also contain a chamber pot. It didn't, and in desperation he was forced to piss out of the window, from the sounds of things onto the metal lid of a dustbin. Then he got back into bed and fell asleep for another hour, woke, shuddered and thought about death and the dying of the England he had loved and how squalid it had all become, and longed to be back in Porterhouse where he would be safe and need never again have to experience the horrors attached to drinking a Dog's Nose in a public bar with the ghastly Pimpole.

How many hours, if they were hours, he managed to sleep he didn't know but at 6 a.m. he could stand the bed no longer. He got up and went in search of the bathroom to wash and shave. There wasn't one or if there was it was downstairs and that damned dog . . . He dressed, thanked God that he'd only brought an overnight bag into the house and that the rest of his luggage was in the boot of his old Rover, and with a murderous courage in his heart went downstairs, braved the growls of Scab, and walked out of the cottage.

*

By the time he got back to Cambridge the Dean had experienced more of the horrors of modern England. Eschewing the narrow lanes and country roads he had so enjoyed on his drive north, he had stuck resolutely to motorways, only to be held up by an accident involving a chemical spill outside Lancaster and an enormous tailback; the old Rover had overheated; the RAC man who arrived to get it started again had been amazed it went at all and wanted to know how it had ever got its MOT certificate; the Service Area he had stopped at for coffee and something to eat had been occupied by eight coachloads of Liverpool football supporters with several police vans in attendance; the sausage and chips he had chosen to fill the vacuum in his stomach disagreed with him and made him wonder if the sausages had been well past their sell-by date; and, to complete his humiliation, he had been called a stupid old wanker by a young lout he had bumped into in a public lavatory near Birmingham. To round off the horrors of the day he had missed the turn-off on the M1 and had had to drive for miles before finally managing to back-track to Cambridge.

By the time he arrived at Porterhouse the Dean was not in a bad temper. He was too exhausted and disenchanted to be in any temper at all. He hadn't had a bath for forty-eight hours and was unshaven and was just glad to be back in a world he understood and could to some extent control. And go to bed in something that did not have quite so much in common with cobbles as the mattress in Pimpole's spare bedroom. Handing the keys of the old Rover to Walter, he slunk up to his rooms and lay down. His guts were telling him something again and this time there was no mistaking their meaning. He would have supper sent up to his room and not go down to dinner that night. He wasn't fit company for anyone.

17

Something of the sort could be said for both the Bursar and Kudzuvine, though in Kudzuvine's case he hankered for the Bursar. It was Skullion's company he was so particularly anxious to avoid. The Bursar on the other hand had come out of his first little chat, as the Praelector insisted on calling it, in such a state of shock and terror that, like Kudzuvine, he had to be given something calming by Dr MacKendly before he could be induced to go into the bedroom a second time.

'This will put some lead in your pencil,' the doctor said before administering the injection. 'They tried it out on some conscientious objectors in America before the war with Iraq and it turned them into some of the finest fighting men in the world.'

The Bursar pointed out that he didn't want to be a fine fighting man, while the Praelector wondered aloud how there could have been any conscientious objectors in the US Army because they were all volunteers and professionals. 'And I'd still like to know the names of the two gunship pilots who shot up two well-identified British armoured vehicles,' he said. 'Our dear transatlantic allies refused to let them give evidence at the enquiry or reveal their identity. Friendly fire my foot. No such thing.'

But it was the Bursar who objected most strongly. He wanted absolutely nothing to do with Americans, especially ones like Kudzuvine who came from Bibliopolis, Alabama, and who told him with such evident relish awful stories about people they'd known who'd been used as shark bait. He particularly didn't want to hear one word more about Edgar Hartang. As he put it in language reminiscent of his last interview with Kudzuvine (the drug was having some curious side-effects), 'Hell, man, that man Hartang is a fucking walking death machine. He finds out I been asking questions about him he's going to have me Calvied by some fucking independents or down the tube from twenty thousand feet the Bermuda fucking Triangle like.'

'There is that to be said for Hartang,' said the Senior Tutor but the Praelector wasn't quite so happy.

'Are you sure you've given him the correct dose?' he asked Dr MacKendly. 'I mean we don't want him going in there and alienating the bloody man by talking like him. It will make it extremely difficult to identify who is saying what when we come to transcribe the tape.'

'Probably just a temporary side-effect,' the doctor assured him. 'Must take people different ways of course but I daresay he'll steady down in a bit and be as right as rain. I got it from one of the medical chaps out at the US airbase at Mildenhall at the time of the raid on

Libya. They gave it to some of the pilots who had the habdabs about being shot down and skinned alive by Arab women. Can't say I blame them. Arab women do that, you know. Pilots went off as happy as sandlarks and perfectly normal.'

'Perhaps that explains why they only managed to kill Gaddafi's children and missed him,' mused the Praelector.

'And what exactly did you get it for?' enquired the Senior Tutor.

The doctor smiled. 'We had one or two fellows who'd done the Senate House Leap and had lost their nerve,' he said. 'Thought it might help them get it back. Didn't have to use it in the end. One of the poor blighters fell off Ben Nevis and the other one gave up climbing altogether, which was a bit wet of him, I thought. Still, it takes all sorts to make a world.'

'It's certainly made a world of difference to the Bursar,' said the Praelector. 'I've never seen such a change in a man.'

'It's only temporary,' said Dr MacKendly. 'He'll be himself again in no time at all.'

'For God's sake don't start on about Selves again,' snapped the Senior Tutor. 'I can't stand it.'

Dr MacKendly looked at him curiously. 'Feeling a bit low, are we?' he asked but, before the Senior Tutor could tell him exactly what he felt, the Bursar was raring to go. 'Let the dog see the rabbit,' he said suddenly, using imagery that didn't come naturally to him, and shot through the door into the bedroom.

For once the metaphor was almost precise. Whatever sort of animal the Bursar had become, Kudzuvine had all the characteristics of a petrified rabbit. Almost an entire day and part of the night with the Master sitting by his bedside had destroyed his confidence as effectively as any anti-psychotic Dr MacKendly could have misprescribed. He was delighted to see his friend Professor Bursar again. And said so. 'Am I pleased to see you, Prof Bursar,' he said. 'I sure as shit am. I've had that Quasimodo update in the wheelchair up to here.'

'You can stop talking about the Master like that,' said the Bursar harshly.

'The Master? You call him the Master too, Prof Bursar? Oh my God. Someone please help me.'

'And you can stop calling me Professor Bursar. I am the Bursar. Get that into your thick head.'

Kudzuvine shrank back in the bed. 'The Bursar? And Quasimodo's the Master? Oh sweet Jesus. Where am I?'

The Bursar ignored the question. '*The* Bursar. Emphasis on the *the*. Got it? And you don't call the Master Quasimodo once more. He's Skullion. But not to you, Kudzuvine. To you he's the Master. Emphasis *the*. And you'd better believe me.'

'Yes sir, I sure do. Anything you say, Professor the Bursar.'

'Not Professor. I am not a Professor. I keep telling

you I am the Bursar. This isn't some academic scumhole in Biblifuckingopolis, Alabama, or anywhere else in the US of A where every asshole who can read and write and produce dumb doctoral theses like they're dungflies laying eggs gets called Professor. This isn't even Cambridge, Massachusetts. This is Cambridge, England, and more to the point this is Porterhouse College, Cambridge, England, and the next time you look at a portrait of one of our great past Masters in the Hall you don't call him human foie gras or you'll learn what force feeding really means.'

'Yes sir, Prof . . . I mean Mr the Bursar, sir,' Kudzuvine whimpered.

'That's better, Kudzuvine,' said the Bursar. 'Now I'm going to ask you some simple questions and you're going to answer them truthfully or you're going to learn . . .'

But the mere mention of force feeding had touched the rawest nerve in Kudzuvine's demented mind. He understood now the reason the Chaplain had produced that disgusting douche bag so readily. It wasn't something he had dreamt up in his mad unconscious. It wasn't a symptom of anything. It was an old Porterhouse custom. 'I swear I'll tell you anything you want to know, swear to God I will,' he moaned.

'Right,' said the Bursar who was obviously on a winning streak for the first time in his life and knew it. 'So what does Hartang do, and don't give me any shit about baby octopuses and turtles and the Galapagos Islands.'

'Well, we do make movies about protected species as well – ' Kudzuvine began but the Bursar stopped him.

'Like you were bringing in a consignment of fucking turtles from the Galapagos Islands like twenty million turtles and they all go play hookie in the Bermuda Triangle? I said truthful, Kadzuvine, truthful answers. Want me to spell it out for you?'

'Jesus, no, I don't want no spelling lessons, Prof Bur . . . *the* Bursar, sir. Twenty million in Bogota Best. You know. Street value twenty million, you know.'

'No,' said the Bursar. 'You tell me, Kudzuvine. Tell me about Bogota Best.'

'Cocaine, man, coke, snow, ice, Colombian marching powder. That's what the consignment was. We got cover Transworld Television Productions. Go anywhere filming and making movies about God for little children. That's how we started. Old E.H. says "What do people want? Like God and a buzz." Necessities of fucking life is what he says. Got it from the Good Book too. He's reading it in prison some place and it says there guys don't live on bread alone they gotta have spirit and this sets old E.H. thinking because he's short on the bread side and he'd sure as hell like some Beluga caviar and a plank steak but what's with the spirit? Shit, he don't want no moonshine gut-rot or whatever they drink wherever he comes from like slivovitz and schnapps I don't know. Got to be some other kind of spirit the Good Book's got in mind. So he sits there thinking but most of the time he's thinking about bread and not just the ordinary crusty kind or pumpernickel but the other sort and he gets the answer to all his problems. Old E.H. gets religion and starts making religious movies and it don't matter what fucking religion so long as people buy it. Jesus, Prof . . . *the* Bursar, sir, you know how much money there is giving people certainty they ain't never going to die, just go along to heaven no questions asked? Shit, man, billions and do I mean billions of dollars, D-marks, pounds sterling, rupees, yen, whatever. I mean it. But old E.H. has some buddies down Lima, Peru or maybe Rio someplace and they're helping him pump out some more of this religious kiddie crap and putting up money provided he runs some Bogota Best for them. How's he going to refuse in the jungle some place with guys like Dos Passos with guns all round and maybe the meat-hook and the piranhas waiting for a snack? No way. So he runs the stuff out once twice and he thinks this is great. Got cover with the Jesus Loves You or Mahatma Gandhi's Got a Place for You in His Heart, we made a movie about this God Gandhi one time and the turtles and rain forests and whales and the baby . . . OK I'll level with you, *the* Bursar sir, they weren't baby octopuses. Didn't have no legs at all. Flippers. Baby seals. Yes sir, baby seals.'

'So why did you say octopuses?' demanded the Bursar.

Kudzuvine tried to remember. 'Had to do with legs. Like they're beating these baby seals to death for the movie and there's blood everywhere and I think "Shit, if they had legs they wouldn't just sit there and let this happen" and I thought one time about octopuses like the fucking monsters they got Alaska, Canada some place and they don't need eight fucking legs. Four or five would do just as well hug something to death and those baby seals could do with two or three. Like they wouldn't just sit there. I got muddled is all.'

'Get unmuddled, Kudzuvine,' said the Bursar. 'So how come Hartang is running Bogota Best and wants to give Porterhouse money? You tell me that.'

'Hell shit, Prof . . . the Bursar, sir, he ain't running dope no more. Daren't and don't any place. He's lost Dos Passos twenty million bucks and that's like death. No, sir, the cartels and the Sicilians and guys out of Russia you don't want to mess with, you name them, is all running the stuff. What they can't handle is the greenbacks coming in in truckloads. Now if old E.H. understands anything it's bread. He don't think words, he thinks dollars, D-marks, francs, pesetas, pounds and yen. You've heard him. You understand him? I don't, except when he wants somebody dead. But figures and numbers is something else. Shoot, like he's got a computer instead of a brain and I mean a real fast number-cruncher. So he washes the stuff for the cartels and the Sicilians and the runners. Got satellites and TV stations all over the world and the You're Going to Live Forever business is spreading and, man, are they ever moving God along with contributions pouring in so who's to know the snow cash from the dollars or D-marks or rupees buying you into heaven? No way. And old E.H. can bounce cash off satellites from one bank in Bombay, India to Santiago, Argentina and back to some bank Stateside by way of London, England, like it's been washed and dried and pressed and it came down with Moses from the mountain only it's easier to handle. Hell, he's even bouncing stuff into Moscow, Russia and out again like it's Yo-Yo Festival time down Santa Fe and he's buying half of the old USS of R.'

'I understand all that,' said the Bursar, whose morale-booster was beginning to wear off. 'But why give Porterhouse money?'

Kudzuvine looked at him incredulously. All this talking had improved his morale no end. 'Giving he ain't. He's buying the place. That old turtle needs another shell. Like I told you, he covers his ass. No time he doesn't. He's got too many guys like Dos Passos want him dead. So he buys protection. Gives a bit first like it's bait and before you know it you're all wrapped up webwise and he's got some new place he can hide. Like . . .'

'He's not hiding here,' said the Bursar. 'You'd better believe that, Kudzuvine, you better had.'

'Shoot, Prof . . . the Bursar, sir, I'll tell him. I'll tell him time I see him, "Mr Hartang, no way you going to Porterhouse College, Cambridge, unless you're fucking crazy. You got your figure to think about and, man, those babies eat. They don't even fucking eat, they devour like . . . like Sumo wrestler vultures been on hunger strike or Lent or some fucking thing. Meat? You think a Texas tenderloin's big you ain't seen nothing." Know what they give me for breakfast this morning? Blood. Said it was pudding, blood pudding. You think I'm going to get AIDS eating a fucking sausage looks like it's tar in a condom or a blacktop turd with lumps of lard in it? No way, Bursar baby, no way.'

He stopped. The Bursar was standing over him and looking livid. 'You call me "Bursar baby" one more time, Kudzufuckingvine, I'm going to wash your mouth out with Harpic. You know what Harpic is, Kudzuvine? It's toilet cleanser. You want to keep your fucking tonsils and your uvula and a tongue that doesn't look like it's been barbecued, you don't call me "Bursar baby" ever again. Right?'

'Yes sir, yes sir, *the* Bursar sir. I ain't thinking clear. I just got carried away. I don't want no wash-out. That douche bag done for me I'm telling you. I don't want to see one of those things ever again. No sir, I'm just a good old American boy don't know nothing I swear.'

But the Bursar was still standing. 'American you may be but good old boy you ain't. You're just poor white trash and don't you forget it.'

'No sir, I'm just poor white trash and I ain't never going to forget it I promise you, *the* Bursar sir.'

The Bursar sat down again. 'Now you're going to tell me exactly how Hartang works and what his telephone number is and you're going to start remembering names and places and bank account numbers and . . .'

Outside on the landing the Senior Tutor and the Praelector looked at one another in amazement. Even Dr MacKendly was astonished. Dr Buscott put a fresh reel on the tape recorder.

'I wouldn't have believed it possible,' said the Senior Tutor. 'I'm not even sure I believe it now.'

'Believe what?' asked the Praelector, who had found the whole episode incredible himself.

'Believed the Bursar had it in him. I've always thought him such a weedy little runt and what's all this about the douche bag? I don't understand.'

But the Praelector didn't reply. He was wondering what exactly was in the Bursar and how they were going to use the evidence Kudzuvine was providing. Even Skullion, sitting behind them, listened with interest. He'd particularly admired the way the Bursar had insisted that Kudzuvine call him '*the* Master, emphasis *the*', and not a Quasimodo update, whatever that was.

18

The Dean was feeling a lot better when he came down to breakfast next morning. He had bathed and shaved and had slept very well and he was looking forward to his porridge and bacon and eggs, toast and marmalade and coffee. But as he crossed the Court to the Hall he was conscious that something was badly wrong with the Chapel. It was surrounded with iron scaffolding and even from the middle of the Old Court lawn he could see that the roof was tilted at a most unusual angle. Evidently the roof timbers had been giving trouble. They should have been treated years before but the Bursar had said there wasn't enough money in the College bank account for anything but the most essential repairs. That was typical of the man. Parsimonious to a degree. Well, he would have a word with him, and not a very nice word either. But that would have to wait. The Dean wanted his breakfast. He sat down and was astonished when, even before he had begun his porridge, the Senior Tutor spoke.

'It is absolutely vital that we have a meeting this morning,' he said. 'You and me and the Praelector. My rooms ten o'clock.'

The Dean looked shocked. It was an unspoken rule at

Porterhouse that no one talked at breakfast. A 'Good morning' grunt was permitted but that was all. The rest of the meal was eaten in silence. Something had to be very seriously wrong for the Senior Tutor, a stickler for tradition, to have spoken as he had. The Dean nodded rather irritably and said nothing. His porridge was getting cold. But when the Praelector arrived and whispered the same message with a significant look at the Senior Tutor, the Dean knew there had to be a major crisis. Something truly terrible had happened. For a moment he stuck to tradition but the strain was too much for him. 'Has . . . has the Master passed on?' he whispered.

The Senior Tutor shook his head. 'Worse than that, much worse,' he said. 'Can't talk about it now.'

'I should hope not,' said the Dean and went back to his porridge. But his enjoyment of the first decent breakfast he had had for some weeks had been spoilt. He couldn't even concentrate on his bacon and eggs. He dreaded to think what they had to tell him. Even the damage done to the Chapel could hardly warrant such extreme talk. The College could always get a grant to pay for the repairs. The Chapel was an important architectural monument and English Heritage would be bound to put up the money. It was with the deepest sense of foreboding that the Dean finished his coffee and went outside into the clear sunlight. He was followed almost immediately by the Praelector and the Senior Tutor. 'Now, what the devil is all this about?' he demanded.

'It's all the Bursar's fault – ' the Senior Tutor began but the Praelector, who, it seemed to the Dean, had changed in some important respect during his absence, stopped him.

'The matter is far too serious to start apportioning blame,' he said, 'and frankly I'm not at all sure we should be seen to be discussing the matter in public.' They went straight to the Senior Tutor's rooms where Dr Buscott had set the tape recorder up and had shown the Senior Tutor how to change the reels.

For the rest of the morning the Dean listened with mounting horror and astonishment to the account, given in the main by the Praelector who seemed the better informed and certainly the more rational of the two, of the extraordinary events that had caused the crisis. He listened with even more astonishment to the recording of the Bursar's two interviews with Kudzuvine.

Only when it was finished and he had asked for something stronger than sherry, preferably a whisky and soda, was he able to speak himself. 'You mean to say this unutterable swine Whatsisname is closeted with Skullion in the Master's Lodge? The bloody man should be behind bars.'

'Exactly my opinion,' said the Senior Tutor. 'But for some reason I cannot fathom the Praelector here seems to think it is to the advantage of the College that he remain in the Master's care.'

'Care? Care?' said the Dean, who couldn't for the life of him see how an elderly man in a wheelchair could possibly be said to be in any position to take charge and keep under control a man who on his own evidence had almost certainly murdered people and had undoubtedly been present when other people were murdered.

'Skullion seems to exercise some peculiar influence over the man,' the Praelector told him. 'It is quite remarkable to watch the creature's reaction when the Master wheels himself into the room. I believe certain snakes have the same effect on their prey. In any case I have gained the distinct impression that Mr Kudzuvine prefers to remain in the Lodge rather than return to the tender care of Mr Hartang. As far as I can gather from his garbled mutterings, and I must say his syntax leaves a great deal to be desired, he regards the College as the safest form of sanctuary.'

'He can regard it how he damned well likes,' said the Dean. 'For my part I want him out of Porterhouse and into the hands of this filthy gangster Hartang and his shredder as soon as possible. I sincerely hope he dies a slow and painful death.'

But again the Praelector asserted his new-found authority. 'I think we should think this matter out and not take any precipitate action we might later come to regret.'

The Dean was baffled, and so was the Senior Tutor. 'What on earth are you talking about? Regret? Precipitate action? These filth come in here and wreck the Chapel and think they can buy the College so that this monster, this drug dealer Hartang, can use us – how did that swine put it? – as another turtle shell. And cover his arse, will he? I'll cover the bastard's arse if he so much as sets foot anywhere near the College. And what did he say about our eating habits?'

'I think he said we devoured . . . like Japanese vultures after Lent or something,' said the Senior Tutor.

'Actually he said Sumo-wrestling vultures had been on hunger strike,' said the Praelector. 'I must say I found it a very striking simile at the time. Most extraordinary way Americans have of using words. I shall never be able to look at black pudding in quite the same light again. Though why he should suppose you can catch AIDS from a sausage I cannot for the life of me imagine.'

'What I don't understand is why he keeps on about rubber douches and forced feeding,' said the Senior Tutor.

'I can't understand a single damned thing. Not one. Not a single damned thing,' the Dean shouted. 'And what's with – bugger the swine, I'm beginning to talk like him. What in God's name has happened to the Bursar? He sounded quite terrifying. Not that I blame him, of course, but he seemed to have gone out of his mind.'

'I think you'll have to ask Dr MacKendly about that,' said the Praelector. 'He gave him some sort of upper, I believe the name is. Unfortunately the after-effects are rather the opposite, an extreme form of lower.'

'Serve the idiot right for getting us into this mess,' snarled the Dean. 'I want a word with Master Bloody Bursar.'

The Praelector looked doubtful. 'I should go easy on him,' he said. 'He's not at all well and his mental state leaves a great deal to be desired.'

'We'll see about that,' said the Dean.

*

He saw precisely what the Praelector meant during lunch. The Bursar suddenly refused a very choice pair of chops on the grounds that he was damned if he was going to eat the Lamb of God. The Dean eyed him warily. The Bursar was clearly a very disturbed person and not the mealy-mouthed creature he had been.

The Chaplain, however, took up the issue. 'That is a very interesting doctrinal point,' he said. 'Now in the Communion Service we are asked to eat the body of Christ and to drink his blood. That is what our Lord prescribed at the Last Supper.'

'Lunch,' said the Bursar, toying curiously with a knife.

'Lunch?'

'The Last Lunch,' the Bursar snarled. 'If you can have a Last Supper, why the hell can't you have a Last Lunch?' There was an uneasy silence for a moment but the Bursar hadn't finished.

'And anyway there's a world of difference between having a sort of biscuit put on one's tongue and munching one's way through a plateful of mutton. And what's the mint sauce for?'

'The mint sauce? My dear chap – '

'I'll tell you what it's for,' said the Bursar lividly. 'It's for covering up the taste of the Lamb.'

The Chaplain nodded. 'Something of the sort, yes,' he said, 'though frankly I think it's going too far to smother a chop with mint sauce. A chop always tastes better on its own or with fresh peas . . .'

'Not that lamb. The Lamb of God, for Chrissake,' the Bursar shouted. 'The mint sauce takes away the taste of . . .'

*

'An interesting point that,' the Chaplain mused, when the Bursar himself had been taken away.

'Which one? They none of them held any interest for me,' said the Dean. 'And I didn't much like the way he kept emphasizing his points with that knife.'

'The one about the Last Lunch,' said the Chaplain, 'or even a Last Dinner. Supper has always struck me as a rather insubstantial meal, more of a snack really. Still, if you're going to be crucified, I don't suppose you want anything too heavy.'

'Christ,' said Dr Buscott in disgust.

'Precisely,' the Chaplain went on. 'We've just been talking about Him. A most peculiar chap, I've always thought. I've often wondered what he'd have done in life if he had come up to Porterhouse as an undergraduate.'

'He might have come in handy to do something for the Bursar. It's going to take a miracle to get him back

223

to sanity,' said the Senior Tutor, and helped himself to one of the chops the Bursar had refused.

*

At the other end of High Table Purefoy Osbert and the Librarian sat eating quietly.

'Do they always behave like that?' Purefoy asked.

'They're always very odd but I've never seen anything like that before,' said the Librarian. 'But then the whole place seems to have gone mad lately. Funnily enough the Bursar has always seemed the mildest of them all.'

'And who is the small round man with the red face?'

'That is the Dean,' the Librarian said. 'The small angry-looking man. Not someone you want to cross, especially when he's in a nasty mood, and by the look of him he's not in a very nice one now.'

'And who is the tall thin old fellow?' Purefoy asked.

'That's the Praelector. He's not a bad old chap. Very old but relatively scholarly for Porterhouse,' the Librarian said. 'The dimmest of the three is supposed to be the Senior Tutor, but I'm not sure he's half as ignorant as he pretends. It's always difficult to know with the Senior Fellows. They are perpetually playing games and pretending to be complete fools and never to do any work and then you find they regard you as an idiot because they've taken you in. But all Cambridge is a bit like that. I call it a "Put-You-Down Town". Everyone is so bloody competitive. Not that I'm bothered, because the Librarian is only a sort of honorary Fellow in

Porterhouse and I very seldom dine in. But as the Sir Godber Evans Memorial Fellow I'm afraid they'll expect you to and they'll put you through it. It is what they call your Induction Dinner.'

*

However, for the moment the Dean was far too pre-occupied to notice Dr Osbert. It wasn't only the Bursar's state of mind that bothered him. In fact that was the least of his worries. Something about the Praelector's manner, and the fact that he was obviously more in command of the situation than the Senior Tutor whose emotions were leading the way, led him to suspect that the Praelector saw more profit for the College in what had happened than was immediately obvious. He would have to have a quiet talk with the Praelector on his own.

19

At the Transworld Television Productions Centre in Docklands Hartang was trying to get Karl Kudzuvine on his own. 'Get me K.K.,' he told Ross Skundler in tones that, had Kudzuvine heard them, would have made sure he wasn't gotten at all easily. The first long letter from Waxthorne, Libbott and Chaine, Solicitors, 615 Green Street, Cambridge, jointly composed by both Mr Retter and Mr Wyve and personally addressed to Edgar Hartang, was not the sort of missive he liked receiving. It set out in numbered paragraphs the list of complaints against Edgar Hartang and Transworld Television Productions in details that covered several pages and requested an early response to their suggestion that in order to save very considerable costs and attendant publicity he pay the sum of twenty million pounds as part payment for the damage done to Porterhouse College buildings and the mental strain placed upon Fellows and undergraduates about to take exams alike.

'Twenty million pounds? Is someone out of their fucking minds? I told Kudzuvine to buy in the fucking place, not smash it to the ground,' he screamed at Skundler who was having to stand in for Kudzuvine and take all Hartang's terrible anger. 'I go to Bangkok a few days and when I get back I find this. Do I need a demand for twenty million pounds sterling? Like holes in my ass I need it. And where the fuck is Kudzuvine?'

'Nobody seems to know, sir,' said Skundler, regretting what he had said about K.K. being up shit creek and needing to paddle. He was nose-deep himself now. He had approved the Porterhouse accounts and by proxy the validity of the scheme. 'He just hasn't come back to work since he went up there with the team, sir.'

'Team? What sort of team? Some fucking demolition one like a wrecking crew? They take a bullfuckingdozer with them? Well, where is he?'

'I'll try and find out some more information, E.H.' Skundler said, sidling towards the door.

'You won't,' said Hartang in tones of unmistakable menace. 'You will stay here and tell me what has been going on while I'm in Bangkok.' He lowered his voice to a terrifying whisper. 'And don't say you don't know, Skundler.' Behind the blue glasses the eyes seemed to shred Ross Skundler already. Only when someone was going to die did Edgar Hartang speak with such clarity.

'All I know is Kudzuvine got the Professor to invite him to make a video of Porterhouse College Sunday and Kudzuvine went to Cambridge – '

'Tell me something I don't know, Skundler. Like who is the Professor? Don't I know Kudzuvine went to Cambridge? Twenty million pounds I know too.'

'Professor Bursar, sir, the one you . . . Kudzuvine

found for you at the fund-raising seminar on account he seemed dumb as dogshit . . .'

'Dumb as dogshit? Twenty million pounds may be dogshit to you, Skundler, but dumb it ain't. Speaks volumes. I don't like what I'm hearing.'

Skundler liked it even less. He wasn't just on the hook now, he was being reeled in. Fast. 'This Professor Bursar, you saw him, sir. He came to lunch Wednesday twelfth, twelve forty-five with you. You remember?'

'You asking me a question, Skundler? Are you asking me a question? Because if you are, I got an –'

'No, sir, Mr Hartang,' said Skundler who didn't want to hear the answer. He knew it. 'I'm just reminding myself of the details and just how dumb he seemed. I mean real stupid.'

Hartang's mind went back to the occasion. 'Ate like a pig,' he said involuntarily, and went into spasms. When he had finally got several pills into his mouth and had washed them down with mineral water, he corrected himself. The pig phobia was subdued by another thought. He was being stung to the tune of twenty millions by some broken-down professors. 'Grotesque,' he muttered, meaning the Bursar. 'Gets his suits from the Salvation Army, thrift shop, some place like that. But dumb he ain't.'

'No sir, I guess not,' said Skundler, wishing to hell he could avoid mentioning the Bursar's next visit with the ledgers.

'Don't guess, Skundler. Tell it like it is.'

'So I told Kudzuvine we had to see the print-out on account we needed to know their financial situation. Like we're not buying a pig in a poke. Jesus, Mr Hartang, you all right? I mean you want me to call the medication team?'

Hartang shook his head – or it shook him. Everything about him shook for a minute and beads of sweat broke out on his face. When he finally pulled himself together again, his voice was shaky but his meaning was unmistakable. 'I am all right, Skundler. You use that word again and you aren't. Next time I'll be putting a long-distance through.'

Skundler tried to swallow. His throat was desert-dry. He knew Hartang's long-distance calls. Like 'Fax me Death'. 'The Professor brings these ledgers, sir, like . . . like they're from before printing.'

'Yes, they would be,' said Hartang. 'Ever know a fucking ledger had printing in it? Because I haven't. Not in a lifetime doing accounts I've ever seen a ledger that's been printed in.'

'No, sir, I didn't mean that. I meant like they were way back. Used quills and all. I said to the Professor – '

'Skundler,' said Hartang very quietly and eyeing him through slits, 'Skundler, are you out of your fucking little mind? Or are you trying to tell me you are way off your trolley? Because I don't believe you. I don't believe one lousy fucking word you are telling me. You are lying, Skundler. And I don't like liars one dead cent. I used to like you, Skundler. Skundler's one of the team,

I said. Not now. Not now you tell me they still use quills to do the books at this Porterhouse College of yours.'

'I didn't say that, Mr Hartang, sir,' Skundler managed to get out, 'I said like they used to. I said to the Professor, "Do you still use quills?" And he said – '

'Yes, we use quills is what he told you. Like they got a million fucking geese running round they can rely on. No way, asshole. You'll be telling me next they don't do double-entry even.'

Skundler seized a final opportunity. 'They do, sir. But with figures that bad nothing coming in and it is all out I don't know why. I said to the Professor – '

'I'll tell you why, Skundler. I'll tell you. Because that fucking Limey shit in the shiny suit like hand-me-downs was pegging you to the ground for the fucking ants to eat. He try and sell you any equity in a New fucking Jersey gold-mine too? Because if he did, you bought. As sure as shit you bought. Well, you and Kudzuvine have bought me twenty million sterling's worth of trouble.' He pressed a button underneath the huge glass-topped desk. 'Get me Schnabel, Feuchtwangler and Bolsover. And fast,' he shouted. Skundler hurried towards the door. 'Not you, Skundler, not you. I want to enjoy your company a little longer. Not much but just a little. Okay.' He paused and the lizard eyes studied Ross Skundler. 'Want a drink, Ross?' he asked. 'Because I sure as hell do. And I don't drink.'

'Yes sir, I could do with one.'

'Well, you're not getting one. Now get me the Chivas

Regal. Where you and Kudzuvine are going you'll have plenty to drink. Like fathoms.'

Skundler crossed to the major bar and fetched the Scotch and one glass. They rattled on the desk top when he put them down.

Edgar Hartang was reading the letter again. He wanted his lawyers' opinion and very fast indeed. It looked real bad to him. Like he'd been screwed.

20

It was late afternoon before the Dean left the Praelector's study to visit the Master and see for himself
what this monstrous gangster Kudzuvine looked like in
the flesh. He had spent the intervening hours listening
to the Praelector explain how he had consulted Mr
Retter and Mr Wyve about damage repair and compensation and he had been impressed by the Praelector's
reasoning. All the same he had his reservations. 'I take
your point about the cost of repairs and compensation,'
he said, 'though frankly I cannot conceive of this dreadful fellow Hartang paying up without a struggle. If what
is on that tape is halfway true the man is in the drug
trade.'

'Which is precisely why he will pay up,' said the
Praelector. 'I don't think he will have any alternative.'

'But money from a drug dealer? I mean the swine
should be in jail. How can we possibly justify receiving
money made in such a way?'

'It is a matter I have given some thought to,' said the
Praelector. 'And I have come to the conclusion that we
must follow College precedent.'

For a moment the Dean could hardly believe his ears.
'Precedent? Precedent? You're not suggesting for one

moment anyone in the College has ever been involved in the drug trade, surely?'

'Not to my knowledge, though statistically I should have thought it was highly likely. No, I was thinking of one of our Masters. Long dead now, though not so long when one comes to think of it. 1749. Jonathan Riderscombe made his money in the Slave Trade. Now I don't know which you think is worse, drugs or slaves. I must say I consider the Slave Trade to have been an abomination. But we benefited from it. I am too old to be entirely sentimental.'

The Dean kept his thoughts on the subject to himself. He disliked being reminded of the dark origins of great fortunes. He was also extremely surprised, and not at all pleased, that a new Fellow had been appointed in his absence. 'The Sir Godber Evans Memorial Fellowship?' he said. 'I don't like the sound of this at all. The damned man Evans didn't deserve a memorial of any sort. He was one of the worst Masters we've ever had. Except for Fitzherbert, of course, but that is another story. I think I ought to have been consulted before any decision was reached.'

'Unfortunately we couldn't reach you,' said the Praelector.

'Cathcart knew where I had gone. You could have asked him.'

'We could have, had we known you were not visiting a dying relative,' said the Praelector with some slight acerbity. 'You could hardly expect us to phone every hospital and nursing home in Wales, and in any case there were other cogent reasons for making the decision very quickly.'

'Were there indeed? And what might those reasons be?' asked the Dean, who disliked being faulted.

'Six million pounds,' said the Praelector, which took the Dean's breath away. 'I think you would describe that sum as a sufficiently cogent reason. We were faced with something of an ultimatum. But the Senior Tutor knows more about the matter than I do. He was the person the donor's lawyers approached. Don't ask me why.'

'Not the Bursar?'

'Not the Bursar.'

'And who exactly is this quite remarkably munificent donor? Do we know that?'

The Praelector shook his head. 'No, we don't, but I think I can make an educated guess. The Senior Tutor would have us believe it to be a group of City financiers who admired Sir Godber Evans' efforts on their behalf. I don't.'

The Dean didn't either. 'City financiers, my eye,' he said, 'the bloody man did terrible harm to the financial interests of the country. Hopeless Keynesian,' he said.

'Quite,' the Praelector agreed. 'On the other hand, a certain woman, I won't call her a lady because in my opinion she isn't one, though she does have the title . . . You take my meaning?'

'I do indeed, and let me make an educated guess as to

the name of the solicitors. It wouldn't be Lapline and Goodenough by any chance?'

'That I don't know. The Senior Tutor was holding his cards very close to his chest. All the same six million pounds is not to be sneezed at. It gives us a fighting fund against this monster Hartang.'

He smiled slightly and the Dean acknowledged the truth of the statement with a nod of the head. 'Unfortunately it also gives us a new Fellow whose antecedents I think we should examine more closely. Where does he come from? I suppose the Senior Tutor was prepared to divulge that information to the College Council?'

'Kloone University. His speciality seems to be in researching crimes and punishments. His main work is a large tome on hanging called *The Long Drop*. I have not read it myself but I am told it is authoritative by those who read such books.'

'And I take it he is against hanging,' said the Dean.

'I imagine so. The widow would not have sponsored him if he'd been in favour of capital punishment,' said the Praelector. 'But you'll meet him tonight. It is his Induction Dinner. I haven't spoken to him myself so we shall just have to see what we have on our hands. In the meantime we have the Bursar in the lunatic asylum where he properly belongs and we have six million pounds in the kitty. And unless Retter and Wyve are totally misjudging the situation we have . . .'

'The gangster Hartang by the scrotum,' said the Dean.

The Praelector acknowledged that this had been his

thought though he would have put it more delicately himself. 'And what is more,' he went on, 'we have the man Kudzuvine at our convenience. I think the expression is that we have taken a hostage to fortune.'

Even the Dean had to smile. 'I must congratulate you, Praelector. For a man of your age you have done splendidly.'

'I don't think age has anything to do with it, Dean, except in one regard. I had the good fortune to be born at a time when Britain was the most powerful nation on earth and the Slave Trade a thing of the past. It was a brief moment in history, I daresay, but the saying "An Englishman's word is his bond" wasn't entirely meaningless in those days. Alas, it is today. Men like Maxwell – though of course his real name was Hoch – and the scum that Wilson ennobled and Mrs Thatcher spawned have made that guarantee derisory.'

'My own recent experiences have convinced me that something has gone terribly wrong,' said the Dean miserably. 'There has been a dreadful deterioration in standards.'

'Yes, there has,' the Praelector went on. 'When I was young and we had to pretend to be gentlemen of honour, we had to act honourably to maintain the pretence. That was the greatest virtue hypocrisy conferred on us. And hypocrisy has always been a particularly English quality.'

The Dean left him sitting and contemplating with sad perception that great past when corruption and lying

were not accepted social norms. Such evils had always
been there and they always would be but they had not
become endemic and socially acceptable. It had taken
war, two Great Wars in which millions had died fighting
for promises that had never been kept, to bring England
to its moral knees. And men like Hartang to the top.
The Praelector would readily die to prevent Hartang and
his ilk destroying Porterhouse and the romantic virtues
it had stood for. Even so he smiled. Englishmen had
been clever in their time and he himself was still no
fool. He just left it to other people to think he was.

*

The Dean approached the Master's Lodge with more
trepidation than he had expected. His nerve hadn't
failed him but he had been subjected to so many shocks
and humiliations in the past few days that his confidence
had been badly shaken. Besides that, he had been truly
alarmed by the violence and disgusting imagery of
Kudzuvine's language on the tapes. Even during his time
in the Navy he had never heard anything quite like the
filth and violence that seemed to be Kudzuvine's natural
way of expressing himself. And it was not only the
manner in which the creature spoke, it was more the
callous acceptance of a world without sense or meaning
that had been so shocking, shocking and alarming. For
once he felt some sympathy for the Bursar and could
understand why he was in the mental hospital, though
that was as far as his sympathy went. The man must

have been mad to begin with to get mixed up with
creatures like Kudzuvine and the even more appalling
Hartang with his phobia about being eaten by pigs and
his insistence on being unidentifiable. Listening to the
tapes the Dean had been confronted by hell on earth
and he did not really want to meet one of its habitués.
Still, it had to be done, so he straightened his short back
and marched across the lawn and was rather surprised
to find the French windows locked. He had to go round
to the side door and ring the bell.

The door was opened on the chain by Arthur. Behind
him stood Henry, the Under-Porter. 'Ah, it's you, sir,'
Arthur said. 'If you'll just wait a mo, I'll undo the chain.'

'Why is it on a chain?' asked the Dean. 'Nobody is
going to break in. Nothing much to steal.'

'It's on account of the American gentleman upstairs,
though I don't consider him any sort of gentleman
myself if you know what I mean.'

'I do,' said the Dean, 'I do indeed, Arthur, and I
entirely agree with you. And where's the Master?'

'Mr Skullion is in with him, sir. He spends most of
his time in there though what he sees listening to that
horrible language I can't think, sir. But it do keep the
American under control. Does everything the Master
tells him.'

The Dean climbed the staircase and met the Matron
on the landing. 'Very nasty business this, Matron,' he
said. 'I'm sorry we're having to submit you to this
dreadful ordeal. Very sorry.'

'It's no ordeal to me,' said the Matron, 'not at all. I find it a pleasant change from dealing with coughs and colds and things. This is much more interesting and I've heard so many weird stories, and I have to say that my vocabulary has been broadened.'

'Yes,' said the Dean doubtfully. He had no wish to have a Matron in Porterhouse whose language had more of the lower deck than was entirely pleasant. 'Yes, I daresay it has. And the Master is in good health?'

'I can't remember when I've seen him looking better, sir. Happier and more like his old self, if you know what I mean.'

'Splendid,' said the Dean. 'Well, I mustn't keep you from your duties, Matron.'

He opened the bedroom door and paused in astonishment. A naked man was kneeling on the floor in front of Skullion's wheelchair with his hands raised in supplication. 'You gotta help me, Master. You got to. You send me away from here I going to die. Like he's passed a death sentence on me. Jesus fuck, what I done, man, he's going to take his time with me too like the slow roast or the charcoal grill and you know about these things, Master, anyone does got to be you. Please, please you got to say you going to help old Kudzuvine. I'll do anything you ask, Master, I'll do it. You just say the word.'

Kudzuvine prostrated himself at the foot of the wheelchair.

Strange sounds were coming from its occupant. Even

the Dean, used as he was to Skullion's inarticulacy immediately following his Porterhouse Blue, found the sounds incomprehensible and alarming. It was all very well the Matron saying she couldn't remember when she had seen Skullion looking better and more like his old self, but the Dean found her optimism distinctly perverse. True, he could only see his back now with the bowler hat pulled well down on his head but if the series of grunts and gurgling noises emanating from him were anything to go by, the Master had never been worse. Even just after his stroke Skullion had been faintly comprehensible, but now whatever he was trying to utter was without any decipherable meaning at all. It sounded like strangulated gobbledygook. And the man prostrating himself on the floor didn't make much sense either, though at least part of what he had been saying was perfectly true. If half the things he had heard about Hartang on the tapes were true, he would undoubtedly have Kudzuvine tortured to death.

All the same, to grovel before Skullion showed such an abject lack of moral fibre that the Dean was disgusted. 'For goodness' sake, get off the floor, man,' he said and strode into the room. Kudzuvine scrambled to his feet and hurriedly got back into bed and sat there huddled up staring at this new dark apparition that had come into his life. The Dean ignored him. He was giving his attention to Skullion and, now that he could see the Master's face, was surprised to see a smile appear and one eye wink at him. And the noises, those dreadful sounds, had stopped.

'If you don't mind, Master, I think we ought to have a little chat in private,' he said, and wheeled Skullion out of the room. Behind them Kudzuvine shook his head. Whatever he had walked into like a fucking monastery with the man in the wheelchair with the hat who made sounds at him had to be in some fucking world he'd never been in before. And it was his only hope.

*

'Tell me, Skullion, if you can of course,' said the Dean, 'and if you haven't had another Blue, tell me why do you make those awful noises?'

'Called me Quasimodo he did. Quasimodo and some bloody hunchback. Now I don't know what Quasimodo means, must be Italian or Spanish or something. Rude anyway. So I thought I'd Quasimodo him back and see how he likes it. Well, that buggered him proper, if you'll pardon the expression. He don't like my gobbledygook any more than I like his bloody Quasimodo,' Skullion explained. 'Not when I go on hour after hour and half the night gobbledygooking the sod. I just sit there and watch him like a hawk and he can't stand it. Broke his spirit I have. Not that he's got much to break. He's one of them Yanks thinks they own the world. Told the Praelector one time he was a true-born American and could whip the hide off the rest of the world. Praelector didn't like it any more than I did. So I thought, "You've come to the wrong place to say a thing like that and I'll whip you into shape, my lad, even if I am in a wheelchair and can't move much." And I have, sir, I have. I've got the bugger gibbering. Another few days and they'll have him in Fulbourn for the rest of his natural, certified insane which is what he is by my book.'

'Well, Skullion – Master, that is – I have to hand it to you, you have been doing a splendid job,' said the Dean. 'You had me very worried when I first came in. But I think you've probably done enough. We are going to want that vile man's evidence and it won't look good if he goes into court gibbering. Let him be for the time being, Master. You've done everything that is needed.'

'Just so long as he don't call me Quasimodo or hunchback again, sir,' said Skullion. 'You'd better warn him. And I don't want him praying to me neither. I'm not some blooming idol. And he calls himself a Christian too. Bloody Yank.'

'Leave it to me, Master,' said the Dean and went back into the bedroom.

*

'I have come to warn you,' he told Kudzuvine. 'I have come to warn you that I have persuaded the Master not to pursue the course he had in mind for you. On these conditions: you will not speak to him one word and you will on no account refer to him as Quasimodo or The

242

Hunchback of Notre Dame. And furthermore you will behave politely and in a civilized fashion. If you fail to meet these conditions, I cannot be responsible for your safety. Do you understand?'

'Yes sir, I sure do, sir. I sure as shit do.'

'And that is another thing,' said the Dean. 'You will moderate your language. It is not customary in Porterhouse to use filthy expressions. Is that clear?'

'I guess so, sir,' said Kudzuvine humbly.

'Don't guess anything. Know it,' said the Dean, and stalked out of the room.

21

That evening Purefoy Osbert dined in Hall for the first time and, because it was his Induction Dinner, he sat with the Senior Fellows. But first he was introduced to the Combination Room and to the Special Porterhouse Amontillado Sherry which was supposed to have been blended at the time of the Peninsular War and which was certainly very old and unusually strong. It was only drunk on special occasions and seldom more than once a year. To begin with the Dean was content to stay in the background and merely observe the Sir Godber Evans Memorial Fellow from a distance while making sure that the waiter with the decanter saw to it that Purefoy's glass was never empty.

Even the Senior Tutor, who was still taking very great care of his liver when it came to fortified wines, had agreed to be genial. 'We have got to find out what this young man has come here to do,' the Dean had told him, resisting the impulse to ask the Senior Tutor why he had not told the College Council that the anonymous donor had employed Lady Mary's solicitors. Some time later would do to score that point.

In fact Purefoy's reception was far pleasanter than he had anticipated. The Praelector and the Chaplain, who was in any case naturally amiable, were particularly friendly. Professor Pawley spoke about the measurement of time from the moment of the Big Bang and even went so far as to attempt an explanation of the importance of his discovery of the nebula Pawley One while Dr Buscott, who wanted to recruit Dr Osbert to his progressive camp, was complimentary about *The Long Drop*, parts of which he had taken the precaution of reading in the University Library. By the time they trooped into dinner Purefoy had unwittingly drunk four glasses of the Special Amontillado and was beginning to think that his first impressions of Porterhouse had been rather too harsh. Only then did the Dean move forward.

'My dear fellow, you must allow me to introduce myself,' he said with a show of bonhomie. 'I am the Dean. You must come and sit beside me. I am so anxious to hear about your work. Your reputation is not an inconsiderable one and we are, I must confess, a rather ignorant bunch of old Fellows and don't keep up with what you young people are doing in your specialized areas of research.'

Through the excellent meat soup, the poached salmon, the deliciously underdone roast beef, the crème caramel, the Stilton and the fruit but, most importantly, through the Montrachet and the Fonbadet – a small but perfect little vineyard, as the Dean was at pains to point out – the Margaux and the Château d'Yquem, Purefoy Osbert gained confidence. He was ready to talk about anything, including his belief that Dr Crippen had been wholly innocent of the crime for which he was hanged. There had been a hiatus in the conversation at that point but a kick from the Dean under the table had silenced the Senior Tutor, who had gone very red in the face and who was on the point of saying he'd never heard such damned tommyrot in his life. The situation was saved by the Chaplain who said he had never been able to think of domestic murder as a capital crime because, as in the case of Mrs Crippen, a great many women were such dreadful nagging scolds that they deserved what was coming to them. Again the Dean had intervened.

'You must excuse the Chaplain,' he said. 'He has always been something of a ladies' man.' The remark left Purefoy so baffled by its implications that he did not know how to reply. By that time the talk had passed on to a discussion of the varying merits of Château Lafite, which the Dean maintained had a delightfully feminine quality about it, and Château Latour, which the Senior Tutor preferred as being more masculine. In other circumstances Purefoy would have found these preferences deeply suspicious. But now he was happy to have another chunk of Stilton. All his prejudices about Porterhouse had been dissipated by the combination of sherry and the various excellent wines and the conviviality with which he was surrounded. 'I'm really enjoying myself,' he confessed to the Dean, who said he was delighted to hear it.

'It is always refreshing to welcome a new face to High Table,' he said, after the Chaplain had mumbled Grace and they were going through to the Combination Room for coffee and port or brandy, whichever one preferred. The Senior Tutor stuck to coffee but Purefoy, who had never in his life drunk so much and who was decidedly tiddly, made the mistake of taking both port and cognac, much to the Senior Tutor's horror and the Dean's delight. He was achieving what he had set out to do. His only worry was that Purefoy Osbert would pass out before he could discover what the Sir Godber Evans Memorial Fellowship really entailed. And when Purefoy accepted a second cognac, the Dean intervened. 'My dear Dr Osbert,' he said, 'let me advise against it. Port is all very well on its own and in moderation but, as it is already fortified with spirit, to add cognac to it is to risk a very unpleasant Morning After The Night Before. Don't you agree, Senior Tutor?'

'I do indeed,' said the Senior Tutor. 'The other night in Corpus . . . But I'd rather not speak about it.'

But Purefoy had seized on the word. 'Talking about corpses,' he said, 'you know what I'm supposed to be researching here?'

'No,' said the Dean with a geniality he did not in the least feel. 'I have been wondering what your particular interest in the College is. Do tell us.'

'You'll never guess.'

The Dean smiled and preferred not to. 'I don't suppose we will.'

Purefoy Osbert swallowed the rest of his port and held out his glass for more. 'I'm here to find out for Her

Ladyship which of you Fellows murdered her husband. He was Master of Porterhouse you know.'

In the silence that followed this appalling revelation the Dean had the presence of mind to say that he had heard Sir Godber mentioned as the Master but that in his opinion the real power lay with Lady Mary. 'I suppose you might say we had a Mistress of Porterhouse rather than a Master and, had I intended to murder anybody, I think I'd have chosen her rather than him. A very ineffectual man, hardly worth murdering.'

A nervous titter ran round the little group. Purefoy concentrated on this argument. It seemed logical to him but there was a flaw in it somewhere. It took him some time to spot it.

' 'S right,' he said with a terrible slur. 'But you kill him and she hasn't got any power, has she?'

'There is that,' said the Dean. 'I can't fault your reasoning. And on which of us Fellows do your suspicions lie most heavily?'

'Don't have any suspicions,' Purefoy managed to say with some difficulty. 'All good fellows as far as I can see.'

'Which by the look of things cannot be very far,' said the Praelector, and got up to leave. 'I must say this is the first time in a very long life that I have been a murder suspect. It's a novel sensation.'

But the Senior Tutor wasn't taking the accusation so casually. 'By Heavens, I've never heard anything so monstrous. Appointing a Fellow to prove that one of us murdered her bloody husband. I'm going to consult my lawyer in the morning. The woman is going to pay for this,' he said, and stormed out of the room after the Praelector.

Purefoy Osbert sat on with the Dean and the Chaplain, who had fallen asleep in his chair and was dreaming of the girls in Boots.

'Drink up, my dear chap,' said the Dean and passed the port. 'And, Simpson, I think Dr Osbert might like another cup of coffee.' The waiter poured coffee. 'And I don't think you need wait up any longer.'

He waited until Simpson had gone before continuing with his questions. Purefoy Osbert was exceedingly drunk now. 'And what makes Her Ladyship think Sir Godber was murdered?' he asked. 'I always understood him to have over-indulged his taste for Scotch, and then fallen and cracked his skull on the grate. That is certainly what the coroner's jury decided.'

'Know they did,' said Purefoy. 'Know they did. I read the transcript she had made. Know all about it.'

The Dean made a note of this. The damned woman had really gone to some pains. And now she was prepared to spend six million pounds. It was all most interesting. Purefoy's next remark was even more revealing. 'Seen the post-mortem report too,' he said.

'Have you indeed? And does that support Her Ladyship's thesis?'

'She says he never got drunk.'

'Yes,' said the Dean encouragingly. 'And?'

'The autopsy report says he wasn't drunk either.'

'But the autopsy report that I remember definitely stated that he had drunk a large quantity of whisky,' said the Dean.

'But it hadn't made him drunk before his head was hit,' said Purefoy.

'Really? How do we know that?'

'You don't, but I do,' Purefoy said. 'Because it wasn't in his bleeding blood.'

'Bleeding blood? I don't quite follow.'

'The blood he bled. It was in his stomach when he died but it hadn't got into his bloodstream so he couldn't have been drunk, could he?'

The Dean said nothing. For the first time he felt a sense of unease about Dr Purefoy Osbert. The man might be very, very drunk, but the clarity of his reasoning told the Dean he was not dealing with a fool. Lady Mary had chosen her champion very shrewdly. 'And do you think Sir Godber was murdered?' he asked.

'Me? I don't know. I only go on facts and I don't have enough of them to know or even think but . . .' Purefoy Osbert paused. He was staring straight ahead of him as though the Dean was not there but his mind was still working with surprising swiftness and concentration.

'Yes?' prompted the Dean.

'Motive,' said Purefoy. 'Supposing he was murdered, *cherchez* the motive. The Dean had one and the Senior Tutor. They were going to be sacked. She said so. Yes, they had motives. But they also had alibis. They'd gone to this General's party and could prove it. Very convenient, that.'

The Dean sat motionless and listened. It was like hearing a man whose mind was sleep-talking. What he was saying had a frightening logic to it.

'And someone else had a motive. The Porter, Skullion. He had been sacked. He wanted revenge. He wanted his job back and he'd get it if Sir Godber died. The Dean and Tutor would see to that. They'd owe him. So where was he that night? There's a question needs an answer.'

It was very still in the Combination Room. Only the Chaplain's heavy breathing seemed to stir the air. A clock ticked loudly. The Dean's unease had turned to fear. The reasoning was impeccable. He and the Senior Tutor had had no invitations to Sir Cathcart's party. They had gone there to force the General to use his influence to rid the College of Sir Godber and, while they were gone, the Master had been mortally wounded. Accidentally, of course. Of course he hadn't been murdered but listening to this drunk young man thinking aloud was eerie and a little frightening. It was as if Dr Osbert were the prosecuting counsel in a trial, slowly but insistently building up his case. On the Bull Tower the clock struck midnight. And still Purefoy followed his line of thought aloud. 'But why didn't the Porter Skullion get his old job back?' he asked.

The Dean didn't reply. He wanted to hear Dr Osbert's answer.

'Because the Dean and Senior Tutor said the dying Master had named Skullion as his successor. But why should Sir Godber do that when he hated him? That doesn't make sense.'

It hadn't made sense to the Dean at the time but he had a terrible idea what was coming next. He was wrong.

'So what does make sense? They only said the dying man named him. No one else was there to prove he really had. Yes, that's more like it. They made the Porter Master to reward him for doing the killing or because they had to keep him quiet. Or both. That does make sense. Much more.' Purefoy paused.

Beside him the Dean was driven to intervene. The charge was too monstrous to be ignored. 'But Skullion had a Porterhouse Blue, a stroke,' he said. 'He was incapacitated.'

Still staring into space Purefoy Osbert waited for an explanation to come to mind. 'Ever hear of a man who's incapac ... incapacitated by a stroke going to prison?' he asked and answered the question himself. 'I haven't. A man in a wheelchair who couldn't even speak, in prison? It doesn't happen. And yet they make the Porter Skullion who's had a stroke and is in a wheelchair the Master? Of Porterhouse, the snobbiest college in Cambridge? There has to be a reason.'

But the reason never came. Without any warning Purefoy Osbert slowly tilted forward out of his chair and fell flat on his face. For a moment the Dean sat looking down at the sprawled figure. There was no contempt on his face now, only a look of fear and something like admiration. His hatred was reserved for Lady Mary.

The Dean got up and went out into the Court and crossed the lawn to the Porter's Lodge. 'Walter,' he told the Head Porter. 'I think the new Fellow needs assisting to his rooms. And wake the Chaplain while you are about it.'

'Can't hold his liquor, sir?'

'You could put it like that, Walter,' the Dean said, but he said it without conviction. Drunk, the Sir Godber Evans Memorial Fellow was capable of frightening deductions. Sober, he might be lethal. Lethal and absolutely wrong. The Dean climbed wearily up the stone staircase to his rooms thinking, as he so often thought, how dangerous pure intellect alone could be. In Cambridge pure intellect was power and like power it tended to corrupt. Something would have to be done about Dr Purefoy Osbert.

22

Edgar Hartang wasn't interested in intellect, pure or otherwise, but he was adamant that something be done about Kudzuvine. He had been in consultation with his legal team for hours and nothing that Schnabel, Feuchtwangler or Bolsover had told him had been to his liking. 'You telling me because that fucking Kudzuvine goes apeshit in this fucking Porterhouse I got to spit out twenty million pounds you got to be as crazy as he is,' had been his first reaction.

'We are merely speaking in terms of the legal consequences of this action,' Schnabel had told him. 'And if the facts as laid out by the solicitors acting for the College are as they state them to be liability certainly lies with Transworld. That is the unfortunate fact of the matter and our unavoidable conclusion.'

Two days later the facts of the matter had worsened and Skundler, who had lost a stone in weight through having to live in the presence of a man who made it abundantly clear he intended to have him killed very painfully, had been ordered to get some independent operatives to find Kudzuvine.

'No, not from Chicago, not yet,' Hartang had shouted

at him. 'Locals. And on the phone, Skundler. You're not leaving this room.'

The operatives' report that Kudzuvine was almost certainly still in Porterhouse, and a further communication from Waxthorne, Libbott and Chaine that they had even more damaging though unspecified evidence, had sent Hartang into a paroxysm of rage. 'You mean the fucker's squealed?' he screamed at the legal team. 'I'll . . . I'll crucify that . . . that . . .' Words failed him.

'Apparently he's given an affidavit of some sort,' Bolsover told him. 'Like it's a sworn statement, a confession – '

'I know what an affifuckingdavit is,' Hartang bawled. 'Whadda they mean by our ancillary activities for shit-sake? That's what I want to know.'

'One can only suppose . . .' Feuchtwangler hazarded to take some of the heat off Bolsover. He preferred to leave the supposition unsaid.

'Suppose? I know. I know what . . .' He turned to Skundler. 'What does Kudzuvine have in that head of his? Like details, you dummy, not fucking neurons. What he's got to have spilt to these fucking shysters?'

Skundler took a desperate gamble. 'As a VP he's got details, sir. Got a lousy mind . . .'

'That I'm learning. Tell me the news.'

'He's got a photographic memory, Mr Hartang sir. Filing cabinet full of account numbers and times of consignments and fund flows and . . .'

'Jesus Christ,' said Edgar Hartang, and wiped the

sweat from his face. There was a long and terrible silence. Finally he spoke. 'Get me some independents Stateside . . .' he began, but this time Schnabel stepped in with remarkable courage.

'I . . . we would strongly advise against any action that might make the situation worse,' he said.

'Worse? Just how much worse can it get you don't think this is worst? I got to take this shit do nothing about it?'

'I did not say that. I just want you to know that there is nothing in this communication from the solicitors to indicate that they intend to move from civil action and initiate criminal proceedings. That's our reading of it.' Beside him his two partners nodded their agreement.

Hartang gnawed a knuckle. 'You mean they're into fucking blackmail? You saying that?' he asked.

'We wouldn't put it in precisely those terms,' said Bolsover. 'Like they're negotiating.'

'You can call it what you like. I call it blackmail.'

'And another thing we'd have to say is that they'll have Kudzuvine under wraps some place we're never going to find him. Any action that might – '

'Don't say make the situation worse. I'm there already,' said Hartang. 'What you're telling me is pay twenty million plus.'

'Negotiate is all,' said Feuchtwangler. 'We don't see any other way.'

'I've been taken. I've been taken by a motherfucking

cuntlapper in a suit I wouldn't be seen dead in. And all because I wanted to help out with their finances. Twenty million is some helping out, and what do I get for it? Zilch. Zero and out.' ('You don't get prison,' the lawyers thought simultaneously, but they kept the thought to themselves.)

'Okay, negotiate. But afterwards . . .'

'Just one other thing, Mr Hartang, we'd like Ross Skundler to come with us.'

'What? To negotiate? Skundler stays here with me. We've got appointments to keep,' said Hartang lividly.

'Not to negotiate,' said Schnabel. 'We need him to tell us everything Kudzuvine knows could harm our case. As Assessmentation Officer he's in a position to make things a lot easier for us in our negotiating posture.'

Hartang thought for a moment. In fact he was heartily sick of the sight of the cowering Skundler. 'Yeah, makes kinda sense to me,' he said. 'Just don't let him out the building. I don't need no more defectors to this Porterhouse.'

They went out into the elevator and, as it shot up and down floors, Ross Skundler thanked them. 'I owe you,' he said. 'I really owe you.'

'Just don't want more bloodshed, is all,' said Schnabel. 'It's not in our line of business. And that old bastard is going to have to watch his back a lot closer with Kudzuvine over the wall. Could be piggy-chops time coming up. I heard Dos Passos is in town.'

'Jesus,' said Skundler. 'I really do owe you.'

'I'll tell you something for nothing,' said Bolsover. 'Someone else in the company owes twenty million plus, plus costs. With what do we negotiate? These guys Waxthorne, Libbott and Chaine have got him by the balls.'

'You reckon he's going to snuff them some time?' asked Feuchtwangler.

Bolsover smiled. 'Going to want to but they're hard to find. Made enquiries. Like they've been dead over thirty years already.'

The elevator shot down from floor ten to zero. Skundler followed them out into the street. His only hope lay with the lawyers.

*

In Cambridge General Sir Cathcart D'Eath's Range Rover was parked in the driveway of the Master's Lodge. There was a horsebox behind it and the doors were open towards the front door.

'It's all right, sir,' said Arthur. 'Streets is empty. No one there. You can bring him out now.'

'Giddy up, Yank,' said the General and Kudzuvine shot into the horsebox. The General's Japanese attendant shut the doors and locked them and presently the Range Rover was on its way to Coft Castle. From a window on the ground floor Skullion watched it go with some regret. He'd enjoyed gobbledygooking the American.

*

In the offices of Waxthorne, Libbott and Chaine, Solicitors, the Praelector read through Kudzuvine's sworn
statement with increasing amazement.

'I must admit I do not understand many of the terms
used,' he said, 'but my overall impression is that he has
fingered – I believe that is the colloquial expression – he
has fingered Edgar Hartang as a banker for a number of
drug cartels. Am I right?'

Mr Retter nodded. 'Of course the accusation is
unsubstantiated,' he said. 'And for that reason we
have taken the precaution of drawing up two affidavits.
In the first there is the full admission of Transworld
Television Productions' responsibility for the damage to
the Chapel and the general fabric of the College,
together with the harm done to the mental and physical
well-being of over four hundred undergraduates studying for their examinations at very possibly the most
crucial moment in their lives, namely just before the
Tripos.'

The Praelector considered the word 'crucial' and
found it inappropriate. 'I rather doubt that,' he said.
'Half of them would get Thirds or what were once called
Specials.'

'Aren't you being overly pessimistic?' asked Mr
Wyve, but the Praelector wouldn't have it.

'The College has never been noted for its academic
excellence. I have always liked to think on the other
hand that we exert a civilizing influence.'

'No doubt about that. However, since there is no way

of knowing what the examination results might have been had this shocking event not taken place, I think we are entitled to assume they would have been excellent. Then again there is the mental suffering caused to the research graduates and the academic staff. We can fairly assert that scientific discoveries of considerable importance have been put in jeopardy.'

'One can assert it,' said the Praelector, 'but I cannot conceive that anyone would find the statement in the least credible.'

'Again, no one can tell. What cannot be denied or quantified is the physical damage done to one of the oldest architectural monuments of Cambridge.'

The Praelector had no argument with this. Porterhouse might lack academic reputation but there could be no doubting the unique qualities of its ancient buildings. 'And how do you rate our chances of getting Hartang to settle out of court?' he asked. 'It would save a great deal of time and money.'

Mr Retter exchanged a significant look with his partner. It was Mr Wyve who replied. 'That is more difficult to say. These things do tend to drag on for months and even years, you know. We can only hope that Transworld will see the justice of our case and not prolong the proceedings.'

'I should have thought this second affidavit would speed things up,' said the Praelector.

'Quite so,' said Mr Retter and took the document from him. 'Let us just say that it will be better to keep it in reserve. I don't think I need say any more. I'm sure you understand.'

The Praelector did. He had revised his opinion of Mr Retter and Mr Wyve. The law might be an ass, but these lawyers weren't.

23

The Dean had risen earlier than usual. He usually stayed in bed rather longer after an Induction Dinner but he had a special reason for being up and about. He had to prevent the Senior Tutor from carrying out his threat to consult his lawyers over the accusation that he had had a hand in murdering the late Master. The Senior Tutor was an impetuous man and, in the light of Purefoy Osbert's dangerous reasoning of the night before, it was essential that neither the Senior Tutor nor the Dean himself should make any real response to what was a manifest absurdity. He waited until after breakfast before broaching the subject.

'Senior Tutor, if I might have a word in your ear,' he said as they passed through the Screens.

'If it's about last night and that impertinent young scoundrel's accusation, I don't think there is anything to discuss. I am seeing my lawyer at eleven. I phoned him at home first thing this morning. I am not taking this sort of thing lying down.'

'Absolutely not,' the Dean agreed. 'Perhaps if we were to stroll in the garden we can discuss what is to be done.' Presently, as they walked up and down the beech avenue and the Senior Tutor had uttered his usual threat to horsewhip Dr Osbert, the Dean got to the nub of the argument.

'Dr Osbert was exceedingly drunk last night,' he said. 'The mixture of port and cognac is a particularly lethal one.' The Senior Tutor said he knew it was from recent experience and it served the little liar right if he felt like death this morning.

'I absolutely agree with you,' said the Dean, 'but the point I am trying to make is that we should in a sense be very grateful to the wretched man for telling us exactly why he has been appointed and what Lady Mary expects for her six million pounds. Forewarned is, after all, forearmed.'

'I'll forearm the bastard. Nobody is going to call me a murderer and get away with it. The damned swine is going to regret making that accusation.'

'I'm sure he is doing so already,' said the Dean and decided that now was the time to take the wind out of the Senior Tutor's sails. 'Frankly, I think it was most unwise to approve his Fellowship at such short notice and without properly examining his credentials.'

'What the devil do you mean by that?' the Senior Tutor demanded angrily. 'There were six million pounds at stake and in any case he came with the very best recommendation.'

'From Lapline and Goodenough, no doubt,' said the Dean, playing his trump.

The Senior Tutor stared at him. 'How the devil . . . how did you know that?'

'Because,' said the Dean, 'I recall that they acted for Lady Mary at the time of the inquest. I am sure you realized that yourself.' Internally the Dean smiled. He was saving the Senior Tutor's face for him. It was important to win the man over.

'Now that you come to mention it,' the Senior Tutor muttered submissively, 'I did wonder at the time . . . The anonymity of the sponsor . . .'

'Not that it matters. We could hardly have turned our noses up at that sort of sum of money.' The Dean had landed his fish. There was no need to use the gaff. 'The crux of the matter is this, that I stayed on last night after you'd left to hear what he was going to say next and I have to tell you that, while his argument is wholly and completely wrong, he has got enough circumstantial evidence to goad us into an action for libel which would do – '

'Goad? Why do you say goad us into an action for libel? We'd be bound to win enormous damages.'

'Possibly. But from whom? Dr Osbert? I think not. The man would be bankrupt and we should receive nothing except the most unpleasant publicity.'

'But Lady Mary has put him up to this. You said yourself she must be his sponsor. The woman is enormously rich.'

'But even if we could prove she sponsored the Fellowship, the libel would be coming from Dr Osbert. Apart from her outburst at the inquest she has said nothing in public and written nothing,' said the Dean. 'We are up against a formidable enemy.'

The Senior Tutor's eyes were on the ground as they walked. He had to acknowledge the force of the Dean's argument. All the same the situation was intolerable. 'But what are we to do?' he asked finally. 'We cannot simply allow a man to go round accusing us of murder and do nothing about it.'

'I quite agree,' said the Dean. 'I propose to do something to put a stop to it but I have had too little time to work out the correct tactics. I only know that we must wait for him to make the next move. In the meantime, I for one intend to pursue a course of insistent friendliness towards him and I would advise you to do the same. It will embarrass him no end.'

By the time they parted, the Senior Tutor had agreed to cancel his visit to his lawyer and to hide his real feelings for Purefoy under a mask of warmth and amiability. 'I'll do my best,' he said. 'But it is going to be exceedingly difficult. The bloody man . . .'

*

And Purefoy Osbert felt bloody awful. His condition was not as extreme as that of the Senior Tutor after his dinner at Corpus – Osbert had youth on his side – but it was awful enough, and made all the more so because he could not remember what he had said to the Dean or even whether he had said anything at all or had merely thought it. Or something. He was sure he had told them all why he had been sponsored by Lady Mary and what she hoped he would achieve. He could remember that as well as the Dean's disarming remark about Sir Godber's ineffectuality and Lady Mary being the Mistress of Porterhouse. And they had taken the accusation so calmly, though the Senior Tutor had been furious and had walked out. But when Purefoy Osbert finally dragged himself out of bed and washed and shaved and went out to go to the Library he came face to face with the Senior Tutor on the stairs.

'Good morning, Dr Osbert,' the Senior Tutor said and smiled alarmingly at him. 'I do so hope you had a comfortable night. If there is anything at all I can do to help make life pleasant for you here, don't hesitate to call on me. I am nearly always in and only too delighted to see you. Do you by any chance row, or play any sport?'

Purefoy managed to smile wanly back and admitted he didn't row and wasn't any sort of sportsman before scuttling off downstairs more than ever convinced that the Senior Tutor fancied him.

And he wasn't too sure about the Dean either when he bumped into him by the Porter's Lodge. He greeted Purefoy almost effusively. 'Such a very pleasant evening and most enjoyable, though, alas, we have to pay for the fun the next morning with a hangover. Small price to pay for such excellent company. Most delightful.' And the Dean passed on, a seemingly merry little man, leaving Purefoy Osbert even more mystified about Porterhouse than before. Whatever else could be said about the Senior Fellows there was no denying their aplomb.

Purefoy went out through the Main Gate into the street and walked slowly over the Garret Hostel Lane bridge towards the University Library. On the river a few punts were out but they were mainly occupied by tourists.

*

Behind him the Dean was doing something he had seldom done before. He was in Purefoy's rooms and reading his correspondence while the Senior Tutor kept watch from the window.

'Here's something interesting,' said the Dean at last. 'Have a read of this and see what you think. I'll keep a look-out.' And he handed a letter and a paper to the Senior Tutor who read them both with growing interest.

'I'll be damned,' the Senior Tutor said when he had finished reading. 'Who would have thought a mousy little chap like that would be so depraved? No wonder the bastard doesn't row or play any decent sport.'

'Well, at least we know his little foibles,' said the Dean, and hurried down to the College office to copy the two documents before putting them back exactly where he had found them.

*

'Coon girls, eh?' said General Sir Cathcart D'Eath later that day. 'Always comes in useful to know what a fellow's tastes are. Not that I blame him. Known some dashed nice black fillies in my time. I remember a very hot little number in Sierra Leone. Name of Ruby. Dear old Rubber Ruby. By God, she knew how to turn a man on.'

But the Dean wasn't interested in the General's sexual reminiscences. He had found Mrs Ndhlovo's advice about masturbation and masturbatory techniques both deeply disturbing and psychologically very revealing. 'Think you can do something?' he asked.

'Don't go in for hand sex myself,' said the General, 'but I daresay the avocado pear method might come in handy if one was ever stuck for company though it would have to be a ripe one. I suppose one could get it up to the right temperature in a microwave.'

'For heaven's sake, Cathcart, I'm not in the least bit interested. I want to know what we can do about Dr Osbert,' he said. There were times when he found the General's preoccupation with the more sordid aspects of life most uncongenial. Of course he couldn't be compared with the appalling Jeremy Pimpole who was in a different league but all the same . . . And Dr Osbert and his lover Mrs Ndhlovo were obviously perverts of the very worst sort. Any woman who could write so enthusiastically about things that had never entered the Dean's mind even in his moments of greatest sexual need, though these were few and far between, had to belong to the dregs of society. And Dr Purefoy Osbert was madly in love with the slut. That was clear from her letter which was obviously in reply to one he had written her. As the Dean had said to the Senior Tutor, 'I must say his parents chose a most inappropriate name for him. Pure of faith, my foot.' But now he had to concentrate Sir Cathcart's mind on matters other than the misuse of avocado pears.

'The point I am trying to make is,' he said, 'can we make use of this information to stop him continuing his investigation into the circumstances surrounding Godber Evans' death? I had the greatest difficulty dissuading the Senior Tutor this morning from instructing his lawyer to issue a writ for libel.'

The General was shocked. 'You mean he's written something saying you and the Senior Tutor murdered – '

'Not written. Said. I told you. Last night in the Combination Room.'

'In that case it's slander, not libel. Got to have it written for libel. Surprised you don't know the difference.'

'Perhaps it is because we don't move in those circles where people write lies about one another so freely,' said the Dean. 'Now, about Dr Osbert . . .'

'You want him taken care of, is that it?'

The Dean hesitated. He certainly wanted something done to deter Purefoy Osbert but he wasn't sure about his 'being taken care of'. The General had rather too many friends in the SAS for comfort. 'In the sense that he is put in a situation which is open to ridicule and which can be used to persuade him not to pursue his enquiries any further. Or at least not to bother Skullion, yes. I do not want him to be physically hurt in any way.'

'I think he's more likely to hurt himself quite horribly if he takes some of the advice that black woman has handed out,' said the General. 'Knew a chappie once got himself trapped in a milk bottle. Couldn't smash it for fear of doing himself a frightful mischief. Had to call a doctor and he was baffled too. Rushed him into hospital and I forget how they got the dashed thing off. Told me just in case, but I've forgotten. Steered clear of milk bottles ever since.'

The Dean winced. 'I don't think we need anything quite so drastic, Cathcart,' he said. 'I was thinking more of his evident need for perverse forms of sex.' He left the General to draw his own conclusions.

'Ah,' said Sir Cathcart. 'Oh yes. See what you mean. Daresay something of that sort could be arranged. I know a dolly bird in Rose Crescent who'll be only too ready to lend us her Torture Chamber.'

'For God's sake, Cathcart, didn't you hear me? I said I didn't want any violence.'

'Not violence, old boy, just a bit of the old Tie-'Em-Up-and-Tickle-'Em stuff. Nothing nasty about it at all. Rather jolly for a change.'

'And is she black?' asked the Dean, who couldn't for

the life of him imagine anything jolly about being tied up and tickled.

'Of course she's not black. White as the driven snow,' said the General. 'But I'll let you into a secret if you really want to know – '

'I don't,' said the Dean, 'I definitely don't.'

But Sir Cathcart couldn't be stopped now. 'Got all sorts of women at a certain training camp not a million miles from Hereford and when they're testing chaps to see if they can stand up to interrogation they strip 'em naked and blindfold 'em and bring in – '

'If you don't mind, I really don't want to hear,' begged the Dean.

'Nothing wrong. Don't hurt the blighters. Bit of humiliation. Anyway it's good for your education to know these things. Can't live your whole life in some sort of romantic dream world.'

'I much prefer to, I assure you. I really do. Man cannot stand too much reality. This man can't at any rate.'

'Just as you like. All I'm saying is they've got all sorts over there. Chinese, Indians, Irish of course. For all I know they've got an Eskimo lass. Russians, naturally, and Jerries. But the one I've got in mind for our young friend is a Zulu woman. Strapping great gal. If you like them big and black, she's right up your street.'

'Not my street,' said the Dean in some annoyance. 'I'm not listening to any more of this.' He got up to go.

'By the way,' he said as the General saw him out to his car, 'how is . . . what did you say you'd changed his name to? The you know who.'

'Oh him. Kentucky Fry. Not a bad chap at heart and I've got to hand it to him, he's very good with horses. I've got him working in the Catfood Canning Factory. Keeps him out of sight and he seems to feel happier with a knife in his hand and all that blood about. Reckons we should start up a pig farm. Extraordinary. Keeps bleating every now and again about Skullion. Seems the Master made a big impression on him. And how is the old rascal?'

'Odd you should ask that,' said the Dean. 'Hasn't been his usual self these last few days. I think he rather misses not having Kentucky Fry about the place.'

24

And Skullion did. He had enjoyed sitting beside Kudzuvine's bed and exercising his authority over him. It was
a long time since Skullion had been able to demonstrate
the power of his personality to any worthy adversary,
and to be called The Thing and Quasimodo and Hunchback by a damned Yank had provided him with the sort
of stimulus he needed. With Kudzuvine to reduce to a
state of gibbering terror he had escaped the boredom he
had suffered ever since his Porterhouse Blue but now
the boredom had returned, made worse by the knowledge of what he was missing. To make up for it he
insisted on Arthur bringing up bottles of Hardy's Special
Ale from the Buttery where very few people knew it
had been laid down twenty years before to mature.
'Piquant yet without a twang,' read the label, 'full in
body.' Which was more than could be said for Skullion,
but it was still his favourite tipple and as the Master he
was free to drink as much of it as he liked and his
obnoxious bag would hold. Or far more if he was out in
the garden with the bag removed from the end of the
pipe and hidden from view under a rug over his knees
where the bottles of ale were hidden too. As Arthur,
who shared his taste in beers, pointed out, 'You can

always have a leak under there and no one will notice. Not out on the lawn they won't. Now, if you was a bitch it would be different, Mr Skullion, but you ain't that. You're an old dog, you are.' Skullion had smiled at the compliment. 'Bitch pee leaves marks on lawns,' Arthur went on, 'but dog's piss don't. Know that for a fact because my old dad was kennel man out Hardingley and old Mrs Scarbell used to carry on something frightful if a bitch peed on the lawn. "What do you think you're doing, Arthur?" she would say to my dad who I was named after. "You know nothing will grow when a lady dog has passed water." And my old dad would say . . .'

It was on conversations such as this that Skullion depended for any interest in his life. And on his daily consumption of Hardy's Special Ale and the memories the ale seemed to encourage. Every day the Chef would come over for a chat or, if there was anything very special for High Table dinner, he would bring some over for the Master's approval. 'Knowed you liked this, Mr Skullion, and I've cut it up small so it's easier to chew,' he would say and Skullion would answer, 'Very nice, Cheffy, very tasty. Always were the best Chef I can remember in this or any college and old Whatsisname in Trinity used to take some beating.' Almost every day the Chef brought over some quails' eggs even when they weren't on the Fellows' menu because Skullion was partial to them like and they went down easy and hardly needed any chewing to speak of.

Most of these little meetings of like minds took place

out of sight of the rest of the College and were held
round the corner on the far side of the Master's Maze
but from his study Purefoy Osbert could only see the
foot of the wheelchair and was intrigued by the routine
of the Chef in his white hat and coat crossing the lawn
bearing dishes on a great silver tray with napkins,
immaculately ironed, laid out over the serving dishes,
just as he was intrigued by the sight of the Master leaning
with infinite patience late into the night against the great
beech tree watching the back gate tipped with formidable revolving spikes over which no one ever climbed.
It was as though he were witnessing some ancient Porterhouse ritual that had been handed down through the
centuries. And always Purefoy wondered what was being
said behind the yew hedge of the maze and what he
might learn if he listened to it. In the end his curiosity
got the better of him and one lunchtime, when Skullion
was safely in the Master's Lodge, Purefoy Osbert sauntered casually through the rose garden before doubling
back out of sight of the Lodge and entering the maze. It
was not a large maze but it was an unusually difficult
one, and the yew was old and dense. It took Purefoy
twenty minutes to reach the corner beyond which Skullion sat in the afternoon and the Chef came with his
offering. Purefoy Osbert sat down and waited.

He had to wait for an hour before the Master wheeled
himself out and stationed himself only a yard or two
away with his bottles of ale and his memories of
Porterhouse past. But this afternoon he was in a bad

temper. He had had a run-in with the Matron who had insisted on his having a bath. 'It's no use your grumbling at me, Master,' she had said, 'we can't have you smelling. You're going to have a bath and a change of clothes. That old suit of yours has got to go to the dry cleaners and if I had my way it would go to the incinerator. Now then, off with your jacket and . . .' Being bathed by the Matron was Skullion's worst moment in the week. It was the ultimate indignity. Deprived of his clothes and the bowler hat, that badge of his office as Head Porter which he had refused to part with even as Master, he not only was naked; he felt naked, naked and vulnerable and in the presence of a woman with none of the sensibilities and respect for human decencies. he demanded. Not that he minded having his back scrubbed – he quite liked that – but there were other areas, his privates as he called them, in which the Matron took what he considered a thoroughly indecent interest and insisted on washing very meticulously because, as she put it so coarsely, if she didn't he'd smell even more like an old dog fox than he did already. Skullion didn't mind being compared to an old dog by Arthur but for a bitch like the Matron to liken him to an old dog fox was going a damned sight too far. And he'd told her so in no uncertain terms. 'You aren't even a married woman and no bloody wonder and, if you want to find out what you've been missing, you go and find some other man to fiddle with because I bloody don't like it. Or you. I can look after them myself.'

Which had done nothing to improve the Matron's temper or her treatment of him.

'You've got a dirty mind, you have, and it's no use your looking at me like that. Call yourself the Master of Porterhouse and you can't even talk like a gentleman,' she had snapped back at him and had then really put the boot in. 'I heard the Dea – well, never you mind who, say the other day, and I did too, that it was about time they sent you to the Park. Oh yes, he did. Where do you think he's been these past weeks? Hasn't been visiting any sick relatives in Wales. Been going round the import-ant Old Porterthusians looking for a Master. That's what he's been doing. And if you don't believe me, you ask Walter in the Porter's Lodge and he'll tell you. In fact I wonder you don't know it already because it's common knowledge in the College. You're for Porterhouse Park and I for one won't be sorry to see you go. I won't have to soil my hands bathing you there.' She had said it with such venom and conviction that Skullion had sensed she was telling the truth. Besides he had suspected some-thing of the sort himself from the way Cheffy and Arthur and Walter had all treated him with more sympathy than they had ever shown before. He had never wanted sym-pathy and until very recently they had not wasted it on him. Instead they had shown him the respect they had shown when he was Head Porter and the most important servant in the College. Not that he was going to ask them. He didn't want them to have to lie to him. That wasn't proper and he had always done things the proper way.

So, now, on this warm afternoon, he sat drinking an unusually large number of bottles of Hardy's Special Ale which Arthur had opened for him, all the time nursing a growing sense of grievance against the world. He even snapped at Cheffy for cutting off the crusts of his cucumber sandwiches for tea which he had never done before. And when Arthur had come out to tell him his dinner was ready, Skullion said he didn't want any.

'Got to keep your strength up, Mr Skullion,' Arthur told him.

'What for?' Skullion demanded. 'What bloody for?'

Arthur was nonplussed. 'Well, I don't really know, Mr Skullion. But you've always been so fond of your grub.'

'Well, I ain't now. You go and get me another half of Hardy's. I've got things to think about.'

For a moment Arthur hesitated. He knew he ought to say he'd had enough already and another six bottles, which was what Skullion meant by a half, and he wouldn't just be half-seas over, he'd be all the bloody way. But he knew better. It wasn't just that Skullion – that Mr Skullion – was the Master. If that had been all, like with the previous Masters, he'd have told him to his face he'd had enough and it wasn't right the Master getting pissed. No, he'd have said that and been cursed for his damned insolence, and maybe he'd have got the Master in to his dinner and maybe he wouldn't, but in the morning the incident would have been forgotten and certainly ignored. But with Mr Skullion it was different. Mr Skullion wasn't just any old Master of Porterhouse, he was Mr Skullion the Head Porter which meant far more to Arthur and Cheffy and the rest of the College servants who remembered him in his prime. It went still deeper, far, far deeper than that. It was that Mr Skullion was Mr Skullion who'd always done things proper and never lied except when he had to save someone else's bacon or the College reputation. He'd have died for Porterhouse, Mr Skullion would have, and no mistake. As Head Porter he'd licked the young gentlemen into shape. 'You'd better get your hair cut, Mr Walker,' Arthur had once heard him tell an undergraduate. 'We can't have them saying Porterhouse is full of nancy boys like King's, can we, sir? And if you haven't got it on you, sir, here's half a crown and I'll put it down against the slate.' And he had done the same with every College servant who'd needed pulling up and told to do it proper, whatever it was. 'Proper is as proper does,' had been Mr Skullion's motto and, if there'd been one word he'd used more than any other – and there was – it was proper. Mr Skullion was proper. There was no other way of putting it and, if he wanted to get properly pissed, Arthur wasn't going to stop him. Mr Skullion was his own man and there weren't many in Cambridge or anywhere else for that matter you could say that about. And so, after the briefest of hesitations, Arthur went back into the Master's Lodge and came back with the bottles and put them down with the tops off on the tray under the rug where Skullion could reach them and all he said was, 'Are you all right, Mr Skullion?' And

Skullion had replied with a strange look, 'All right, Arthur? All right? Oh I'm all right. It's the others is all wrong.' And as Arthur had walked away back to the Lodge he'd heard Skullion call out, 'And thank you, Arthur, thank you,' which was only proper.

*

Three yards away behind the yew hedge Purefoy Osbert sat on the mossy grass and wished he could move. He was getting hungry himself and cold and he had learnt nothing except that the Master was drinking halves and didn't want his dinner or the crusts cut off his cucumber sandwiches for tea. Above him the sky darkened – it was already dark in the maze – but still Skullion sat there and Purefoy Osbert with him, each keeping a vigil the other would not have understood, they were such worlds apart. He was still there after ten o'clock when the Dean came out of the Combination Room and walked towards the Master's Lodge. He had dined well and had had another talk with the Senior Tutor about Dr Osbert and had assured him without going into any detail at all that he need not worry any longer because the matter was being attended to. Now he wanted a word with Skullion to warn him about not talking to the new Fellow. Skullion didn't seem to hear him coming.

The Dean's footsteps were soft upon the lawn and it was only when he had passed the maze that he became aware of the dark shape behind him and heard the clink of a bottle. 'Good Heavens, Master,' he said. 'What on earth are you doing out here?' It was a silly question. Skullion nearly always sat out at night but usually by the back gate.

'Sitting,' said Skullion, slurring the word more than usual. A whiff of Hardy's Special Ale reached the Dean. 'Sitting and thinking.'

'Sitting and drinking?' said the Dean, choosing to interpret the word differently. It was an unwise remark.

'Sitting and thinking and drinking,' said Skullion and there was no friendliness nor the deference the Dean had come to expect. This was no way for the ex-porter to speak to him.

'Mostly drinking, by the sound of it,' he said.

'Mostly thinking. The drinking is my business, not yours. I'm entitled to it.'

'Of course, Master, of course,' said the Dean hurriedly. He realized he had gone too far. 'You have every right to drink.'

'And think,' said Skullion.

'That too, of course,' said the Dean. 'And what have you been thinking about?'

'About you,' said Skullion. 'About you and the Park. Porterhouse Park where you send all the old Fellows you want to get rid of, the loonies like old Dr Vertel.'

'Dr Vertel? What utter nonsense, Skullion. You know perfectly well – '

'Oh, it's Skullion now, is it?' There was no mistaking the savagery in Skullion's voice. 'And I do know perfectly well. Old Vertel turned dirty, didn't he? Started flashing the bedders and the kiddies over at the Newn-ham swimming pool so he had to go.'

'You're drunk and you don't know what you're saying,' said the Dean angrily.

'I'm drunk and I do know what I'm saying because I was in the Porter's Lodge when the police came and I held them off till you got him out the back into the Senior Tutor's car and down to the Park where they couldn't find him or want to. Under the carpet you said, under the carpet. And the Praelector made a joke and said, "Under the Parket," and you all laughed over your coffee in the Combination Room. So don't tell me I don't know what I'm saying. And don't think you're sweeping me under the carpet because you ain't. And that's a fact.'

In the darkness, and silhouetted against the lighted windows of the Master's Lodge, the Dean felt that strange feeling of alarm he had felt listening to Purefoy Osbert a few nights before. But this time he felt an even greater threat. There was a strength about Skullion and a depth of anger that had been absent in the younger man. The Dean tried appeasement. 'I assure you, Master, that there is no question of your being sent to the Park. The idea hasn't crossed anyone's mind. It's absurd.'

From the wheelchair there came a sound that might have been laughter. 'Bullshit,' said Skullion, 'bullshit. Where've you been the past weeks? Visiting someone sick in Wales? My eye and Betty Martin. Been going round asking the O.P.s, the important ones, who's to be the new Master. And don't tell me you haven't because I know.'

'How do you . . .' The Dean stopped himself but it was too late. The hair on the back of his neck was tingling. Skullion's knowledge was terrifying and somehow the Dean knew there was worse to come.

'How I know is my business,' Skullion went on. He didn't sound in the least drunk now. He was frighteningly sober. 'And what I know is my business and what you'd better know is you aren't sending me to Porterhouse Park not never.' He paused and let the statement sink in. 'Know why?'

The Dean didn't and he didn't want to know. But there was no stopping Skullion now. He was the Master of Porterhouse and for the first time the Dean knew it. He was the lesser man. 'Because I've got you by the short and curlies,' Skullion said. 'Know what that means?'

The Dean thought he did but he said nothing.

'By the balls,' said Skullion. 'By the bloody balls and you want to know how and why?'

'Skullion, you've said enough . . .' the Dean began but Skullion's voice merely rose.

'Don't you Skullion me,' he said. 'It's Master from now on.'

The Dean gasped. Something had happened to Skullion but he had no idea what it was.

'You ask yourself this question,' Skullion said. 'You

ask yourself this question. Who put up six million quid to send the new Fellow here, the one they call Oswald or something? Sir Godber Evans Memorial Fellow. Who did that?'

The Dean seized what he supposed briefly was his opportunity. 'That is exactly what I was coming to talk to you about, Master.'

'Well, you came too late, you did,' Skullion continued. 'That bloody Lady Mary sent him. And why? I'll tell you why. Because she still wants to know who murdered her husband and this fellow's here to nose about.'

He paused. The Dean was stunned. Skullion seemed to know everything. Didn't seem to. Did know. It was a long pause full of horror.

'And I can tell him,' said Skullion. 'And if you try to sweep me under the carpet to Porterhouse Park I will tell him. Want to know why?'

'No, Skullion, no,' the Dean pleaded.

But Skullion was ready with the *coup de grâce*. 'Because I did. I murdered the bastard. So put that in your fucking pipe and smoke it.'

And before the Dean could say another word the Master had pressed the button on his wheelchair and was moving implacably towards the Master's Lodge, leaving a trail of empty beer bottles behind him on the lawn.

*

In the maze Purefoy Osbert had forgotten how cold he was. What he had just heard had stunned him almost as much as it had stunned the Dean, who still stood rooted to the spot. Through the thicket of the yew Purefoy could see part of him outlined against the lights of the Lodge and he still didn't move. In a long lifetime of College intrigue and bitter contest the Dean had never before been outmanoeuvred so completely. Outmanoeuvred was the wrong term. Skullion hadn't been manoeuvring: he had been fighting a battle tooth and claw. And brain. And the Dean had been crushed. Against the power of Skullion's verbal onslaught he had been destroyed, and made to eat humble pie in a way that had never happened to him before. And all this by a man in a wheelchair who was largely paralysed and who had drunk numerous bottles of strong ale and was a mere college servant. The Dean had always thought of him as that. He knew better now. Skullion had spoken no more than the truth. He was indeed the Master of Porterhouse. It was five minutes before the Dean could recover sufficiently to stumble away across the lawn. As he went, he stepped into a damp spot where Skullion had been but he didn't notice. What thoughts he had left, and they were bitter ones, were concentrated on other things.

To Purefoy Osbert the Dean's going came as something of a relief. Only something, because he was freezing cold and so stiff that he had trouble getting to his feet and, when he tried to walk, he staggered. The maze was no place for staggering. It was pitch dark and, while Purefoy could vaguely see the night sky and the lights of Cambridge reflected in the clouds that had gathered, he could see nothing else. He had had enough difficulty getting through the maze to the corner where Skullion sat. Finding his way out proved impossible. Time and time again he thought he was about to succeed because he could see the lights of windows through the peripheral yews, only to find he was back in the corner he had set out from an hour before. Somewhere nearby the clock on the Bull Tower struck midnight. Purefoy tried for the umpteenth time to remember the route he had followed to get in. It had entailed going almost to the very centre of the maze and then turning to the left and then the right and then after some yards going left again – or was it right? Not that it mattered. He had no idea where to start or in which direction to go. Thought failed him entirely. With hands outstretched he crept along banging into the yew thicket up dead ends and having to turn round and try to find some other turning. The clock struck one, and then two, and Purefoy had to sit down and shiver for a while until the cold night air and fear of pneumonia forced him to his feet and another hour of stumbling in the darkness. It was well after three when he finally found his way to the very heart of the maze. At least that was where he thought he was. There was no way of telling. He was up another cul-de-sac of yew. Many times he had thought of trying to fight his way through the hedge itself to get out, but the yew was old and had been planted in staggered rows of three around the edge so that it was impossible to squeeze between the thick trunks.

He even tried climbing, but he had never been anything of an athlete and the cold had sapped what strength he had in his arms. In any case there were no proper branches to grasp. He was in a thicket of yew. He was also in a thicket of fear. He had sat within a few yards of a murderer and heard his confession, if that was what Skullion's revelation had been. It hadn't sounded like a confession to Purefoy Osbert. It had been far too threatening to be called that. And the man had shown no remorse. 'Because I did,' he had said almost with pride and certainly with terrible menace. 'I murdered the bastard. So put that in your pipe and smoke it.' To Purefoy Osbert, whose whole career had been spent finding reasons for crime, and in particular for murder, that shifted the onus of guilt from the criminal onto the police and the judiciary and the law and the prison system, those words had come as a frightening refutation of everything he believed in. The sheer brutality and cold-blooded nature of the words had chilled him almost as much as the night air. They had done more. They had gone to the very centre of his being and unlike the cold of the night their cold would never leave him. He was trapped in a maze of knowing that was at the same time unknowing. His theory about Sir Godber's death had been almost entirely logically right – he had been wrong about the Dean's complicity, but that was all. And he knew, as certainly as he knew he would never get out of the yew maze until dawn brought some light, that he would never be able to prove it. The murderer in the wheelchair was harder than anyone he had ever encountered. He was adamantine. Nothing and no one had it in their power to break his will. Purefoy Osbert had heard that hardness in Skullion's voice and he hadn't required his intellect to tell him the strength of will that was in the mind of the man in the bowler hat. His understanding of it was more primitive than rational thought. It was like hearing death speak.

Now cold and hungry and lost, he was filled with terror too. Everything he had ever heard about Porterhouse had been an underestimation of its awfulness. As dawn began to break and the yew sides of the maze slowly changed from black walls to reveal their dark green leaves, Purefoy Osbert fought down his panic and made his last attempt to find the way out. He listened to the clock on the Bull Tower and tried to position it in his mind. The entrance had been on that side of the maze and he set out towards it. Even so the clock had struck five before he stumbled utterly exhausted onto the lawn and made his way to his rooms and collapsed on the bed. He was no longer capable of thinking. Pure instinct told him he had to get out of Porterhouse before the place destroyed him. Even, perhaps, in the way it had destroyed Sir Godber Evans.

25

Had Edgar Hartang had his dearest wish fulfilled he would have had Kudzuvine murdered. He might have included Schnabel, Feuchtwangler and Bolsover in the massacre for allowing Ross Skundler to get out of the building. Then again, he didn't find their advice to his liking. But he depended on them. They knew too much and Schnabel was laying it on the line.

'It seems they've got a sworn statement out of Karl Kudzuvine that doesn't leave much room for manoeuvre,' Schnabel told him.

'Like what? And who's to believe the bastard?'

'Like everything. And as to who's to believe him, I'd say just about everyone.'

'What he's got is say-so. Circumstantial,' said Hartang.

Schnabel shrugged. 'He's got corroboration from Skundler. From what we've seen from the Porterhouse lawyers, Kudzuvine had the schedule of various consignments and Skundler confirms them with payments.'

Behind the blue glasses Hartang's eyes had narrowed. 'You took a statement from Skundler? You did that?'

'No, no need. He's seen this coming and bought himself some insurance. Like copies of financial movements and transactions locked in a bank deposit. All we've seen are the copies.'

Hartang wiped his face with a handkerchief. 'Comes of helping people,' he said. 'The bastards. The bastards. So what do we do?'

'Depends,' said Schnabel. 'They aren't pressing criminal charges and they could. That's a hopeful sign. I mean you don't want to be standing trial at the Old Bailey or having the DEA investigating Stateside. At least I don't think you do.'

Hartang didn't.

'So they're dealing off the top of the deck,' Schnabel went on. 'They're not interested in your business dealings, they're only after compensation for the damage done.'

'How much?'

'Forty million.'

'Forty million?' squawked Hartang. 'Forty million only? Where'd they get that figure from? Last time I heard, it was twenty.'

'Could be Kudzuvine,' said Schnabel. 'What he's given them. Could be he wants his cut. I don't know. I'm just reporting what their lawyers are saying.'

'Fucking blackmail,' shouted Hartang and knew he had been screwed. To make matters worse, Dos Passos was in London and still out for his blood over the loss of the consignment of Bogota Best. Now Schnabel was telling him he had better settle the Porterhouse claim out of court or face the unpleasant alternative of standing in the dock in the Old Bailey or even of being deported to the United States and standing trial under RICO.

'And I don't mean Puerto Rico,' Schnabel said. 'I heard a rumour that the FBI are interested. And the source is good.'

'How good?'

'Like Lord Tankerell,' Schnabel said. 'You've heard of him, Mr Hartang. Just happens to have been the Attorney General some years back.'

'Him? You call an ex-Attorney fucking General over here a good source? Those shysters can't barely spell their names they're so dumb.'

'Sure. Don't have to spell what Karl K. and Ross Skundler signed their sworn names to,' said Schnabel. 'Just read it out and you'll go down twelve to twenty. Stateside more like ninety-nine and some. They've got a containment unit for RICOs, place called Marian. Real safe down there. No one gets you till the morticians are sent for.'

There was a long silence while Edgar Hartang digested this information and felt sick. 'What's with this Rico?' he asked.

'Racketeering and Incitement to Corruption Act. But you know that, Mr Hartang. Like tiny mesh for big fishes and you don't ever come out.'

Hartang said nothing. He was thinking of a way out.

'Another thing I have to advise. I wouldn't be thinking of taking a powder.'

'Powder? What the fuck you talking about, powder?'

'Like trying to leave the country. There's too much known about another sort of powder. Like the talcum you flew in from Venezuela June fifteenth 1987. Or the load shipped out of Ecuador to Miami November eleventh '89. Like it's all here and no loopholes. So if you are thinking of Learing it some place, don't. Ross Skundler saw that situation coming and he bought himself some more life insurance. Like a miniature video in your bathroom so he knows who he's working for. Bald guy without glasses, uncircumcised, got a mole on his right shoulder, appendix scar, gives himself a hand job with pictures of little boys. You know anyone like that, Mr Hartang? Because if you do, you'd better pay your forty million and be thankful.'

'Forty million? Jesus.' He paused and looked venomously at the lawyer. 'Schnabel, just who are you working for? Me or fucking them?'

Schnabel sighed. It was always like this with mobsters. Consequences had to be spelt out for them when they were in deep shit. 'Mr Hartang,' he said patiently, 'I am working for myself and you have hired me to lay it on the line so you can make a rational choice. If you want me to feed you a weather report says it's going to be sunshine all day and every day for ever and ever and only rain nights, that's fine with me only I lose a valuable client whose doing all the time he's got left and I don't earn my regular fees when he's in trouble again. That is how it is. I just want you to make a rational decision is all. I've given you the information. You make a choice. I cannot do it for you.'

'You have,' said Hartang bitterly. 'Like forty fucking million and you call that a rational choice?'

'Matter of fact, no. I call it a necessity. Like of life.'

'Shit,' said Hartang, with his usual economy.

'And just one more thing, Mr Hartang,' said Schnabel. 'A minor matter but it's down in black and white. You ever been in Damascus, Syria? Khartoum, Sudan? That neck of the woods?'

A grunt from Hartang signified that he could have been.

'Ever had drinks with a guy called Carlos?'

'Of course I've had drinks with hundreds of guys called Carlos. I do business with South America. You think I can avoid having drinks with Carloses?'

'Just enquiring, Mr Hartang. Abu Nidal mean anything to you? Like you bank-rolled one or two of their operations for insurance in the Arab world? You got friends in mighty strange places but I don't think they'll help you in this situation.'

'So what exactly are you trying to tell me, Schnabel? Tell it like it is.'

'Like it is is this,' said Schnabel. 'You pay the forty million plus all costs, you buy yourself immunity in London. Money comes in and no one asks why. Bank of England is happy you're such a big investor in Britain. Chancellor of the Exchequer is in love with you because you pay some taxes and everyone loves you because you're respectable and have helped a Cambridge college out. Even Bolsover loves you, and that's difficult with what you've called him. You pay our fees and we all love you. Right?' He paused for a moment and then went on. 'But you take the talcum route and nobody is going to love you. British Government, the United States Attorney General and the FBI and of course the DEA, the Drug Enforcement Agency, but you knew that, didn't you, Mr Hartang? You've made enemies, and with friends like Carlos and Abu Nidal you could be in worse places than Marian, Illinois. There's some story going the rounds the Israelis have the idea you've been buying insurance with some bad guys, and a bomb explodes in Tel Aviv. With the video Ross Skundler took you can have all the plastic surgery in the world, and that includes a sex-change operation, and they're still going to get you. Mossad, Mr Hartang, Mossad.'

The sweat was pouring down Hartang's face now. He took another pill and Schnabel went on. 'Just a rumour of course and maybe there's no truth in it but if there is, I'd say you're in deeper shit than you know. I don't say it is but rumour has it that way. And if you don't believe me, you take a look out the window at the two cars out there, because one thing is as certain as death itself, those guys aren't Transworld groupies, you better believe me.'

*

By the time he left the building Schnabel felt good. 'He's paying,' he told Feuchtwangler and Bolsover when he got back to the office. 'Through the nose. Those two cars and the private heavies in them were a good idea of yours, Bolsover. I have to hand it to you. Put them down to the bastard's expenses.'

'What's all this about Skundler's video?' asked Feuchtwangler. 'First I heard of it.'

But Schnabel only smiled enigmatically and was thoughtful. 'Let's go some place for coffee,' he said. 'I think our own position needs considering.'

Feuchtwangler and Bolsover nodded. The same thought had crossed their minds. They went out into the street and took a taxi.

'The point we've got to bear in mind is that we are dealing with a man who's lost all sense of reality,' said Schnabel.

'Genius tends to,' said Feuchtwangler. 'And financially, that's what he is. He's got more money than sense and he's lost what little sense he ever possessed. He has become a no-hoper and a loner.'

'Precisely my point. And the investigation of his affairs isn't going to stop with him. He's involving us. All right, we merely represent him legally but the shit about to hit the fan is likely to cover us too. I think we are going to have to start our own negotiations with certain influential authorities ourselves.'

'He'll kill us if he finds out,' said Bolsover.

Schnabel shook his head. 'He isn't going to find out, and he's going to be too scared to think at all clearly.'

'In short we are going to trade. I take it that is your proposition,' said Feuchtwangler.

'We are going to cover ourselves and, if my conversations with Lord Tankerell are anything to go by, and I think they are, the situation can be contained without too much trouble. Which is what I told Hartang just now.'

'You old fox, you've started negotiations already,' Bolsover said.

But Schnabel only smiled enigmatically again.

*

There was hardly a flicker of a smile on the Praelector's face when Mr Retter and Mr Wyve brought him the news. 'Forty million pounds? Are you absolutely sure? It's quite extraordinary. Transworld Television must be coining it.'

'I think you could almost literally put it like that,' said Mr Wyve, 'and Edgar Hartang is, without any qualifications, filthy rich.'

'And to think that it all comes from television programmes about whales and dolphins,' said the Praelector. 'I saw the most interesting programme the other day about bears in Alaska. They wade out into rivers and catch leaping salmon. One would not think a bear had so much quickness of eye and hand. Or should I say paw? Most remarkable. But then so many wonders of nature depend on something approaching brilliance in the most unexpected places. I once read Darwin, and while I found it hard going, I think I learnt what he meant by the survival of the species.'

'That,' said Mr Retter as they walked solemnly but with joy in their hearts across the Fellows' Garden, 'that is a quite remarkable old gentleman. I use the word in its best sense. Did you notice how tactfully he had forgotten everything that madman Kudzuvine had said onto the tape recorder. And he read both affidavits most carefully too and yet he has put all the filth out of his mind. It has been a privilege to have worked with him.'

Mr Wyve agreed most heartily. He had been impressed by the story about the bears catching salmon in the swiftest-flowing rivers. The unspoken comparison had been a nice one. 'I don't think the Praelector and his ilk could possibly come into the category of a species that needs protecting,' he said. 'As you so rightly say, it has been a privilege to watch an old educated mind at work.'

'Until these last few days I would have questioned your use of the word "educated". Now I don't,' Mr Retter agreed.

*

The Praelector was worried. It was of course nice to know that the College had been rescued from bankruptcy but there were still problems ahead. The Bursar was in Fulbourn Mental Hospital, and the Praelector felt strangely sorry for him. After all the Bursar had inadvertently been responsible for the forty million pounds and, while the Praelector couldn't be said to like the man, the Bursar had done his best to keep Porterhouse solvent and would keep it so now that it had adequate funds.

In the afternoon the Praelector sent for a taxi and had himself driven out to the hospital to see the Bursar.

'He has recovered from the effects of whatever drug he had taken but all the same I have my doubts about discharging him quite so soon,' the psychiatric doctor in charge of detoxification told him. 'He is still extremely anxious and suffers quite severe episodes of depression. He seems to have an obsession about the oddest menagerie of animals.'

'Let me guess what they are,' the Praelector said. 'Pigs, turtles, baby octopuses, sharks, and possibly piranhas. Am I by any chance right?'

The doctor looked at him in astonishment. 'How on earth did you know?' he asked.

But the Praelector's discretion prevented him from telling. 'As Bursar I am afraid he has been under the most fearful strain about our finances. Porterhouse, as you must surely know, is not a rich college and the poor chap felt responsible for our problems. But all that is past and thanks to his magnificent efforts we are quite solvent again.'

'But why are his obsessions centred on pigs and turtles and – '

'Simple,' said the Praelector. 'At our annual Founder's Feast we do tend to do ourselves very well and sometimes a little too exotically. I don't know if you realize the cost of genuine turtles these days. And sharks are by no means cheap and of course we always have a wild boar. It was all too much for the Bursar.'

'I'm not in the least surprised,' said the doctor. 'I cannot think of a more breathtakingly indigestible menu. And you really have piranhas too?'

'Only as a savoury at the end of the meal. Served on toast with a slice of lemon they make a very fine digestive. If you'd feel like accepting an invitation one of these days . . .'

But the doctor excused himself and hurried away. The Praelector went into the Bursar's room, where he found him studying an immigration form for New Zealand. 'You're not seriously thinking of leaving us, are you?' he asked. 'At the very moment of your greatest achievement? Besides, they tell me it is an exceedingly dull country.'

'That's why I'm going there,' said the Bursar. 'I'd go somewhere even duller if I could think of it.'

'But my dear Bursar, you can be as dull as ditchwater in College. And besides, it is precisely now that we have forty million pounds from Transworld due to us that we need your expertise.'

'Like a hole in the head,' said the Bursar bitterly. The anti-depressants he was on had slowed his thinking. 'I . . . Did you say forty million pounds?'

The Praelector nodded. 'I did. Mr Hartang has very generously doubled the amount of compensation in return for a promise that there be no publicity. He has for his own good reasons undergone what I believe is known as a change of heart.'

'I don't believe it,' said the Bursar. 'He hasn't got a heart. He's got a beating bank vault. And even if he had, what about that bloody man Kudzuvine? If he is still in the Master's Lodge, there is no way I am coming back to Porterhouse.'

The Praelector smiled benignly at him and patted his shoulder. 'I give you my word of honour that Mr Kudzuvine is no longer with us,' he said. 'He is immersed in – '

'The Bermuda Triangle tubewise. Don't tell me,' squawked the Bursar.

'I was going to say in a totally different occupation and one in which he can exercise his talents to the full and find complete satisfaction.'

'Like he's killing things,' said the Bursar.

But the Praelector was not to be drawn. 'He is engaged in work that is utterly removed from anything he has done previously,' he said. 'You will never see or hear from him again. And no, he is not dead. He is very much alive and, I am told, happy. Now then, I have a taxi waiting . . .'

The Bursar was finally convinced. Something quite astonishing must have happened to the College finances for the Praelector to keep a taxi waiting with the meter running all this time. 'You've really been very good to me,' he said emotionally as they went down the corridor and out into the open air. 'I don't know what I should have done without you.'

'I'm sure you would have done just as well,' said the Praelector, 'but I really don't think you'd have found life in New Zealand to your taste. All that lamb.'

The Bursar agreed. He'd gone off lamb.

26

For the Dean the next few days were as hellish as any
he had known. He sat in his room trying to come to
terms with Skullion's threat. Everything he had ever
believed in had been put in jeopardy by that confession.
He was confronted by a disgustingly brutal world in
which the traditional virtues he held dear had been
swept aside. Duty, deference, honour and justice had all
gone. Or were in conflict with one another. 'It is my
duty to inform the police,' he said to himself, only to
hear another part of his mind tell him not to be such a
fool. 'After all, the fact that Skullion told you he killed
Sir Godber is no proof that he did. He has only to deny
it and then where would you be?' The Dean could find
no answer to the question. Then again there was the
honour of the College to take into account. Even an
unsubstantiated accusation would create a scandal and
Porterhouse had had too many scandals in recent years
to withstand another. A fresh crisis would only provide
an excuse for those who wanted to change the whole
character of the College, and the Dean and the Senior
Tutor would be ousted by the likes of Dr Buscott and
brash young Fellows. The Prime Minister would appoint
a new Master and Porterhouse would become nothing

more than an academic forcing-house like Selwyn or Fitzwilliam. The Dean put his duty to one side and with it went his belief in justice.

There were other consequences. All his life the Dean had seen Skullion as a servant, a social inferior whose deference was living proof that the old order had not fundamentally been changed. Skullion had destroyed that comforting illusion. 'Don't you Skullion me,' he had said. 'It's Master from now on.' With that command, and there could be no other term for it, the Dean's world had been turned upside down. Coming so shortly after his encounter with the drunken Jeremy Pimpole living in squalor in the gamekeeper's cottage, Skullion's assertion of his own authority had shattered the Dean's dream of society. Little islands of the old order, where deference was due, undoubtedly remained but the tide of egalitarian vulgarity was rising and in time would swamp them all. The Dean had seen that barbarism in action at the motorway service areas and had been appalled. To encounter it in Porterhouse was more than he could bear. To add to his sense of disillusionment there was also the knowledge that he had been wrong about Sir Godber's death and Lady Mary had been right. Her husband had been murdered. And to compound that awful realization, the Dean had misunderstood the meaning of the dying man's last words and had interpreted them to make his murderer the Master of Porterhouse. There was a horrible irony about that error but the Dean was in no mood to appreciate it. Instead he kept to his rooms and thought the darkest thoughts, dined silently in Hall and took long melancholy walks to Grantchester debating what on earth to do.

It was on one of these walks that he encountered the Praelector. He too seemed preoccupied. 'Ah, Dean, I see you too have taken to doing the Grantchester Grind,' the old man said.

The Dean did his best to smile. 'I take my constitutional,' he said. 'I find it helps my rheumatism to get some exercise.'

'That too,' the Praelector agreed. 'Though in my case I come to try to clarify my thoughts about the state of the College. It is not good.'

'In what respect?' enquired the Dean cautiously.

'I do not know precisely. Though in the Bursar's absence I have had occasion to examine the accounts and our expenses and I have to say they are as bad as the poor man has always maintained. Even to my untrained eye the situation looks desperate. I fear we are facing bankruptcy.'

'Bankruptcy? But the College can't go bankrupt. Such things don't happen. We are not some sort of business company or any individual. Porterhouse is an institution, one of the oldest in Cambridge. They won't allow us to go bankrupt.'

'They, Dean, they? May I enquire who this, or more precisely, these ubiquitous "They" might be?' The Praelector paused to allow the Dean to pass through a kissing gate first.

The Dean went through and stopped. He had never before had to face such a direct question about the nature of society. To his mind, a mind as drilled in deference as Skullion's, 'They' were anonymous and all-powerful and at the very heart of Britain, an unperceived amalgam of, to use one of his clichés, the Great and the Good who ran the City and Whitehall and gathered together at the Athenaeum and the Carlton and the better clubs and in the House of Lords and were united in allegiance to the Crown. To be asked who 'They' were was to put in question the very existence of authority itself and render nebulous unspoken certainties. 'I cannot answer that,' he said finally and stared out across the meadows to a pollarded willow on the river bank.

The Praelector made his way through the gate and stepped aside to let a jogging undergraduate go by. 'The powers that be,' he said, 'are no longer on our side. They have been supplanted by purely mercenary men who have no social interest. My lifetime has encompassed our decline. A sad, dispiriting epoch and one that leaves us wholly at the mercy of the market. We've fought two wars and won a hollow victory at the cost of millions dead and all our independence lost. Sparta and Athens went that way and Greece's greatness perished. Like them we have nothing to sell but ourselves.'

'I do not follow you,' said the Dean. 'How can we sell ourselves? I have nothing to offer a buyer. I am an old man and everything I hold dear is in the College.'

'I was speaking in more general terms. Personally I daresay we are all provided for by pensions and small private means. I have in mind the College. It is ourselves collectively.'

'But that is out of the question,' said the Dean. 'The College cannot be put up for sale. We are not some marketable commodity.'

The Praelector poked a molehill with his walking stick. 'I shouldn't be too sure of that. In the present climate of opinion it would be a brave man who would predict what was a commodity that might be up for sale. Who would have thought a few years ago that water would be sold to private companies, some of them foreign at that, and that each English family would have to pay for a necessity of life and put a profit in the hands of individual shareholders? And water is a monopoly as well. We cannot pick and choose which tap to use. And if water, why not air?'

'But that's absurd,' said the Dean. 'Air is for everyone to breathe. It's everywhere. It needs no pipes or reservoirs, no pumping stations or filtration plants as water does.'

'Can you be sure? I can't,' said the Praelector. 'There's talk of air pollution all the time. The fumes from car exhausts and factory chimneys and even the boilers for domestic central heating. A perfectly valid case could be made out for processing the air and making it fit for human consumption. The men who think only of money could make out that case. "Clean air," they'd say. And what needs cleaning costs money and must be paid for. And where there's money to be paid there must accordingly be profit to be made. One has to have material incentive if market forces are to work. That is the principle our masters in the "powers that be" apply. They recognize no other.'

'It is an obnoxious one,' said the Dean heatedly. 'I fail to see how it can be applied so generally. Some things cannot be quantified in terms of money.'

'Name me one,' said the Praelector.

The Dean stood still and tried to think of something beyond price. 'A man's life,' he said. 'I defy you to calculate a human life in monetary terms. It can't be done.'

'It can and is,' replied the Praelector and pointed his stick at a distant concrete tower. 'Addenbrooke's Hospital, the new one over there. Go there and ask the doctors in the geriatric wards or in intensive care what determines when they turn a life-support machine off or why some patients are deemed not to warrant certain complicated operations? Or better still, ask them why foreign patients who can pay vast sums for liver transplants are given preferential treatment over English ones who've paid their taxes all their lives into the National Health Service. They'll tell you why, those doctors will. Because the Treasury uses all those NHS payments for other things like roads and civil servants' salaries. It goes into the general fund and only a portion goes to nursing British patients. So now the surgeons charge rich foreigners to raise the funds they need to operate on us.'

They walked in silence for a while and the Dean's thoughts grew darker still. The old man's arguments had served to reinforce his own conviction that something had to be done about Skullion. If the Praelector could face the grim realities of life without recourse to comforting pretence, the Dean felt he ought to take up the challenge himself and say what was preying on his mind. And if the College finances were in such a terrible way, and for the first time he did not doubt it, the question of the Master became more urgent still. 'I wonder if you would come down to the river with me,' he said when they reached the last gate. 'It is more private there and what I have to say must be said in absolute confidence.'

They turned off the path and made their way down to the river bank. There, standing by the water and the waving weeds swept by the river's flow, the Dean told the story of Skullion's confession and his threat to make it public. The Praelector stared at the water weeds for some time before he spoke.

'It fits,' he said at last, 'it fits the facts. I can't say I'm entirely surprised. There is a streak of violence in us all and Godber Evans had sacked Skullion who had more violence in him than most of us. Still has it, by the sound of things. You say he threatened you?'

The Dean nodded. 'Skullion was drunk. He said he had us by the short and curlies and by the balls, the bloody balls he said, and when I asked him why or what he meant he said he knew that Lady Mary had sent this Dr Osbert to find out who had murdered her husband. God knows how he finds out these things.'

'Because he's clung to his authority,' the Praelector said. 'In his own mind he is still Head Porter. All the servants know that too. They tell him everything they hear. The Chef, the waiters, the gyps and bedders doing our rooms. They don't miss much, and what they don't tell Skullion he deduces for himself. What words exactly did he use about Dr Osbert? Can you remember them?'

The Dean searched back to that bad night. 'He asked a question,' he said. 'I remember that. Something to this effect, "Who put up six million pounds to send the new Sir Godber Evans Memorial Fellow here?" That's what he said and when I said I did not know he said, "That bloody Lady Mary did because she wanted to know who'd murdered her husband and this Fellow is here to nose about." Yes, that was what he said. In just those words. "To nose about."'

'And then?'

'Then he said he could tell him,' the Dean went on. '"Because I did. And if you try to sweep me under the carpet to the Park, I'll tell him. Because I murdered the bastard." He told me to put that in my pipe and smoke it.'

The Praelector sighed a long sigh. 'He said to sweep him under the carpet, did he? He's got a long memory, has Skullion. I made a joke once along those lines.'

'And he remembered it,' said the Dean. 'He said you'd called it under the Parket.'

'And that's the truth,' the Praelector said and whacked a tuft of grass with his stick. 'That was when Vertel had to go away before the police arrived.' He paused for a moment. 'So Master Skullion has us by the short and curlies, has he? I think not.'

He turned and led the way up to the tarmac path and the Dean followed. He was relieved to have confided in the Praelector. There was a strength in the older man he knew he'd somehow lost himself, a strength of purpose and a terrible clarity of thought. And this time the Praelector led the way through all the gates.

They neither of them spoke for a long while and it was only when they had crossed Laundress Green and reached the Mill that the Praelector turned aside. 'You have told no one else, not even the Senior Tutor?' he asked.

'No one, Praelector, not a soul.'

'Good. And now we'll go separate ways into the College. We don't want to be seen together going in. I'll speak to you later. Things cannot rest like this.' And with what appeared to the Dean to be surprising energy, the Praelector strode off down the lane towards Silver Street.

For a moment the Dean lingered by the Mill looking at the water churning over the weir and under the bridge beneath him, remembering nostalgically the time a South African undergraduate had swum the Mill Pond in midwinter for a five-pound bet. That had been in 1950, and the young man's name had been Pendray. A Cat's man, the Dean seemed to recall, and wondered what had become of him. He looked up in time to see the Praelector disappear down the public lavatory on the far side, which explained his sudden hurry. With a fresh sense of disillusionment the Dean turned away and went the other way down Little St Mary's Passage. He would have a cup of tea in the Copper Kettle before going back to Porterhouse. There, sitting unhappily, he understood now why in earlier times the Praelector had been known as the 'Father of the College'. The term 'Grantchester Grind' had taken on a new meaning for him too.

*

At Kloone University Purefoy Osbert finished his day of Continuous Assessment, the monthly process of reading his students' essays, appending a short commentary to each of them and giving them grades. He had driven up from Cambridge with the satisfying feeling that he had something to tell Mrs Ndhlovo that would surely convince her he was a proper man. It had taken him some days to get over his cold and the fear he had experienced in the maze but during that time his view of himself had changed. He had come to Porterhouse to find out who had murdered Sir Godber Evans and in the space of a few weeks he had succeeded where lawyers and trained private detectives, who had spent months and even years, had failed. He had recorded the time and place, the Dean's presence and the circumstances surrounding the event most carefully and had even gone to the expense of hiring a safety deposit box in Benet Street in which to keep these documents. On the other hand he had rejected his first impulse to go down to London to tell Goodenough and his cousin Vera, on the grounds that they would either consider his findings inconclusive or take immediate and, in his opinion, precipitate action. He needed time to think things over, and besides his own theories about the causes of crime and the role of the police and law as being responsible for criminal behaviour had been thrown in doubt. Worse still, for the first time in his life Purefoy had, if not met a murderer face to face, seen his shape and heard the violence in his voice. There'd been no reasoned argument, no plausible excuse or even explanation for his action, only the threat to tell Purefoy that he had murdered Sir Godber if the Dean and Fellows tried to send him to Porterhouse Park. Purefoy Osbert had never heard of Porterhouse Park before. Now he knew it was where old Fellows went when they became a nuisance or got in trouble with the police. That much he had learnt. But basically the mystery of Skullion's motive remained unsolved. There was a lot of groundwork still to do before he could submit convincing findings to Lady Mary and to Goodenough and Lapline.

The more he thought about the problem the more he found fresh snags. He had disclosed his reasons for being the Sir Godber Evans Memorial Fellow to the Dean and to the other Fellows in the Combination Room and they would be on their guard. Purefoy cursed himself for his drunken indiscretion. It meant that every question that he asked would meet with silence or a deliberately misleading answer. In short, he had learnt what he had come to learn, but could do nothing with it. There was another reason for not knowing what to do, and one that weighed upon him all the time. Skullion was old and crippled, a tragic figure in his wheelchair and his ancient bowler hat, and to expose him now would do no good to anyone. Only Lady Mary's sense of vengeance would be satisfied and Purefoy had come to feel no sympathy for her. The murderer would never kill again and, even if the case against him could be proved, what good would prison do? Not that, in Purefoy's informed opinion, prisons did any good to anyone. They were the symptoms of society's failure and infected what they were supposed to cure. Skullion was already punished and imprisoned by his immobility. With so many conflicting thoughts colliding in his mind Purefoy Osbert sought escape by concentrating on his love for Mrs Ndhlovo. He would explain it all to her and, being a woman who had seen so much of life, she would be bound to know exactly what to do.

Having finished his marking and made arrangements to meet all fourteen students the following day for lunch in the University Canteen to discuss any problems they might be having with their reading list, he went off rather more cheerfully to visit Mrs Ndhlovo. On his way he bought some red roses. Mrs Ndhlovo's flat was on the first floor of a large Edwardian house. Purefoy climbed the stairs and was about to knock on the door when it was opened and he found himself looking at a woman who resembled Mrs Ndhlovo, but wasn't, and who didn't seem surprised to see him. She was dark-haired, wore glasses and was dressed rather formally in a skirt and a high-necked sweater. 'Oh my God, it's you,' she said. 'I might have guessed it. You don't give up do you?'

With a feeling that something was very wrong, though for the life of him he couldn't think what except that he had somehow come to the wrong house and that the woman must suppose he was a rent collector, or someone who looked like him and who had been making a nuisance of himself or even sexually harassing her, Purefoy stammered his apologies. 'I'm terribly sorry,' he said. 'I was looking for a Mrs Ndhlovo.'

'Mrs Ndhlovo doesn't live here any more,' said the woman.

'I see,' said Purefoy. 'Do you happen to know her new address?'

'You want to know Mrs Ndhlovo's new address? Is that what you're asking?' said the woman with what

Purefoy could only consider rather gratuitous repetition and an almost sinister emphasis. He had a feeling too that her voice had changed.

'Yes, that is what I'm asking for,' he said staring at her blue eyes behind the thick lenses of her glasses. 'I'm an old friend of hers from the University.'

'So,' said the woman, and looked him up and down rather rudely. 'How old?'

'How old?' said Purefoy, feeling even more peculiar. The woman's accent had changed with that 'so'. It sounded middle-European. 'Oh, you mean how long have I known her? Well, actually I've known her – '

'Not vot I meant,' said the woman. 'I vant your age.'

Purefoy stared at her. Something was terribly wrong now. Her accent changed from relatively normal if upper-class English to something he had only heard before in movies featuring KGB interrogators. He glanced past her into the room. Mrs Ndhlovo's clothes were scattered on the sofa and an empty suitcase was lying open on the floor. 'Now look here – ' he began, but the woman interrupted him.

'Mrs Ndhlovo has disappeared,' she said. 'Do you know where she has gone?'

'Of course I don't,' said Purefoy. 'I wouldn't be here if I did, would I?' Again the feeling hit him that whatever was going on made no sense. The woman's accent had changed once more. It was distinctly English.

'But you could identify her body?'

'Body?' said Purefoy, horribly alarmed. Within a very

315

few minutes he had been assailed by the conviction that he had come to the wrong address, had met a total stranger who seemed to have been expecting him and who had then changed from talking normal English to something guttural and who had now switched back to English with a question that implied Mrs Ndhlovo was dead and if she hadn't entirely disappeared was in such a mutilated state that it required an old acquaintance to identify her. 'Body? You don't mean . . .'

'How often vere you intimate viz ze voman? You vere her loffer, ja?'

'Jesus,' said Purefoy, and clutched the side of the doorway for support. The beastly woman's changing accents, not to mention the appalling implications of her questions, had him reeling. And now she had taken him by the arm and was dragging him into the room. Purefoy Osbert clung to the doorway. 'Look,' he squawked. 'I don't know what you're talking about. I haven't a clue –'

'Ah, that was what I was waiting for. Clue,' said the woman. 'We rely on these little mistakes in cases of this sort, Dr Osbert. You said "Clue."'

Purefoy Osbert's hand left the doorway partly as a result of the woman dragging him but far more because she had just called him Dr Osbert, and had added to his sense of utter horror by speaking about cases of this kind and clues. He staggered into the room and leaned against the wall. The woman locked the door and pocketed the key, then, with a distinctly sinister movement which involved keeping her eyes on him, sidled across the room to the bedroom door and shut that too.

'Sit down,' she said. Purefoy remained standing and tried to marshal some reasonable thoughts. They didn't come easily. In fact they didn't come at all. 'I don't,' he tried to say, only to find that his voice wasn't responding properly. It sounded extraordinarily high-pitched and tiny. He tried again. 'How do you know my name? And what's going on? And why are Mrs Ndhlovo's clothes all over the place?'

'I said sit down,' said the woman. She pulled a chair from Mrs Ndhlovo's desk, turned it round so that its back faced Purefoy, then straddled it, showing a good deal of leg in the process. Purefoy Osbert crept away from the wall and sat on the arm of the sofa.

'Right. Now then, Dr Osbert, I want you to start at the beginning and tell me in your own words how you first became acquainted with Mrs Ndhlovo.'

From the arm of the sofa Purefoy eyed her and tried desperately to think. It was almost clear to him that he was either in the presence of some sort of plain-clothes police person or, since she was apparently alone and had multiple accents, most of them foreign, a member of a secret intelligence service. Either way she was alarming. 'How do you know my name?' he asked in an attempt to get some bearings.

'You will answer my questions,' she said. 'I am not

here to answer yours. If you are not prepared to co-operate with me, I will have to call my assistants.' She glanced significantly at the door into the bedroom.

Purefoy shook his head. The woman was bad enough without any assistance. He looked miserably round the room at all the familiar African ornaments and knick-knacks Mrs Ndhlovo had decorated it with, but they gave him as little comfort as her clothes and the empty suitcase. 'I just met her at the University,' he said. 'In the Common Room or the Canteen. Somewhere like that.'

The woman reached across the desk for a notebook and opened it. 'We have reason to believe that is not the truth,' she said. 'You attended her evening class on Male Infertility and Masturbatory Techniques in Room Five in the Scargill Block. The excuse you gave at a later date was that you mistook it for a lecture on Prison Reform in Sierra Leone.'

Purefoy Osbert swallowed drily. This was infinitely more awful. The woman shut the book and put it back on the desk. 'That is what happened,' he admitted. 'It was a genuine mistake.'

'The following week you returned. Would you please explain why?'

Purefoy looked round the room again and tried to think of a suitable answer. 'I just – ' he began and stopped.

'You just what? You just wanted to learn how to masturbate?'

'No, of course not,' said Purefoy angrily. 'This is insufferable.'

'Insufferable? How you mean insufferable?' said the woman, lapsing into middle- or eastern-European English again. 'Like you don't suffer from von Klubhausen's Syndrome mit der hairy hands?'

'Jesus,' said Purefoy, breaking out into a cold sweat and beginning to think, in so far as he was able to think at all, that he was going mad. The next question convinced him.

'Tell me, Dr Osbert, tell me about your interest in clitoral circumcision. Have you ever had any experience of it personally?'

'What?' Purefoy shouted, and for a moment it looked as though the woman hesitated herself. 'What did you say?'

'You heard me,' she snarled. 'Answer the question.'

'Personally?' yelled Purefoy. 'How the fuck can I have had any personal experience of female circumcision? I haven't got a bloody clitoris for God's sake.'

'Yes, zere is zat,' the woman admitted switching to Lubianka 1948. 'Afterwards, of course not, but before . . .'

'Afterwards? Before?' yelled Purefoy. 'Any time I couldn't have a clitoris. I'm not a woman.'

'You think not?' said the woman doubtfully. 'To go to evening classes on Clitoral Stimulation and Female Circumcision and you're not a woman? We can see about that at a different stage of the investigation.'

Purefoy was about to say she could see about it now, but he thought better of it.

'So,' said the woman, 'when did you last see Mrs Ndhlovo alive?'

Purefoy Osbert felt sick. The significance of that 'alive' had not been lost on him. 'You mean she's dead?' he stammered.

The woman stood up. 'You should know, Dr Osbert, in what condition she was when you last saw her. Was she alive, Dr Osbert? Or was she already . . . All right, I will rephrase the question.' She stopped and said nothing for half a minute. It seemed longer to Purefoy. Like half an hour. 'Well?' she snapped at him suddenly. 'What is your answer to that?'

Purefoy blinked. 'To what?' he asked shakily. 'You said you were going to rephrase the question.'

'Rephrase the question, Dr Osbert? Why should I do that?' Purefoy's fingers tightened on the back of the sofa. It was the nearest he could get to keeping a grip on reality. Whatever he was involved in didn't begin to have anything real about it. To make matters worse, he thought he could hear someone sobbing at the back of the flat. 'I don't know why you said you were going to rephrase the question,' he said. 'How could I know? I didn't even know what question you were talking about.'

'Very clever,' said the woman. 'Your evasive technique is psychologically interesting. You have evidently prepared yourself for just this sort of interrogation. And the flowers are not without significance. You brought them as an indication that you did not know what had happened. Is that it?'

'I didn't. I brought them for Mrs – '

'Not true,' snarled the woman, her pale eyes glinting behind the spectacles. 'Not true. It is time you were brought face to face with the facts.' She got off the chair and moved towards the door into the bedroom, and for a moment Purefoy's hopes rose.

At the door the woman paused and looked back at him. 'It is not nice vot you vill see,' she said thickly. 'Three veeks viz ze central heating turned up high and ze refrigerator door open iz not nice. But then you will know about deliquescence, the liquefaction that takes place when . . .'

Purefoy had gone ashen and he was sweating profusely. 'For God's sake, get it over with,' he squeaked. The sound of sobbing was clearly audible now. The woman opened the door with a flourish and pushed Purefoy Osbert into the room. Mrs Ndhlovo was lying on the bed with a handkerchief pushed into her mouth, and she was red in the face with tears running down her cheeks and with her knees doubled up in a spasm. For a moment Purefoy gaped at her and a surge of relief swept over him. It was a brief moment. There was absolutely nothing the matter with her. It was simply that she was howling with laughter.

With a final spasm she rolled off the bed and took the handkerchief out of her mouth. 'Oh Purefoy,' she said weakly, 'you were delicious.'

But Purefoy Osbert hardly heard her. The other woman was doubled up with laughter too. In blind fury he pushed past her and out of the flat and was presently striding angrily down the street. He had had Mrs Ndhlovo and Kloone University and the whole damned lot. They could stuff themselves for all he cared. Without even bothering to collect his papers from the University he made for the car park and began the long drive back to Cambridge. And as he drove he composed in his mind a letter that would say exactly how he now felt about Mrs Bloody Ndhlovo.

*

Behind him in the apartment the woman he had thought of as Mrs Ndhlovo, and who had insisted on being called by that name, looked up from the red roses still lying on the floor and said sadly to her sister, 'We seem to have gone too far this time. Poor Purefoy. I suppose he's never going to forgive me. And you have to admit that he did face the facts terribly well.'

'If he's really in love with you, he'll get over it,' said her sister. 'And he has to have a sense of humour somewhere or he wouldn't be worth marrying anyway.'

'It's not going to be easy to explain,' Ingrid said. 'Oh dear. How the past comes back to haunt us.'

27

Getting hold of a black woman who was prepared to do what General Sir Cathcart D'Eath wanted done to Purefoy Osbert was proving harder than he had expected. His contacts in the SAS had not been able to help him at all. 'Financial cuts,' he was told. 'Half our chaps are on secondment somewhere or helping the Americans out. We're practically becoming a self-financing service. Bloody diabolical state of affairs. Sorry not to be of any use but there it is. Recruitment is down to nearly zero.' As a result the Zulu woman had been made redundant and had gone back to South Africa to stiffen up the new Defence Force there, and none of the General's chums in London was able to suggest an alternative. In the end he was forced to make do with a hefty white woman from Thetford whom one of his stable boys recommended as being hot stuff and not particular.

The General, inspecting her across the bar of the pub in which she worked, could see what he meant. She was an elderly peroxide blonde well past her sell-by date whose best days had been in the Sixties and Seventies when the American airbases had been at their busiest and she'd had ever so much fun with the boys at

Mildenhall and Alconbury and all, know what I mean?
The General thought he did, and arranged for her to
come to the safe house opposite the Botanical Gardens
he kept for his own peculiar practices. Surrounded by
offices and occupied on the ground floor during the day
by a firm of architects, it was virtually indistinguishable
from all the other buildings in the street and had the
added advantage of being approachable through a garage
in a lane at the back. Here in a pink and padded bedroom
the General discussed the choice of costume and the
scenario he had in mind for her. 'He's quite a young
man,' he said, conscious that he wasn't sure how old Dr
Osbert was.

Myrtle Ransby said she liked young men too. She also
liked older men. 'More experienced like, know what I
mean?'

The General preferred not to. His diverse tastes did
not run to anyone quite as ripe as Myrtle. He preferred
to concentrate on Purefoy Osbert's supposed preferences. In the next room behind the mirror Sir Cathcart's
attractive secretary had already sited the video camera
and arranged the sound. 'The thing is,' he continued,
'he's spent a long time in Africa, in fact he is South
African and he is both attracted to and terrified of black
women. The point of this therapy is to prove to him
that colour is completely irrelevant . . .'

'It isn't,' said Myrtle, but the look in the General's
eyes silenced her.

'In other words we are all exactly the same under the

skin which is why you are to wear this . . . er, confection.' Sir Cathcart indicated a black latex costume on a chair. 'It will lessen the need for you to black up and help to contain your charms which, you must admit, you do have in abundance.'

'Ooh, you are awful, General, you are and all,' said Myrtle Ransby.

Sir Cathcart confined himself to dubious compliments. Awful was not the way he would have described Myrtle Ransby. Time and the ravages of long tempestuous nights and alcohol had told on her. She was infinitely worse than awful. Her hairstyle was particularly affecting.

'I don't see how you're going to get me into the rubber hood and it still look natural,' she said. 'I mean it's going to spoil my en bouffant, know what I mean?'

'There is that,' said the General, beginning to wonder if he would ever feel quite the same about black latex. Certainly the suit would never fit the smaller women he preferred, and there was no doubt in his mind that Dr Osbert would find his sexual perspectives fundamentally altered. Then again, naked and white, Myrtle might well send him clean off his trolley.

Behind the screen he had insisted she use to change, Myrtle was struggling. 'It's ever so difficult to get into,' she called out. 'You sure this wasn't made for a much smaller girl? I mean I've got my proportions and all.'

'You have indeed, my dear,' said Sir Cathcart, 'and very lovely they are too.'

Ten minutes later Myrtle appeared round the screen and fulfilled his worst expectations. Wrinkled pink skin was apparent through the slits where her nipples were supposed to be. They were evidently squashed up over her shoulders. 'It's because I had to pull it up from below,' she explained breathlessly. 'They're all squeezed up. Now if you was to put your finger through and sort of hook it round you could pull them down so that they poked out proper.'

The General gritted his teeth and did what she suggested. It wasn't pleasant, and Myrtle made it no easier by pressing herself urgently against him and murmuring what a lovely man he was. But in the end her enormous teats bulged through the slits and behind them her breasts assumed a more orthodox if knobbly appearance. The only trouble was that the nipples were not black ones.

'We'll just have to dye them,' said the General. 'Can't see any other way round it.'

'You can't dye my eyes, dearie. What are you going to do about them?'

The General considered the problem for a moment. 'The best thing would be if you didn't look at him too closely. The hood will help and we'll keep the lights down low. Besides, I daresay his attention will be focused on other parts of you which will be much nearer to him.'

Myrtle giggled. 'Ooh, fancy that,' she said. 'You want me to give him the old cough medicine, do you?'

'Cough medicine? I don't quite follow.'

'The cunning linctus, you know. Some fellatios like it, know what I mean?'

'Yes, yes, absolutely,' said Sir Cathcart with a shudder, 'though I can assure you that it's not my cup of tea.'

'Ooh, you are awful, General. Fancy thinking of that too. Do you think he'd like a nice – '

'I'm sure he'd find it delightful, but I think we'll give it a miss all the same. Now then the game plan is this – '

'I've got to go wee-wee,' said Myrtle. 'This costume is ever so tight and my – '

'Quite,' said the General loudly, and wondered how long she was going to take. If she had to get out of the costume, she'd be gone for hours.

In fact she was back almost at once. 'Ever so handy having that hole down there,' she said, 'though if you ask me it could do with a bit of widening if he's to get the full benefit of the old oral, know what I mean?'

'I'm sure you'll manage somehow,' said Sir Cathcart, beginning to feel rather squeamish himself. 'Now, as I was saying, he's got this ambivalent attitude towards women and in particular – '

'Oh dear, he's one of those is he?' Myrtle interrupted. 'So many of them are these days, aren't they? I don't know what the world's coming to. I said to my hubby only the other day – '

'I daresay you did, but let's get this over with,' said

the General irritably. 'The point I am trying to make is he's heavily into bondage and he may struggle a bit when he first sees you come in. Not that there'll be trouble. My man will be there to help.'

'Ooh, it's couples, is it? I didn't know it was going to be couples. Still, makes a change, I always say.'

'I'm sure you do. But as a matter of fact it's only one couple. You and this young man. Now once you've got him starkers you may find he's got an arousal problem. In fact seeing you dressed up like that he's almost certain to – '

'That's not a very nice thing to tell a girl, I must say,' said Myrtle. 'I may not be as young as I once was but – '

'Not that,' the General said hurriedly. 'Because he'll think you're black. I've told you he's a South African and he's got a problem about women who are black. Which of course is why we're going to all this trouble for the poor fellow. And that, Myrtle dear, is why you're just the right person for him, the mature and beautiful woman with experience who can alter his sexual outlook quite dramatically.'

Myrtle Ransby preened herself. 'That's different of course. I always did want to be an actress,' she said. 'You know, like Barbara Windsor. Ever so sophisticay.'

Sir Cathcart glanced once again at her curious proportions and doubted the comparison. Hattie Jacques. With bits of her into anorexia nervosa.

'Well, now is your opportunity. At first you will

pleasure him as a black woman and of course he may struggle a bit as a result of his phobic reaction. But then you will slowly reveal yourself in all your radiant beauty as the lovely white woman you are.'

'You mean I've got a chance to do a bit of the old striptease? Ooh, I do like that. You undress ever so slowly like, and do a bit of a dance in between.' She stopped and looked puzzled. 'Will he have a gag in his mouth? Bondage freaks usually do.'

'Of course,' said the General. 'I should have mentioned that before. Why, what's the problem?'

'Well, I don't see how he's going to give me the old cough medicine with a gag in his mouth.'

'That is a bit of a problem, come to think of it, but I'm sure you'll find a way round it somehow. You know, improvise. After all he's got a nose and things. That's when you are a black woman. When you've revealed yourself as a white one, you can dispense with the gag. He's bound to give you all the pleasure he can in that area then. And one other thing. You'll be wearing this little earpiece under the hood. It's got a tiny radio in it and I'll tell you what I want you to do and things like that. They use them all the time on film sets and TV, you know. Well, I think that's about all. You can get out of the latex togs and back into those lamé trousers of yours. Very fetching, I must say.'

Myrtle Ransby disappeared behind the screen and took a great deal longer getting out of the costume than she had getting in. But at least Sir Cathcart didn't have to use his finger again. Instead he gave some thought to the need for discretion. Not being acquainted with Dr Osbert he couldn't be at all sure how he would feel about being tied to a bed in a strange house and subjected to the sexual favours Myrtle was going to offer him so fulsomely. In the long run, when he had seen the video, it would be different, but all the same it was best to be on the safe side. 'By the way, I think you had better have a stage name,' he said. 'I mean, if he knew your real name was Myrtle Ransby, he might start making a pest of himself by falling in love and all that sort of thing.'

There was a giggle behind the screen. 'Ooh, you are silly, Sir Cathcart. You don't think my real name is Myrtle Ransby, do you? Course it isn't. Like the Yanks used to say, I only use it for special assignments. My hubby wouldn't like it if I went around saying who I really am. He's got a very good job with British Telecom.'

'Oh well, that's all right,' said the General. 'And how many children did you say you had?'

'Didn't say any,' said Myrtle, still involved in a battle with the costume. 'Though actually it's nine not counting the miscarriages.'

'Ah,' said Sir Cathcart who had suspected she was the mother of a very large family. All the same, there was something still troubling him. If she was shrewd enough to use a false name for special assignments and had nine children to cater for plus a husband in British Telecom, she was also shrewd enough to have found out who he was. It suddenly dawned on him that she had been calling him 'General' and 'Sir Cathcart.' With the thought that the wretched woman was in a position to blackmail him, the General decided to take precautions.

'If you don't mind, my dear,' he said when she reappeared in her gold lamé trousers, crimson see-through top and leopardskin coat, 'I just want to check up on a partner of mine. We've got a little enterprise going and I'd like you to make his acquaintance. He's an interesting fellow with rather special expertise and I'm sure he'd like to see you looking so lovely.'

They went out to the garage at the back and drove out to Coft Castle.

'Ooh, ever so posh,' said Myrtle appreciatively. Sir Cathcart drove past the sign to Cathcart's Catfood Canning Factory and they got out.

'In here, my dear,' said the General and ushered Myrtle into the abattoir where Kudzuvine was skinning an ancient stallion which he had only recently dispatched.

'Kentucky Fry, I want you to meet Miss Myrtle . . .' the General began, but the message of the horrible scene and of Kudzuvine's bloodstained knife and hands had not been lost on Myrtle Ransby. 'You needn't worry about me, Bishop,' she whimpered when she had been helped out of the shed. 'I ain't going to say nothing to nobody. Swear to God I won't.'

Sir Cathcart beamed at her. 'Of course you won't, my dear,' he said. 'And no doubt you'd like to be paid in advance.'

Myrtle brightened slightly. This was the sort of gentleman she appreciated.

'Half now and half afterwards suit you?'

'Oh yes. Ever so generous of you,' she said and was surprised when the General took out a bundle of large-denomination notes and tore them in half.

'You need have no fear. The banks accept torn notes with no trouble at all. You simply tape them together,' he explained and gave one half to her.

'Yes, Bishop, anything you say. And I ain't going to say a word to anyone.'

'Then I'll call you when our young friend is ready,' said the General. Myrtle Ransby got into the car and was driven away.

*

Sir Cathcart's next move was to consult his secretary, a blonde from Las Vegas who was just crazy about generals and horses and not being anywhere near certain guys in Nevada. 'Now, my dear,' he said, 'what have you been able to find out about Dr Osbert? Did you phone the Porter's Lodge like I told you?'

'Gee, General, the guys there say he's a loner and a weirdo. You know what he's into? You're not going to believe this.'

'Tell me, my dear,' said Sir Cathcart, helping himself to a large Scotch to rid himself of the memory of Myrtle Ransby bulging in black latex. The gold lamé and the leopardskin hadn't been too pleasant either. 'What is he into?'

'Like penises.'

'Like penises, dear? Are you sure?'

'That's what they said. I mean it's something different, I guess.'

'You can say that again,' said the General and took a large swig of whisky. A man who could elicit letters from Mrs Ndhlovo in which she recommended masturbatory techniques involving avocado pears, and who was also heavily into penises, combined so many sexual inclinations he might even find Myrtle Ransby's elderly and over-ripe eroticism attractive. Weirdo was definitely an understatement. 'What exactly did they say?' he asked. 'And first of all they didn't know who you were, did they?'

'Oh no, General, I said what you told me to. Like I was calling from the Embassy on account of a visa application by Dr Osbert and needed verification of his subject specialty.'

'And they said penises? They must have been having you on. The blighter is an expert on crime and punishment. He's written a book on hanging. I can't see where penises come into that. Unless . . .' He paused for a moment and gave the matter some thought. 'Of course, they do say you get an erection and have an orgasm at the moment of death. Not that that's much consolation in the circumstances.'

The girl consulted her notes. 'I've got it here,' she said. 'I said what's his subject specialty and they said he's the Sir Godber Evans Memorial Fellow and he's a penologist.'

'Oh that,' said Sir Cathcart and relaxed. 'As a matter of fact it's nothing to do with penises. It has to do with prisons. P-E-N-A-L as in penalty not penile as in ... whatever. Natural mistake for a gal to make. Now let's see, what have we here?'

He riffled through the copies of Purefoy's correspondence the Dean had given him. 'Ah, here we are. The American Association for the Abolition of Cruel and Unusual Punishment. Entirely appropriate. The President is coming to England in August and would value a meeting with Dr Osbert whose book etc. Illegible signature belonging to the Secretary. That should do very nicely. The letter-heading is easy to copy and there shouldn't be any trouble with the envelope and stamp. Well, my dear, now that you've got it clear in that pretty little head of yours that penology has nothing immediately to do with John Thomases, you are about to be enrolled as a member of the American Association for the Abolition of Cruel and Unusual Punishment over here to arrange for the President's meeting and eager to meet the distinguished Dr P. Osbert, author of *The Long Drop*. I'll get a copy from Heffer's and you can mug it up. That shouldn't be too difficult for you, should it?'

'Oh gee, General, it's such a privilege to be of help to you,' the blonde said. 'Just anything you say.'

'Very good of you to say so,' said the General and
went upstairs, wondering not for the first time what it
was about Americans that made them such amazing
experts in some of life's most complicated operations
and absolute ignoramuses in simple matters like geog-
raphy. He put it down to specialization. That and not
being European. Not that Myrtle Ransby was any
brighter. God alone knew what she'd have made of
penology.

28

At Porterhouse there were frequent occasions when the grosser tastes of past Masters seemed never to have gone away. This was particularly true on Thursday nights. Thursday dinner was always a very good one. Friday was fish day, fish for lunch and fish again for dinner originally for religious reasons but now simply a tradition followed implacably by the Chef. However, fish being an insubstantial dish when filleted or with too many bones to make for large mouthfuls and easy eating, on Thursday nights the Fellows could fill up on meat and something especially nutritious and with body to it. And on the second Thursday after Easter *Canards pressés à la Porterhouse* was always on the menu. It was on Thursday that General Sir Cathcart D'Eath came to dine in College. 'Got to put in an appearance for the good of the Society, that great community of Old Porterthusians whose spirit spans the continents,' he boomed in the Combination Room where the Fellows had gathered for sherry. There was one of those sudden silences that inflicts itself at random on such gatherings.

The Chaplain broke it. 'What did Cathcart say?' he yelled. He had forgotten to turn his hearing aid on.

Dr Buscott took the opportunity he had been waiting

for ever since the General had mistaken him for a junior porter and had told him to get his hair cut or lose his job. 'General Sir Cathcart D'Eath,' he announced in tones that would have done credit to a toastmaster at a rowdy banquet, 'General Sir Cathcart D'Eath, KCMG, etcetera, has just stated that the spirit of the Old Porterthusians spans the continents.'

'What on earth can he mean?'

'I've no idea,' said Dr Buscott, and moved away into the company of his fellow scientists where he felt safer.

The Senior Tutor prevailed upon the General to have some more Amontillado. 'It's the Special Old one, you know. We only bring it out on certain occasions,' he said.

'Where's the Dean?' asked the General, who felt like saying he hadn't come to be insulted by long-haired louts who only deemed his DSO worth an etcetera. In any case he had a special reason for being there that night. He was hoping to meet Dr Osbert and assess his suitability for the ordeal of Myrtle Ransby. 'No use wasting a perfectly foul old bag on some swine of a sexual athlete who doesn't mind being filmed under half a ton of lard trussed up in rubber. Got to gauge his psychology, don't you know. Some chaps like that sort of thing,' he had said to his secretary, who already knew it. Now, clutching his sherry, he peered round the exceptionally crowded Combination Room in search of the Dean.

'I don't seem to see him here,' the Senior Tutor

commented. 'Mind you, he's been a bit off colour lately. We all have. Those terrible American TV people and the damage to the Chapel, you know.'

'Well of course,' the General boomed, 'but the rumour I've heard is that the compensation is going to be enormous. Bound to be. Kentucky Fry tells me they're worth billions.'

'Kentucky Fry?' said the Senior Tutor. 'I can't for the life of me understand how people can stomach that stuff. I made the mistake one night in London somewhere. Most indigestible.'

'Really?' said the General and looked at the Senior Tutor suspiciously. He had the feeling that someone was taking the piss out of him.

It was confirmed by the Chaplain who had got his hearing aid going again. 'Colonel Someone's Chicken,' he shouted. 'I had some once. You had to lick your fingers afterwards. I can't remember why. Mind you, the waitresses were most attractive. Lovely legs and things.'

'What's this new chap, the Godber Evans Fellow, like?' the General asked, to change the subject.

'He died, you know,' bellowed the Chaplain. 'I'm surprised no one told you. Murdered, they say.'

'What?' said the General. 'Murdered? Already?' He looked round for the Senior Tutor but he had disappeared in the crowd.

'I'm surprised nobody informed you,' the Chaplain continued. 'It happened quite a long time ago. I found it most distressing. Of course none of us liked him

but . . .' Any further information that might have
cleared the matter up was prevented by the arrival of
the Praelector.

'I've just been hearing about Dr Osbert,' the General
told him.

The Praelector looked at him curiously and shook his
head. 'A nasty business,' he said. 'I blame the Senior
Tutor myself.'

'The Senior Tutor?' said the General. 'You're not
seriously telling me . . .' A waiter with the decanter slid
between them and filled his glass.

'He should never have allowed the Fellow to be
appointed,' the Praelector continued. 'We weren't properly informed. All we were told was that some City
friends had put up the money. Now, of course, it's too
late. The damage has been done.'

'It is never too late to repent,' bawled the Chaplain,
who had been elbowed aside by the waiter and had only
just rejoined them. 'On the other hand, when you're
murdered you don't have much opportunity.'

This time it was the Praelector who was shocked.
'Don't use that word,' he told the Chaplain sharply. 'It
isn't generally known. We can't have rumours
spreading.'

'I should damned well think not,' said Sir Cathcart. 'I
for one had no idea.'

'None of us did,' the Praelector said. 'I only learnt
about it this afternoon.'

The Chaplain looked at him in some astonishment.

'But you were there when he admitted it. We all were. It was after his Induction Dinner. He got pickled.' But before the matter could be satisfactorily cleared up dinner was announced. They filed into the Hall and the Chaplain shouted Grace.

'Praelector,' said Sir Cathcart in a conspiratorial whisper when they were finally seated. 'I know we can't talk about Dr Osbert now, but perhaps we should have a word in private afterwards.'

'Just as you like,' said the Praelector with an insouciance that took the General's breath away, 'though frankly I should have thought it was the other . . . er . . . matter, you know, we should consider.'

Sir Cathcart glanced cautiously around. 'The other matter?' he asked through gritted teeth. 'Other matter?'

'Can't talk about it now for goodness' sake,' said the Praelector hurriedly. 'I just hope to God the Chaplain keeps his trap shut. I told the Dean only this afternoon not to mention it to anyone. If it got to the Senior Tutor's ears the fat would really be in the fire. The fellow's in a bad enough state already without provoking him any further. He's as unstable as the very devil.'

'Yes,' Sir Cathcart agreed, with the private thought that a man who had so recently murdered the Sir Godber Evans Memorial Fellow was bound to be in a pretty bad way. Unstable was putting it mildly. Mad as a hatter was more like it. He peered down the table at the Senior Tutor and was relieved to see him talking quite naturally to the Fellow beside him, exhibiting no signs of homicidal mania. He was so engrossed in the thoughts this news had provoked, and in particular how he was going to get back the half of the two thousand pounds he had given Myrtle Ransby, that he hardly noticed what he was eating until *Canards pressés à la Porterhouse* was served.

Even by Porterhouse standards it was exceptional. In the belief that, with the collapse of the Chapel and the gloom emanating from the Bursar's office about the state of College finances, this was in all likelihood the last time he would be allowed the chance to do a Duck Dinner, the Chef had gone to town. To be exact, he had gone to three of East Anglia's largest duck farms and had returned with over one hundred and thirty plucked Aylesburys and the determination to so concentrate them that this last Duck Dinner would go down in the gastronomic annals of Porterhouse. For days the ancient presses had been groaning under the strain of achieving the greatest possible mass of duck in the least possible volume or, to put it another way, that three overweight ducks should be compressed into an oblong no larger than a matchbox. And while he hadn't entirely succeeded in this remarkable compression, what was finally placed in front of General Sir Cathcart D'Eath had so little resemblance to a duck or anything vaguely capable of flying or floating that he had munched his way with some difficulty through the first forkful before realizing what he had just swallowed. He turned a bulging eye to the menu and then looked down at his plate. 'Dear God,

I thought this was some sort of pâté,' he muttered, and tried to dislodge a compacted feather from his dentures. 'This isn't pressed duck, it's triple-distilled cholesterol. God alone knows what it does to the arteries.'

'An interesting point,' said the Praelector, finishing his first helping and signalling for a second. 'The calorific value is quite astonishingly high. In my younger days I did some slight calculations into the matter. I forget what the exact figures were but I do remember concluding that a starving man of medium build adrift on an icefloe could survive perfectly well on one portion every third day.'

'I daresay, but since I'm not on a damned icefloe,' the General began and was about to push his plate away when the waiter intervened.

'Anything wrong, Sir Cathcart? Chef's special, sir.'

The General picked up his knife and fork again. 'Momentary hiccup,' he said. 'Give the Chef my compliments and tell him this duck is delicious.'

'These,' said the waiter enigmatically, and went away.

'As I was about to say,' continued the Praelector happily, 'I have always found duck a very delicate dish. Goose tends to be a bit on the greasy side but with far more flavour to the meat whereas duck, unless it's wild mallard of course, has always struck me as a bit bland. On the other hand with sage and onion . . .'

Sir Cathcart picked at his duck and tried to shut out the words. Never a great trencherman – his interest in the less savoury qualities of the opposite sex inclined

him to pay attention to his figure – he was feeling
decidedly liverish. He wasn't helped by Professor
Pawley, who pointed out that he had known people
drop dead immediately after a Duck Dinner. 'Dr
Lathaniel was one, I remember, and then there was
Canon Bowel. A question, I suppose, of the individual's
metabolism.'

'Canon Bowel?' said the Praelector. 'Another rotten
Master. I must say we've had more than our fair share
of bad Masters. Not that he died at a Duck Dinner. Had
an ulcer and wouldn't attend.'

'He tried to introduce compulsory Compline,'
shouted the Chaplain. 'We had to do something about
him, you know. Now what was the menu that night? I
know we had devilled crabs with Tabasco sauce to start
with but . . .'

'It was the jugged hare and the zabaglione . . .'

'Oh yes, the zabaglione,' sighed the Chaplain ecstati-
cally. 'It was a special recipe I remember. A dozen yolks
of goose eggs and a pound of sugar and instead of sherry
we had Cointreau. Oh, it was wonderful.'

'And we had a special cheese with peppers on it,' the
Praelector said.

Down the table the Senior Tutor had pricked up his
ears. 'You're talking about Canon Bowel, I can tell,' he
called out. 'It was the cigars that finished the man off.
They were enormous ones. We had to budget for them.
Ah, those were the days. We were a proper college then.
Used to call us Slaughterhouse.'

By the end of dinner Sir Cathcart's sympathies had gone out to Canon Bowel, and he could fully understand the Dean's absence. To have to sit down to a Duck Dinner knowing full well that the Senior Tutor was a murderer, and so evidently revelled in the College being called Slaughterhouse, was more than enough to put any man off colour. It was with an ashen, though mottled, face that he followed the Praelector into the Combination Room. 'I won't have any port or coffee, if you don't mind,' he said. 'Perhaps a breath of fresh air might help.' They went out into the Fellows' Garden and the Praelector lit a cigar.

'Now then, about this business of the murder,' said Sir Cathcart. 'What on earth are you going to do?'

'Get rid of him of course,' said the Praelector. 'Can't have him in the College any longer.'

'You mean to say he's still here?'

'Of course he is. Can't simply sneak the damned man out at dead of night,' said the Praelector and intensified the General's mental and physical discomfort by adding, 'actually I intend to talk to him about it some time tonight. It won't be easy but I'll have to try. Of course it all depends on the weather.'

'Really? Does it?' said Sir Cathcart. 'How very remarkable. Of course one's heard about, well . . . this sort of thing before but I never realized communication could be affected by the weather.'

'Only possible when it's fine, according to the Dean,' said the Praelector. 'He's the expert. I can't be bothered myself. It's so difficult to make out what the damned man's saying. Not surprising in his condition but I suppose I'm too squeamish or something. Beastly state to be in. I always feel so sorry for the poor devil. A dreadful way to go.'

Sir Cathcart said nothing. He was feeling dreadful himself. He had always thought of the Dean and the Praelector as perfectly rational men, not at all inclined to superstition, and to discover now that they were both convinced spiritualists was almost as disturbing as the knowledge that the Senior Tutor had murdered the man the Praelector was hoping to talk to that night if the weather was fine. And the fact that the corpse or cadaver or whatever murdered bodies were called was still in the College, and in a beastly condition to boot, did nothing to put his mind at rest. It was no longer a question that things in Porterhouse might be in need of change. They bloody well had to be changed before the police and the media were swarming all over the place and all the Senior Fellows had been arrested. That sort of thing was going to do the College no good at all. The old name of Slaughterhouse would become a permanent one. For the first time in his life Sir Cathcart regretted his own name. It was bound to be up on the billboards.

He pulled himself together and placed a kindly hand on the Praelector's arm. 'Listen, old chap, why don't we go inside and sit down quietly somewhere and I'll see if I can get hold of the College legal fellows. I really do think it's time to get them in on this. I mean this is a spectacularly awful situation. Now what are their names?'

'Waxthorne, Libbott and Chaine,' said the Praelector shaking himself free rather irritably. He disliked being called 'old chap' and patronized quite so openly, as if he were in some sort of geriatric ward. 'Though you won't find them in at this time of night.' He gave a nasty chuckle. 'In fact you won't find them in at all. Waxthorne has been dead for the past sixty years. Buried in the cemetery on the Newmarket Road. And Libbott was cremated a couple of years later. I don't know exactly what happened to Chaine though I once heard a rather peculiar story about him ending up in King's. Something about his skull being used as a drinking mug. Waxthorne's widow told me that. I used to keep in touch with her, you know, on a regular basis. Nice woman.' For a moment his mind wandered back to those happy afternoons in her house in Sedley Taylor Road.

Beside him Sir Cathcart adjusted himself to another set of deaths. It was turning into a singularly ghastly evening. All the same he tried again. 'I thought the College lawyers were . . . Retter and . . . Wyve,' he said at last. 'Perhaps if I were to telephone them . . .'

'Oh, them,' said the Praelector. 'I shouldn't do that. They've got enough on their hands with this other business. Besides, the fewer people who know about it the better. No, no, we've got to handle the matter ourselves. And it is a fine night, so we should be able to find him.'

Sir Cathcart looked balefully up at the sky and gnawed the end of his ginger moustache. 'When you say "we",' he said. 'I'm not at all sure I want to get any further involved . . . in . . . well, you know what I mean.'

'Suit yourself. I know my duty. And in any case I can't see how you can slide out of it now. We're all involved. Question of the College's reputation. And frankly . . . well never mind about that. Least said soonest mended. We'd better go and talk it over with the Dean.' And on this curiously ambivalent note the Praelector led the way across the garden to the Dean's staircase.

They found him drinking a cup of coffee. A plate of half-eaten sandwiches was on the table beside him. 'Ah, hullo Cathcart, Praelector. Sorry I wasn't at Duck Dinner. Wasn't in the mood somehow. Couldn't bring myself to face it. Cowardly, I daresay.'

'Not at all, my dear chap,' said the General. 'Know just how you feel. All that damned grease and this fellow Osbert still on the premises. Ghastly business. Mangled too, according to the Praelector here. And the Senior Tutor sitting there chatting away cheerfully and acting perfectly normally. First thing I heard about it was from the Chaplain.'

The Praelector addressed the Dean sternly. 'I told you not to mention it to anyone. And there was the Chaplain practically shouting the odds from the house tops. Fortunately no one takes much notice of what he says.'

It was the Dean's turn to look decidedly uneasy. 'I

can assure you I haven't said a word to the Chaplain. Last person I'd tell. You don't think . . .'

'I don't know what to think,' said the Praelector. 'All I know is that someone's been talking.'

The General tried to take command of the situation. 'Now then, you fellows, we're not going to get anything done nattering about it. We've got to think how to protect the College reputation. If it got out that we were sheltering a murderer, the gutter press would have a field day. And the broadsheets too. Letters to *The Times* and television programmes. We've got to be practical and find some way of keeping the police out of it. The best way of doing that is to get the body off the premises. Where is it at the moment?'

'Well, at a rough guess,' said the Praelector, now convinced that Sir Cathcart was a great deal drunker than he looked, 'at a rough guess I'd have to say it was still in the Crypt. Of course I haven't been down to have a look lately but that's where they're usually kept.'

'The Crypt, eh? Well, I suppose it's as good a place as any. Not many people go down there. Probably kept locked in any case.'

'Invariably,' said the Dean. 'I can't see that it matters much. The really important thing is to get Skullion out of the Master's Lodge. Now he has already threatened to tell the world he killed Sir Godber if we even think of having him shifted to the Park and – '

'Excuse me,' said Sir Cathcart, sliding slowly into an armchair. 'I don't feel awfully well. Must be that damned duck, though how the hell all that fat can affect the brain so quickly I'm damned if I know. You don't think I'm having a Blue, do you?'

'A Blue? Oh no, no,' said the Praelector. 'A Porterhouse Blue always attacks the speech first. You wouldn't be making any sense if you'd had a Blue.'

'And how does it affect the hearing? I mean, I'm not hearing any sense half the time. I thought I heard the Dean say Skullion had threatened to tell the world he killed Sir Godber Evans.'

'Quite right too. That's what I did say,' said the Dean. 'What's wrong with that?'

Words failed Sir Cathcart. Slumped in the old leather armchair he looked pucely up at them and shook his head. 'I don't understand,' he muttered. 'I don't begin to understand.'

'We none of us do,' said the Praelector. 'That is one of the problems but it's not one we can get to grips with now. We have to take immediate action. No matter how many threats he makes Skullion must go, if necessary by force. We simply cannot afford to have a murderer as Master.'

'Of course we can't but don't you see he may say something to the Press,' the Dean said anxiously.

But Sir Cathcart D'Eath had overcome his temporary lapse. The words 'immediate action' and 'force' had reawoken his military spirit, and the clear statement that the Master of Porterhouse was a murderer had driven all other considerations out of his mind. The Senior Tutor's killing of Dr Osbert was by comparison a minor misdemeanour. He got to his feet and stood with his legs apart in front of the empty fireplace. 'Right, the first thing is for one of us to go and explain the situation to him,' he said. 'Now I've known Skullion a long time and I think I can say with some confidence that he trusts me. I shall speak to him man to man, soldier to soldier, and . . .'

'Oh for God's sake,' muttered the Praelector but the General ignored the interruption, '. . . and I shall put it to him that his duty now is to go. He has always been a loyal College servant and I daresay the action he took, however regrettable, against the late Sir Godber Evans was done for the sake of Porterhouse. Frankly I have a great deal of sympathy for the old boy and, speaking as a military man, I have little doubt that in the same circumstances I would have done the same thing. Can't say fairer than that. We had to put some of the Watussi Rifles down in Burma one time and I can say with some confidence that I did not shrink from putting my hand to the wheel. Now you chaps just wait here and I'll go and look Skullion up. Daresay I'll find him on sentry duty by the back gate.'

And before either the Dean or the Praelector could say anything to stop him he strode from the room and could be heard clattering down the staircase into the night.

'Did he have an awful lot of pressed duck?' the Dean asked.

The Praelector shook his head. 'Hardly any, unfortunately. Hardening of the arteries is an occupational hazard that seems to affect cavalrymen in particular. We'll just have to wait and see what this charge of the heavy brigade results in.'

29

Out in the darkness under the old beech tree by the back gate Skullion followed the General's progress across the lawn and round the rose beds by the occasional glow of his cigar. Sir Cathcart had lit it almost as soon as he was in the open air partly to give him time to think what he was going to say but also to give Skullion warning that he was coming. 'No point in alarming the old bugger,' he'd said to himself.

But Skullion wasn't alarmed. He'd known this would happen sooner or later. He'd given the Dean his marching bloody orders and the Dean wasn't ever going to forgive him for that. Given him a nasty shock into the bargain telling him about killing Sir Godber Blooming Evans. Only done it because he was drunk and pissed off. But what was done was done and in some ways Skullion didn't regret it. He'd had enough of being called Master and them not thinking of him as the Master. Somehow the Bursar's telling that bloody Yank not to call him a Quasimodo update but the Master had cleared the air and let him see his position in the College in a new light. There wasn't any pride in being Master of Porterhouse and being helpless in a wheelchair. The fact that he'd missed sitting by the bed and gobbledygooking the Yank had told him that too.

It had been different when he'd been Head Porter. He'd had real power then even if he did have to hide it and call the young wet-behind-the-ears 'Sir'. He'd learnt that lesson in the Royal Marines from watching the sergeants saluting young wet-behind-the-ears officers and calling them 'Sir' to their faces and then seeing to it they didn't lead them into any trouble. In France Skullion had seen a corporal put a bullet through a second lieutenant who'd wanted to be a hero and get them all killed taking on a company of Panzergrenadiers waiting for them in a sunken lane. He'd heard the corporal mutter, 'Him or us. And it ain't going to be us,' just before he shot the officer. And at Lympstone – or was it Deal? – Sergeant Smith had asked him one wet afternoon standing in the drill shed, 'What's your most important job in this bloody war, boy? I'll tell you what it fucking is. To kill the fucking enemy. And to do that you've got to be alive, see? So keep your swede down and remember your blooming mother wants to see you again even if I don't and she ain't going to do that if you're a dead Marine and some fucking Jerry's done to you what you're being paid to do to him. And what are you fucking smiling at, boy? Tell your ruddy uncle here because I'm sure we all want to share the joke.' And 3rd Class Marine Skullion PO/X 127052 had said sheepishly, 'It's just that a dead Marine is an empty bottle, isn't it, Sarge? Like a bottle of beer.' And even Sergeant

Smith had almost smiled for a moment. 'Well, you're going to see plenty of both where you're going, and for your sake I hope you live to drink plenty of the one and aren't one of the others.' That had all been such a long time ago, but Skullion had never forgotten it nor what he'd seen in France. And people like General Sir Cathcart D'Eath talked about having a Good War. As if being cold and wet and hungry and shit-scared was fun. And hearing someone screaming wasn't fun either even if it was a bloody wounded Jerry.

So now in the darkness Skullion waited underneath the great tree for Sir Cathcart and wasn't sorry it was over.

'Ah Skullion,' the General said, peering at the dark shape against the trunk of the beech. 'Still waiting for us to climb in, what?'

'You, Sir Cathcart, yes, you were a one for climbing in, you were. I caught you many a time and let you go some more, though I don't suppose you ever knew it, sir.'

The end of the General's cigar glowed in appreciation. 'You're an old devil, Skullion, you know that, a wicked old devil.'

Skullion grunted, or chuckled. It was impossible to tell which.

'Bad business, Skullion, bad business,' the General continued. 'The Dean's upset. Praelector too. Can't have it, you know.'

'No, sir,' said Skullion.

'Can't say I blame you myself. The bloody man wasn't a fit and proper person to be Master. In your own way you were trying to do the College a service.'

He stopped. Somewhere behind him there was a sound of raucous laughter.

'Boat club,' Skullion explained. 'Getting ready for the Bumps. Senior Tutor's got them in training.'

'Yes,' said the General, suddenly remembering that Skullion wasn't the only killer on the premises. 'And that's another thing. College reputation's at stake. This business is bound to leak out and once the police start poking their noses in there'll be no stopping them. We can't afford to let that happen. Can't have you making threats to the Dean. He's not a young man, you know. We none of us are and things are going to change pretty damn drastically. So, no matter what you say . . . well, to put it bluntly, Skullion, man to man and so on, your innings is over. Ran yourself out or played on, whichever you like. Now, I understand from the Dean you don't want to go to the Park.'

'No, Sir Cathcart, I don't. Not with all them loonies like old Dr Vertel. I'd rather die here and now and be done with it. I mean it, sir. I'd rather die now.'

Sir Cathcart mulled this over for a moment, but ruled it out. 'Tell you what,' he said finally. 'There is no question of your going to Porterhouse Park. Give you my word as a gentleman that you won't even be asked to. What do you say to that?'

'Very good of you, sir, very good.'

'On the other hand, the College needs a new Master. You must see that.'

'Oh I do, Sir Cathcart. I've never been the Master the College needed. I've always known that.'

'Good man. Now if you were to retire, of your own free will of course . . .' Sir Cathcart let the question hang on the still night air. For a moment Skullion said nothing.

'If I retired, Sir Cathcart, I'd have the right to name my own successor, wouldn't I? That's the Master's right, isn't it?'

Sir Cathcart nodded. 'You would indeed have that right,' he said. 'It is your absolute right as Master to name the person to succeed you. And you could come and live at Coft Castle with me, and occasionally we could drive over to visit the College, if you so wished. That is what I've come to tell you.'

'In that case I'm prepared to go,' said Skullion solemnly, 'go whenever you want, sir. And I will name my successor now.'

'And who is it to be?' Sir Cathcart asked.

'Lord Pimpole, sir, Lord Pimpole.'

'Very good, Master, very good. And I can go and inform the Dean of your decision?'

'Yes, Sir Cathcart, you can tell him. And you can tell him this too, he doesn't have to worry about the Sir Godber Evans Fellow, Dr Osbert, about him knowing I killed Sir bloody Godber, because he already does know.'

Sir Cathcart hesitated. 'Knew' would be a more appropriate word in the late Dr Osbert's case.

'He knows because I told him,' Skullion continued. 'He was sitting in the maze when I was telling the Dean. Been there all afternoon, waiting and listening, and he heard every word I said.'

'Good Lord,' said Sir Cathcart and understood why the Senior Tutor had acted with such precipitate violence.

'What's more, the stupid bugger was in the maze all bloody night, crashing about and trying to find the way out.' Skullion chuckled at the memory.

'And you knew he was listening all the time?'

'Course I did. I haven't been Skullion the Head Porter and not known what's going on in College all these years. Yes, I heard him and I thought to myself, "I'll tell you what you've come to find out and it isn't going to do you any good at all because you ain't going to be able to do anything about it." And it hasn't done him any good.'

'Hmm,' was the only comment Sir Cathcart was prepared to make. He had begun to regret with a new and fearful intensity ever having come near the College in these unfathomable circumstances. He certainly had no intention of incriminating himself any further by asking questions. 'Well, I'll be getting back to the Dean,' he said hurriedly before there could be any fresh disclosures. 'I'm sure he'll be delighted to learn of your decision. We can make arrangements for your moving

357

out of the Master's Lodge at some other time.' And with a hasty 'Goodnight' he was off across the lawn.

He found the Dean and the Praelector sitting in gloomy silence.

'Well?' asked the Dean without getting out of his chair, but Sir Cathcart needed a quick restorative.

'Mind if I help myself?' he asked, and without waiting for an answer poured himself a large cognac. Only when he had drunk it did he resume his stance in front of the empty fireplace.

'For goodness' sake, Cathcart, put us out of our misery. What is his answer?'

'Good man, Skullion,' he said finally, having decided that even among old friends there was a great deal to be said for deception. The Praelector's 'Least said soonest mended' made perfect sense to him now. 'He's agreed to go. I said the timing of his leaving the Lodge could be left to a later date.'

'And he didn't make any difficulties?' the Praelector enquired.

'None whatsoever. Regrets the whole business and apologies all round for making such a damned nuisance of himself.'

'It's unbelievable,' said the Dean. 'He didn't threaten any disclosure if he goes to the Park?'

'None whatsoever. Of course he's reluctant to go but I made it plain that, for the good of the College, it was the best thing for him. I suggest we get a move on. Like tomorrow. Leave it to me. Private ambulance and some hefty attendants to lift him into it and then straight down the motorway. You can put it about that he's had another Porterhouse Blue.'

'Well I must say, Cathcart, you've done sterling work this evening,' the Dean said, rising and reaching for the brandy. 'I think this calls for a celebratory drink.'

'I must say it comes as a great relief,' the Praelector agreed, 'though it does leave us with the question of who is to be the new Master.'

Sir Cathcart raised a hand. 'No need to trouble yourself about that either. Skullion has exercised his traditional right and named his successor.' He paused for effect. The two old men looked at him with amazement.

'Well, it is his right, you know. I could hardly refuse him,' Sir Cathcart continued.

'Absolutely his right,' the Dean agreed. 'One of our oldest traditions as a matter of fact. Dates back, I believe, to 1492.'

'Yes, well there you are. I suppose I'd better be on my way. It's been a difficult evening, but at least you don't have to worry about Skullion any more.'

'But you haven't told us whom Skullion, the Master that is, named as his successor.'

'It is rather important to know,' said the Praelector.

'Oh that. Of course, how stupid of me. Jeremy Pimpole. That's who he's named. Lord Pimpole . . .' He stopped and looked at the Dean. 'Are you all right, Dean?'

It was a stupid question. It was obvious that the Dean

was far from all right. He was clutching the edge of the table and had dropped the brandy. 'No, no,' he gasped. 'Not him. For God's sake, not the Dog's . . .' He staggered for a moment and almost collapsed.

'Not the what?' asked Sir Cathcart as he and the Praelector helped the Dean to a chair.

'Not the Dog's Nose man,' he whimpered.

Sir Cathcart bent over him solicitously. 'The Dog's Nose man?'

'Pimpole. It isn't possible. Not Pimpole.'

'He doesn't seem to be very well,' the Praelector said. 'Perhaps the strain has been too much for him. And I shouldn't give him any of that brandy.'

But Sir Cathcart had reached the end of his own tether. 'I'm not going to give him any,' he snapped. 'I need some myself. Come here for that infernal dinner and find the place has been turned into a human abattoir. And then when I've managed to persuade one murderer to get the hell out . . . Damn it, what the hell is wrong with Lord Pimpole? Knew his father. Charming family. Pots of money, too. Just the chap.'

'No, he's not,' moaned the Dean. 'He is nothing like the man he used to be. He's a filthy soak. Pimpole Hall and the estate have been sold to meet his debts. He has drunk a fortune away. He doesn't even wash. Pimpole lives in a dilapidated cottage with a vile dog and drinks Dog's Noses.' He paused and looked wildly around at them. 'Have you ever drunk a Dog's Nose?' Both men shook their heads.

'Heard of 'em,' said Sir Cathcart, 'but – '

'Then don't,' the Dean continued. 'Not ever. If you value your sanity. Pimpole drinks them all the time. Seven ounces of gin to thirteen of beer.'

'Dear shit,' said Sir Cathcart, 'the bugger must be off his head.'

'Cathcart, he is. And what is more . . . no, I can't tell you how depraved Pimpole is. It's too awful.'

'Try, old fellow,' Sir Cathcart said. 'Try and tell us. You've done jolly well so far.'

'I don't think we need to hear any more,' said the Praelector. 'Seven ounces of gin . . .' His voice trailed away in disgust and disbelief. But Sir Cathcart wanted to hear about depravity.

The Dean told them. And even Sir Cathcart understood. 'Sheep?' he said slowly. 'Sheep and dogs? Well, that does put a rather different complexion on the matter.'

He helped himself to some more of the Dean's brandy and sat down. It was the Praelector who spoke. 'It also puts an entirely different complexion on Skullion's apparent willingness to retire. He has, in old-fashioned golfing parlance, laid us a perfect stymie.'

There was silence in the room as they took this in. Again from somewhere in the College there came the sound of raucous laughter. It reminded Sir Cathcart of the Senior Tutor. 'I know why the Senior Tutor . . .' He hesitated for a moment and chose his words with care. 'I know why the Senior Tutor took the desperate action

he did. Skullion had told Dr Osbert that he had murdered Sir Godber. Obviously the Senior Tutor realized
he had to act immediately. All the same this second
killing has made things damnably awkward. Still, if the
body is in the Crypt I daresay we can buy time.' This
time there could be no mistaking the Dean's and the
Praelector's unease. They exchanged a glance and turned
back to Sir Cathcart.

'Cathcart my boy,' said the Praelector, 'have you ever
had any allergic reaction to duck? By that I mean, has
the ingestion of concentrated fat ever affected the way
you perceive things?'

Sir Cathcart D'Eath's eyes bulged in his purple face.
'Have I what?' he bellowed. 'An allergic reaction to
duck? Are you quite insane? Here we are with dead
bodies littering the damned College and you want to
know if the ingestion of digitalized duck affects the way
I perceive things. Well, as a matter of fact . . .'

'Hush, my dear chap, do keep your voice down,' the
Dean intervened.

Sir Cathcart did. 'As a matter of fact the way I
perceive things has changed,' he said hoarsely. 'I perceive that the College has gone collectively off its trolley.
Not only have we an ex-Head Porter as Master and one
who admits to killing his predecessor but we also have a
Senior Tutor who has beaten, anyway mangled, another
Fellow to death and put his body in the Crypt and to
top it all . . .'

'What on earth are you talking about? What makes

you think the Senior Tutor has beaten anyone to death? Bodies in the Crypt? Of course there are bodies in the Crypt. The Masters are buried there. No one else.'

Sir Cathcart eyed them with a doubtful and extremely cautious suspicion. 'Then why did you tell me before that damned dinner that the Senior Tutor had butchered this new Fellow, Osbert?' he demanded of the Praelector.

'Me? I never said a word about the Senior Tutor murdering Dr Osbert,' said the Praelector indignantly. 'I've never heard such a farrago of nonsense in my life.'

'You bloody well did. You said you blamed the Senior Tutor . . .' Sir Cathcart hesitated. In his befuddled mind a fresh doubt had arisen.

The Praelector took advantage of the pause. 'I said I blamed the Senior Tutor for allowing Dr Osbert to be appointed without properly investigating who was putting him up for the Fellowship. I said nothing about him murdering anybody.'

'And to the best of my knowledge Dr Osbert is still alive,' said the Dean.

Sir Cathcart stirred unhappily in his seat. 'There has evidently been some sort of ghastly cock-up,' he said. 'All the same some stupid bastard told me . . .' His voice trailed away as enlightenment slowly dawned.

'The Chaplain, perhaps?' hazarded the Dean.

Sir Cathcart nodded.

'Ah,' said the Praelector significantly and reached for the brandy. 'That explains everything. Which still leaves us with the vexed question of a Master to succeed Skullion. I take it that we are all agreed that he has not nominated Lord Pimpole.'

For a moment it seemed as though Sir Cathcart was going to object on the grounds that he had given his word as a gentleman et cetera, but he backed away. Sheep and dogs were too much even for his sexual eclecticism. 'Good,' continued the Praelector. 'In that case I shall convene an emergency meeting of the College Council to have the Master declared *non compos mentis*. This will negate any future nominations he might attempt. It is the only method open to us and it will have the additional advantage of rendering any ridiculous assertions that he murdered Sir Godber Evans nugatory. And now, if you'll excuse me, it is long past my normal bedtime.'

'And mine,' said Sir Cathcart.

As he made his way out past the Porter's Lodge a figure hurried by into Porterhouse. It was the man the General had come to identify.

30

It was a very different Purefoy Osbert who came into
Porterhouse that night. He no longer felt strongly that
crime was a product of the law or that human misbehav-
iour existed only as a side-effect of police brutality and
social repression. He had moved beyond these generali-
zations into a more personal world in which his own
anger dominated everything. He had been deliberately
humiliated and made to look an idiot. All the way back
from Kloone he had faced the fact, the evident fact that
Mrs Ndhlovo, far from loving him or even feeling fond
of him, had made a mockery of his feelings for her. Just
as evidently she had always regarded him as a fool. And
Purefoy was prepared to agree with her. He had been a
damned fool to have been taken in by her stories of a
black husband in Uganda who had ended up as various
portions of President Idi Amin's late-night snacks. A
woman who could hoodwink the University authorities
into believing such an unlikely story by speaking pidgin
English had to be an experienced charlatan. It wouldn't
have surprised him to have learnt that she had never
been anywhere near Africa and that her encyclopaedic
knowledge of sexual practices had been obtained
entirely from treatises on the subject or from hearsay.

Whatever the case she was definitely a liar and a fraud as well as a heartless bitch and Purefoy wanted no part of her. She belonged to a past that he intended to forget. He had even given up the idea of writing her a letter in which he told her what he thought of her. She wasn't worth the trouble, might even find some satisfaction in knowing how much she had hurt him, and besides he had more constructive things to do.

For one thing he was going to make his presence felt in Porterhouse. The place was worse than an anachronism, more than an archaism, it was decadent, possessed a diseased arrogance to disguise its abysmal banality and lack of any academic distinction and to hide from the outside world the fact that it was morally as well as financially bankrupt. What other colleges in Cambridge hid from the world Purefoy had no idea but, whatever that might be, they did produce educated graduates and distinguished scholars. It was even claimed, though Purefoy found the statistic incredible, that one college, Trinity, had produced more Nobel Prize winners than the whole of France. In short, other Cambridge colleges could afford to parade a sense of superiority without appearing wholly ridiculous. Porterhouse had no such right. It was ridiculous. Worse still, it had as a Master an ignorant brute who could admit to having murdered the previous Master without a vestige of remorse or regret. Well, all that was going to change. Maddened by Mrs Ndhlovo's laughter and the recognition it had brought with it of his own ineffectuality, Purefoy Osbert had

lost all fear of the place and of the elderly buffoons who
were the Senior Fellows. He intended to fulfil his
contract as the Sir Godber Evans Memorial Fellow and
make his presence felt. With this dominating thought
he strode past Sir Cathcart D'Eath without noticing him
and went to his rooms. It was too late to do anything
now but in the morning he would tackle the Dean and
tell him what he knew and what he intended to do. He
had in mind to announce that he was going to the police
with his knowledge and he would see how the Dean
reacted. It was this reaction that would actually be his
purpose. Purefoy Osbert had discovered gifts of provo-
cation. He would force the Dean to admit the truth of
Skullion's confession. Or to deny it. It hardly mattered
which. His own position didn't matter to him either. All
his life he had pretended to accept only certainties. But
now in the space of half an hour in Mrs Ndhlovo's flat
he had learnt that nothing was so unsettling as some
prior knowledge mixed with absurdly inconsequential
accusations. He would apply the technique to the Dean
in the morning. Exhausted by the day's events Purefoy
Osbert slept soundly.

*

The Praelector slept too, though in short bursts. He
always went to sleep quickly only to wake an hour or
two later to lie awake dwelling on the previous day's
events or simply lying quite happily in the darkness
letting thoughts roam. He rather enjoyed his broken

nights. They gave him an opportunity to ponder things uninterruptedly and without the feeling that he ought to be doing something useful. But this night his thoughts were focused narrowly on the question of the new Master. Unlike the Dean and Senior Tutor he had no illusions about Porterhouse. He had, as he had told the Dean on their walk, been shocked at the state of the College finances. And then on top of that had come the shock of Skullion's crime and his imminent removal to Porterhouse Park and the need to decide on a successor. Finally, and in its own way most disturbingly, the multiple misunderstandings at Duck Dinner and in the Dean's room had proved once and for all the incompetence of those who were supposedly in charge of the College. The Senior Tutor had become childishly emotional, the Dean was demoralized and Sir Cathcart D'Eath's changes of mood and identity suggested he was beginning to suffer from senile decay. The time for radical change had obviously come. As the sky began to lighten at dawn the Praelector went to the nub of the problem and with a sudden grasp of essentials found a startling solution.

In fact it was so startling that he hoisted himself up the bed and sat upright against the pillows to consider it more carefully. But though he looked at it from as many angles as he could think of he could not fault the solution. On the other hand it was so extraordinarily wild and daring that he could hardly bring himself to believe in it. Besides, the risks were tremendous. For an hour he lay there propped up against the pillows searching for a more moderate alternative and failed to find it. Then with the clearest picture in his mind of what he must do and with the certain knowledge that he had found a way to save Porterhouse, he slid down the bed and went back to sleep.

At half past seven he was awake again. He got up, had his bath and shaved, and then, as he did every day, he stood naked in front of the wardrobe mirror and studied his long, lean body with a dispassionate acceptance that was the tribute he paid to reality. What he saw was what he had become, an old man with spindly legs, a slight stoop but with clear blue eyes above a long nose and a firm, if shrunken, mouth. Having done that he dressed more carefully than usual and chose a suit that was so old that it seemed to have no perceptible style at all. It was his favourite suit and one he wore so seldom that Dege might have cut it for him only a week before. Having dressed and checked that his tie was as imperceptibly smart as the suit he went down to breakfast by way of the Porter's Lodge.

'Kindly inform the Senior Fellows that there will be an Extraordinary Meeting of the College Council at 11.30,' he told Walter. 'It is vital that as many as possible attend.' And leaving the Head Porter to wonder what was in the offing he walked across the Old Court to the Hall.

'Something serious is up,' Walter told the Under Porter. 'When they use Extraordinary they don't mean

Maybe. And when the Praelector calls the tune, you jump to it.'

*

For the rest of the morning the Praelector went about various errands. He visited the offices of Waxthorne, Libbott and Chaine, Solicitors, and spent half an hour with Mr Retter and left that gentleman in a state of consternation and alarm, and in no doubt that it was make-or-break day at Porterhouse. After that the Praelector took a taxi to the Bursar's house and, after a short and bitter exchange in which the Praelector spoke with lethal clarity of the alternative futures facing him, the Bursar took three pills and went back to Porterhouse with him.

'I have some telephone calls to make but you can come to my rooms and sit there while I make them,' the Praelector said. 'And so long as you do as I say you will be quite safe.' The Bursar said he felt quite safe, but he spoke without conviction.

On the other hand, as they passed beneath the Dean's windows the sound of raised voices clearly indicated that a very different form of conviction was being discussed. The Praelector stopped to listen. He disapproved of eavesdropping as much as he did the reading of other people's letters but he had shed all moral and social conventions during the night.

'You . . . you . . . dare to come in here and . . . and

threaten me . . . you . . . have the effrontery to . . . to suggest that I instigated the mur . . . murder of the late Master?' the Dean stammered.

'You tell me,' a quiet, calm voice replied. 'You tell me and I'll tell you what you did.'

There was a silence in the room. Even the Praelector felt the menace of that cold and calculated statement. The Bursar whimpered.

For a moment the Praelector hesitated before ordering the Bursar to go to his room and stay there. Then he hurried through the doorway and mounted the stairs. As he reached the top he heard the strangulated voice of the Dean. 'You . . . you infernal little whip . . . whipper-snapper,' he tried to shout. 'I'll have . . . the . . . the law on you. I'll . . .'

'By all means,' Purefoy Osbert interrupted in a tone of voice that was as icy as it was confident. 'By all means call the police. The telephone is there beside you. Do you know the number?'

The Praelector had heard enough. Opening the door he stepped into the room. 'Ah, Dr Osbert,' he said with a geniality he did not feel, 'how very convenient. I hope I am not interrupting anything important?'

Purefoy Osbert was standing in the middle of the room with his back to the window. He said nothing and against the sunshine outside the Praelector could not see the expression on his face. He could see the Dean's face well enough though. It was purple with ashen patches.

'He's accusing me of ... of ... of having organized Sir Godber's murder,' the Dean managed to say. 'He's saying – '

'Oh surely not,' the Praelector began, still maintaining an air of unconcern. 'I'm sure Dr Osbert knows better than to make unwarranted accusations of that sort. He is merely fulfilling the terms of his contract as the Memorial Fellow, and we all know Lady Mary's views on the matter. They are understandable in a widow and the fact that we have a Master in the last stages of senile dementia brought on by alcoholism makes such assumptions unfortunately all too plausible.' He turned to Purefoy. 'I suppose you have been talking to poor Skullion?' He paused for a moment and smiled. 'Alas, the poor man has developed a sense of guilt, an obsession caused no doubt by his stroke and the terrible misfortune of his position as the so-called Master. He was an excellent Head Porter in his time. We can hardly blame him for taking to drink.'

Purefoy Osbert looked into the blue eyes which might have been smiling at him and he knew he had met his match. 'I have made no accusation,' he said. 'I merely wanted to know what the Dean thought. I think I have found out.' And without another word he left the room. As his footsteps retreated down the staircase the Praelector helped the Dean out of his chair.

'Come,' he said, 'we must hurry. The Council is due to meet in five minutes and I have still a telephone call to make.'

'That bloody man – ' the Dean began but the Praelector raised a finger to his lips and listened. The sound
of an ambulance siren was growing louder.

'They have come for the Master,' he said and led the
way down into the Court.

*

The Extraordinary Meeting of the College Council was
a solemn occasion. Even the Senior Tutor and Dr
Buscott, evidently sensing that something unprecedented was in the air, were in a subdued mood, while
the Dean, still shaken by Purefoy Osbert's calm assumption that he had conspired with Skullion to murder Sir
Godber, was incapable of doing more than agreeing with
everything the Praelector proposed even though he did
not follow the argument or understand the consequences any more than the Bursar did.

'In the first place we are here today to mark the
passing of the Master,' the Praelector announced.
'During the night his state deteriorated to the point
where he was no longer capable of fulfilling those few
statutory duties he has been limited to. This, together
with his state of mind, obliged him to relinquish the
position of Master on the grounds that he is *non
compos mentis*. We are therefore in a state of interreg-
num until the new Master has been appointed. Yes, Dr
Buscott?'

'I was just wondering if Skul . . . if the late Master exercised his right to nominate his successor,' Dr Buscott

said. 'And, if he did, being as you say *non compos mentis*, whether his nomination had any validity.'

'It is a perfectly proper point to make and one on which I have this morning consulted the College solicitors. They have given it as their opinion that in the circumstances of the Master being unable to make a rational decision the choice of a new Master devolves upon the College Council and in the event of the Council failing to agree, the matter automatically reverts to the Crown. Or, to put it more precisely, the choice of a new Master will be decided by the Government of the day.' He paused and looked round the table. 'I, for one, am wholly opposed to such a course of action. We have had previous and catastrophic experience of a Prime Minister's choice.'

There was a murmur of agreement from the Fellows, all of whom remembered the late Sir Godber Evans.

'It is therefore essential that we show a degree of unanimity in the interest of the College and at the same time accept the indisputable fact that a wholly unprecedented and catastrophic financial crisis faces Porterhouse. I won't go into the history of it. Rather than look back, I would ask you to look to the future. We are now in a position to ensure that, from being the poorest college in Cambridge and one that is in fact on the point of total bankruptcy, Porterhouse can be among the very richest.'

A gasp of amazement ran round the table. The Praelector waited until he had their full attention again.

'You will, I am afraid, have to take my word for it. I have been a Fellow of Porterhouse for more years than I care to remember and I think I can claim to have the interests of the College at heart.'

For twenty minutes the Praelector went on presenting facts and figures obtained from the Bursar's office to show the College debts and the temporary nature of the reprieve offered by the Transworld Television compensatory payment when and if, as he implied, it was finally settled. And all the time the Fellows sat mesmerized by his strange authority. For years the Praelector had gone quietly and inconspicuously about his little business and had been ignored as a force in the College. But now, in an Indian summer of the intellect, he had come to dominate them all. Even Dr Buscott recognized that he was in the presence of someone, even some thing, that was too powerful to be doubted. And at the end when the Praelector asked for their unanimous consent that he be allowed to conduct negotiations with the candidate of his own choice and with no questions asked, the Council passed the motion without a single dissenting voice. As they filed out into the spring sunshine there was a new confident mood among the Fellows of Porterhouse. They had surrendered their authority to a man they could trust and they felt a sense of freedom.

*

Which was more than could be said for Skullion. Seated in his wheelchair in the ambulance, he knew he had been betrayed again. He wasn't going to Coft Castle as the General had promised. They had been on the road too long for that and they were moving too fast. They were on the motorway and heading for Porterhouse Park and there was absolutely nothing he could do about it. He had been taken for a mug again. And they had done a good professional job getting him out of Porterhouse too, sending Arthur off to the chemist for the prescription of his blood-pressure pills and then as soon as the Master's Lodge was empty coming in without so much as a by-your-leave and having him through the doorway into the ambulance before you could say Jack Robinson and then off through the traffic as if everything was hunky-dory.

Oh well, it was his own bloody fault. He shouldn't have got pissed and threatened the Dean. And he shouldn't have listened to Sir Cathcart fucking D'Eath. He should have known those bastards would stick together. Always did and always would when it came to saving their own skins. Not that they were above slitting one another's throats if it came to that. And now that he was gone they'd say he'd had another Porterhouse Blue and Cheffy and them wouldn't know any better. They wouldn't know he'd been taken off to Porterhouse Park and if they did it wouldn't do any good. No one ever visited the Park. It was just somewhere they sent you when you'd lost your marbles like old Dr Vertel and Mr Manners who'd become an embarrassment with his incontinence and his nasty habit of suddenly attacking undergraduates with his umbrella because he thought they were sniggering at him behind his back. And now it was his turn and no doubt they'd have some hard old woman in charge to give him his pills and order him about and give him baths. Doubtless too they would wheel him out on sunny days to stare out over the landscape and listen to the other old loonies mumbling to themselves. He'd have to eat with them too and they'd call him Skullion and treat him like dirt just as they used to do when he was a porter. Old Vertel had never liked him, and he must still be alive because there'd been no obituary in the Porterhouse magazine. Skullion sat in his wheelchair and stared at the curtain they'd pulled across the rear window of the ambulance, and cursed himself for a fool.

31

Purefoy Osbert watched the Fellows file out of the old Library with interest. For a moment he thought they had been discussing the threat he posed to the Master but the meeting had been called before his confrontation with the Dean. Something else was in the wind. Some undergraduates passing him in the Court had spoken about the Master having another Porterhouse Blue and of an ambulance arriving at the Master's Lodge. Whatever the cause of the air of excitement in the College, Purefoy was determined to make use of it. His visit to the Dean and the Dean's impotent and stammering fury had done surprising things for Purefoy's confidence. He no longer felt overawed by the atmosphere of Porterhouse and in his own mind saw it as having no more importance than some casual roadside café. Its ceremonies and rituals like the Induction Dinner, its archaic terminology – 'the Dossery', 'the Fellows' Combination Room', 'the Buttery', 'the Dean', 'the Master' – were mere devices, theatrical and phoney, having the intention of fooling immature and impressionable minds and masking, like some masonic ceremony, the littleness of the officials who hid behind such titles. In all the other colleges Purefoy had visited at one time or another there

had been at least some slight self-mockery. Not at
Porterhouse. Here the dense seriousness of small minds
prevailed. Purefoy Osbert saw through the pretence and
chose his next target. It was to be the Senior Tutor. He
caught him as he came up the stairs to his room.

'Ah, there you are,' Purefoy said, coming out of his
doorway. 'I'd like a few words with you.'

The Senior Tutor looked at him angrily. He didn't
like being accosted without a title. It smacked of rudeness. And he certainly didn't want any words with Dr
Osbert. 'Busy at the moment,' he said and turned into
his doorway.

Purefoy Osbert followed him before the Senior Tutor
could shut the door in his face. 'It's about the allegations
the Dean has made,' he said.

'Allegations? What the devil are you talking about?'

'I was hoping you could explain exactly what your
role was,' Purefoy said.

'My role? What role?' demanded the Senior Tutor.

'In the light of Skullion's confession it is important to
get things in their proper perspective,' Purefoy continued. 'Now the Dean says that ... Well, perhaps it
would be fairer to hear your account. That way you will
be saved the need for denials.'

The Senior Tutor backed unsteadily into his study.
'Skullion's confession?' he gasped. 'What has Skullion
confessed to?'

'To being responsible for the actual murder of Sir
Godber Evans. Only the act of murder. He puts the

responsibility . . . Now, if you'll just state for the record what part you played . . .' Purefoy hesitated and waited for the Senior Tutor's reaction to the imputation that he had played any part in a murder. It was a long time coming. The Senior Tutor was staring at him in horror.

'Sir Godber Evans' murder?' he managed to say finally. 'I had no idea.'

'That is not what the Dean has said in his statement. Now, at the time of the murder you were not in College yourself. According to the evidence you gave at the inquest. If you want to change that now . . .'

'Change it? But I was at Coft Castle visiting Sir Cathcart D'Eath. There were people there who saw us.'

'Us?' said Purefoy with a look of some doubt on his face. 'You did say "us"?'

'Of course I said us. The Dean and I.'

'Really? That is not what the Dean has said,' Purefoy replied. 'Still, if that is your story . . .'

'Of course it is my story,' shouted the Senior Tutor. 'It's the bloody truth.'

'There is no need to shout,' Purefoy told him. 'Why don't you sit down and tell me about this so-called alibi? You'll feel much better when you've got this off your chest.'

Without thinking the Senior Tutor sat down. His mind was a maelstrom of hopelessly conflicting emotions. Thought hardly came into it. 'I haven't got anything to get off my chest. I don't know anything about Sir Godber Evans' murder. I didn't even know he had been murdered. No one told me.'

Purefoy Osbert smiled, and his smile seemed to imply that the Senior Tutor had hardly needed telling. 'Now, when you spoke to him earlier on the fatal evening what did you actually say to him?'

'Say to him? Say to whom, for God's sake?'

'Skullion of course.'

'But I didn't speak to him that evening. Why the hell should I have spoken to Skullion?'

'That's for you to tell me,' said Purefoy Osbert. 'Now according to the Dean you were the one . . .'

'Fuck the Dean,' shouted the Senior Tutor. 'I don't care what that stupid bastard says, I'm telling you I never went anywhere near Skullion that evening –'

'Right,' Purefoy interrupted. 'So the Dean is a liar and . . .'

'Look,' the Senior Tutor yelled, 'I don't know whether the bloody man is a liar or not. What I am . . .'

'So you're saying his account of your actions is correct now?'

The Senior Tutor stared wildly round the room. Purefoy Osbert recognized the symptom. It was exactly what he had experienced in Mrs Ndhlovo's apartment. He decided to strike another blow at the Senior Tutor's morale. 'As you know the Master, Skullion, was taken away this morning . . .'

There was no need to say more. The Senior Tutor

clearly did know, but until that moment the full implications of the Extraordinary Council meeting hadn't
occurred to him. He could understand only too well the
Praelector's statement that Skullion was *non compos
mentis*. Frankly the Senior Tutor found the Latin totally
inadequate to describe the man's state of mind. He was
clearly as mad as a hatter. But then so was the bloody
Dean, if it came to that. In the Senior Tutor's imagination the police were already interrogating Skullion and
would shortly continue their investigations in Porterhouse itself. And the Dean must have had some hand in
the murder or he wouldn't be making allegations against
him to this swine Osbert. The Senior Tutor made up his
desperately confused mind.

'All right, I will tell you this,' he said. 'The Dean was
the one who suggested we go out to Coft Castle that
night. He suggested it at Dinner and I remember being
most surprised. In fact I said it was not on and wouldn't
work but he insisted in spite of my objections.'

'I see,' said Purefoy after a significant pause. 'That
isn't the story the Dean provided us with. He said you
were the one who insisted on being out of the College
that night. He says . . .'

'Then he's a bloody liar,' shouted the Senior Tutor.
'I'll tell you exactly what he said.'

Ten minutes later Purefoy Osbert left the room. The
Senior Tutor had given him some very surprising information, had in fact opened up an entirely new can of
worms and one that would almost certainly provoke

General Sir Cathcart D'Eath to an ouburst of fury and
indiscretion. Purefoy couldn't imagine what it would do
to the Dean. In his room he checked his pocket tape
recorder and changed the tape. Then he went down into
the Fellows' Garden well pleased with himself. Mrs
Ndhlovo and her friend had done him a good turn after
all.

*

The Praelector travelled down to London by train and
caught a taxi to the Goring Hotel. It was not where he
usually stayed, preferring a more modest establishment
near Russell Square on his very infrequent visits to the
capital, but the Goring had a solid respectability about
it and in the circumstances the Praelector knew he
needed all the solidarity and respectability he could
muster. It was there that he received Schnabel and
Feuchtwangler for the informal meeting he had
requested. The deeply alarmed Mr Retter had advised
against it. 'You're going to be talking to men . . .' Mr
Retter had hesitated over the word and almost said
'shysters' '. . . who would skin their grandmothers alive
for the sort of fees they're earning from Transworld.
You really must be most careful what you say to them.'

'I always am,' said the Praelector, and decided not to
add 'when talking to lawyers'.

And so that evening a seemingly benign old man
greeted Schnabel and Feuchtwangler in a corner of the
lounge. 'I am sure this whole wretched business can be

settled more amicably,' he told them when they had made themselves relatively comfortable. Mr Schnabel said he doubted it. Mr Feuchtwangler nodded his agreement.

'Our client is not an amicable man,' Schnabel said.

The Praelector smiled. 'So few of us are,' he said. 'But we must try to accommodate ourselves to circumstances, don't you think?'

Schnabel said he didn't think their client understood the word.

'"Accommodate," or "Circumstances"?' the Praelector enquired.

'Both,' said Schnabel.

'All the same he must have a well developed sense of self-preservation to have survived so long,' the Praelector went on. 'Is Mr Passos still in town?'

Schnabel blinked and looked at the old man with new eyes. Feuchtwangler swallowed drily.

'I wouldn't know about anything like that,' said Schnabel.

'Of course you wouldn't,' the Praelector agreed. 'It is outside your remit. However, I imagine it is a matter of some concern to your client, and I rather think he wouldn't welcome deportation to Thailand or Singapore. I believe the death penalty there is mandatory for certain commercial activities. Of course I'm by no means an expert in these matters but . . .'

'Shit,' said Schnabel. This wasn't a benign old man with gravespots on his hands. This was death itself.

The Praelector signalled to a waiter. 'I wonder if you'd care to join me in a drink,' he said. Neither of them wanted anything stronger than water. The Praelector ordered a fino. 'Now, as I said at the start, I am sure this whole affair can be dealt with on an amicable and mutually beneficial basis and one that your client will find most acceptable. I shall, of course, need to put the proposal to him personally and I daresay he would prefer me to visit him in his office. I have one or two important appointments to keep tomorrow morning but perhaps four o'clock tomorrow afternoon would suit him.'

'I don't think any time is going to – ' Schnabel began but Feuchtwangler cut in. 'Listen,' he said. 'When you say "a mutually beneficial basis", it would be helpful to us in arranging this meeting to know where we stand in the matter.'

'Of course, of course,' said the Praelector. 'I quite understand your concern. Let me just say that the financial consequences of the proposal I have been authorized to put before your client will not adversely affect your firm in the slightest. Quite the contrary. As you know we have been represented by Waxthorne, Libbott and Chaine in Cambridge and naturally for purely minor matters we shall continue to use their services. However, in the hoped-for eventuality that your client accepts our proposal, the College will need the expertise of a firm with wider experience in the field of finance and commercial law. And now if you will excuse me I must leave you. I have a dinner appointment with my godson.'

Accompanied by the two lawyers the Praelector went out to a taxi. 'Downing Street,' he told the driver in the clearest voice. 'Number Eleven.'

Schnabel and Feuchtwangler stood on the pavement and stared after the taxi. There was no doubt now in their minds that their client was going to keep the appointment the following afternoon.

In the taxi the Praelector smiled to himself and, as they drove down Whitehall, leant forward. 'I have changed my mind,' he told the driver as they drove down the Mall. 'There's a rather good restaurant in Jermyn Street. I think I'll dine there.'

32

By luncheon the freedom the Dean had felt on leaving the Council Chamber had evaporated. In its place there was a sense of uncertainty and the feeling that things were occurring in a mysterious and secretive way which would change the College entirely. The situation had passed beyond the Dean's control. One shock after another had left him exhausted – too exhausted to notice that the Senior Tutor kept looking at him with such poisonous hatred that Sir Cathcart's belief the night before that the man was a homicidal maniac seemed perfectly plausible. Certainly the Senior Tutor had murder in his heart and only the established practice of not having full-blown rows at High Table (a practice that went back to the seventeenth century when two Fellows had fought an impromptu duel between the game pie and the roast beef over a misunderstanding of the word 'Bestiary' which duel had resulted in the death of a talented theologian with a harelip) prevented the Senior Tutor from telling the Dean exactly what he thought of him. In any case, the Friday lunch fish had its usual moderating influence. There were far too many bones in the red mullet to attend to.

Only the Chaplain was in conversational mood. 'I am

most concerned about the Master,' he said. 'I tried phoning Addenbrooke's to find out his condition and they assured me he hadn't been admitted.'

'Hardly surprising. I don't suppose they recognized him,' said Dr Buscott. 'Not as the Master of a college at any rate. Possibly as a tramp or something of that sort.'

'What the devil do you mean by that?' asked the Senior Tutor, glad to be able to vent his feelings fairly legitimately.

'Simply that Masters of other colleges are rather more distinguished and don't wear bowler hats.'

'I don't suppose he was admitted in a bowler hat,' Professor Pawley commented. 'Even if he was wearing it when he had this latest stroke, which strikes me as doubtful, they would have removed it when he was put on the stretcher.'

'Nothing wrong with bowlers,' said the Senior Tutor. 'They used to be very fashionable. Guards officers in mufti had to wear them. Still do, for all I know.'

'I remember seeing Larwood when I was a small boy,' said the Chaplain. 'He was really fast. But it was Jardyne who caused all the rumpus over the bodyline bowling. Now they wear helmets.'

'We weren't talking about those bowlers. We were talking about Skullion's hat.'

'Of course I asked for him by name. They wouldn't have known who I was talking about otherwise. They still said he wasn't there.'

'Perhaps he's in the Evelyn,' said Professor Pawley. 'They say it's very comfortable there.'

The Dean ignored their talk. As far as he was concerned Skullion no longer existed, and in any case he had no intention of telling them where Skullion had gone. The fewer people who knew, the better. He was wondering where the Praelector had got to and whether it had been wise to give the old man the authority to conduct negotiations with a candidate of his own choosing. It was too late now to do anything about it, but all the same he couldn't help feeling anxious. In the end he excused himself before the end of the meal and went for a quiet walk along the Backs.

For a moment the Senior Tutor almost followed him but thought better of it. There was time enough to have it out with the Dean and for all he knew the police were keeping an eye on the College. He had never for one moment believed the story about Skullion being taken to hospital. With a sense of tact that was surprising, or perhaps for the practical reason that a wheelchair could not be got into a police car, the police had made use of an ambulance to take Skullion to the Parkside Police Station where they were undoubtedly questioning him. For a moment the Senior Tutor wondered if he ought to do something about getting him a solicitor before remembering that the Praelector had mentioned visiting Mr Retter that morning ostensibly to consult the partner about the constitutional position of a successor to a mentally incompetent Master. Again he was astonished at the tact and care the Praelector had shown in avoiding unwanted publicity. It only went to prove the College Council had been correct in putting so much trust in him.

All the same the Senior Tutor was still in a filthy mood when he set off for the Porterhouse Boat House across Midsummer Common and as he rode his bicycle his thoughts were centred on Dr Purefoy Osbert. He would dearly like to find some way of making that young man regret the day he had ever set foot in Porterhouse. He was still considering the possibility of somehow incriminating the damned Dr Osbert when, having vented his fury on the First Boat, he cycled back to the College.

As he passed the Porter's Lodge Walter came out with an envelope.

'Sorry to bother you, sir,' he said. 'Urgent message for Dr Osbert and since you're on the same staircase I wonder . . .' The Senior Tutor took the envelope and hurried on. He was anxious to see what the urgent message was. It might prove to be useful.

Once in his room he switched the electric kettle on and steamed the envelope open and read the letter inside. It held little interest for him. It was simply an invitation from the President of the American Association for the Abolition of Cruel and Unusual Punishment to meet with the author of *The Long Drop*, a work that

she had read with great interest and appreciation etc.
Unfortunately her schedule was very tight and the only
free evening available was Friday. She was staying with
friends in Cambridge overnight but would be honoured
to meet Dr Osbert outside the Royal Hotel at 8 p.m.
The Senior Tutor folded the letter and put it back into
the envelope before changing his mind and tearing it up.
That was one appointment Dr Osbert was not going to
keep.

*

In London Schnabel was on the phone to Transworld
Television. 'I'm telling you they are evidently offering
you a way out,' he told Hartang. 'This guy's the genuine
article and he's got real influence.'

'Like how real?' Hartang wanted to know.

'Like Downing Street,' Schnabel told him.

There was a long pause while Hartang considered this
extraordinary statement.

'He's got that sort of influence, what's he want from
me?' he asked finally.

'I don't know. He's got some sort of proposal to put
to you. He stated quite specifically that he thought that
the matter could be dealt with on an amicable and
mutually beneficial basis. Feuchtwangler was with me.
He can tell you.' Feuchtwangler told him and handed
the phone back to Schnabel. It took another half hour
to convince Hartang to agree to see the Praelector and

even then he remained highly suspicious. It was the mention of extradition to Singapore as an alternative that finally persuaded him.

'You get this one wrong, Schnabel, and I won't just be looking for some new legal advisers, I'll be needing the help of some contractors from Chicago. Know what I mean?'

Schnabel said he did, and hung up. 'Number Eleven Downing Street and the stupid bastard talks like that,' he said.

*

The Praelector rose late and had a leisurely breakfast. Then, in case his movements were being watched, he paid a visit to a nephew who did have a job in the Home Office. After that he had lunch with a retired bishop. All in all his day was spent building up in any watcher's mind the belief that he was dealing with a man of very considerable influence. When he returned to the Goring Hotel, an invitation to meet with Mr Edgar Hartang at the Transworld Television Centre was waiting for him. The Praelector had a rest and then took a taxi to Docklands where he was subjected to a body check and the attentions of the metal detector before shooting up and down in the elevator to the unnumbered floor and Hartang's bleak office. Hartang greeted him with an ingratiating concern and a sickening servility that fully substantiated the Bursar's account of his meeting with him. Hartang had slipped into his middle-European

charm mode. It didn't fool the Praelector for a moment.
On the other hand he was pleased to see that Hartang
had discarded the blazer and the polo-neck and even the
white socks and was dressed slightly more formally in a
light suit with a plain tie.

'I am authorized,' said the Praelector when the slight
courtesies were over, 'by the College Council of Porterhouse College to offer you the position of Master of the
College.' He paused and looked at Hartang with all the
solemn benevolence he could muster. Hartang was
staring at him through lightly tinted glasses – the dark
blue ones had gone with the white socks and moccasins
– with a mixture of incredulity and extreme suspicion.

The Praelector savoured his astonishment for a
moment and then went on, 'My purpose in doing so
is to achieve two objects, the first beneficial to the
College and the second, I believe, very much to your
standing as an eminent financier and as an individual.
Let me say that the gift of the Mastership at Porterhouse
is the Crown prerogative and it is only in exceptional
circumstances that the Crown, or to be more precise
the Government of the day, that is to say the Prime
Minister, is prepared to derogate its authority in these
matters to the College Council. It has done so in the
present case for reasons that we need not go into and
which, in any event, I am not at liberty to divulge.
Suffice to say these reasons have to do with the national
interest. Treaty obligations with certain countries can be
obviated by your acceptance while at the same time

your recognized financial expertise will remain inviolate.' The Praelector paused again and this time he assumed the most solemn expression to emphasize the seriousness with which he had spoken. He hadn't tickled trout as a boy without learning when to take particular care. Edgar Hartang hardly breathed at the other end of the green sofa.

'Naturally you will want to consider the proposal at your leisure and consult your advisers before giving an answer. However, I can assure you that the position of Master is not offered lightly or capriciously. Nor does it involve more than formal duties. You would have as your residence the Master's Lodge, the provision of College servants and of any amenities you chose to provide for your own comfort and security. At the same time your social position would be assured. I cannot put it more highly than that. Porterhouse College is one of the oldest in Cambridge and, if I may be permitted a moment's frankness, your contribution in the field of electronic communications would be invaluable to us, to say nothing of your financial expertise. I will leave you now. I shall be staying at the Goring Hotel for three more days and will await your answer there.'

The Praelector rose and took his leave with a slight diplomatic bow. As the elevator doors shut Hartang loosened his collar and then sat down again and tried to come to terms with the extraordinary mixture of threats and promises he had just heard. In a life full of crude alarms and brutal opportunities he had never experi-

enced anything in the least like this. For an hour he tried
to find a snag in the Praelector's offer and failed. Maybe
Schnabel would know. He picked up the phone and
punched the lawyer's home number.

*

It was an altered Edgar Hartang who went into conference with Schnabel, Feuchtwangler and Bolsover that
evening. The realization that something fundamental
had occurred in his life had softened Edgar Hartang's
approach to his legal advisers. 'You believe it's for real,
the old guy having the authority to negotiate like he's
an ambassador or something?' he asked them.

'We do,' said Schnabel.

'It's a very great honour, sir,' said Bolsover.

'It's helluva good protection,' was Feuchtwangler's
comment. 'I never heard of them extraditing a college
President yet.' Hartang gnawed a knuckle. He hadn't
liked that talk about treaty obligations one bit. A godson
at Number Eleven Downing Street and what the fuck
had the old geezer been doing with the guy who worked
in the Home Office and bishops and all?

'It's the way the Brits have always done things,'
Feuchtwangler explained. 'They tie you up tight and
then say "Join the club, old boy." Don't have to mention
what the option is because you know. How do you think
Dick Whittington became Lord Mayor of London?'

Hartang said he didn't know any Dick Whittington.
'What's in it for them?' he wanted to know.

'What he said, your expertise. First, money. Information highway stuff costs. You've got to hand it to Kudzuvine. He's done you a favour.'

It was a risky statement. Hartang wasn't ready to think of Kudzuvine doing him any favours yet.

'And one thing is certain,' said Bolsover. 'Dos Passos will be on a flight out the moment you officially accept. They've got him under surveillance now.'

It was a convincing point. Hartang agreed to become Master of Porterhouse.

*

'It is amazing how things work out,' Schnabel said as they drove away. 'I won't say he's at all civilized yet but the process has begun. In two years I daresay he'll be house-trained.'

'Porterhouse-trained,' said Bolsover.

33

The Praelector sat on a seat in the spring sunshine and watched some children fighting on the grass. It was a great many years since he had indulged in such an enjoyable activity, rolling over and over and trying to get the upper hand in a tussle with another boy but he could remember vividly what fun it had been even when he had lost. And now for the first time for many years he was having fun again though this time it was the fun of genuine conquest. Of course there would be more battles to come. For one thing Hartang would have to be tamed and even in these gross days it would never do to have a Master using the word 'motherfucker' at High Table too often. But the Praelector intended to leave that aspect of Hartang's development to the other Fellows and to the atmosphere of the College with its many little formalities. His more immediate problems were quite different. He had to persuade the College Council to ratify Hartang's appointment and he had never faced a more difficult task in his life. Even the most brilliant Cambridge academics had no grasp of the political implications of finance and industry. Brought up in a Welfare State they had not lived through the Twenties and Thirties when the poor had been genuinely hungry and men and women and children had pinched white faces and there had been Salvation Army soup kitchens. Some of them had read about such things but they had never experienced them. Instead they indulged in nostalgic charades and mock hunger-marches, their plump comfortable faces glowing with health and their feet shod in warm well-soled shoes, and went home afterwards filled with a sense of self-righteous concern and satisfaction to congratulate themselves on their moral stance over smoked salmon and coq-au-vin in centrally heated houses. And everywhere television and glossy magazines insulated and to some extent inoculated them from real pain and misery. The Praelector had lived too long to forget the world before Beveridge and the need to produce manufactured goods for export. Now Porterhouse had to come to terms with his decision or it would go under. It would be his last struggle. He got up and walked back to the hotel relishing the thought of the Dean's face when he heard the news.

*

Purefoy Osbert and Mrs Ndhlovo sat in the sunshine too on a bench under the wall of Peterhouse with the old river gate behind them. It was blocked up now and the river over a hundred yards away but it had been from that gate that the Masters and Fellows had stepped into boats centuries earlier to travel down to their colleges and avoid the mud and filth of the streets.

'I had to come and explain,' she was saying. 'After all it was only a joke, and all right it wasn't in the best taste but really good jokes so seldom are.'

Purefoy scowled at some horses browsing in the grass in front of them. He still hadn't made up his mind about Mrs Ndhlovo and her sister. And he was no longer sure he believed a word she said. On the other hand he was secretly pleased she had never been the third wife of the late Mr Ndhlovo.

'It was the only way I could get into the country,' she had explained. Purefoy said he didn't understand.

'How do you imagine someone without a birth certificate or a passport can pass through Immigration Control without any papers? It is impossible.'

'But you must have had some sort of identification. You must know who you are.'

'I know who I am now, but I didn't then. Nobody knew. You have never lived in a country like Argentina under the Generals where people quite literally disappeared. That's what happened to my mother and father. Brigitte and I were found one morning on a picnic table on the bank of the Rio Plata in a town called Fray Bentos. We had labels tied to us with the word "Unknown" in English written on them. So we went to a Catholic orphanage where the nuns called us Incognito. That was a joke too, to begin with, but the name stuck and I became Ingrid Natasha Cognito and Brigitte was more fortunate. All the same we hated the orphanage and the nuns and we ran away and went to Paraguay.

And that wasn't nice at all because we had to live with some very poor Germans in a really strange settlement. We had blue eyes and fair hair and spoke English.'

Purefoy listened with a drowsy fascination. The River Plate, Fray Bentos and the meat-packing factory which had closed, the Golf Club with the Coronation Plaque for George VI on the wall and the distances of the holes still in yards, Paraguay and Stroessner's German-helmeted troops goose-stepping in a dusty plaza, the dilapidated farmhouses of the descendants of nineteenth-century German settlers, strange South African sects in modern buildings, heat and insects, and then back through Uruguay to Montevideo, a city which was frozen in the 1950s and where Anglos still gathered in the English Club with its cracked and pasted dining-room window and the plaster ceiling in the bar broken and partly fallen and its bound copies of the *Montevideo Times* piled in the library next to the ancient and unused fencing gallery. From there to Africa, this time with the help of the South African sectarians.

The white horses grazed on the meadow grass and Purefoy's imagination followed the story of Miss I. N. Cognito's wanderings with the growing conviction that she must be telling the truth. All the same he was still suspicious. In the modern world everyone in faintly civilized society had to have some means of identifying themselves even if it was only some nuns in an orphanage or someone who had known them for a time.

'That doesn't help you get into the UK,' Ingrid said.

'You try coming into Heathrow with no passport or birth certificate and no one to vouch for who you are. It's weird. Those immigration officers don't even pretend to think you're telling the truth. We tried it one time on a cargo flight from Lusaka. That was a mistake. It got the crew into terrible trouble and they gave us the most gruesome body searches. And laxatives in case we'd swallowed condoms of drugs or diamonds. Not nice.'

'What on earth were you doing in Lusaka?'

'I told you we had become born-again members of the Benoni Sect. Some woman had visions or something back in 1927 and the people thought this was a good time to move out of South Africa with some money to build missions in South America.'

'They could have given you some means of identification . . .'

'Could have. Didn't because we told them the religion was a phoney and it's amazing how intolerant religious people can be when you refuse to believe. They cast us out into outer darkness, in this case Brakpan, and we had to make it on our own.'

'So how did you get into this country?'

'By making friends with a nice Greek who had a corner store and two sisters who didn't mind losing their passports. We had to give them back to him in Athens. After that it wasn't so difficult. We worked our way along the Mediterranean to Spain, on yachts mainly, and a sweet old man in Palamos needed crew. His wife didn't like crossing the Bay of Biscay in winter and went home by air. So one day we sailed into Falmouth and came ashore when no one was looking.'

'And you still have no papers? You don't have a passport or a birth certificate or anything?'

'Oh, but I have. Once you're here it's easy to get a birth certificate.'

'How?' Purefoy asked. He wanted certainty. She gave it to him.

Purefoy looked at her in amazement. 'You didn't,' he said. 'At least, I hope you didn't.'

'Well, we had to do something. And he was such a pathetic man. All alone in the world and slaving away in Somerset House and no one had been nice to him before.'

'So you got a passport in the name of Mrs Ndhlovo?' said Purefoy suspiciously.

'Oh no, not Mrs Ndhlovo. She was only a temporary expedient much later. I'm Isobel Rathwick and I was born in Bournemouth. I'm entirely legitimate now. All the same I much prefer Mrs Ndhlovo. I don't want you to call me anything else. It gives me a lot of fun with all those serious people who are concerned about the Third World.'

'I'm sure,' said Purefoy. 'And what about your sister? What's she doing now?'

'Being frightfully respectable in Woking. She's married and has two daughters, but every now and then she has to break out and go back to being herself.'

'It all sounds very odd to me. I don't see how you can live a lie.'

'Because we've had to invent ourselves, Purefoy dear, just like everyone else.'

'Not me,' said Purefoy. 'I'm certain I know who I am.'

'You only think you do,' Mrs Ndhlovo thought but she didn't say it.

They strolled back up King's Parade and looked at the stalls in the market and had tea in a little café behind the Guildhall, and this time Purefoy told her about his sparring rounds with the Dean and the Senior Tutor, and how Skullion had been taken away.

'Oh Purefoy, how brilliant. And it's all because of me and Brigitte. I think I shall become something called . . . What shall we call it? A Provocator, yes, a Provocator and conduct classes for shy young men who believe everything they are told or read in books. I'm tired of Male Infertility and Masturbatory Techniques and all those earnest women feeling deeply about Female Circumcision and not a smile among them.'

'But you are an expert on it. You can't just give it up like that.'

'I took it up just like that,' said Ms I. N. Cognito. 'I got the slides in London and read up on all the rest. And if you want to know why, because I was bored with being a stewardess on airlines and being polite to people I would never want to see again. Oh, the lies one had to tell! And they were always the same boring lies. At least as Mrs Ndhlovo I could be more imaginative, but that's got boring too, and people, usually most unattractive ones, will come up to me afterwards and ask questions. The number of really awful women who have tried to proposition me! But now it's all going to be different. I want you to show me your Porterhouse. I'm going to apply for the post of Provocator. Junior Provocator. Do you think they'll accept me?'

'They've got enough troubles already,' said Purefoy.

*

In the bedroom at General Sir Cathcart D'Eath's 'safe house' near the Botanical Gardens Myrtle Ransby was experiencing a sense of the unreal combined with a hangover that was the worst she had ever known. She had arrived at the right time the night before as the General had ordered, having had one or two brandies to steady her nerves which were still affected by meeting the American with the bloodstained apron, the awful knife and the partly dismembered stallion at the Catfood Canning Factory. She had let herself in the back door and after one or two more brandies – there was no one else about – she had managed with great difficulty to get into the black latex suit and had put the hood on over her en bouffant. Then she had sat down and waited, every now and then helping herself to some more brandy. The client hadn't turned up. Myrtle rummaged in her bag and read the General's instructions again. He had definitely said Friday at 8 p.m. It was now nearly nine. Well, she'd get paid whatever happened. Those torn notes were going to become whole ones even if she had to sit there all night. Two hours later she decided to take the hood off and get some fresh air. This entailed removing the rubber gloves first and they wouldn't come. She was interrupted in her struggle with the things by the need to go wee-wee and she was fighting another battle, this time with the bottom half of her costume, when the phone rang. Myrtle told it to go fuck itself and stayed where she was. Then, when it was too late, she made an attempted dash for the thing and tripped over. The phone stopped ringing. Myrtle reached for the brandy bottle and drank quite a lot more. It was almost midnight when she tried to go to the bathroom again and inadvertently switched the light off and couldn't find the switch again. By now her efforts to rid herself of the gloves, the hood and the rest of her costume had become a waste of time. In the darkness she crawled about the floor and found the brandy bottle and finished it. Presently she passed out and spent the night where she lay, happily unaware of time, place and her own condition.

Morning, not a bright morning in the shuttered room, was very different. It took her some time to work out why she could hardly breathe, could only see out of part of one eye – the hood and en bouffant had both changed position – and was encased in something that was at once cold and sticky. Slowly and painstakingly she managed to get to her feet and make it with the help of the wall to the bathroom and turn the light on. The image in the mirror did nothing to restore her self-esteem. Used to fairly awful mornings in the company of boys at the airbase with peculiar tastes in fetish costumes, she had never seen herself in anything approaching this bizarre condition. Myrtle Ransby sat down on the lavatory and began to cry before dimly remembering that she had promised her husband she'd be back by one o'clock at the latest. She had also been promised the other half of the two thousand pounds. For a moment fury rose in her. She had been betrayed, was in a strange house and in a rubber suit that was far too small for her. She felt like death. Worst of all it was the weekend and somehow she had to get home. At that moment the effects of the brandy made themselves felt in various ways.

Ten minutes later, feeling only slightly better, Myrtle rallied and tried to find something to help her cut her way out of the costume but apart from an old tooth-brush which was no help at all, the only thing was a double-bladed plastic razor but even in her desperation she couldn't get it to cut anything. Once again she set to work trying to get the gloves off and when that failed, she spent a fruitless and frequently painful twenty minutes dragging at the various slits in the costume which kept recoiling violently. There was nothing for it. She wasn't going to risk having her nose broken or being choked to death on her false teeth. She'd just phone for help. She sat on the edge of the bed squinting down at the telephone and wondering what her husband Len would say or, more importantly, do if he came and found her like this. Knowing him, he'd either knock her about a bit, and quite a bit at that considering she was in no condition to fight back or, even worse, laugh himself sick and tell all his rotten mates down the local and she'd be the laughing stock of Thetford.

Darker thoughts slowly made their way into her mind. She'd been left in the fucking lurch, which was bad enough, and she'd been made to look a bloody idiot, but, worst of all, she had been robbed blind by an old poncey General and a Sir. Oh no, she hadn't. Myrtle Ransby had been through too many sordid squabbles and downright wars over payments for services rendered to be done out of her two thousand nicker by an old fart called D'Eath, Sir Cathcart fucking D'Eath. Well she'd D'Eath the bugger before she'd finished never mind that Yank who killed horses. After much thought Myrtle rang her sister and told her to come over from Red Lodge and not to say anything to anyone, not anyone at all. Maggie wanted to know what was wrong with her voice 'cos she sounded all hoarse or something and anyway she couldn't come until Perce got back from Newmarket with the car and Myrtle knew what Perce was like when he'd been to Newmarket. Worse when he won of course. Anyway she'd come when she could. Rather than enter into a prolonged argument with her sister, Myrtle put the phone down and checked her handbag to see if the envelope with her half of the two grand was still safe. She'd brought it to compare the way it was torn with the other and make sure she wasn't being done. She also looked at her watch and found it was 3.15. She lay on the bed and thought even darker thoughts until 7 p.m. when Maggie drove up in front of the house and blew the horn. Myrtle put on her leopard-skin – the gold lamés were too tight to fit over the latex leggings – and went downstairs and made a dash for the car.

'Lumme,' Maggie said, 'Lumme Myrt, what's with the Michelin tyre outfit? You been to a rubber lovers' fancy-dress ball or something?'

A very nasty blue eye warned her not to laugh. They drove out of Cambridge on the Barton Road.

*

Sir Cathcart D'Eath had had a tiring two days. Duck Dinner and the shocking events afterwards had given him a sleepless night and he'd had to be up early the following day to make arrangements for Skullion's hasty removal from the Master's Lodge. It had involved a number of phone calls and awkward questions about covert operations of that kind and the difficulties involved in getting an ambulance with a suitable crew up from London at a moment's notice. But in the end and at considerable personal expense he had prevailed. After the lightest of lunches he rested and prepared himself for a small dinner-party with a number of old and distinguished chums who were coming up for the

weekend with their wives. Most importantly, Sir
Edmund and Lady Sarah Lazarus-Crouch had been
invited. The General was particularly anxious to ingra-
tiate himself with the Lazarus-Crouches because his
niece, Katherine D'Eath, was engaged to their son Harry
and Sir Cathcart was anxious to avail himself of Sir
Edmund's financial acumen which, since he had advised
the Queen to sever all connections with at least three
merchant ventures which had later collapsed, was considerable. In short the gathering at Coft Castle that
evening was of the unostentatiously great and the ostensibly good. Even Sir Cathcart's secretary had been given
the weekend off while Kentucky Fry had been sent to a
pig farm in Leicestershire for a holiday. And all the time
Sir Cathcart had a nagging feeling that he had forgotten,
in the horror of Duck Dinner and the distractions of the
day, something he ought to have done and hadn't. He
very soon discovered what it was.

The General and his guests had just sauntered out
into the old Orangerie with their drinks when Myrtle
Ransby drove up with Maggie in the battered Cortina.
Conversation in the Orangerie came to a sudden halt as
Myrtle staggered out of the car and peered horribly at
them. Never, in Sir Cathcart's opinion, a pleasant sight,
she was cataclysmically awful now. With her leopardskin
draped over her shoulders, and with her distorted en
bouffant bulging under the hood, she advanced on the
little group. In her hand she held the torn notes and
even her protruding nipples and swollen thighs had a

menace about them Sir Cathcart could not fail to recognize.

'Oh my God, what on earth is that?' Lady Sarah gasped as Myrtle approached.

'There must be some mistake,' Sir Cathcart muttered and then, with a quickness of thought that sprang from desperation, 'Perhaps she's collecting for some charity.'

But before he could usher his guests back into the house Myrtle was through the door. 'You fucking owe me,' she shouted and waved the torn notes. 'Two fucking thousand smackers. And you're going to pay me or else . . .'

The threat was superfluous. Nothing else could be more disastrous to Sir Cathcart than her appearance now. Purple and speechless, he tried to mouth to her to go away but Myrtle wasn't having any. She had come for her money and her revenge and she was determined to get both. She turned hideously to the guests.

'Says he likes nigger women and he wants me in the old rubber,' she told them. 'He's got this house in Cambridge, see, and he wants me to give him the old oral and I've got to dye my teats. And you know what he does then?' She advanced, with evident social perception, on the Lazarus-Crouches. 'Ties me up so I can't move and leaves me there all night and all day so he can –'

'I did nothing of the sort,' stammered Sir Cathcart most inadvisedly. 'I . . .'

But it was too late for any escape. Myrtle had backed

Lady Sarah against a camellia and was breathing stale brandy in her face. 'He likes the old waterworks, know what I mean?' she mouthed through the hood. 'Really dirty. Disgusting I call it. Know what I mean?'

It was obvious that Lady Sarah had some idea, but would have preferred not to. 'Well, really,' she said.

'Yes, really,' said Myrtle, and waved the torn notes under her nose. 'Why else would he pay two grand? Dirty old men don't pay that sort of money for the old missionary, do they?'

'No, I'm sure they don't,' Lady Sarah murmured weakly.

'I say – ' one of Cathcart's chums tried to intervene but Myrtle turned on him with the money. 'Two grand. That's what he owes me,' she growled through the hood. 'I ain't going till I gets it.'

'Oh quite,' said Sir Edmund diplomatically and helped his wife towards the door. Several of the distinguished old chums and their wives followed. Only one remained.

'Now, my good woman, if you'll just excuse us for a moment,' he told Myrtle, and took Sir Cathcart apart. 'For goodness' sake, give her the money,' he said. 'Only decent thing to do.'

Twenty minutes later Sir Cathcart sat slumped in a chair in the library and watched the last of the cars depart. He did not even want a drink. He had been unmasked.

34

The College Council met in plenary session two weeks later to hear the Praelector's report and come to a decision. There had been other more informal meetings and a great many heated arguments. But the Praelector had prepared the ground with a thoroughness that had left the Dean and the Senior Tutor furious but without any reasonable argument. The Praelector no longer relied on his undoubted authority. He had employed power and had done so through the strangest and most unlikely medium, that of Purefoy Osbert.

'This is pure blackmail,' the Dean said lividly when the Praelector told him that Dr Osbert's suspicions were a weapon he was quite prepared to substantiate if the need arose.

'You may call it that if you choose,' the Praelector replied. 'It is the truth and I shall use it if I have to.'

'You would bring the College down if you did. You would destroy the very thing you claim you want to preserve.'

'Again, that is your choice to make. Stand in the way of Hartang's nomination as Master and Porterhouse will be destroyed in any case.'

'But the man is a criminal and a monster.'

'I don't deny it. He is also immensely rich and vulnerable. By providing him with the protection of respectability we will earn far more than his gratitude. We will have him at our mercy.'

The Dean sneered his disbelief.

'I mean it. At our mercy,' the Praelector continued. 'You have not seen the almost ineffable surroundings in which he exists and which the pitiful man supposes must be style. The great glass tables, the long and most uncomfortable sofa in green leather, the wrought-iron chairs, the black leather, the windows of armoured glass. You would shudder at vulgarity of his minimalism. Thank God he doesn't collect paintings.'

'I can't see that any of this matters,' said the Dean. 'You want to introduce this murderous gangster into the College and you call that having him at our mercy. You are mad.'

But the Praelector merely smiled. 'Charles the Fifth of Spain and Holy Roman Emperor, the most powerful man in Europe at the time and therefore probably more unlikeable than Edgar Hartang, withdrew to a monastery for the last few years of his life. I haven't put that comparison to the new Master – I doubt if he would understand it – but I like to think we can play a similar role in Mr Hartang's life. A quiet period of contemplation combined with the satisfaction of knowing that one is paying compensation for the excesses of one's past by contributing to the cultural achievements of the present.

I am sure our future Master will come to view life here in that gentle light. After all he has no family.'

'How do you know? He has probably spawned frightful offspring all over the world.'

'Boys,' said the Praelector smugly. 'And since you want to know how I know, I can say that Mr Schnabel has been most cooperative. As the new College legal advisers, the firm of Schnabel, Feuchtwangler and Bolsover, has been most helpful. They share my feelings about Mr Hartang's future. I think he has uttered one threat too many. But you will meet them when they come up to prepare the documentation. Everything must be done in the proper manner.'

'But what are Retter and Wyve going to say? You can't just throw them over like that.'

'They are not being thrown over,' said the Praelector. 'They will continue to deal with local matters and besides they are being paid, which is an entirely new experience for them as far as Porterhouse is concerned. I don't suppose you realize how much we owe them but . . .'

*

To Dr Buscott the Praelector spoke rather differently, and to Professor Pawley he explained, 'This will ensure that Porterhouse will be in a position to make a very munificent contribution to the scientific funding of the University and naturally your advice will be much sought after.'

*

414

But it was with the Senior Tutor that he had the greatest difficulty.

'Drugs? Heroin, cocaine, and you want to let a drug trafficker become Master of Porterhouse? I shall most certainly oppose the nomination,' said the Senior Tutor. 'After all we have always prided ourselves on our athletic prowess, particularly on the river. You are setting a fearful precedent. No, I refuse to be party to such a vile conspiracy. Over my dead body.'

For the briefest of moments the Praelector thought of saying that that could be arranged, but he desisted. 'There will be no drugs in Porterhouse,' he said. 'Funnily enough, Mr Hartang shares your feelings exactly. True, in the past he has had some dealings with the drug trade but he has long since seen the error of his ways.'

'Not according to those tapes. How else do you think he has made so much money? He's hand in glove with the Mafia and the drug cartels of South America. He has people murdered, he hires killers, he commits the most monstrous crimes . . .'

'True, Senior Tutor, very true. Anyone who opposes him does tend to come to a sticky end.' He paused for the inference to sink in. 'However, he has learnt from history that there is advantage to be gained from respectability. Take President Kennedy's father. Started life as a bootlegger and a gangster selling gut-rot gin and whiskey during Prohibition and almost certainly had competitors murdered. He ended up as Ambassador over here during the war.'

'The bastard said Hitler was going to win,' the Senior Tutor retorted, 'and in any case they had to repeal the Prohibition law because they couldn't stop people drinking and they were putting money into the hands of gangsters like Al Capone and Joseph Kennedy.'

'Exactly the point I was going to make,' said the Praelector. 'Do you seriously suppose that the present American authorities, in so far as there are any, with their incredible financial deficit are going to succeed in stopping the drug traffickers? Do you really think that?'

The Senior Tutor said he sincerely hoped so.

'Ah, but think of the financial advantages that will accrue to the Governments when drugs are legalized,' the Praelector told him. 'And the social benefits will be enormous too.'

'What social benefits? The wholesale consumption of crack cocaine does not strike me as having any social benefit whatsoever.'

'I can think of one. The elimination of the criminal coterie that controls the trade now. And besides, I have never believed in the regimentation of society by a self-appointed and supposedly moral elite. If people choose to indulge tastes that hurt only themselves, they are entitled to do so. To attempt to dragoon them into moral perfection always fails. Or ends in war.'

'You are a cynic,' said the Senior Tutor.

'I have fought in one war and, while I cannot claim to have known what I was fighting for, I think I knew what I was fighting against,' said the Praelector. 'So far I have always found myself on the side of right. An accident of birth and history, I daresay, but one that doesn't incline me towards cynicism.'

'Not this time,' the Senior Tutor said. 'This time you are on the side of wrong and I shall oppose you.'

'It is your right to do so,' said the Praelector. 'Though I must warn you that you may come to regret it.'

*

The Senior Tutor did, almost immediately. Two days later he found a letter demanding immediate payment of far more than he had expected in connection with repairs, renovations and the re-roofing of the Porterhouse Boat House.

'This has nothing to do with me,' he told the Bursar, who had finally been persuaded to resume his duties. 'The College funds the Boat Club. I don't.'

'I daresay in the past . . .' the Bursar began, but the Praelector came out of the Secretary's office in support.

'You've evidently not boned up on the College ordinances of 1851 lately.'

'Ordinances of 1851? Of course I haven't. I didn't know there were any,' spluttered the Senior Tutor.

'Oddly enough, I have a copy of the relevant clause with me,' the Praelector said and handed him a page of numbered paragraphs. 'Number 9 is the one that applies to your position with regard to the expenses you have incurred without the authority of the College Council

Bursarial and Finance Committee. Most unfortunate of course, but there you are.'

The Senior Tutor read the offensive paragraph and was appalled. '"In the event of an officer of the College in whatsoever capacity acting without the consent of the Bursarial and Finance Committee to incur expenses . . ." Are you mad? I can't pay forty thousand pounds and I'm damned if I'm going to. I've never even heard of this fuck – ' (Mrs Moreland had added her presence to that of the Bursar and the Praelector) ' – of . . . of this Committee.'

'It meets every term, doesn't it, Bursar?'

The Bursar nodded weakly. He was too frightened to speak. He had horsewhips on his mind.

'Of course, in the past these matters have been a mere formality,' the Praelector continued, 'but in the light of the financial crisis now facing the College, I am afraid that Clause 9 has become obligatory. Our creditors are insisting on immediate payment and since you are legally responsible . . .'

The Senior Tutor retreated and consulted his own solicitor. 'I'm afraid there is very little we can do,' he was told.

By the time the College Council met in plenary session the Senior Tutor had capitulated. A bankrupt Porterhouse was one thing, but he was not prepared to be a bankrupt himself. Hartang was set to become the new Master.

35

It was morning and Purefoy and Ingrid lay in bed late. 'You're wasting your time here, Purefoy darling,' she said. 'You aren't going to find out anything more and even if you did what could you do about it? They're all so old.'

'I just want to know what actually happened.'

'The truth, is that it? Is that really what you want to find out? Because if it is, you'll be wasting your time. They are never going to tell you.'

'Perhaps not, but I still want to know where Skullion is. He's not at any of the hospitals or nursing homes in Cambridge, and that night he spoke about the Park. He threatened the Dean that if they sent him to Porterhouse Park, he'd tell me he murdered Sir Godber. And then three days later he suddenly disappears and hasn't been heard of or spoken about since. The next thing they've chosen a new Master who is as rich as Croesus. That wasn't a coincidence. I don't believe that for a moment.'

They got up and went out for coffee at the Copper Kettle.

*

In the Council Chamber the Praelector laid down his pen. He had been thinking about writing his letter of resignation. He had achieved his purpose and the Council had accepted his nomination of Edgar Hartang as the new Master. The other Fellows had left and only the Dean and the Senior Tutor remained behind. They were neither of them in a good mood.

'On your own head be it,' the Dean said. 'God alone knows what sort of monster we're landed with, but we'll have to cope with the man as best we can.'

'We've had such men before. It was either that or bankruptcy. In any case I shan't be here to see it,' said the Praelector. 'I am resigning.'

'And not before time,' said the Senior Tutor bitterly.

'I agree. I have hung on uselessly for too many years now. It is time for younger, more talented Fellows to take over.'

'And do you intend to stay in Cambridge and occasionally dine in Hall?' the Dean asked with a little malice.

'No. I have a niece in Chichester and there is a pleasant guesthouse nearby. I had always thought of going there. But I daresay the Park will suit me well enough. I shall see the term out, that is all.'

They went out into the spring sunshine, conscious that an era had ended. The Dean and the Senior Tutor were thinking of their own futures. They had no wish to stay on and watch the changes that were coming. Even now in the Bursar's office Ross Skundler was busy installing the screens and electronic equipment that he insisted were essential. His appointment had been one of the conditions laid down by Schnabel. 'He was invaluable to you in the past,' he had told Hartang at their last interview at the Transworld Television Centre. 'And he had nothing to do with any of this. Forget the past. You are Master of Porterhouse and a free man.'

'Free fuck,' said Hartang.

'And I wouldn't use that sort of expression. As a respected member of the Establishment you've got to moderate the force of your language.'

'I'm not there yet,' Hartang said, but already in his mind he was. He'd been up to Porterhouse and seen the place for himself with Schnabel and Bolsover and while he hadn't liked the look of it, he knew there was no safe alternative. In fact he had paid two visits, on each occasion without his wig or the dark blue glasses and dressed in a very quiet suit.

But before that he had had a visit from four people, two men and two women, who had very tactfully handed their cards sealed in envelopes at the reception desk for Mr E. Hartang's perusal only. They had also arranged for Schnabel, Feuchtwangler and Bolsover to accompany them. The legal team had looked suitably subdued. They recognized Intelligence when they saw them.

'You've got your legal advisers here, Mr Hartang, so that you don't feel under any pressure to answer questions you don't want to or which you feel might incriminate you,' the older woman who had blue-rinsed hair had explained very politely. 'We just want you to know that.'

Hartang knew better. Like they were telling him the lethal injection wouldn't hurt one little bit.

But he had known a lot more than that and the one thing he knew most clearly of all was that he wasn't going to walk away from this situation except by telling them what they had come to hear. Schnabel and Feuchtwangler had tried to intervene as a matter of form, and Hartang had had to tell them to lay off. They didn't know the score. Not that he put it like that. He had simply said that he didn't require their presence and he had business to do with the two men and the two ladies, no problem. Cooperation for protection. And when the lawyers had gone, he had made only one request: that when they found all the information he was about to give them they would have found it from the persons he had already chosen for that role. All those persons, though he didn't say this, had expressed intentions so violently antipathetic to him that he had had to take certain precautions about intruders and so on. Agree to that simple request and they could have every micron of information he possessed, though not by word of mouth. He wasn't going to talk but they would find what they had come for on computer files composed under such electronically secure conditions that even the most sophisticated devices could not pick up the signals from the CPU. Again he didn't give them the full explanation any more than he intended to give them every scintilla of information he possessed. That might come later if they kept to their side of the bargain and allowed him time and opportunity to cover himself with safety and protection. Again he didn't say this but then he didn't have to. They knew it and, provided he gave them those files and what was on them met their need for arrests and satisfactory verdicts, that was fine with them. They said they understood his requirements and, after some slight delay during which Hartang left the office and went elsewhere in the building to fetch the disks, they went away.

A week later Schnabel arrived to say that the Mastership of Porterhouse was his for the asking.

*

On his first visit he had been treated with solemn courtesy by the Fellows and shown over the College. He had been reassured by the revolving spikes on the walls and the barred windows which were, they told him, to prevent intruders climbing in. He had found the Crypt under the Chapel rather more disturbing.

'This is where the Masters are buried,' the Dean had told him as they went down the steps. Hartang had surveyed the stacked coffins with distaste. He had expected proper stone sarcophagi, not this higgledy-piggledy arrangement of wooden boxes. Still, if the Crypt lacked orderliness and the Chapel was impossible to visit because of the scaffolding and the plastic sheets, something about Porterhouse lent credence to Schnabel's assurance that as Master he could shed all connections with his own past.

Even Hartang couldn't see Mosie Diabentos or Dos Passos sending contractors into these ancient courts to blow him away. Like rubbing the Archbishop of Canterbury out in Westminster Abbey. There had been only one moment of unease when they were being shown the Combination Room by the Head Waiter. 'This is where the dons take their coffee after dinner,' he'd said.

'Dons?' Hartang whispered hoarsely to Schnabel. 'You never said nothing about dons being here. Who are the dons for fucksake?'

'Not that sort of don. It is Cambridge slang for the Fellows of the College. Like the Dean and the professors and so on.'

'And I'm the top don?'

'You are the Master. They won't even call you Mr Hartang. They will address you as Master. It is a great honour.'

'Five hundred million of honour, Schnabel.'

'So it's your pension fund out of petty cash, Master. Look at it that way.'

*

Hartang looked at it a great many ways, but his mind had already been made up for him. He still had Transworld Television Productions and he would never be poor. All the same, as he waited in his bleak suite in Docklands he regretted the days when he could telephone someone on the other side of the world in the dead of night and talk and the someone would listen dutifully to whatever he had to say and their fear would reassure Hartang that he had achieved power. That was out of the question now. They, the ubiquitous 'They', would pick up the call and even with the scrambler would know every word he was saying and analyse even his most guarded statements. He knew it just as surely as he knew his various names were being pronounced in police interrogation rooms in Rome and Palermo, New York and Los Angeles and in towns in South America by men who wanted to finger him just as he had fingered them. They couldn't, of course, because the computer disks had been found in a garden in Colombia and the death of Dos Passos had been announced in the papers and on television. He was said to have died in a car crash after a week in custody. On his way home after such a short time being questioned in Bogota Dos Passos has a blow-out? And the disks with all that info were in his garden. Just went to show you couldn't trust nobody . . . anybody, these days.

There was another question that obsessed him. Whoever had set this thing up had known precisely what they were doing. There hadn't been anything accidental about it. They had seen Kudzuvine coming and had used him because he was a cretin and by using him they could get to Hartang. He didn't doubt that for a moment. And they had targeted Hartang himself because it suited more ends than one: they'd taken him because he knew the source, the sums and where the money went which no one else, but no one else, knew. For why? Because the information, all the information, was in his head or so broken into completely unconnected pieces that no amount of putting figures together by the most sophisticated computer, one doing sixty billion calculations a second like the Cray they were said to be developing, would be able to find the answers. Because it wouldn't recognize any conceivable pattern. Or even if it found the patterns – and for all he knew it might – the pattern itself wouldn't make sense, wouldn't be recognizably different from all the other patterns it came up with because the numbers it needed weren't there to be fed into it. Only in the multiple mnemonics of his own mind were the connections to be found and when he died or got Alzheimer's the full picture would fade with him. He'd got the idea from a crazy in an automotive dump outside Scranton looking for the meaning of life. That was what he had said, 'It's got to be here, the meaning of life,' and he'd picked up a hub-cap and laughed. 'Could be this is it. Could be, couldn't it?' And Hartang had agreed that the meaning of life could be a hub-cap from an old Hudson Terraplane they didn't make any more. Yeah, that crazy had shown him the way to hide what needed to be hidden in the confusion of calculated madness.

So 'They' had targeted the right man and had 'taken'

him, and in return he had given them enough of what they wanted without giving everything away. But who had 'taken' him? Who had set this trap up? Had to be a government agency. Couldn't be anything else the way they treated him nice. Scary just the same, being treated that nice. No use worrying himself sick.

Edgar Hartang turned on the tape recorder and began his elocution lesson again. Got to remember to speak properly. Got to learn to keep the 'fucks' and 'shitsakes' out.

427

36

Skullion was sitting in the verandah staring grimly out over the garden and the mudflats at the sea beyond when Mrs Morphy took Purefoy and Mrs Ndhlovo through the house.

'I have to say he's a very difficult one is Mr S,' she told them. 'The others, Dr V and Mr L, well they have their nasty little ways which is only to be expected at their age but I wouldn't say they were unfriendly. Just a bit messy and so on, you understand, but as I say to Alf, he's my husband, when you get to their age, not that he's likely to the way he smokes and drinks, you'll be the same, and I hope there's someone around like me to clear up after you. I mean the cost of the laundry. Of course we've got a machine but . . .'

'When you say he's unfriendly . . .' said Purefoy to change the subject.

'You'll see for yourself,' said Mrs Morphy. 'Down-right rude, but then he's only been here a short time and he hasn't got used to it yet. But he will. They all do because we don't stand on ceremony here and never have. Just the same, Mr S hardly opens his mouth and when he does what comes out isn't fit for decent hearing.' She paused at the glass doors of the verandah and said, 'I won't come out if you don't mind. He'd only tell me to . . . well, you know what.'

She slouched back into the kitchen and left them standing in what was evidently the dining-room. Next door a television was on. Purefoy and Mrs Ndhlovo looked out at the dark figure in the bowler hat hunched in his wheelchair on the verandah. This was not the Porterhouse Park they had expected but a red-brick house standing on a little promontory by itself and with a dilapidated wooden fence separating it from the gorse and tufted grass of the sand dunes on either side. There was nothing parklike about it and Purefoy had driven up and down the main road half a mile away several times before stopping at a petrol station and asking for Porterhouse Park.

'There's a house they call the Park,' the woman at the till had said. 'Don't know anything about Porterhouse. It's the old folks' home down Fish Lane, you know, one of them geriatric places. I wouldn't want to go there.'

Now, standing hesitantly in the dining-room filled with dark furniture, and made darker still by the roof of the verandah, they could understand her reluctance to have anything to do with the Park. Purefoy opened the door and Skullion expressed his feelings for the housekeeper. 'What do you want now, you old bitch?' he asked, without moving his head. 'Come to see if I'm fucking dead yet? Well, I'm not so you can bugger off.'

Purefoy coughed diplomatically. 'Actually, it isn't the old bitch,' he said and moved forward so that Skullion could see him. 'My name is Osbert and I've come up from Porterhouse . . .'

From under the rim of the bowler hat Skullion peered up at him and Purefoy found himself looking into two eyes dark with hatred and contempt. For a moment he almost backed away from such open hostility but he stood his ground and presently, much to his astonishment, Skullion grinned.

'Dr Osbert? So you're Dr Osbert. And you've come up from the College. Well I never. Wonders never cease.' He paused and grunted, possibly with pleasure. 'I've been looking forward to meeting you. I have indeed. Get a chair and sit down so I don't have to break my neck looking up at you.'

Purefoy pulled up a wooden chair and sat. At the back of the verandah Mrs Ndhlovo stood motionless. 'And you can tell her behind me to sit down too,' Skullion said and there was no doubt about his amusement now. 'Want to know how I know she's there?' he went on and didn't wait for an answer. 'Because the old cow in there stinks, and I mean stinks, and her behind me washes. Makes a change. She your secretary?'

'Not exactly but all the same we'd like to talk to you.'

'Daresay you would,' said Skullion. 'I daresay you would.' He transferred his gaze across the unweeded flowerbeds and the stunted roses to the brown mudflats and the silver runnels of water flowing through them. The tide was far out and only a few seabirds moved on the mud. It was a dispiriting prospect. 'They call this

Porterhouse Park. Funny sort of name for a dosshouse but then they've got a funny sort of sense of humour, dons have. That or they want to fool you into coming here without a fuss. But you're a don, aren't you?'

'I'm supposed to be. I'm not sure I am, though.'

'No more sure than I am,' said Skullion. 'No, you're not a don. Not yet. You're Mr Nosey Parker who's being paid by that Lady Mary to find out who killed her husband. And now you know.'

Purefoy said nothing. He was waiting to hear Skullion tell him.

'And shall I tell you why you know? I will anyway. Because you were sitting in the maze the night I got pissed on Hardy's and warned the Dean what I'd do if they sent me here and you were listening.' He chuckled. 'I could practically hear you listening. Know that?' Again he paused. 'I could hear you because I knew you weren't hardly breathing. And if that doesn't make sense to you, work it out.'

Purefoy tried to. He was still afraid of the man in the wheelchair who had spoken without any guilt about murdering Sir Godber and his fear had returned now. With a difference. There was a mind at work underneath that ridiculous bowler hat. An old mind intelligent from years of watching and listening and waiting for someone else to do something and then suddenly doing something nobody would have expected. He'd just done it now by telling Purefoy he'd known he'd been in the maze that night.

'So now you want me to tell you all about it,' Skullion went on. 'And I'm prepared to. I'm even prepared to tell you everything I know, everything. But not for nothing. And I'm not talking about money. I've got what they call a sufficiency in my bank account. I'm talking about something else.'

'Yes?' said Purefoy. 'What else do you want?'

Skullion squinted at him for a moment. 'I want out of here. That's what I want. Out of here. And I can't do that on my own. Except the only way I've worked out is to wheel myself down there when the tide's in and drown in the mud and I don't intend to do that unless I have to. No, you go back and get a van I can get into and some rope and a torch and come back here tonight at one o'clock and pick me up at the gate and we'll go somewhere and I'll tell you everything I know. That's my terms.'

'I suppose we could do that,' said Purefoy a little uncertainly. 'But the gate is locked. There's a chain and a lock on it. The woman came out and unlocked it.'

'And there's a key here,' Skullion told him. 'And even if there wasn't, the fence is so rotten you could kick it in. Anyway those are my terms. A van big enough to get this chair in and don't forget the rope. That's all. One o'clock.'

They left him there and walked back to the road, got back into the car and drove up Fish Lane to the main road.

'I wonder what he has in mind,' Purefoy said. 'You ever seen anyone like that before?'

'Whatever he's got in his mind he's going to give it to you so long as you get him out of there. What a terrible place. And that awful woman.'

'And you really think we ought to do what he wants? I mean supposing he dies or something.'

'Purefoy, your trouble is you think too much. Just do something for a change.'

*

They hired a van in Hunstanton and bought some nylon rope. Then they spent the rest of the day walking along the beach and sitting in cafés and wondering what Skullion was going to tell them. And, in Purefoy's case, worrying. He had never done anything like this in his life.

At eleven o'clock they left the Renault in a side street, drove along the coast road towards Burnt Overy and the mudflats and parked up a lane inland and waited. At ten to one the van was outside the gate with the headlights off. Over the fence they could see the silhouette of the house. A light in a window at one end was still on but presently it went out.

Purefoy got out and tried the gate. It was locked. 'I hope to goodness he's got the key,' he said. 'I don't fancy having to kick the fence in. It would make a hell of a noise.'

From the sea there came the slop of the waves on the mudflats. The tide was in and the wind had risen, and far out the lights of a ship coming from the Continent and heading for King's Lynn could be seen. Purefoy shivered and went back to the Transit van to check that the doors at the back were already open so that they could hoist Skullion and the wheelchair in quickly. He didn't want to hang about. He had the feeling that what he was doing was somehow illegal like kidnapping and if the police came along it would be difficult to explain. Mrs Ndhlovo had no such worries. She was enjoying herself. Skullion had impressed her. Even in his wheelchair and semi-paralysed she had recognized him for a proper man though understandably a nasty one.

It was one o'clock exactly when they heard the wheelchair and saw the dark shape coming slowly towards them up the old tarmac drive.

'Gates open inwards or outwards?' Skullion asked.

'Inwards, I think. Yes, inwards,' Purefoy said.

'Right, then here's the key. It's the one I've got in my fingers. You open them while I back off.' He handed the bunch of keys over and Purefoy used the torch to find the lock. When it was undone and the gates open, Skullion came through. 'Now lock them again and with the chain and give me the keys. That'll teach them what it feels like to be locked in when you want to go to work.'

'I thought you didn't want them to come after you,' Mrs Ndhlovo said and made Skullion chuckle.

'Come after me, duckie? They wouldn't turn out to look for me, not unless I was the only poor bugger down there and their jobs depended on it. Glad to see the

back of me. The same as I am of them. And they keep
the phone locked too, so only they can use it or hear
what you say. And I've got the key of that too and of
the cellar and the kitchen cupboards. Mean as cats'
whiskers. Now this is the difficult bit, getting me up
into the van. You do the chair first. I'll prop myself up
here.'

He got out of the chair and stood leaning against the
side of the van. By the time Purefoy and Mrs Ndhlovo
had lifted the chair in and Purefoy had tied it securely
to the passenger seat with the rope, Skullion had worked
his way round to the back to watch.

'Now give me the end of the rope and I'll pull and
you shove. I still got some strength in my arms. One of
them anyway. Here, put my bowler somewhere out of
the way.'

It was a struggle getting him in but they managed it
and presently, with Skullion seated in the wheelchair
and breathing heavily, they started up Fish Lane.

'Where do you want to go, Mr Skullion?' Mrs
Ndhlovo asked.

'Home,' said Skullion. 'Where the blooming heart is.'

'You mean to Porterhouse?'

'Oh no, not there. Not yet, any rate. Just drive down
to Cambridge and I'll show you. Take the Swaffham
road. Won't be much traffic on it this time of night.'

37

It was late when Purefoy and Mrs Ndhlovo woke that morning. It had been after three before they reached Cambridge and left Skullion with a couple who lived in a side street near the Newmarket Road and who had seemed to take his unexpected arrival in the middle of the night quite calmly and as if it was the most normal thing in the world.

'Old friends,' was all that Skullion had to say about them. 'You come here when you want to and I'll tell you everything you want to know. They won't find me here if you don't say anything. And I don't think you will.' They had left him there and Purefoy had parked the van on the other side of the river before walking wearily back to Porterhouse.

Now in the morning the whole interlude had an air of unreality about it, at least to Purefoy. To Mrs Ndhlovo helping a man in a wheelchair escape from a so-called retirement home in the middle of the night was apparently the most normal thing in the world. 'That place gave me the creeps, and as for that Mrs Morphy, I'm sure she's in favour of involuntary euthanasia. I like your Mr Skullion, though. He's different.'

Purefoy didn't disagree. Skullion was different but he

still wasn't at all sure he liked him. There was a hardness about him that alarmed him and in any case he couldn't forget the menace in Skullion's voice when he threatened the Dean. 'That's because you've lived such a protected life, Purefoy,' Mrs Ndhlovo told him. 'When are we going to take the van back and fetch the car? Not today, please. I'm too tired and anyway I think you ought to hear what he has to say first.'

They went out to lunch and it was four when they finally went to the house in Onion Alley off the New-market Road. A plump woman let them in. 'He's in the front room because of the stairs and we never use it really,' she said. 'Special occasions. So we made up a bed for him. He's still in it. I'll just go and see he's tidy. Oh, and I'm Mrs Rawston. Charlie, my husband, went to school with Mr Skullion.'

They found Skullion sitting up in bed with his bowler on the table beside him. 'Wondered when you was coming. Thought you might have got cold feet.'

'There's no need to be rude,' said Mrs Rawston.

'Not being rude,' said Skullion. 'Dean'll know by now I'm gone from the Park and you gave that B-I-T-C-H your name didn't you? So they'll have a fair idea.'

'Nobody's said anything to me,' said Purefoy. 'But it's true. That dreadful woman does know my name.'

'Just so long as you don't let them know I'm here. If they ask you can say I told you to get lost. They can go on searching the mud for a bit. Do them good. And it'll do them good at the College to wonder what's become of the Master. It's all right, Mrs Charlie, you don't have to wait unless you want to hear a lot of history.'

'I'll make a pot of tea,' said Mrs Rawston and went out.

'We'll get round to why I did what I did to Sir Godber Evans in a bit,' Skullion went on. 'First I'll tell you what they're like and why I'm here and not where that General Sir Cathcart D'Eath promised I'd go if I kept my trap shut, out at Coft Castle which isn't any sort of castle and he trains horses.'

They listened as he told the story and presently Mrs Rawston returned with the tea tray and some biscuits and left them to themselves.

'You do shorthand?' Skullion asked Mrs Ndhlovo who said no but she wrote fast. 'Right, then you'll have to use a tape recorder and I'll go slow because I've got a lot to tell if you want to hear it. The history of the College from a different point of view than any you'd get from anyone else. As it really is or was and not dolled up with things left out because they wouldn't look nice. Forty-five years I was there in the Porter's Lodge and what the porters and the College servants don't learn in forty-five years isn't worth knowing. More than the Dean, more than the Praelector, more than anyone. And I'll tell you if you want to hear.'

'Oh, but I do,' said Purefoy. 'I don't suppose anyone has written a history of Porterhouse from that angle.'

'Course they haven't. Haven't asked and the Dean and them wouldn't have allowed them to if they had.

They won't allow you to either, not have it published at any rate. But you can write it down for the record. Just be careful and don't keep it in your room. Dean and Senior Tutor went through your stuff one day you were out.'

'What?' said Purefoy in astonishment and anger. 'Went through all my notes and . . . Are you sure?'

'Dead certain,' said Skullion. 'Watched them from my bedroom in the Master's Lodge. Saw them through the window and they came out looking shifty and went to the Secretary's office. Want to know why?'

'Yes, I bloody well do.'

'Because there's a copier there. Then the Dean went back up again and came out looking smug. 'Skullion laughed.' I may miss some things but not a lot and what I don't see or hear, other people tell me. But that's not for anyone else's ears. Right?'

'All right,' said Purefoy, still fuming. 'Just the same they had no right – '

'Oh come off it. Right? Right doesn't come into it. You come up here all of a sudden as the Sir Godber Evans Memorial Fellow, get appointed when the Dean's away and the Senior Tutor gets me to sign my name to your appointment without telling me what you are or who put up the money, and they're still not certain, and you think they're not going to want to find out? Was there anything in there said Lady Mary was behind you?'

'No, no I don't suppose there was.'

'Must've been something, because the Dean drives

out to Coft Castle to see Sir Cathcart that afternoon and he don't do that just for a chinwag. Never mind that. Just don't leave what I'm going to tell you lying around. Put it somewhere safe out of College.'

He finished his tea and handed the cup to Mrs Ndhlovo. 'And you'd better not be seen around,' he told her. 'You'd be better off in digs. Mrs Charlie'll recommend some. The Dean and the Senior Tutor don't hold with women in College.'

'I don't care what they hold with. I'm entitled – '

'Entitled? You may be entitled but they can dig up something in College Rules and Regulations says you're not and cause him a lot of trouble arguing about it. Take my word for it. When I've finished, that'll be different. For the time being keep your head down. They can think what they like but there'll be nothing they can do. And I don't want them finding me and trying to stop me spilling the beans.'

'If you say so, Mr Skullion, if you say so.'

'Sensible,' said Skullion, pleased by the 'Mister'. 'Now you'll be wanting to get that van back and fetch your car and you don't want to be all night about it. Ask Mrs Charlie about the digs and I'll see you tomorrow. Any time in the morning.'

It was almost midnight when they got back to Cambridge and slipped up to Purefoy's rooms. 'Just this once,' Mrs Ndhlovo said. 'I'll move into the digs in the morning.'

*

Dinner in Hall had been a sombre affair. Mention of Porterhouse Park was normally avoided as being an unsuitably morbid topic but there could be no avoiding it now.

'Dr Osbert and a woman went up to see him? How the deuce did they find out how to get there?' the Senior Tutor wanted to know.

'It seems our young colleague is rather more ingenious than his manner suggests,' said the Dean. 'Someone claiming to be from the hospital phoned to say that blood was needed for a transfusion, Skullion had burst an ulcer or some such nonsense, and they needed the address. Walter gave it to them. And now Skullion has disappeared and the police tell me that all the gates were locked and the keys have gone.'

'Nasty, very nasty. He couldn't by any chance have taken himself off?'

'One hardly supposes a man in his condition in a wheelchair would get very far without being spotted. No, I think the presumption must be that Dr Osbert agreed to help him get away from there.'

'But what on earth for? I shouldn't for a moment imagine he and Skullion have anything in common. Just the sort of young man he most dislikes.'

The Dean kept his thoughts on the matter to himself and glanced significantly at the Praelector but the Praelector had preoccupations of his own. The Bumps were coming up and after them the May Balls, and for the first time in several years Porterhouse was having its own May Ball. By that time Hartang would be installed in the Master's Lodge – for once the Inauguration of the new Master was being postponed until the Michaelmas Term in case certain 'rearrangements' had to be made – and the Praelector had spent part of the afternoon with three people from London whose IDs suggested they were Customs and Excise but whose questions and inspection of the College and in particular the Master's Lodge seemed to have more to do with security. The woman had been the one who had impressed the Praelector most. In her forties, she had the air of a perfectly ordinary housewife on her way back from a supermarket – she actually carried a shopping bag – or the local library to collect a new historical romance. Her hair was permed and slightly blue, she was short and plump and at first sight she appeared happily absent-minded. By the time they had finished that first impression had been replaced by another. The patina of cheerful absent-mindedness had been overlaid by too much intelligent questioning and the authority she obviously possessed. The Praelector preferred not to wonder what was in the shopping bag. She seemed particularly interested in the May Ball.

'Anyone who pays for a ticket is entitled to come,' the Praelector told her, and was promptly assured that this year there would be certain unspecified measures taken to keep the rowdier element away.

'We want it to be a happy occasion,' she said. 'I think

you can safely leave the staff arrangements to us. We have some excellent caterers we can provide and it will save the College authorities extra work. Now about the Master's accommodation.'

The Praelector had taken them to the Master's Lodge and had left them there. 'I shall be in my room if you need me,' he said.

They had spent several hours there and had come away apparently satisfied. 'Such a very pleasant house. And so handy having a lift. Of course it needs rewiring and a few refinements added. We will send some electricians up in a day or two. There is no need for the College to concern itself. They will use the main door of the house and Bill here will be with them. He knows about these things.'

Bill was the taller of the two men, and looked as though he knew a great deal about a great many things.

'And now if we could just have a word with the porters?'

The Praelector had taken them down to the Porters' Lodge and had gone back to his rooms uncomfortably aware that he had just made the acquaintance of three very hard people. It was going to be a very odd May Ball. And when that evening he had gone down to see if there was any mail in his pigeonhole Walter had been in an unusually serious mood.

'Bloody coppers,' he said with uncharacteristic frankness when the Praelector asked him if the visitors had stayed long. 'Telling me how to run my own business.

Going to put a bloke in here with Henry and me for May Week. What do they want to do that for?'

'I think they may be looking for pickpockets and people using the occasion to come into College to steal,' the Praelector said tactfully. 'I'm sure they'll keep out of your way.'

'They'd better. Got enough to do without having the place crawling with flatfoots. Stick out like sore thumbs they do, and rude with it.'

*

Sir Cathcart would have found the comment precise. His feelings about the police were even less friendly. He'd had two uniformed officers and a plainclothes man in a patrol car drive up without bothering to make an appointment that morning and he hadn't liked their manners in the slightest. They had said they had received a complaint from a Mrs Ransby and had reason to believe he might be able to help them.

Sir Cathcart had tried to laugh it off. 'You mustn't believe anything you read in the papers. An utter travesty of the facts. As a matter of fact she was trying to blackmail me.'

'Oh yes, sir. Was she indeed? Blackmail you? And how was she trying to do that?' the Sergeant had asked in a tone of voice the General hadn't heard from a policeman before. The CID man said nothing. He had just stood there looking at the furniture in the hall and seeming not to be interested. Something about him annoyed Sir Cathcart, who had had two drinks for breakfast.

'Mrs Ransby tried to blackmail you and you didn't feel inclined to pay her. Very natural, sir, and may one enquire what your reaction to her demand, I presume it was for a sum of money, what your reaction was?'

'I told her to fuck off,' said the General. 'And frankly I'd be glad if you would go and make yourselves useful somewhere else. If you want to discuss anything more with me, you can make an appointment. I am extremely busy and . . .'

The plain-clothes man introduced himself. 'My name is Dickerson, Detective Inspector Dickerson, and I have here a warrant to search premises in Botanic Lane . . .'

It had been an appalling moment, and the morning had got worse. Sir Cathcart had reacted angrily, the police had asked him if he wanted to speak to his solicitor and have him present when they searched the house, Sir Cathcart had said he did although it was the last thing he wanted, and had then changed his mind and had tried a different approach. That hadn't worked either.

'The Chief Constable is in London today, sir. If you'd like his deputy . . .' Sir Cathcart didn't, and had suffered the ignominy of being driven to Botanic Lane because as the Sergeant had pointed out it wouldn't look good if he was stopped for driving over the limit.

Nothing had looked good. The architects on the ground floor had watched his arrival with interest and when they got up to what Sir Cathcart had in the past jovially referred to as his little love nest he had been shocked by the mess it was in. Evidence of Myrtle's drunken struggles with the latex costume was everywhere and the brandy bottle was still on the floor of the bedroom. In the bathroom things were worse still. The consequences of the brandy were in the basin, the toothbrush was on the floor with the old razor, and the smell was most unpleasant. There was worse still to come.

'A one-way mirror, eh? And a video camera. Well, well. Someone is into porno by the look of things. I think we are going to need a photographer and the print man,' the Inspector said, and suggested they wait outside in the car. The General went downstairs and ran the gauntlet of the architects' office and sat in the police car. He'd changed his mind about his solicitor.

'You can use the car phone, sir,' he was told. An hour later with the solicitor, a very respectable solicitor who, if he had known General Sir Cathcart D'Eath in happier circumstances, didn't show it, they all climbed the stairs and inspected the rooms once again. The leather straps and the inflatable gag were placed in plastic bags.

'There is no need for you to say anything, and I strongly advise you not to,' the solicitor informed Sir Cathcart and requested that his client be allowed to go home. The General had to wait for a taxi and the Inspector said he would make an appointment to see him when they needed to ask him any further questions.

Or perhaps he would prefer to come to the police station instead when they let him know. The solicitor said his client would prefer to be interviewed at home. Sir Cathcart went back to Coft Castle and was photographed by a young newspaperman who just happened to be there.

Alone in his study Sir Cathcart D'Eath sat with a revolver and a bottle of Chivas Regal and thought about shooting Myrtle fucking Ransby. And possibly some policemen at the same time.

38

As the end of term drew near and the Porterhouse Eights, no longer near the Head of the River, rowed over or moved up one, and as the marquees for the May Ball arrived and preparations were made for erecting them, Hartang came almost unnoticed to Porterhouse. His car, no stretch limo with black windows but a three-year-old Ford as nondescript as Hartang himself, slipped into the Old Coach House and the Master-to-be climbed out and stared around at the motley of old cars, the Dean's humpbacked Rover and the Chaplain's ancient Armstrong Siddeley and Professor Pawley's even older Morris. In the space of sixty miles he had stepped from the safety and sterile modernity of Transworld Centre into a mausoleum of antique machinery. Even the large iron bolts on the Coach House doors alarmed him by their simplicity while on the whitewashed wall at one end a wooden hay-rack spoke of even older means of transport. And the floor was cobbled and stained with oil. Hartang looked at it all distrustfully and with a sense of defeat.

'If you'll just follow me, sir,' said the taller of the two men who had driven up with him. 'We can walk across to the Master's Lodge unobserved.' He opened a side

door and stepped outside. Hartang followed nervously
and blinked in the bright sunshine. Without his dark
blue glasses the light hurt his weak eyes and he walked
with head down to avoid the glare until they were in the
hall of the Master's Lodge. Here evidence of the past
was all too apparent. The furniture he had seen on his
previous visits had been comparatively modern but in
its place there was solid black oak and dark mahogany
and even an old curved wooden hatstand. On the wall
the portrait of Humphrey Lombert, Master 1852–83,
stared through small metal spectacles sternly into the
distance over his head. The floor was shining parquet
with a dark red Afghan rug. Behind him the smaller man
shut the door quietly and they went through into the
drawing-room where a woman with permed hair and
wearing a brown tweed suit was sitting on a chintz sofa
looking through a copy of *The Field*. 'Ah, there you are,'
she said. 'I do hope you had an uneventful drive.'

Hartang tried to smile and said it had been all right.
'Well, now that you're safely here,' she said without
introducing herself, 'you can make yourself at home.
Your luggage is upstairs and everything has been
unpacked. You'll find it in the wardrobes and the chests
of drawers. I'll show you that in a moment. In the
meantime here are your new passport and birth certificate. And your curriculum vitae. There is nothing in it
that should cause you any difficulties. We have tried to
keep as close to your natural characteristics as possible.
You are an obsessional recluse with very few outside

interests. A number of suggested hobbies have been listed. There is, for instance, the collection of eighteenth-century American law books that you might like to have. Or there's . . .'

Hartang sat in an armchair and knew he was trapped. Until this moment and until this woman with the plump legs and the permed hair he hadn't been sure. He knew he'd been in deep shit, but you might get out of deep shit if you thought enough about it and had people out front. This was different. He was alone and in an environment he didn't begin to understand and she was telling him how he was going to live his life and what he was going to think and all she was allowing him to do was to choose some hobbies. Worst of all, she was doing it all with an air of absolute certainty that he had to do exactly what she was telling him. Even in prison all those years ago Hartang had felt freer than he did now. And even when they took him up in the elevator and explained how the doors and the roof and floor were bullet-proof and if he ever felt threatened all he had to do was get in there fast and press the yellow button, he could find no comfort in the knowledge. Quite the opposite. The metal walls were like a cell, they weren't even like: they *were* a cell. The bedroom was full of old-fashioned furniture too and it was only when they went through it to a small room with no windows that Hartang began to feel in surroundings that he was used to – computer screens and printers and white wood tables and comfortable executive chairs.

'You have your communications centre here and you can get all the information you need and talk to whoever you want to worldwide,' the woman told him. Hartang doubted it. Whatever he said and whatever messages he sent or came in would be recorded. The information he wanted was what the fuck was going on.

Finally, just before the woman left, he asked about Transworld Television Productions. 'How are they going to run without me being there and telling them what projects to do? They need me to make decisions. There's no one down there can make them except me.'

'I'm sure they'll manage somehow. They understand you've got a serious health problem and in the past when you've been away in Thailand or Bali things have gone on very well.'

'You mean I can't communicate with them?' said Hartang.

'Of course you can. You've got all the equipment you need upstairs and Mr Skundler will take whatever instructions you want to give him every morning. When you have settled in you'll find it works extremely well. Is there anything else?'

'Yes,' said Hartang. 'I want to talk with Schnabel.'

'That is no problem. The telephone is in the study,' said the woman and walked out the front door.

Hartang went through to the study and dialled Schnabel's office. He got an answerphone. 'Mr Schnabel is not available to take messages,' a man's voice said, and the phone went dead. It was the same in the case of

Feuchtwangler and Bolsover. Hartang knew he had something more than a health problem. Like being in solitary confinement. He looked at the collection of books on the shelves. They all dealt with American law.

For a while he sat at the desk and stared out through the window at the Master's Maze. From somewhere near by there came the sound of people playing croquet. Someone had once told him that croquet, for all its apparent gentility, was a vicious game, and the sound gave him no comfort. In the kitchen the shorter of the two men was sitting at the deal table helping Arthur peel potatoes. In the cellar the tall man, Bill, was watching a bank of television screens which showed the road, the drive, and views of the garden and the doors.

*

In the front room of the house in Onion Alley Skullion was explaining why Dr Vertel had had to go to Porterhouse Park in a hurry. He had already talked about Lord Wurford and how the College money had been lost by Fitzherbert when he was Bursar. For three days he had sat in a chair talking about Porterhouse and what it had been like in the old days while Mrs Ndhlovo took notes and the tape recorder ran silently beside him. In the past Skullion had glorified those days when Porterhouse had been a gentleman's college. Now he saw things differently. The years he had spent in the Master's Lodge confined to a wheelchair had given him time to think and reflect on the way he had been treated. He had always accepted the patronizing attitude of the Dean and Fellows and even the undergraduates as a necessary evil and had put up with it because that was part of the job of being a porter and because it gave him a curious sense of his own superiority. He wasn't educated, didn't know anything about science or history or any of the subjects they were interested in. Instead he had made a study of the men who passed through the College or stayed and became Fellows. As Head Porter he had been proud of Porterhouse and had accepted his role because he was serving gentlemen. It had been a necessary illusion but a partial one. He had never succumbed to it entirely and, as he explained through many digressions and byways of memories suddenly recalled, he had seen the illusion slowly dissolve until only the shell of the College remained and the gentlemen were dead and gone.

'They stopped dressing properly and getting their hair cut, not that some of them, especially the real scholars, had ever really known what they were wearing. There was that chemist Strekker, brilliant reputation he had and we'd heard him called a genius, F.R.S. and all that, and his gyp, name of Landon, had to lay his shirts and underpants out and tell him to wash his neck or have a bath or he wouldn't have from one year's end to the next. Wouldn't say boo to a goose, Strekker wouldn't, but he'd been what they called a boffin during the war and he'd gone to America and ended up at some College in Oxford. Funny thing was he wasn't in *Who's Who* because I looked him up but I heard the Senior Tutor say once that often the very best people didn't want to and only the nouveaus made a point of getting in. Strekker would be like that. It wouldn't concern him being known or clean. But a gentleman for all that. Never rude though that wasn't always a sign. No, where it went wrong was after the war. A lot of ex-servicemen and half of them only National Service who'd never been in the war but were older in their twenties when they came up and couldn't be taught to be proper Porterhouse men. On grants too. You've no idea, you youngsters, what it was like then. Grim. With whale-meat in Hall and snoek, and all some of them seemed to have learnt was to skive in the army. I rate the rot from then with their something-for-nothing attitude. And even the ones who could afford to pay going to the NHS for nothing. Not that the National Health Service was a bad idea. It was the fact that everyone even the rich got everything free and they came to think life was like that.'

Purefoy almost argued about that, but he stayed silent and let Skullion keep talking and having the cups of tea Mrs Charlie brought in to whet his whistle. And give Mrs Ndhlovo time to rest her writing hand. By the third day she couldn't keep it up and bought a second tape recorder to back up the first. 'It's going to cost a fortune to have all this typed out,' she said and Skullion said they mustn't have it done in Cambridge. Someone in London who wouldn't know what he was talking about.

He thought Purefoy had been wise to move into digs too. 'They'd question you otherwise. Or even have you followed and we don't want that. I'll go back in my own good time when you've got everything you need down.'

So they went through the story of Sir Godber wanting to sell the College servants' houses in Rhyder Street and the sense of betrayal when Skullion was sacked and how they had made him Master after he'd killed Sir Godber and he'd had a Porterhouse Blue with the Dean and the Senior Tutor there in the room and they hadn't realized what it was and he might have died if Cheffy hadn't come round later that night and sent for the ambulance. And then the years in the wheelchair and how he had stayed sane remembering who lived in what room and in which years. 'I sat and thought about it all and that's what you're getting now so it won't go to waste or get doctored up to look nice because it wasn't.'

Purefoy's interest waxed and waned with the topics. He found Skullion's assessment of the Senior Fellows most fascinating. 'Dean's not the man he was. The spirit has gone out of him and he's only left with his deviousness which he's always had. Made up for his lack of scholarship. Never published anything the Dean hasn't. Just run the College and he can't do that any more. Senior Tutor's different. He got a Two One and he did have a brain. Published a doctoral thesis on tides or rivers or something a long time back but he gave it up and became a Hearty. Wasn't Porterhouse being a scholar and he wanted to be one of them. Now I don't suppose he can think properly. Lost the habit cycling up and down the towpath with the Eights. But he fitted in which is what he wanted though he and the Dean used to fight like cat and dog. Hated one another which is what most of them do if you ask me. Spend hours thinking up things to say to one another that'll be like pinpricks. Only natural having to live on top of one another like that. Chaplain's deaf, or pretends to be. He's the one that's human. Likes the girls, the Chaplain does, girls in Woolworths and Boots. I've seen him sniffing around the perfume counter many a time just to size them up. Used to take photographs of them too. Not their bodies, just their faces when they'd let him. He loves a pretty face and who can blame him. Never did anyone any harm, the Chaplain.'

'And what about the Praelector?' Purefoy asked. 'Is he a nice man?'

'Nice? The Praelector? No, I wouldn't say he was nice. Nice isn't the word for him. He's a strange old stick, he is. Didn't say boo to a goose for years and then suddenly he's something you've never expected. English, if you know what I mean. Lost his wife when she was only forty-five and for several years he was a broken man. Took rooms in College and never looked at another woman. Something in anti-tank during the war though you'd never think it to look at him. Was a military historian and wrote books on the First World War and what fools the generals were. I ought to know. Lost my dad the second day of the Somme and two uncles at

some muddy place where they had to use duckboards
and if you fell off you drowned.'

*

That evening in the digs in City Road Mrs Ndhlovo
wondered how they were going to organize the mass of
material Skullion had provided in such a disorganized
way. 'There's a tremendous amount and half of it is
overload.'

'Once we have the transcript, then I'll edit it,' Purefoy said. 'I won't cut too much out, but he does repeat
himself. It must be a unique account of life in a college
from an entirely different point of view.'

'And what about Lady Mary?'

'I'm not thinking about her at the moment, and
anyway she'll get a full report. I don't really care if she
likes it. I'm doing what she asked me to.'

39

'I've had a very peculiar letter from the Senior Tutor,'
Goodenough told Mr Lapline over coffee one morning.

Mr Lapline said he wasn't in the least surprised.
'Disgusting business. You'd think a man in D'Eath's
position would have more sense. If he wants to tie
women up in black latex, he could at least have maintained some degree of anonymity. It makes the worst
sort of impression on the public.'

'I wasn't actually talking about that,' said Goodenough who was surprised Mr Lapline read the *Sun*. 'It's
about that silly fellow Purefoy Osbert.'

Mr Lapline shuddered. 'I always knew that was a
terrible mistake. What's the filthy brute done now?'

'I think if you read the letter yourself, you'll get a
better picture of the situation,' said Goodenough and
put the letter gingerly on the desk. The solicitor read it
through twice.

'Abducted the Master? Abducted the Master from
Porterhouse Park? Is the man completely insane? And
where the devil is Porterhouse Park? I've never heard of
it,' said Mr Lapline at last.

'I've no idea. He merely says that Skullion, that's the

458

Master, was convalescing there and that Dr Osbert turned up with some woman – '

'I know what the Senior Tutor says. Not that it's a coherent letter for a supposedly educated man. But to abduct the Master, who's in a wheelchair? And what's all this about locking the whole place up so no one can call the police? And the man's gone a week and neither of them have been seen? It's utterly appalling. Goodenough, I hold you responsible for ever letting this damned swine loose on Porterhouse. I do indeed.'

'Steady on,' said Goodenough grimly. 'If you remember, you were the one who insisted on keeping Bloody Mary's account and then you went sick with that wretched gall bladder you won't have out and handed the problem over to me.'

'You volunteered,' said Mr Lapline, who still hadn't had his gall bladder out: it was playing up again. 'You specifically said you could handle the matter and keep Lady Mary happy. You then sent her a collection of sexual psychopaths and neo-Nazis knowing full well she'd reject them out of hand and finally you offer her a blighter who is into the most disgusting details of hanging and who's convinced Crippen was innocent.'

'Now wait a moment – ' Goodenough began but Mr Lapline hadn't finished.

'Anyone in his right mind could have seen catastrophe coming and, as a matter of fact, you did. You said it was called putting the cat among the pigeons and now we have this bloody man abducting – I wonder he didn't call it kidnapping – the Master from his sickbed and for all we know hanging the poor chap.'

'Actually, Purefoy is very much against hanging. That's one of his pet aversions.'

'I'll tell you one of my pet aversions,' said Mr Lapline viciously, but stopped himself just in time. After all, Goodenough was a partner and very successful at handling the clients Mr Lapline least liked. 'Anyway the damage is done and you'll just have to tell Lady Mary – '

'Not yet, for God's sake,' said Goodenough. 'I mean there may have been some mistake.'

'May?' said Mr Lapline.

But in the end it seemed better to wait on events and hope for the best.

*

At Coft Castle General Sir Cathcart D'Eath had lost hope entirely. All the women servants had walked out, including his American secretary, and only the Japanese butler and Kudzuvine were left, though there was nothing for Kudzuvine to do now that the Cathcart's Catfood had been closed down. The knowledge that Sir Cathcart made a habit of having old racehorses slaughtered and consigned to tins, cats for the consumption of, had alienated everyone in the district. He had been cut in Newmarket by old friends and there had been a disturbance outside the house when some Animal Rights activists broke in and had to be dispersed by the police. Worst of all the rumour had spread that he had been breeding horses simply to satisfy the nation's cats and because horses grew faster than cows. Even his milder neighbours had been so enraged that on one occasion his Range Rover had been pelted with rotten eggs as he drove through Coft.

Sir Cathcart stayed in his study and drank with Kudzuvine, who didn't know what all the shit was about. Horses were horses though frankly he preferred pork himself. More human he reckoned. You could keep fucking turtles and baby octopuses but fucking pigs was something else again. Sir Cathcart said he supposed it must be, though even in his drunken state he couldn't think it was very pleasant and talking about fucking pigs that Myrtle Ransby ... Kudzuvine said she hadn't turned him on either. Old bag like that dress her how you like and that black rubber hadn't done anything for her except stop you having to see her face. Still some guys he'd known liked their meat well hung. Sir Cathcart said he'd have hung the bitch a long time ago if he'd known what she was going to do to him. Kudzuvine said Hartang would have Calvied her no mistake the way she'd acted. It was a most unedifying conversation.

*

The talk in the Master's Lodge between Hartang and Ross Skundler had been only slightly more civilized. The Bursar, the Dean and the Praelector had been present in part to reassure Skundler that he was *persona grata* with the new Master but also, as the Dean put it, to find out if there was any little thing they could do to make the new Master more comfortable in the College and, of course, to welcome him.

'Drop dead,' said Hartang, looking at Skundler but evidently including the Bursar, the Praelector and the Dean in the injunction. He had had an appalling two nights in the Lodge in the company, by the sound of it, of a colony of enormous rats in the attic above his head. Certainly some things had spent their time scurrying about up there and making very strange noises. Arthur had tried to reassure him at breakfast (Hartang had been downright rude about the cholesterol effects of two fried eggs and a Porterhouse portion of fatty bacon, not to mention the fried bread which had been Skullion's special favourite) that they were merely squabs.

'In the roof? Squabs in the roof?' Hartang had said incredulously. 'I don't believe it. That where these eggs come from?'

'No, sir, those are hen's eggs. We do not keep chickens in the attic.'

'And if squabs aren't chickens, what are they?'

'Young pigeons, sir. In the old days pigeons were a Porterhouse delicacy and some of their descendants still inhabit their predecessors' home. You will see the entrances on the end gables. I believe there may be a colony of pipistrelles up there too.'

'Bats? Bats?' said Hartang who did at least know what a pipistrelle was. 'Are they a Porterhouse delicacy too? Shit.'

'No, sir, bats are a protected species. It is unlawful to kill them,' Arthur said, and went back to the kitchen to see if he could find some oatbran and skimmed milk yoghurt that Hartang insisted was all he ever ate for breakfast. Hartang was not in a good mood when Skundler and the Senior Fellows arrived. He'd had to have muesli and even that had sugar in it. And the coffee had been foul.

Arthur hadn't been too happy either. 'Very uncouth gentleman, the new Master,' he told the bodyguards who had heard the exchange on the wired sound system. What they were now hearing had the same acrimoniously uncouth quality about it. The Dean's use of the word 'amenities' had been the last straw.

'What amenities? Amenity? I haven't seen a single amenity since I got here. The fucking bath is big enough to drown in and it takes an hour to fill and the water's goddam cold by the time it's full.'

'Well, we've had some rather large Masters in the past,' the Dean explained. 'They needed a sizeable bath. I'm sorry about the water but Porterhouse men are used to it being on the lukewarm side.'

'I'm not,' Hartang assured him. 'I like my water hot and if what that old fool of a waiter tried to give me for breakfast is anything to go by, like it would fur up an elephant's arteries in no time at all, I'd say the Masters you've had in the past had to have been sick men. Didn't think what they were doing to their bodies.'

'Very possibly,' the Praelector said pacifically. 'As

you've undoubtedly noticed we are a very old College and some of our ways may seem rather out of date. I am sure we can accommodate you in circumstances more to your liking.'

Hartang didn't say anything. He had found the Praelector daunting when he had met him at Transworld Television Centre and he had found that 'accommodate' uncomfortable. 'I'd be glad if the boiler could be fixed,' he said. 'Most grateful.'

For the rest he talked earnestly with Skundler who took notes and only answered questions, none of which the Fellows understood. By the time they left the Master-to-be had remembered his elocution and etiquette lessons, and was quietly polite, and thanked them for coming.

*

'This is not going to work,' the Dean said when they were out of earshot. 'That man ought to be behind bars. I still find it difficult to believe such people exist. What on earth are we going to do?'

'For the time being nothing,' said the Praelector. 'I suggest we keep out of his way and ensure that his bathwater is hot. And I think we must persuade his lawyers to come up and talk to him. I have found them most helpful.'

It was not an opinion Hartang shared.

*

In the listening-room the tape of the conversation was locked away and the older taller man was on the phone. His views were exactly the same as the Dean's. The Master-to-be was not shaping up. 'She says it's going to take time and there's no point in rushing things. There are still things they need from him. Just keep him safe.'

In the kitchen Arthur explained to the Chef that 'Him-over-there' wanted something called Noovell Couiseen.

'Never heard of it,' said the Chef. 'Best see if they've got some at Marks & Sparks by the Market. We're having beef with dumplings tonight in Hall with a Stilton soup to start with and omelette for savoury.'

Arthur said he didn't think 'Him-over-there' was very fond of eggs and Cheffy said he didn't care what he was fond of, he wasn't Master yet and never would be till Mr Skullion gave his say-so because Mr Skullion was the Master still whatever anyone said.

'I wonder where he went to, Cheffy. Him and that Dr Osbert.'

'That'd be telling, Arthur, that'd be telling,' was all the Chef would say. 'And don't you tell anyone I said so.'

40

'I can fully understand your feelings, Master,' said Schnabel when he finally came up to Porterhouse. Hartang said he couldn't. No one could live in a fucking mausoleum with a whole lot of deadbeats who didn't know a dollar from a peso and had to use their fingers to count to ten, and even begin to understand what it felt like.

'I don't think you should allow appearances to mislead you,' said Schnabel. 'Academics are deceptive people and the English have always been known for their understatement. It's part of the national character. They don't like to show their feelings. You mustn't take them at face value.'

Hartang looked out of the window at the marquees on the Fellows' Lawn and wished he could express his feelings. He had never taken anyone at face value except maybe in movies. Some of the best contractors from Chicago and Miami had nice faces. 'Have you ever met a fat woman with a blue hair rinse and a shopping bag who doesn't give her name?' he asked. 'Artificial pearls and a voice like a pointed Luger. Has two men with her who could be SAS. They're living in the house with me. Not the woman. The men.'

'For your protection, I'm sure,' said Schnabel. 'They'll see you through this early period until you're settled in and then they'll pull out. That's the agreement. You wouldn't want non-professionals who don't know their job.'

'I certainly hope so. Anyone show around Transworld? You know "anyone"?'

'My information is no. You're keeping the money flowing into the same accounts so there's no reason to think you have been involved in any way. If you'd blown with it, that would be different. There's a man in your office your height and dressed the same, lives the same way you do. So you're there if they ask the staff. And one day, say in six months, he'll have an infarct and they'll have a big cremation at Golders Green and an obituary in *The Times* about how you built Transworld up from nothing.'

'Someone's going to want to see the body.'

'Naturally,' said Schnabel. 'No one will stop them. Same build, same face, wig and glasses. They'll be able to take photographs but no touching. The people protecting you have morticians who could make Boris Karloff look like Marilyn Monroe. How do you think they get IRA informers new identities?'

'You going to tell me they embalm them? Shit, I don't want to know.'

'They embalm some dead guy. Plastic surgery like you wouldn't believe. The real guy's different too. So who's to know? No one. Got a new identity and could be living in the same street as always. That's the way they are. Professionals.'

'Just so long they don't change their minds about me. I don't want to end up this place Golden Green.'

'You aren't going to,' said Schnabel. 'You're too valuable. So Hartang's dead, long live the Master of Porterhouse.'

Hartang thought about it for a bit. 'I'm not making a will,' he said finally. 'They want my money they keep me alive.'

'Very wise. They want your financial genius. That's what they're buying – keeping you alive and out of circulation. Ross Skundler making out all right?'

'That shit,' said Hartang and felt better.

And Skundler was. Every few days he would look at the old bound ledgers and ask the Bursar for a quill but the new financial position was good. The Bursar was happier too. He didn't have to worry about money or the College debts but could go and inspect the work being done in the Chapel and see how much better the College looked. Even Skullion's disappearance didn't bother him. He'd never liked him and Skullion had never bothered to hide his contempt for the Bursar. In fact from every point of view things were working out very well.

*

In Onion Alley Purefoy was exhausted. So was Mrs Ndhlovo. For a week they had sat and listened to

Skullion and they felt they had been living in Porterhouse for ever. It was the repetition that had this effect, repetitions and digressions, trips Skullion took them on down the tributaries of his main concern, the treachery he had suffered, not just once, not even twice, but from the moment he had set foot in Porterhouse and had doffed his cap to the gentlemen there. It was that sense of betrayal, stronger now than it had been even when Sir Godber had him sacked, that gave him the strength to keep talking, dredging his memory for details of those slights and little insults he knew now to be the pilot fish for the greatest betrayal of all.

'That bloody Sir Cathcart D'Eath promised me, swore on his oath as a gentleman, that I wouldn't go to the Park. Gave me his word I could stay at Coft Castle if I agreed to retire. The bloody bastard,' he told them any number of times. 'And I said I had the right to name my own successor as Master and I have, and he agreed. Had to. College tradition since time immemorial. The dying Master has the right to name his own successor. And I did. "Lord Pimpole," I said, "The Honourable Jeremy Pimpole of Pimpole Hall in the County of Yorkshire." That's who I named and a nicer young gentleman you never met. Came up in 1959. Him and Sir Launcelot Gutterby were the best.' Skullion paused, recalling their ineffable superiority and arrogance.

Then he spat into the fireplace. 'So what happens next? That bastard Sir Cathcart has me bundled into an ambulance and I'm locked in the Park and they've got some fucking Yank or something in the Master's Lodge.' The enormity of this final betrayal overcame him and he was silent, staring into the meaningless abyss of hatred this final act of treachery had led to. Worst of all he had only himself to blame. He could have kept his independent mind, he'd always believed he had, but he hadn't. He'd surrendered it to Porterhouse, to his cosy job and his self-indulgent consciousness of doing his duty. Duty! About as much duty as a fucking poodle jumping through hoops in a circus and walking on its back paws and doing tricks to satisfy an audience of idiots. That's what his duty had been. He knew that now. He knew it because they had betrayed him.

He knew it even more because they had betrayed Porterhouse by their stupidity. Any fool could have seen what was happening to the College years ago and taken measures to protect the place and keep it independent. He'd seen that himself and had denied it too because he'd trusted them. And because there'd been nothing he could do about it. He hadn't wanted to think about it and had told himself it would all come right in the end. Instead it had all come wrong. There was a worse thought at the back of his mind: that it had always been wrong and that his life had been wasted in the service of the rotten. That was what he thought now but he didn't say it to Purefoy and Mrs Ndhlovo and the tape recorder. They were young and there was no point in hurting them so early. Life would do that. Besides, he needed them for what he had to do.

*

'Still no news of Skullion?' the Praelector asked, looking out of the Fellows' Private Dining Room at the marquees and the tables and wooden dance floors arranged on the lawn. A group of sound technicians were setting up speakers, and lights were already installed round them.

'None,' said the Dean. 'And Osbert hasn't been into College since that first night. None of the College servants has any idea where they've got to.'

'Wouldn't tell you if they knew,' the Senior Tutor said. 'They've always kowtowed to Skullion even before he became Master.'

'True, but they're worried too. If they knew and weren't telling, they'd be in a different mood. I'm certain they have no idea.'

'The police have no information either. All they have found out is that Dr Osbert hired a van in Hunstanton and brought it back two days later. They've contacted hospitals but he hasn't been admitted. It is all most disturbing.'

'Since there is nothing we can do about it, I don't think we should waste time worrying about it,' said the Praelector. 'I have to confess the new Master is giving me more cause for concern. He is an even more unpleasant individual than I had supposed.'

'He was your choice and you have no one to blame but yourself,' said the Senior Tutor.

'I accept that responsibility and I do blame myself. On the other hand he is yet to be inaugurated and if anyone can think of a suitable alternative, someone who can provide the College with the financial resources we so desperately require, I daresay we can persuade the authorities to take him off our hands.'

'By "authorities" I take it you mean the people with him in the Master's Lodge,' said the Senior Tutor. 'I have to say they are not very pleasant themselves. I gather they body-searched Professor Pawley when he made the mistake of going to pay his respects. He hasn't got over their thoroughness yet.'

'Well, at least they are subduing the wretched man they are looking after,' said the Dean. 'We must be grateful for that, and they are on our side.'

The Praelector left them and walked pensively across the Court to the College kitchen. He wanted a word with the Chef.

41

For the next four days the Praelector was a busy man. He consulted Mr Retter and Mr Wyve; he telephoned a number in London and met a plump woman with a Liberty shopping bag in Grantchester and had a long talk with her walking in the meadows; he even went to Coft Castle and had a most distasteful hour with Sir Cathcart who wept maudlin tears about Skullion and finally agreed to go to a Spa. He also spoke to Kentucky Fry who said Shit he wasn't going to do any such fucking thing. The General had bought him some weaners and he was going in for hog raising in a big way. Guy he'd met said they were selling off land from the airbases for Transcendental Meditation but he reckoned hogs was better like fifty thousand piglets rootling would give a good living and living was what he was into, staying living. The Praelector agreed it was a good idea but in the meantime all he wanted him to do was think about it. Kentucky Fry said he couldn't think about anything else except . . .

'How about deportation? To Singapore,' said the Praelector and switched his attention away from hog raising. Kudzuvine said he didn't want to be deported. Hadn't done nothing wrong in Singapore. The Praelector smiled and gave him two days to go on thinking about it. Kudzuvine didn't need two days. No sir, if that was what they wanted, like a ceremonial role and he didn't have to do anything else, his answer was in the affirmative. The Praelector took his taxi back to Porterhouse and spoke to the Chef who said it wasn't usual but he didn't see why not. And finally the Praelector visited Onion Alley by appointment and talked to Skullion for a long time.

But his hardest task was one he put off to the end, waiting until the May Ball was in full swing and the telephone in the Porter's Lodge was being deluged with calls from people in the neighbourhood who couldn't stand the appalling din and at the same time weren't able to make their complaints audible to Walter.

'A word in your ear,' he shouted at the Dean who was standing mesmerized by a band from the Caribbean who didn't need the loudspeakers to make life intolerable for anyone within earshot. In front of them on the dance floor undergraduates hurled themselves about in an ecstasy of savagery under pulsating multi-coloured strobes in a way which so disgusted the Dean that even if he had been able to hear the Praelector, and he couldn't, he would have been unable to reply at all rationally. The Praelector shouted some more but the Dean himself, affected by the insistent beat, only nodded.

'Anything you say,' he yelled back after the Praelector's third attempt to communicate.

'Thank you,' bellowed the Praelector. 'I am delighted you agree.' And he went away in the direction of the Master's Lodge and was promptly admitted by the shorter and more intimidating of the two men on duty.

'He's up in the communications room,' the man said when he'd shut the door. 'He never seems to sleep. Spends his time surfing the Internet for stuff I didn't know existed and I used to be on the Porn Squad before I joined this outfit. I'll buzz him you're coming.'

The Praelector waited in the drawing-room, staring out into the pulsating night and thinking about the May Balls he had known in his youth. They had been sedate affairs and he had enjoyed them enormously, swinging round the Hall doing the quickstep or a foxtrot and, most daringly of all, the tango with a polished liveliness and delight that was a world away from the mechanical Bacchanalia the young now seemed to crave. Not that he blamed them. They were drowning out a world that seemed to have no structure to it and no meaning for them, a monstrous bazaar in which the only recognized criteria were money and sex and drugs and the pursuit of moments of partial oblivion. Perhaps it was a better world than the one he had known when Europe had gone to war and discipline was everything. He didn't know and wouldn't live long enough to find out.

He was interrupted in his reverie by the arrival of Hartang. He was smaller than the Praelector had remembered him, seemed to have shrunk and had a haggard look about him. 'You wanted to see me?' he asked almost humbly, his weak eyes blinking in the bright light of the drawing-room.

The Praelector nodded deferentially. 'Good evening, Master,' he said. 'I trust I am not disturbing you. I'm afraid our May Ball this year is unusually noisy. The students are celebrating the change in the College fortunes and your appointment.'

Hartang smiled slightly. He was never too sure about the Praelector. 'It's nice to hear kids enjoying themselves,' he said. He indicated a chair and the Praelector sat down.

'I have come, Master, to say that your Inauguration Feast has been fixed for Thursday and to find out if this suits you.'

'Inauguration Feast?' Hartang sounded uncertain.

'Yes, it is a necessary part of the formal ceremonies which are traditional in Porterhouse with the appointment of a new Master. We take sherry in the Combination Room and then proceed to the Hall where you will take your place in the Master's chair.'

'I've got to do this?' Hartang asked.

'No Master has ever been known to absent himself,' said the Praelector. 'It is considered a great honour. The College is closed for the evening and no guests are invited. It is a purely private Porterhouse function.'

Hartang considered the matter for a moment. 'I guess it'll be all right,' he said at last. 'Yes, I guess so. Thursday?'

'We gather at 7.30 and the Senior Fellows will escort

you to the Combination Room. You will not be required to make a speech.'

'Sounds fine with me. 7.30?'

'Thank you, Master, we will be honoured by your presence.'

The Praelector left the Lodge well satisfied, and Hartang went back to his communications room. He wanted to find out what the yen was doing. It was up and the Tokyo Stock Exchange was down 100 points. He'd got it right again.

*

Purefoy and Mrs Ndhlovo sat on the bank of the river on the way to Grantchester watching the punts go by. It was 6 a.m. and the revellers were going happily up to the Orchard Tea Garden for breakfast before drifting wearily back to Cambridge and bed. It was the custom and in their evening dresses and dinner jackets they struck a discordantly gay note against the pollarded willows and the flat farm fields on the far bank. 'Not our scene,' said Purefoy. 'But worth seeing. Like going back fifty years and probably much more. Weird.'

But Mrs Ndhlovo was a little envious. She would have liked to dance the night away and be lying in a punt while Purefoy poled it up the river with the one-handed twist some of the young men affected before leaving the punt pole dragging in the water for a moment to steer. All the same she knew what Purefoy meant. Even at their dances the English lacked the vivacity of the people she had seen in South America and Africa. Their laughter was different too and hadn't the same joyfulness about it. To her ear it didn't seem spontaneous, merely an awkwardly conventional response that was required of them. But these were young people whose year had been spent in pursuit of academic excellence and in serious discussions and the world weighed heavily upon them. They were recruits in the army of the intellect, drilled and disciplined in thinking. And after a week listening to Skullion she was confused. Behind the façade of convention so many dark inhibitions found expression in the weirdest ways. Nothing was what it seemed. She and Purefoy had been taken behind the scenes into a little world full of the strangest inconsistencies and disguised animosities that was both sad and alarming and full of hidden unhappiness. It was not her world.

She turned over and looked down at the grass. Some ants were busily going to and fro along a path of their own devising, never deviating for more than a moment from some unknown and interminable purpose. Mrs Ndhlovo wondered if she looked like that seen perhaps from a satellite. It was certainly how Purefoy behaved, busily pursuing his facts and placing so much reliance on the written word. Skullion had shaken that solid confidence with his oral history of forty-odd years in Porterhouse and perhaps Purefoy would change. It wouldn't be enough. He was already working furiously, editing the typescript that had cost so much, cutting a digression here and noting it for future use, removing unnecessary repetitions and even once – and in her eyes unforgivably – removing a double negative 'in the interest of clarity'. Mrs Ndhlovo sighed and rolled over again to look up at some passing clouds in the blue summer sky.

'Purefoy my love,' she said, 'you aren't the Sir Godber Evans Memorial Fellow any longer. You're the James Skullion Memorial Fellow. You'll write a book from what he's given you and with all the checking of cross-references it will be your life's work. Your *opus dei*.'

But Purefoy Osbert didn't get the allusive pun. His had been a strictly Protestant upbringing. 'Ours,' he said and lay down beside her. Mrs Ndhlovo smiled but said nothing. She wasn't going to stay in Cambridge and she wasn't going to stay with Purefoy, but she had no intention of telling him that now. He was too happy. It would be soon enough when he had his nose in the book to give him a sense of real achievement and lessen his feelings of loss. Besides, it would never have worked. Purefoy was far too easy to lie to and far too gentle to hurt. She would find an improper man who would understand her.

*

In Porterhouse the marquees were gone and only the marks on the lawn remained where the dance floors and the pegs had been. The courts were silent again and the tables and benches had been brought back into the Hall when Kudzuvine presented himself nervously at the Porter's Lodge and was admitted.

'Shoot, what's happened to the grass?' he asked Walter as they went through to the Buttery. 'That stuff has been there hundreds of years. Like it's a protected species. How come it's all fucked up?'

'It was the May Ball last week.'

In Kudzuvine's head the words had a sinister ring to them. 'Last week? Last week was June.'

'Yes sir,' said Walter. 'Last week was June.' He wasn't going to bother explaining things to the Yank. He'd had them up to the eyeballs. Only Mr Skullion knew how to handle them and he was in the Combination Room sitting in his wheelchair with his bowler hat still defiantly on and eyeing the Fellows with a hard unyielding authority. Even the Dean was solemnly deferential now. He knew when he was beaten.

Only the Chaplain's bonhomie remained unchanged. 'Ah, Skullion, my dear old fellow, how splendid to see you again. It seems ages since we had a chat. What have you been doing?'

'Oh, this and that,' Skullion said. 'Mostly this, but a bit of that.'

'A bit of that, eh? And at your age! How I envy you. I remember once years ago now . . .' But he stopped himself in time and looked puzzled. 'A bit of this and that, eh? Well I never.'

Presently, when everyone was assembled, the Praelector and the Dean and the Senior Tutor in their festal

gowns and silk hoods walked slowly across the Garden
to fetch the new Master. Hartang walked back between
them. In the background the two men kept a discreet
watch on the procession and then followed.

'We are deeply honoured . . .' the Dean was saying
but the words meant something else to the security
men. They had no time for Hartang and would be glad
to get back to some real work. They took their places in
the Hall, the shorter one in the Musicians' Gallery and
the older man in the shadows behind High Table where
Arthur was lighting the candles and the silver gleamed.
They didn't have long to wait. The new Master said he
didn't drink amontillado and no one offered him whisky.
Then the door of the Combination Room opened and
the Fellows filed in. This time the Dean and the Praelector preceded Skullion in the wheelchair and Hartang
followed. He was feeling really awful. This was it, his
future life and it was his idea of hell.

The Chaplain said Grace and Hartang was offered
the Master's Chair. On either side of him the Fellows
took their seats and at the very end Skullion sat in his
wheelchair looking down the table with approval. At
least the standards he had known were being kept up.
The silver had been polished and the old oak table
gleamed with wax. That gave him some sense of accom-
plishment but he had greater cause for satisfaction. All
the same he was still afraid. The Fellows of Porterhouse,
of Porterhouse past, had not been men who gave way to
threats – not easily at any rate – and there was still the

danger that they would deceive him. Even the Hall played a part in his apprehension by calling up memories of feasts and great occasions when he had been a servant of the College and proud of his position. Skullion closed his mind to the siren call of that past with its deference and its social wiles and steeled himself with a contempt for the present. He was helped by the occasional anxious look the Dean gave him. They were all as old and feeble as he was in his body but theirs was a worse weakness: they had lost their spirit. They were going to see that he hadn't.

'I hope we are not going to have anything too rich,' Hartang said to the Praelector.

'I can assure you, Master, that the menu has been carefully chosen with your constitution in mind. I trust you like German wine. We start with Vichyssoise and we have a delicate Rhein wine to go with it. Then there is the cold salmon, one of the Chef's specialities and a great favourite with the Queen Mother.' He broke off to allow the Dean to tell the story of his meeting with the Queen Mother or the Queen as she then was and the King on the battleship, the *Duke of York*, then Flagship of the Home Fleet during the Fleet Review on the Clyde in 1947 and how when the Prime Minister, Mr Attlee, was piped on board he didn't know whether to take his hat off or leave it on and he held it sort of hovering above his head. To make matters worse, King George VI and the Queen and, of course, the young Princesses with Prince Philip in tow had been round the

Fleet on a motor torpedo boat which made a terrible din and was so loud when it came alongside that the Royal Marine Guard of Honour on the quarterdeck had barely heard the order to Present Arms. The Senior Fellows knew the story off by heart and Hartang wasn't interested in kings and queens unless he held them in his hand, but the story saw them through the soup and the salmon. All Hartang was thinking was that he was safe. Safe and bored. His thoughts drifted to Thailand and the beach house he owned there and what he would do if he were there instead of sitting with these stuffed shirts.

A moment later he knew with a terrible certainty that he was not safe. The doors at the far end of the Hall under the Musicians' Gallery had been flung open and four waiters entered carrying on their shoulders like some monstrous bier a vast pig, a tusked boar with a blackened apple in its mouth. Behind them came waiters with two more great roast boar. And beside the first pig came Kudzuvine dressed from top to toe in black with an enormous carving knife and fork in his hands. For several seconds Hartang gazed at the ghastly beasts in frozen terror. At the long tables the undergraduates were shouting and clapping enthusiastically. It was bedlam in the Hall. Then with a scream only he could hear – his mouth opened but no sound came out – the financier struggled to his feet unable to take his eyes off the approaching monstrosity. This was death and Kudzuvine was its herald. The Master's great Chair fell back with a crash and Hartang recoiled in horror. The Fellows had no eyes for him. They stared at the boar with astonishment and delight. The Chaplain's simple Grace, 'For what we are about to receive may the good Lord be thanked,' had been answered in full measure. So had the Praelector's intention. Hartang staggered a few steps and fell.

'Kudzuvine, attend your Master,' ordered the Praelector and Kudzuvine came round the table, but there was no need for his appearance to complete the charade. Hartang was already dead.

*

'A Porterhouse Blue, do you think?' the Senior Tutor enquired when the body had been removed and the great boar had been carved by the Chef.

'Less a Blue than a yellow, if you ask me,' said the Dean, who had suddenly remembered Hartang's phobia about pigs on the tape.

'It looks as though we are going to have to look for another source of funding,' said the Bursar sadly. 'It's really most unfortunate.'

'I don't somehow think we need to worry about the College finances,' the Praelector said as he helped himself to some more apple sauce. 'I happen to know he died without making a will.'

'You mean . . .' the Senior Tutor began.

'Intestate. No next of kin. And in such cases the Crown, as you know, is the beneficiary. I think we will find we have not been forgotten. After all we have been most cooperative in dealing with a very unpleasant situation.'

The Fellows gazed at him in amazement and almost stopped eating.

'But that will mean the Prime Minister will appoint the new Master,' said the Senior Tutor. 'We may well end up with Tebbit.'

'I can think of worse choices,' said the Dean with unintended perception.

'You seem to forget that the Master is still with us,' said the Praelector and directed his gaze at Skullion. 'He has the traditional right to name his successor, and I can think of no better moment.'

At the end of the table Skullion raised his head and made his pronouncement. For one terrible moment it looked as though the Dean was going to follow Hartang's example, but he had merely swallowed a piece of crackling the wrong way and tried to say something. When he had stopped coughing and had been given another glass of Fonbadet he was still incapable of speech.

'What did the Dean say?' shouted the Chaplain.

'God knows,' the Praelector said with the utmost tact.

42

It was mid-summer before Purefoy Osbert had completed the first edition of what he now thought of as Skullion's memoirs. It was by no means the final version, was ostensibly no more than the punctuated transcript of the long monologue, but he felt it was enough to indicate to Lady Mary that he had not been wasting his time. Mrs Ndhlovo typed it out for him – Purefoy was far too busy cross-referencing the College archives even to look at the final version. Then to save him the trouble she took it down to London and delivered it to Lapline and Goodenough. Mr Lapline read the manuscript over and over again and on each reading was more and more appalled. 'We can't possibly let her see this,' he told Goodenough. 'It's out of the question.'

'I don't see why not. After all, she asked for the facts and she has obviously got them.'

'Yes, but she didn't know she was going to get the most scurrilous account of her husband's time as an undergraduate. I had no idea he was capable of such things. This bit about blackmailing the Praelector would be enough to kill her. The man was an absolute shit.'

'We knew that already,' said Goodenough. 'Married for money and all that sort of thing.'

'I daresay, but not all this sort of thing.'

'Quite a different kettle of fish, eh?'

Mr Lapline winced. 'I wish you wouldn't use expressions of that sort, Goodenough. It is painful enough having to digest this filth without additional culinary references. You'll be telling me next that Porterhouse was a positive stew.' He smiled bleakly at his own pun.

'It certainly makes Sir Cathcart D'Eath's peculiar tendencies slightly more understandable,' Goodenough said. 'Though why he should fancy large middle-aged women in rubber beats me.'

'Bedders and bedwetters,' said Mr Lapline and left it at that.

'Bedwetters? I missed that bit. Where is it?'

'Never mind. The point is that we cannot possibly allow Lady Mary to see this . . . this document. It would destroy what few illusions she has left. God knows she can't have many since the end of the Cold War. She shall carry her happy memories of her marriage to Sir Godber to her grave.'

'Reading that little lot I'd qualify the use of the word "happy". Still, you're probably right. She's old and there's no use larding the bacon. Sorry, I meant rubbing salt into the wound.'

*

In the secretary's office Mrs Ndhlovo was explaining to Vera why she was leaving Purefoy without telling him. 'I don't want to hurt him,' she said.

Vera said she understood but doubted Purefoy would be hurt for long. 'He falls in and out of love all the time. He was once passionately in love with me or thought he was. And my poor dear cousin is incapable of love or passion. He thinks all women are physical versions of words. It's the worst mistake possible. I doubt if he'll ever get married to anything more practical than a library. And at least you've got him off hanging. His mother will be ever so grateful. She had a bad enough time with his father who was always changing his mind. Purefoy's mind never changes. He clings to consistent falsities.'

*

At Porterhouse Park Skullion and the Praelector sat on the verandah together and stared out to sea across the mudflats and said nothing. It was high summer and a few holidaymakers wandered the coast path in search of escape from the boredom of having nothing to do. The two old men knew better. There was no escape for them now. They had had the good fortune to have had something to do and, each in his own way, they had achieved something. The illusion sustained them now. There were no fishing boats out to sea and few fish left to catch. Only the little dinghies and yachts remained aimlessly trawling the wind for pleasure.

*

In the Master's Lodge the new Master was explaining to Arthur the right proportions needed for a really good

Dog's Nose. It was not easy. Arthur refused to understand that a concoction made up of seven ounces of gin and thirteen ounces of beer could possibly add up to three thirds. As he told Cheffy, 'You'd think he had never been properly educated. Talk about vague.'

'Never known a don who wasn't,' said the Chef. 'Not in their natures.'

*

Out on his rock garden the Dean decided to get rid of the gunnera next to the pond. It was gross and fleshy and coarsely out of place. Like so much he had come to detest, it came from the Americas. He would replace it with something small and simple and elegant and hardy. He was also thinking of the next Master. The Dog's Nose man couldn't last long. He was drinking himself to death. It was the Dean's one consolation.

His thoughts, inspired by the coming fate of the gunnera and the loathsome Pimpole, turned towards the Japanese. What that infernal man Lapschott had said was true. The Japanese were an island people, were in fact what the British had been, at once hard-working and violent and ruthlessly efficient. They were inventive, and their engineering was superb. They learnt from their mistakes, and they persevered. They were immensely rich, they believed in discipline and the need for authority, and they understood the vital importance of ritual and ceremony in preserving the decencies of life. Above all, they had the virtues of courtesy and courage. They did their duty to the death. For the first time in his life the Dean looked without shrinking into the face of the inconceivable and was undismayed. He would work for the appointment of a Japanese Master of Porterhouse. And for him.

It would be an honour.